LYRICAL
BEA PAIGE

CONTENTS

Blurb	vii
Bea Paige's Books:	ix
About Bea Paige	xi
Author note	xiii
Prologue	1
Chapter 1	5
Chapter 2	16
Chapter 3	19
Chapter 4	26
Chapter 5	32
Chapter 6	34
Chapter 7	41
Chapter 8	50
Chapter 9	62
Chapter 10	76
Chapter 11	84
Chapter 12	92
Chapter 13	106
Chapter 14	119
Chapter 15	127
Chapter 16	134
Chapter 17	143
Chapter 18	149
Chapter 19	161
Chapter 20	169
Chapter 21	179
Chapter 22	188
Chapter 23	200
Chapter 24	211
Chapter 25	219
Chapter 26	228

Chapter 27	237
Chapter 28	245
Chapter 29	259
Chapter 30	270
Chapter 31	278
Chapter 32	286
Chapter 33	288
Chapter 34	300
Chapter 35	308
Chapter 36	318
Chapter 37	325
Chapter 38	337
Chapter 39	347
Chapter 40	357
Author Note	367

Copyright ©: Kelly Stock writing as Bea Paige
First Published: 23rd September 2020
Publisher: Kelly Stock
Cover by: Everly Yours Cover Designs

Kelly Stock writing as Bea Paige to be identified as author of this work has been asserted by her in accordance with sections 77 and 78 of the Copyright, Designs and Patents Act 1988.
All rights reserved. No part of this publication may be reproduced, stored in retrieval system, copied in any form or by any means, electronic, mechanical, photocopying, recording or otherwise transmitted without written permission from the publisher. You must not circulate this book in any format.

This book is licensed for your personal enjoyment only. This e-book may not be resold or given away to other people. If you would like to share this book with another person, please purchase an additional copy for each recipient. Thank you for respecting the hard work of this author.

BLURB

From the gutter to the stars…
Dance is in my blood.
Once upon a time it ran through their veins too. Xeno, York, Zayn, and Dax.
The Breakers and I were a crew until bad decisions and circumstances ripped us apart.
Now the Breakers are back.
And they've brought trouble.
They're not here at the Stardom Academy to dance.
They're here on a mission for Jeb, the leader of the Skins.
He wants something, and me…? I'm just a pawn in their game.
To make matters worse, my psychotic brother wants something too.
I must befriend the Breakers and find out what they're up to.
If I refuse, my brother will hurt the one person I love more than life itself.
I cannot allow that to happen.

Dance was always the cure to our pain, the foundations of our friendship and love.
It brought us together once before.
Can I go through the cycle of friendship, love, and heartache all over again?
Will I survive the Breakers a second time? Will they survive me?

BEA PAIGE'S BOOKS:

Academy of Stardom (academy reverse harem romance)

#1 Freestyle https://books2read.com/AcademyStardom1

#2 Lyrical https://books2read.com/AcademyStardom2

#3 Breakers https://books2read.com/AcademyStardom3

Academy of Misfits (academy reverse harem romance)

#1 Delinquent https://books2read.com/AcademyMisfits1

#2 Reject https://books2read.com/AcademyMisfits2

#3 Family https://books2read.com/AcademyMisfits3

Finding Their Muse (dark contemporary romance / reverse harem)

#1 Steps https://books2read.com/Steps

#2 Strokes https://books2read.com/Strokes

#3 Strings https://books2read.com/StringsFTM

#4 Symphony https://books2read.com/FTM4

#5 Finding Their Muse boxset https://books2read.com/FTMBoxset

The Brothers Freed Series (contemporary romance / reverse harem)

#1 Avalanche of Desire https://books2read.com/AvalancheOfDesire

#2 Storm of Seduction https://books2read.com/StormSeduction

#3 Dawn of Love https://books2read.com/DawnOfLove

#4 Brothers Freed Boxset https://books2read.com/BrothersFreed

Contemporary Standalones

RH Fairy tale retelling

Cabin of Axes https://books2read.com/CabinOfAxes

Age gap romance

Beyond the Horizon https://books2read.com/Beyond-the-horizon

The Sisters of Hex series (paranormal romance / reverse harem)

Prequel to The Sisters of Hex series:

Five Gold Rings: https://books2read.com/FiveGoldRings

Sisters of Hex: Accacia

#1 Accacia's Curse https://books2read.com/AccaciasCurse

#2 Accacia's Blood https://books2read.com/AccaciasBlood

#3 Accacia's Bite https://books2read.com/AccaciasBite

#4 Accacia's Trilogy https://books2read.com/AccaciasTrilogy

Sisters of Hex: Fern

#1 Fern's Decision https://books2read.com/FernsDecision

#2 Fern's Wings https://books2read.com/FernsWings

#3 Fern's Flight https://books2read.com/FernsFlight

#4 Fern's Trilogy https://books2read.com/FernsTrilogy

The Infernal Descent trilogy (co-written with Skye MacKinnon)

#1 Hell's Calling https://books2read.com/HellsCalling

#2 Hell's Weeping https://books2read.com/HellsWeeping

#3 Hell's Burning https://books2read.com/HellsBurning

#4 Infernal Descent boxset https://books2read.com/InfernalDescent

ABOUT BEA PAIGE

Bea Paige lives a very secretive life in London… she likes red wine and Haribo sweets (preferably together) and occasionally swings around poles when the mood takes her.

Bea loves to write about love and all the different facets of such a powerful emotion. When she's not writing about love and passion, you'll find her reading about it and ugly crying.

Bea is always writing, and new ideas seem to appear at the most unlikely time, like in the shower or when driving her car.

She has lots more books planned, so be sure to subscribe to her newsletter:
   beapaige.co.uk/newsletter-sign-up

   facebook.com/BeaPaigeAuthor
   instagram.com/beapaigeauthor
   bookbub.com/authors/bea-paige

AUTHOR NOTE

Dear Reader,

As an author music plays an important part in my creative process. I *always* listen to music whilst I write, and with these books, in particular, music has become even more important to the creative process. The title of this book is aptly named *Lyrical* for a number of reasons but most significantly because of the style of dance that is a theme throughout this book.

In the barest of forms lyrical is a dance used to express emotional moods with emphasis on song lyrics. It embodies various aspects of ballet, jazz, acrobatics, and modern dance. In this book there are several songs that I picked both for their lyricism and how well they fit the mood of the scene. I thought I would point these out below as you may wish to listen to the song before reading, or if you're like me, whilst reading (writing).

All these songs can be found on my Spotify playlist. Music helps me to visualise a dance, I hope it helps you to do that too.

I want to take this opportunity to thank my amazing

readers of **Queen Bea's Hive**, my reader group on Facebook. *Thank you*. Thank you for all the song recommendations, the links to incredible dance videos on YouTube. Thank you for getting behind this story and immersing yourself in Pen and the Breakers' world. Thank you for waiting patiently. I had to get this right. I hope you love it.

Special thanks to the following people who found some beautiful songs that really encompass the feel of the scenes I wrote them to.

Erica Marie Beavor, my goodness, woman, you literally supplied me with THE BEST songs. I am so grateful to you!!! Lyrical's playlist is made up mainly of your suggestions. You're a queen and I'm forever grateful for your enthusiasm and support. Several of your songs have given me inspiration for scenes in Lyrical. One of my favourites that you suggested was *Paralyzed* by NF. That song was perfect for a dance I had in mind and summed up how the character felt perfectly.

Lori Todd, thank you for suggesting *Elastic Heart* by Sia. I hope you enjoy the scene that goes with it. Sia is one of my favourite artists and this song was absolutely perfect for Pen and her emotions and feelings in this particular scene.

Brittany Graham, thank you for suggesting *You Broke Me First* by Tate McRae. It was absolutely the most perfect song for the scene I had in mind. Can't wait for you to read it!

Noteworthy songs that inspired specific scenes:

Arsonist's Lullabye by Hozier – Chapter three

Elastic Heart by Sia – Chapter Nine

Paralyzed by NF – Chapter Seventeen

Running Up That Hill by Kate Bush – Chapter Twenty

You Broke Me First by Tate McRae – Chapter Twenty-three

Let Me Down by Jorja Smith and Stormzy – Chapter Twenty-four

I Can't Make You Love Me by Teddie Swims – Chapter Thirty

Dancing with a Stranger by Sam Smith – Chapter Thirty-one

Demons by Jacob Lee – Chapter Thirty-Three

Halo by Beyonce – Chapter Thirty-six

Play with Fire (feat. Yacht Money) by Sam Tinnesz & *Fire on Fire* by Sam Smith – Chapter Forty

Happy reading.

With love,

Bea xoxo

For dance and music.
For expression and self-love.
For hopes and dreams.
For courage and strength.
For friendship and love.
For kindness and empathy.
This book is dedicated to all those things.

Set your life on fire. Seek those who fan the flames
   ~ **Rumi.**

PROLOGUE

Xeno

My mum was a wise woman.

She often told me that the strongest, most courageous of us all are not the ones that mete out blood and violence but kindness and understanding in the face of opposition.

She was a good person, unlike me.

I learnt the value of kindness and understanding from her.

I learnt the importance of friendship and loyalty from the Breakers.

And I learnt to be a ruthless, violent bastard from the Skins.

Right now I bet my mum's rolling over in her grave, praying to anyone who'll listen to save my wretched soul. Some nights when I'm stuck in my head, I sure as fuck feel her disappointment. It weighs as heavy as the bad choices I've made and the souls of the men I've killed.

I've killed people.

I might not wear the tattoos beneath my eyes like Jeb does, but it doesn't make it any less true. Sure, they might have been bad men. They might have deserved to get a bullet between the eyes, but that doesn't change the fact that *I* took their lives. It also doesn't change the fact that I used a dance I love to seduce their wives to find out as much as I could about them. I never slept with the women, not ever, but being their private bachata teacher was how I learned their husbands' secrets. It's amazing what a woman will say when they think they're going to get fucked. I don't feel any guilt. Those women have better lives without their sadistic, violent husbands ruling over them. The truth is, I've done many things I'm ashamed of but killing those men, so the rest of the Breakers didn't have to, isn't one of them.

Zayn, Dax, York, they're my ride or die.

The choices I make are for those motherfuckers, *my brothers*. Every damn time.

When we were kids our crew gave us purpose and dance held us steady, it gave us an outlet that didn't end in violence. We tried so fucking hard to fight the inevitable, and for a time we stayed out of trouble. We were the best dance crew in London, and when Pen joined us, we became a goddamn family. That tiny little girl who'd walked into our basement battered, bruised and with balls of steel, had done something no other girl could.

She made us love her.

With her by our side we found solace in dance. *Peace*. We formed a bond that meant something, that meant fucking *everything*, and over time our friendship grew into more. We would all do anything for her.

She taught us how to love, and then she broke our fucking hearts.

I told her that we'd returned to reclaim what's ours. She believes that's her.

She's wrong.

I let her destroy us once before. There isn't a chance in hell I'll allow her to do that again.

She can tempt me with her fire and her fury. She can kiss me and almost bring me to my goddamn knees. She can dance until the very fucking pit of my soul starts to revive but I cannot, *will not*, let her back in.

And neither will they. I'll make sure of it.

We aren't the boys she once loved anymore.

They're dead.

And when we're done, a part of her will be too.

I don't get off on that fact. It's just a certainty that none of us can avoid.

We're the Breakers and we break things after all.

1

Pen

I have a choice. I know that.
Fight back and sign Lena's death warrant.
Obey and get raped.
Running is no longer an option. It never was.
"That's it, Penelope, do the right thing," Jeb sneers as I turn to face him. His warm breath curdles the air that's already filled with the heady scent of sex and debauchery. Around us people are fucking like animals, all sense of decency left at the entrance to Grim's club. Not that any of these fuckers had much to begin with. They're all gangsters, fucking criminals. They don't give a shit. Their sense of right and wrong is skewed to suit their own sense of morality. This is probably an average night out for them.
"I'm sure Zayn will make you feel good, Penelope. I've heard he's quite the lover." Jeb's laughter scratches down my spine, making me stiffen as bile burns my throat.

My instinct is to fight back, but if I do that then David will be the least of my problems. He's in fucking Mexico, after all. Right here and now, Jeb is just a short car ride away from my little sister who has no fucking clue about the target on her head.

"Did you think I'd forget? That I'd let this go?"

"No," I bite out. Of course I didn't. Jeb hasn't got to this position by backing out of his threats. He collects his debt in blood, tears, and death. Everyone knows that, including me. I just wish I hadn't allowed myself to fall into the false sense of security that the last three years have afforded me. Now, after all that time, Jeb's cashing in part of my debt.

Tonight Zayn is playing his doppelganger for the sole purpose of fucking me in front of all these bastards. What I don't understand is why Jeb gives a shit anyway? Why does he feel he needs to hide his sexual preferences? What difference does being gay make? This is the twentieth century for fuck's sake.

"Pretty girl, just fucking relax. You loved him once. I'm sure he'll make it good for you..." Jeb has the gall to say, his blasé attitude boiling my blood.

"I can't believe Zayn would agree to this. I know I hurt him, but *this*?"

"You know you want it. Don't lie to yourself, Penelope. I bet you're wet thinking about Zayn fucking you in front of the Breakers. Isn't that what pissed your brother off so much, knowing that you were a whore for them?"

"Fuck you," I seethe, holding onto the anger because tears are unthinkable. I will not shed *any* for this man, and I refuse to shed any more for the Breakers.

"It ain't me who's getting fucked tonight, pretty girl. Though admittedly, your feistiness is turning me on just a little," he admits, with a surprised laugh. "Who would've thought it?"

"You're sick. This is *rape*," I snarl back, yanking my arms from his grip. My gaze flicks to the table beside us and the empty bottle of champagne. If I could just reach it, I could use it as a weapon.

Jeb smiles lazily beneath his mask, even though his black eyes flash with warning. "Nuh-uh-huh," he says, wagging his finger in my face. "Grim's men will take you out, and your little sister will be dead within the hour. The only fighting in Grim's club is in the cage. Those are the rules. Of course, hate sex is positively encouraged." He tips his head back and laughs like a fucking bloodthirsty hyena.

Around us the patrons are oblivious to the war raging within me, too busy fucking like animals, or snorting long lines of coke laid out onto plates of mirrored glass in front of them. The trouble is, there's no winning side. Not for me. I'm fucked any way you look at it. Knowing that, my hands remain by my side. I want to scream, my fists curl and uncurl and my jaw aches from clenching it so tightly, but nothing compares to the anger and betrayal I feel. *Nothing*.

It burns inside of me, ripping through my chest like an out of control fire gutting a home filled up with memories. Jeb might be the instigator, the guy who holds all the strings, but the Breakers, *they're* the ones who agreed to this.

Zayn agreed to this.

And that's unforgivable.

"So what's it to be, Penelope? We could do this the easy way or the hard way, but either way, you're getting fucked right here in front of all these people."

"Why does it even matter? Why do you care so much about what people think of you? Fuck a man, Jeb. Grow some goddamn balls," I hiss, trying to buy some time, not caring that my words will piss him off. The longer he's standing here arguing with me, the better. Maybe I can keep him occupied long enough for this debauchery to be over. I might pay for it later, but I'm going to take my chances. Jeb steps closer, gripping my upper arm as he yanks me towards him.

"Don't try and psychoanalyse me, *bitch*. It doesn't matter why I do what I do. It only matters that *you* fucking obey!" he sneers.

Twisting on his feet, he pulls me towards Zayn and my worst fucking nightmare. I know I'm strong. I've survived years of abuse, but this. How can I survive this? I loved Zayn. I still love him despite everything, but that love is quickly draining away like water through sand.

As I walk through the dense heat of the warehouse, I remember that time when Zayn and I had made out on Xeno's bed. I remember how I'd adored his kisses, relished his touch. I remember how I revelled in his words of affection and love. My heart had been so fucking full. Back then, Xeno had watched and it had turned me on knowing he was there. Back then, I'd been a willing participant.

Back then, they had *both* loved me.

Those boys would never, *ever* have contemplated rape, let alone agree to it. Surely they're not so different now, right? Surely, what we had meant *something*? Then again, a lot can change in three years, especially when you're part of the Skins. Perhaps they're beyond repair, so damaged by this life they've led that there's no coming back from it. My steps falter as we near their table, my body trembling.

"Don't fight this, Penelope. You need to put on a convincing show; your baby sister's life depends on it," Jeb reminds me.

I clamp my mouth shut on the sob that threatens to break free. I will do anything for Lena. *Anything.* I survived what happened before. I'll survive this. My feet feel leaden with every step, but I don't fight. I keep walking. On the far side of the warehouse, I see their red skull masks. They look like the devil's henchmen, waiting for my return.

Waiting to *break* me.

The closer we get, the more I feel their gaze penetrate my skin like tiny nicks from a knife. Every slice has my heart stuttering for breath and my soul crying out for some kind of intervention. Around us, the fucking has become frenzied, dark, feral. One gangster has a woman gripped by the throat, her mouth slack in desire and the skin around her lips dusted a shade of blue. If he hadn't just released her throat, so that she could scream out her orgasm, I have no doubt death would've taken her.

Directly to our left, the same female gangster who was getting eaten out earlier is now straddling a burly man, and is riding him hard. She catches my eye and must see something because mid fuck she reaches out to grab my wrist. I yelp at the tightness of her grip as she yanks me down to her mouth, the scent of her desire is pungent and far too intimate. Jeb stills, looking between us, but for some reason he doesn't pull me away. He gives her a moment to say what she wants to say.

"I see the fear in your eyes, girl. This isn't the place for that. Do what you need to survive." Then she lets me go, leans over the man beneath her and grips his jaw before fucking his mouth with her tongue and his dick with her pussy.

Jeb whistles low, his fingers digging into my upper arm as we move away from them. "You've caught the attention of The Belladonnas. Interesting."

"The Belladonnas?" I ask, again trying to distract him.

"Yeah, those bitches run Manchester. No one moves drugs in or out of that city without their say so, but their time will come," he explains, the arrogant arsehole.

He's so fucking sure of himself. Of his power and his reach.

But he's still flesh and blood, muscle, and bone. Jeb has a weakness, and I'm the one who's aware of it. That gives *me* power. I didn't understand that when I was a kid. I do now. Gritting my jaw, I straighten my spine and hold my head high as we walk back to the table, a plan forming.

"Here we go, *Sir*," Jeb says, smiling with glee as he pushes me towards Zayn.

I stumble a little, keeping my gaze fixed on Zayn, the boy I found friendship with first. His onyx eyes flash with anger and something else, something close to pity. It makes a fire burn inside me.

Well, fuck him.

I don't want his pity. I want him to stand up against Jeb. I need him to do the right thing. I have to hope he's still capable of it.

"Where have you been?" Zayn asks, flicking his gaze between us both. There are questions in his eyes that remind me of the night I broke his heart. Questions he should've voiced back then instead of holding inside. Not one of the Breakers questioned my actions.

They let me go.

They. Let. Me. Go.

"We were just having a little... chat," Jeb shrugs, sitting at the table. He leans over and grabs the bottle of whisky and pours himself a shot of the golden liquid, smacking his lips after swallowing it down. "We're back. Now the fun can really start."

Not one of the Breakers speak up. All four of them remain

tight-lipped. Out of everyone here I thought at least Dax would do something. He was the one who always protected me, who came to my rescue first. My Dark Angel.

Not this time.

This time I have to save myself.

With a calmness that I didn't know I possessed, I turn to look at Jeb, locking eyes with the man that is using me like a whore who can be loaned out at his whim.

"You wanted a show. I'm going to give you one you'll never forget," I say, then remove my mask and place it on the table. My trembling fingers linger over the shiny plastic as I hold back the tears pricking my eyes. There are too many memories bound up in that mask. That night, three years ago, I might have removed this mask, just like I have now, but I hid behind another of my own making to save my sister, to save these four men sitting before me now. Tonight, I'm going to lay myself bare to save myself and buy some time. Right now I need the Breakers to see into the very heart of me. They can hide behind these glowing red skull masks like fucking cowards, but I sure as fuck won't hide. Let them see my anger. Let them see my pain, my fear.

Let them see me.

I look at Dax first, my eyes boring into his. He holds my stare, his mouth pressed into a hard line. On the table, his leather-clad fingers curl into a fist. He's barely holding onto that anger he's so famous for. *Teardrop Dax*, the man who can make grown men cry, but who's never once shed a tear of his own. I can't tell if his anger is aimed at me or Jeb, or something else altogether. Either way, he's on edge. Good. Maybe it's going to take something like this to push him to *act*.

Next I turn to face York. He studies me closely, and this time when he looks at me, I don't hide a thing. I lay myself bare. If he can still read me like he could so well when we were kids, he'll know exactly how I'm feeling now. In fact, I'm counting on it.

Beside him, Xeno meets my gaze with a hard stare of his own. He was always the most difficult to reach and now it's no different. I swallow hard, my heart aching for everything we had and all that we've lost.

"Come on, Penelope, we haven't got all night," Jeb says from behind me.

I ignore him. With a shaky breath, and my head held high, I finally focus on Zayn who is glaring at his uncle.

"*Jeb*, I need you to look at me," I say to Zayn, barely holding onto my disgust for his part in this charade. There's a firmness to my voice that's sharp, lethal. To feel this way towards Zayn isn't something I'm used to. Hurt and disappointment, yes, but never disgust. Feeling like this cuts me deeply, and I want to hurt him back.

Tonight, I'm going to do that.

He twists his torso, canting his head to look at me, but he doesn't say a word. The speakers blast out *Arsonist's Lullabye* by Hozier, adding to the already oppressive atmosphere. The moaning around us intensifies. The fucking becomes even more frenzied, feeding into the sin and carnal pleasure that unravels at every table. It's a cocktail of violence, passion, and brutal sex. Chairs fall to the floor, glasses smash and tables rock under the weight of rampant desire. The heat in the room rises and a light sheen of sweat spreads out over my skin. I don't know whether the Breakers are enjoying this moment or if they're as uncomfortable as I am. Either way, the tension rises with every second that passes and my skin prickles with apprehension.

I can't back out now.

Blocking out everyone around us, I concentrate on Zayn. "Turn your chair around and face me," I repeat, lowering my voice and softening those sharp edges just enough to give him pause.

"I don't take orders from you," he replies, the tone of his voice dark, glittering with challenge and *lust*. Behind us, Jeb sniggers. He's fucking loving this. Screw him.

"I have something you want, and I can't give it to you if you're tucked beneath the table."

"*Fuck*," York grinds out, and I can hear the disbelief in his voice.

I ignore him. I ignore the heat of the Breakers' stares. If this is going to work I'm going to need more than their eyes on me. I'm going to need the whole fucking warehouse to take note.

Zayn shifts his chair around to face me, his legs widening so that I can step into the space he makes. He leans back, his hands on his thighs, his fingers relaxed as he watches me.

I wait for his gaze to run up my body before resting on mine and swallow hard when I see the flash of pain he's holding onto. It makes me hesitate. Could I have read him wrong? But just like hope, that look is fleeting, gone before I can even grab hold of it, tuck it inside my chest and let it grow.

"What is it that you think I want?" he asks, not taking his eyes off of me. His ebony irises bore into my skin, piercing flesh and bone, aiming right for my heart.

It's now or never.

I have to keep Lena safe.

"This," I whisper, then twist away from him, part my legs and bend at the waist, my dress riding up around my hips with the movement. My hands grab my ankles as I look up at him from between my calves. My hair falls in a shroud around my face as Zayn stares at the silky material of my black, lacy underwear that rides up my arse and wraps around my pussy lips, leaving little to the imagination.

His mouth parts and his teeth bite into his bottom lip. That chipped tooth I love leaving an indent.

He *wants* me.

And I've never wanted to kill someone more than right at this moment.

This bastard actually thinks I'm going to fuck him willingly.

Betrayal bleeds like acid into my veins, fuelling me with a rage that overwhelms me. I want to claw at his face. I want to rip him to shreds. I want to rip all of the Breakers to shreds just like they've done to me with their barbed comments and their cruelty over the past few weeks. Well, screw him. Screw *them*. This is as close to my pussy they're ever going to get.

On the next beat, I straighten up. Twirling on the ball of my left foot, I spin around to face Zayn, my loose hair flaring around me as I move, lashing at my skin. My chest heaves, my face flushes with heat and my fingers curl into my palms. I'm aware that the skirt of my dress has hitched up to reveal the bottom of my arse cheeks, and the mound of my knicker-covered pussy, but I don't pull it down.

Let them look. Let them *all* fucking look. If they didn't see my emotions before, then they sure as fuck can't mistake them now. My anger is a living, breathing beast that reveals itself in the baring of my teeth, the flaring of my nostrils, the narrowing of my eyes and the raggedness of my breath. Zayn's gaze snaps up to meet mine just as the words of the song hang in the air around us, a heavy shroud of truth, precise in its timing. When I was a kid, I was fooled by the Breakers. I'd believed that they'd loved me. I'd believed they'd always have my back, would always fight in my corner. It was all lies. Now all I'm left with is this fire burning inside of me ready to eviscerate everything in its path.

"Pen..." Zayn murmurs, his fingers gripping hold of the material of his trousers tightly as I glare back at him.

Pressing back the bitter tears that threaten to fall, I lean over, rest my hands on Zayn's shoulder and whisper into his ear. "You cannot take what isn't freely given, Zayn Bernard. You fucking disappoint me."

With that I place my bare foot on the chair between his open thighs and step up onto the table, kicking the glasses and bottles out of my way. I get a feeling of satisfaction as one of the goblets hits Jeb on the arm, before crashing to the floor. I'm going to pay for that, but right now I don't give a shit. He jerks towards me, baring his teeth but Zayn holds his arm out, preventing him from getting close. I don't get to think about that too much because with the next beat, I slam my left foot on the table and proceed to follow up with an angry time-step. I might have slowed down the step a little to compliment the beat of the song, but it still conveys the emotion I wish to get across. In bare feet it doesn't have quite the same effect that it would have with tap shoes on, but when I glance down at York, I can see he's beginning to understand. Thoughts whir behind his icy-blue eyes as he watches me intently.

In fact they're all watching me.

If they wanted a show, they're going to get one, just not the one they expected. Dance has saved me countless times before. I've no doubt in my mind that it's going to do the same tonight.

It has to.

2

Zayn

Pen stands before me, a fucking *goddess*. Wild, beautiful, *angry*.

The glow of our masks, and the orange flames flickering in the oil barrels around the warehouse catches the auburn lights in her long dark hair and dusts her skin in a fiery glow.

Her wrath, her fire and fury, it all bleeds out of her, scalding me with a passion that is raw, powerful, and oxygen stealing.

I can't fucking breathe.

She just bent over provocatively. Her shapely legs, her rounded arse and the slash of her knicker-covered pussy bared for me. I damn near fucking came in my pants like a teenage boy. I wanted to press my face against her slit and fuck her with my tongue. I wanted to do that so fucking bad. I'm hard for her. So fucking hard. I don't doubt that everyone around this table is too.

But everything about this is *wrong*.

So fucking wrong.

When Jeb had asked me to stand in for him, I'd agreed because I knew that this warehouse would be filled with his enemies. I don't think that there's a crew here that the Skins haven't clashed with over the last few years. Grim might think she has control of these fucking arseholes, but I know better. Any one of the gangsters here will take a hit for their crew just so they can take Jeb out and whilst I know he fucking deserves it, he's still blood, he's still the leader of the Skins. Besides, I took an oath — just like the rest of the Breakers did — one we can't break. But *this*, I sure as fuck didn't agree to this. It doesn't take a goddamn genius to see why he invited Pen tonight. Now his words from earlier make sense.

"Zayn, you've had my back all this time. I owe you. Tonight, I've got an extra special gift for you," he'd said with a fucking wink and a smile.

I figured he was talking about a new ride.

Not this.

The music adds to the potency of the moment. The beat of the snare drum pounding in time with my bastard heart. Hozier, might not produce music that I usually listen too but he sure as fuck knows how to write a song that gets your blood pumping.

I'm itching to move. To let go. Really let go.

I lost my passion for dance the night Pen walked away from us.

We all did.

The only one who continued to dance was Xeno and that wasn't because he wanted to, but because he had to. Now, as Pen stares at me with a rage befitting the music flooding my senses, all I want to do is dance with her just like we did when we were kids. She's lit a match between all of us. Xeno can deny it all he wants, but I know him, and he wants Pen as much as the rest of us. Fuck, if I thought she wanted it, I'd take her here and now.

"Pen..." I murmur, my fingers curling into my trousers so tightly I think my knucklebones might just rip through my skin.

Her eyes glisten in the dim lighting. I see the rage brimming on her lashes, but she holds back her angry tears. She's so fucking strong. She always was. I hold her gaze, forcing myself to take on her wrath. This is the first time since she danced in the studio that she's allowed us to see her. And, boy, do I fucking see her. When she rests her hands on my shoulders, and leans over, I bite down on this feral need I have to take her. Gritting my jaw, I hold back not because I don't want her, not because I'm afraid to finish what we started all those years ago, but because Pen hasn't agreed to this. She doesn't want me to fuck her and to give in to my base needs. There's a pang in my chest that has never, *ever* fucking gone away when it comes to this woman. To fuck her now like this would be rape. Plain and fucking simple.

I'm *not* that kid she once knew. I'm *not* a good man. None of us are.

But I sure as fuck am not a rapist.

Her fingers squeeze tighter as her lips graze across my ear. "You cannot take what isn't freely given, Zayn Bernard. You fucking disappoint me."

And even though her words sting, her naivety floors me because I could take, I just *choose* not to. With one last fleeting look, she steps up onto the table, then takes my fucking breath away.

3

Pen

My anger is loud.

My rage is a beast that dances with the intent to maim.

My steps are ruthless, timed to perfection with the thumping beat of the song.

My bleeding heart knits together with every thrust of my hips, every flare of my arm, every turn of my head and kick of my leg.

My soul screams like a warrior as I use the table as my platform and dance as my weapon.

I'm not a victim.

Not tonight.

Fuck that.

Dax might knock his opponents out with lethal punches and kicks.

Zayn might slash his victims with the sharpened point of a knife.

York might crucify his enemies with fists that break bones.

Xeno might torture his adversaries with something far worse.

And Jeb might ruin lives with threats to the ones I love.

But tonight I'm fighting back.

Fucking like animals in front of each other isn't a display of dominance. It's for the weak, the vain, the narcissistic. I'm going to show everyone here what it really means to be powerful, because that's why they're here, right? Instead of, *'my gun is bigger than yours'*, it's *'my cock is bigger than yours'*. Even The Belladonnas have played into that mentality and it's bullshit. Fucking bullshit.

Tonight, all eyes are going to be on me.

But it will be on *my* terms.

They can look, they can want, but they sure as fuck can't touch.

I've had to endure years of my brother *beating* me. I've had to suffer a lifetime of my mum's words *belittling* me. I've had to withstand *judgement* from people who don't even know me. I've had to live the past three years in a permanent state of *fear*.

This is my chance to take a little of my power back.

The song intensifies and so do my dance moves. I'm freestyling, yes. But this is more than a kid in a nightclub battling against other kids for kudos. This is me dancing for my life, for Lena's life.

Jeb might have brought me here to be fucked, to keep up appearances, to hide who he really is, but what shows more strength, to follow the crowd or to act in defiance? When I arrived people just saw a vagina fit for fucking, and fucking alone. Grim had looked at me like I was a whore, and so did every other person in this place.

I'm *not* a whore.

I'm Pen and these bastards can kiss my arse.

By the time I've finished I'm going to be wanted by every man and woman in this place, but only owned by one. Jeb, the leader of the Skins. Well, at least that's what I'll allow him to think.

Because no one truly owns me.

No. One.

But if I can appease Jeb's pride, his vanity, and his need to keep up appearances by being a spectacular dancer and becoming something other people covet, then I'd rather that than be used as a whore.

So I dance.

The table is large enough, and stable enough for me to move freely. I'm careful not to look at Jeb or the Breakers. Instead, I look out over the warehouse, my gaze skating over the different tables. Slowly, one by one, I gain the attention of the crowd. The fucking stops and the staring starts. Men tuck their cocks away. Women pull down their dresses and adjust their masks. All eyes are on me.

Good.

My movements evolve from angry tap steps to the fluidity of contemporary dance. The pounding of my feet on the table is replaced with the pounding of my fist against my rib cage as I jerk my whole torso forwards and back showing the Breakers how my heart beats with so much rage that it feels like it's about to burst free of my chest.

Before long I'm covered in a sheen of sweat as I twist and turn, moving my body in such a way that shows both sensuality and strength. I'm careful not to be too overtly sexual this time.

I need to be desired, but untouchable. A rare, precious piece of jewellery brought out to be ogled, but not touched. Like the Crown-fucking-Jewels.

The emotive form of contemporary makes way for ballet and the perfection and poise of such a dance that juxtaposes beautifully with all the imperfect and untamed gangsters surrounding me. I'm using this dance like a metaphorical middle finger to all these bastards. I'm rising above the grime and the grit, the violence and the aggression, and showing them what it truly means to be powerful with grace and beauty.

Most won't get it, but my Breakers. They *will*. I'll make sure of it.

Rising up onto my toes in a demi-pointe, my arms held outwards, I breathe in deep before spinning on the ball of my left foot and kicking out with my right leg in a fouetté turn. My arms spread wide, before I draw back in both my arms and my right leg, my pointed toe touching my left knee. I repeat the move over and over again, thankful for Sebastian, his ballet lessons, and words of wisdom. Thanks to his recent tutelage and hours of practicing alone in a studio, my core muscles are able to hold me steady and I have enough stamina to dance this fight. I dig deep, using that muscle memory, that energy, to showcase what I've learnt from him.

My skirt is now hitched up over my hips, but I don't care about that, at least I'm still wearing my knickers. Besides, I'm practically dressed as a nun given the state of undress the rest of the crowd has been in over the course of the night. With every spin, the warehouse rushes by, the flames in the oil drums blurring within the darkness. Heat radiates around me, my movement parting the air with purpose.

I allow the dance to take over, my soul speaks through my

limbs and the movements I make with my body. Heat pervades the air alongside a desperate kind of longing. I've longed for the Breakers' return. Deep down inside, all I've ever wanted is for them to come back into my life, to beg for forgiveness, to allow me the opportunity to beg for theirs. I've never wanted to fix what was broken more than I do now. This need I have for them, the friendship I yearn for, the *love* that breaks my heart, is all encompassing. Hate and fear still bubbles within my chest. The concoction makes me feel ill, confused, uncertain about everything.

I *love* them.

I fucking *hate* them.

I *want* them.

I *never ever* want to see them again.

Too many conflicting emotions bleed into my dance steps until the only thing I can grasp hold of is the need to save myself from something that I might never recover from and the absolute determination to keep Lena safe from harm.

So I keep moving, spinning, jerking my body with every last ounce of strength I have left. Tap merges with ballet and contemporary. I even throw in some hip-hop just because I can. Black spots dance at the edges of my vision, the lack of food and the flood of adrenaline a dangerous cocktail that will make me crash and burn the second I stop moving. But I keep dancing until I'm not conscious of my moves, until the dance truly and completely takes over.

I feel powerful. Strong.

Maybe it's foolish to believe that my talent will get me out of trouble. Maybe it's just prolonging the inevitable, but I have to try. I have to hope that Zayn, that the Breakers will be reminded of who I am, who I was to them. I dance with every last part of my soul, every last drop of energy as anger and love burns inside my chest. I grab hold of those feelings with gritted teeth and clawed fingers and don't let go. We all have a demon within us, just like Hozier sings. My demons have been eating away at me for three fucking years. It's time to set them free.

Bending backwards in an arch, my palms nearing the edge of the table between York and Dax, I flip over, landing on my feet between them. The air zings with energy, and I'm very aware that every single pair of eyes in this warehouse are on me now. Even the topless women in the cage are gawking at me. That's where I head next. Striding over to the cage unaccosted, I step into the space and nod. I see something within them, a respect that comes from a love of dance. These women might remove their clothes for money, hell, some of them probably even spread their legs for it. But right now, all six of them acknowledge what this is. They see something in me too.

The need to *fight*.

To be seen as something other than a sexual object. None of us want to be lusted over and discarded like trash the minute these arseholes are done with us.

No more.

The women surround me, small smiles pulling up their lips.

"Get it, girl," a tall blonde says to me before she spins away from me in impossibly high heels and towards the edge of the cage. The rest of the women follow suit and like caged animals finally given freedom, really fucking let loose. Pride fills me as I watch them move with purpose, resolve, and a proverbial fuck you to all these bastards watching us.

I don't know them, but that doesn't matter. I understand them in this moment, just like they understand me. Right here and now, we're bonded by our anger, by our love of dance, by our need to be fucking *seen*.

Standing in the centre of the cage, my chest heaving, my bare feet tacky from the not yet dried blood, I glare at my Breakers with curled fists and fierce determination. All four of them are hidden in the shadows, their expressions unseen from this distance, but I know I've hit them where it hurts. I fucking *know* it.

A feral, animalistic feeling blooms inside of me. Something as dark as the violence that had bled into the canvas beneath my feet just minutes before. I feed off of it. I let it fill me up and with the last remains of my energy, I let it all out. Hozier sings about internal strength, a fire that burns within us all. He sings about the demons we fight inside of us, about controlling them. But tonight I'm not controlling anything. Tonight, I'm showing my strength.

Tonight, that's what I give them, *my fire*.

Every. Last. Fucking. Drop.

4

Pen

My hands and knees slam onto the bloodied canvas, my chest heaves as I draw in precious oxygen. I'm shaking all over. My teeth chatter and sweat pours from my skin. The soles of my feet are raw, blistered from dancing barefoot. I'm spent. Every last ounce of energy is gone, and blackness threatens to take over.

I don't want to faint. I don't want to be that vulnerable, so I give myself a moment to breathe as my head drops between my shoulders and my hair falls over my face. All I can hear are my laboured breaths as I suck precious oxygen in and out of my lungs, drawing on it so that I don't fall into darkness. Then, slowly, as I sit back on my haunches with my head still lowered, other sounds trickle in. Someone close by begins to clap. I peer to the side, not lifting my head, but looking through the curtain of hair that falls over my face. A pair of shiny, black shoes approach me as I try to steady my thundering heart. They're buffed to perfection and sit beneath a pair of dark grey suit trousers, coming to stop directly beside me. Beyond them I see the strippers walk out of the cage leaving me alone with this man and it's definitely a man given the size of his feet and the clothes he's wearing.

"That was quite incredible. You are an outstanding dancer," a deep male voice says to me, proving my point.

This man has an accent. I'm no expert, but it sounds Russian or eastern European with the way his lips wrap around the *w* making it sound more like a *v*. I don't respond to his compliment, focusing instead on getting my pulse back to a less dangerous beat and trying not to succumb to the black spots threatening my vision. He slowly lowers himself into a crouch beside me and I see a white shirt rolled up to the elbows to reveal tan skin and dark hair covering thick forearms.

"Look at me, *piękna tancerka*," he says, lifting my chin with his finger. There's something in the tone of his voice that sends warning bells ringing. I listen to my gut, it's never wrong. This man is dangerous, but then again, what man isn't? All the men in my life are dangerous. I'm used to the predators. Can smell them a mile off.

I peer at him through my messy strands of hair, some of which are sticking to my forehead with sweat. He's wearing a mask, but it isn't much of one. Just a thin length of red silk wrapped around his eyes with holes cut into the material so he can see. There's really no effort to hide his identity and that only makes me more wary of him, not less. He's older than I expected, maybe in his early fifties with dark hair smoothed off his face in a sharp style that greys around the sides of his temple. A short, clipped beard covers the lower half of his face, wrapping around plump pink lips and teeth so white and straight they must have been paid for. He's handsome, there's no denying that, but I can see the truth of who he is deep in the dark recesses of his cobalt eyes.

Like Jeb, like David, this man is vicious, cruel, calculating.

There's something else too, something darker, something that hints at a wickedness that surpasses both Jeb and David, if that's possible. He smiles slowly, his fingers pushing back my hair before he lowers his hand over my shoulder and trails his fingers down my arm, cupping my elbow.

"My name is Malik; I'd like you to accompany me to my table. There are matters I wish to discuss with you," he says, and though on the surface it sounds like a request, it comes out as an order, one I'm betting most people will follow or lose their life for disobeying him.

Except I'm not most people and I'm done with being ordered around tonight.

"I'm with someone," I respond, pulling my arm out of his hold and pushing to my feet, hoping to God they hold me upright. My body betrays me, and I wobble from sheer exhaustion and light-headedness. Malik grabs my elbow once more and steps closer, an elegant smile plastered on his face.

Beyond the spotlight lighting up the cage, I hear a commotion, though I can't make out what's going on. It's too bright where I am, and too dark in the rest of the warehouse to see clearly.

"Do you think that matters to me, *Stopy Płomieniach*?" he asks, ignoring whatever the fuck is going on behind us. I have no idea what *Stopy Płomieniach* means but I'm guessing it's some kind of disparaging remark. Not that I give a shit. I've been called so many names that I've become immune to the harm they cause.

"It will matter to the people I came here with," I retort, yanking my arm free from his hold and stepping away from him so that I can pull my dress back down over my hips.

"Oh, I'm not sure that I give a fuck," he retorts with a shrug.

"Grim will have you shot if you start shit here tonight."

"Hmm, yes, that is quite a predicament. Then again, everyone has a price. I'm certain whoever owns you now would gladly hand you over to me if the reward was high enough, wouldn't you say?"

I take another step backwards, but he just enters my space again, unperturbed. Reaching for me, he grasps my hand before pressing a kiss against my knuckles. The second his lips brush against my skin, I can hear the familiar sound of Dax's roar and York telling him to calm the fuck down. "See, you're pissing them off," I point out.

He smiles lazily at me. "Regardless, I tend to get what I want, by using force or by spending money. I have a lot of both."

"I'm not someone you can buy, and if you try to take me then there'll be consequences," I bluff. Jeb would sell me out in a heartbeat and I no longer have faith in the Breakers to protect me like they once did. Still, putting up a front is a better option than crumbling.

"Everyone has a price, even you."

He taps my nose and anger whirls inside my chest once again as another man tries to own me. It pisses me the fuck off. Maybe I brought this on myself. I knew dancing the way I did just now would garner attention, but it was because I couldn't face the alternative. I'm just trying not to get raped, for fuck's sake.

"I'm not for sale," I grind out.

"Let's see, shall we?" he asks, yanking me against his chest and kissing me on the mouth. I try to break free from his hold, but his arm wraps around my back as he crushes me against him.

I can feel the hard edge of his cock pressing through his trousers and against my lower belly.

Fuck. Fuck. *Fuck!*

I'm about to bring my leg up and knee him in the balls when he's forcefully pulled backwards by Dax who now has his throat gripped in a tight stranglehold.

"You do not fucking touch her, motherfucker!" Dax growls, his teeth bared in rage beneath his mask as he pushes Malik up against the wired fence of the cage. His body is whip tight and the veins beneath his skin popping with tension.

Malik smiles, the slow spread like black ink in water. He's not afraid, not in the slightest. This is a game and I have the sense that he's always the victor. He narrows his eyes at Dax and mutters something I can't hear. Dax pulls back then slams his body into the wire once more, all whilst his grip on Malik's throat tightens.

"Don't!" I say, finding myself in the position of trying to prevent Dax from doing something that's going to have consequences. Consequences that will end very swiftly in his death. Half a beat later, Beast walks into the cage with a gun held out in front of him and Grim by his side. I'm too shocked to do anything but stare at the unfolding events. Beast aims the gun at Dax's head, pulling back the safety.

"Let him go or get a bullet in your brain," he grinds out.

"He touched what isn't his," Dax grunts, not loosening his hold, but not tightening it either.

"Let. Him. Go. Or. Die!"

LYRICAL

Dax doesn't let go.
Beast doesn't back down.
And my heart? My heart fucking splinters.

5

Dax

Motherfucking cunt! I will rip his heart out and gut the bastard for laying his hands on her.

I'll fucking *kill* him.

I'll kill the cunt.

I don't care who he is. I don't fucking care!

My fingers close around his throat and I squeeze, willing to get a bullet in my brain. In fact, I welcome it. Death doesn't scare me. What's happening inside my goddamn chest, *that* fucking scares me. I was done with her.

DONE.

Except now I'm not.

Her passion, her anger, her fear, her *rage*, it cut me deep and I'm fucking bleeding from the wounds. I'm bleeding out like a motherfucking soldier ripped apart in the crossfire of some fucking war he never wanted to be a part of.

It pours out of me. My blood drips from every goddamn pore.

She *slayed* me. Slayed *us* with one motherfucking dance.

She punched her fists into my chest and wrapped her fingers around my heart and squeezed. She's reignited feelings that I've long since buried.

Right there in front of me, she just danced for her goddamn life and I saw her clearly for the first time since returning.

I saw her.

Kid.

My Kid.

She was afraid, angry, and utterly fucking breathtaking.

And now this dick, this fucking *prick*, put his hands on her.

No! No fucking way!

Not again.

Not again.

NOT AGAIN.

The only person who has the right to touch her is us. She's fucking ours.

Ours.

Our Pen.

Our lucky penny…

You're wrong. She doesn't belong to the Breakers. She belongs to HIM.

To Jeb.

MOTHERFUCKER!

I squeeze tighter and wait for death.

6

Pen

Dax isn't letting go. I can see the rage taking over. So I do the only thing I can, I step in. Tentatively, I place my hand on his arm. "Let him go," I coerce, looking at Beast and begging him with my eyes not to pull the trigger. Beside him, Grim frowns and I know she sees something in me that she hadn't before.

"Stay out of it," Dax bites out, anger billowing off him, thick and pungent. He doesn't look at me, he keeps his gaze fixed on Malik, refusing to release the arsehole. I wish I could see more of his face to try and gauge just how close he is to exploding. Then again, it doesn't take a genius to know how he's feeling. I just wish I knew why.

He doesn't give a shit about me. *Unless…*

My heart stutters in my chest, but I refuse to let hope take hold. This could all be because Jeb has ordered him up here. This could all be a part of their game and not because my Dark

Angel has returned to protect me. I swallow the hope that tries to make me weak and force a firmness into my voice.

"You don't need to die tonight."

I don't say his name, and I don't beg, but I'm sure he hears the plea in my voice all the same. No matter how angry I am with him, I don't want Dax to die. I don't want any harm to come to any of them, no matter how they've behaved. Deep down, I'm still that girl who loved them fiercely even if they aren't those boys anymore.

Nausea twirls in my stomach, threatening to burst free. I sway on my feet, stumbling a little. Dax flicks his gaze to me, slamming his lips together in a hard line.

"They have guns," I press. I know he knows that, but he doesn't seem to give a shit, and that scares me more than anything else does. He has no regard for his life right now. It's like he *wants* to die. That was never Dax. He had a shit upbringing, yes. He endured a life that would have led any kid to harm themselves, to want out, but he *never* succumbed. He fought to keep his sanity. Why so different now?

"I don't motherfucking care," Dax grinds out, confirming my worst fears. Malik eyes us both with interest, coming up with his own conclusions despite the fact he mustn't be able to breathe all that well right now. He's eerily calm. I don't like it.

"Five, four," Beast counts down. I see his thumb pull back the safety and urgency snaps at my heels. I step closer, ignoring Malik and focusing on Dax.

"Stop," I say gently. "Stop. Don't die tonight. Not for me." I can't hide the sheer exhaustion from my voice. The physical, emotional, and mental exhaustion. I'm about done.

Dax tips his head back and roars, losing his shit right in front of everyone and my throat tightens as Beast continues to count down.

"Three, TWO..."

"Let him go," I choke out, hating that I'm showing vulnerability but knowing it's the only thing that might stand a chance at getting through to him. My eyes flick to Beast, honing on his trigger finger. *"Please..."*

Dax's shoulders slump, and just like that, his hand releases Malik's throat as he steps back. I breathe out a sigh of relief whilst Malik just laughs, his voice tight, croaky.

"She's quite something. I can see why you wish to protect her."

Dax doesn't respond, he just keeps glaring at Malik. Behind him, Beast lowers his gun. I reach out, my fingers curling around the wire, holding myself upright as my heart really does try to escape my chest.

"Out of the cage, *gentlemen*," Grim says with anger, her attention focused on the two men. Though there is less strain in her voice now that the situation is under some semblance of control.

"As you wish, Grim," Malik says with a broad smile that makes Beast growl in warning. He watches both Malik and Dax closely as they pass by, his gun still clutched in his hand. Once they've stepped out of the cage, he follows.

Grim looks at me, her chin jerking. "You too, *Stopy Płomieniach*," she says, repeating the same phrase Malik used to describe me earlier.

"What does that even mean?" I mumble as I follow her instructions and exit the cage on wobbly legs and painful feet. They begin to throb as the adrenaline starts to wear off. I'm not really expecting an answer, given Grim dismissed me the moment we met, so I'm surprised when she falls into step beside me, allowing Beast to deal with Dax and Malik.

"It means *feet of flames*," Grim replies, moving closer so I can hear her over the music that has been turned up a notch. "Malik Brov is otherwise known as *The Collector* and is the head of a powerful Polish crime family."

"I see," I respond, not really knowing what the fuck to say to that.

"You don't," Grim insists. "Malik's side hobby is to collect *women* like other men might collect cars or jewels. Rumour has it he has a castle in the Scottish Highlands filled with women talented in the arts. Most of them are dancers, some are artists, others are musicians but *all* of them are prisoners. Malik and his three sons, *The Masks*, are a force to be reckoned with. Don't doubt there will be some kind of retaliation against the Skins for this—"

I nod, wondering if she knows that Jeb and Zayn have switched places. When I look over at the table, I notice that the only person still sitting is Zayn whilst the rest of the Breakers and Jeb are on their feet, standing toe-to-toe with three mean-looking arseholes with the same mask as Malik. Zayn appears to still be playing the part of gang leader and gives Malik a deadly look as he approaches. The rest of the gangs in the warehouse are watching everything unfold with interest. The tension is thick, cloying, and I'm finding it hard to breathe.

"Are they his sons?" I ask, indicating the three men.

"No. Bodyguards. His sons rarely leave the castle."

She reaches for me, stopping us both in our slow walk back to the table. "You are here under duress, aren't you?" she asks, her voice low and her fingers cool on my forearm.

I nod my head. What would be the point in lying?

Her jaw grits, anger flashing across her gaze. "I'm sorry for that."

"Why?"

"I assumed, and I was wrong. I'm guessing you didn't want

to fuck Mr Bernard tonight," she says, canting her head towards Zayn. I can't tell whether she genuinely doesn't know that Zayn is playing Jeb or does and is protecting that secret for some reason I'm unaware of. I'm not sure I care either way.

"No, I didn't," I bite out.

"And you dancing was a way to get out of that?"

"Yes."

"You think that's going to prevent him from taking what he wants regardless?" Grim asks, her voice low, angry. Her reaction surprises me. I really didn't think she'd give a shit.

"The moment's over. Besides, who wants to fuck with a gun aimed at their heads?" I say with false bravado as I nod towards Beast who still has his gun clutched in his hand. My gaze flicks to the men standing high above us, all of them pointing at the Breakers and the men opposing them. I bite down on my lip to stop it from trembling as I focus my attention back to the face-off unfolding in front of us. Dax has joined Xeno, York and Jeb. Zayn maintains a relaxed posture at the table, looking almost bored. He plays the role of Jeb well. Too well. My stomach flips over at the thought. I catch Zayn's eye. I can't read him, won't allow myself to. I need to keep my head rather than try to digest everything that's passed between us tonight.

"You'd be surprised," Grim answers sharply, a flash of disgust passing over her features. That one look tells me more about who she is than anything else that has passed between us tonight. Grim is tough, there's no denying that, but she has her own set of principles too. Maybe I judged her wrongly just as much as she judged me.

"Who are these people?" I ask, a shiver tracking down my spine as Malik barks an order at his bodyguards. They immediately step away and follow him to whatever hole he crawled out of. Good fucking riddance.

"People you don't want to get mixed up with." Grim leans in close, taking the opportunity to keep talking with me whilst Beast has a conversation with the Breakers and Jeb. Now that Malik and his bodyguards have walked away, the tension dissolves further. The rest of the gangs resume talking as more girls come pouring out from the corners of the warehouse. I tense. Grim notices.

"They're not here for sex. Just to serve. None of my girls fuck these men, unless they want to, of course," she says, as more drinks are poured, and drugs consumed.

"I'm not with the Skins because I want to be…"

"Yeah, no shit…" She sighs heavily, looking at me as though making a decision. "Fuck sake, I'm getting soft. Those damn delinquents have screwed me up for life."

"Delinquents?" I frown. What's she talking about?

"Don't worry about it. Look, I can get you out of here right now," Grim offers, but I shake my head. As much as I'd love to run, I can't, for Lena's sake. I need to see this night through. I need to face whatever Jeb has planned for me because even though I've managed to dodge a bullet, there's a whole load more aimed at me and I have a feeling more than one is going to hit their mark sooner rather than later.

"That won't help me in the long run," I reply.

"That bad, huh?"

"Yeah. That bad."

She nods. "I can make shit difficult for them…"

"What do you mean?"

"Jeb's an opportunist, I've never liked him. He likes to use kids to do his dirty work just like another wanker I used to know."

"No one likes him," I say, with a hint of a smile.

"All the more reason for me to take him down. He stepped on a few toes recently and whilst I'd normally keep the fuck out of bullshit like this, I will step in if I have reason to. Lately I have reason to."

"No offense, but you don't know Jeb. He's a fucking maniac."

"I don't need to know Jeb. I've dealt with men like him all my life," she says looking at me intently. "I see you have too. Am I right?"

I nod. "Yes."

"What's your name?" she asks me, changing the direction of the conversation.

"Pen. I'm Pen."

"Well, Pen. You ever need a friend. You come find me."

My stomach swirls with apprehension. I'm not sure of her motives, not at all. She might appear to be someone I can trust, but I've not lived the life I have to throw myself at the feet of someone I've only just met. Fuck that. Instead, I proceed with caution.

"Friends can turn their back on you without a moment's hesitation, so forgive me if I don't jump at the offer."

I expect some kind of caustic reply or a revoking of her offer, but all I'm given is a wide grin. "Yeah, I like you, and because of that I'll make sure Jeb doesn't fucking touch you tonight or any other time he brings you to my club."

"Thank you," I respond.

Not that it'll make much difference. If the leader of the Skins wants to fuck with me, he can do that at any point. Gritting my jaw, I make my way back to the table ready to face the Breakers and Jeb.

7

Pen

Keeping my shoulders back and my head held high I approach the table aware of the heated gaze of every single one of the Breakers, as well as Jeb. I don't make eye contact with any of them, all my concentration is on placing one foot in front of the other and keeping myself upright. I need to eat. I need to sleep. But most of all, I need to cry in the privacy of my own room. I blink back my tears. Showing weakness here isn't an option. I need to hold my shit together for a little while longer. Just a little longer.

Beside me, Grim folds her arms across her chest, looking directly at Dax. I'm grateful for her presence, even if I'm not sure whether I trust her yet. "You seem to enjoy being in the cage, don't you?" she says.

Dax grunts, still too wound up to respond beyond that guttural, dismissive acknowledgement. It's the wrong thing to do because Beast snarls, stepping into Dax's space, chest to chest. Dax doesn't flinch, his lip curls up in distaste.

"You've already pushed your fucking luck tonight. Answer Grim, right the fuck now!" Beast scowls, his thick finger pressing into Dax's chest. They're equally matched in size and fierceness, but there's an edge to Beast that I wouldn't want to test. The guy is named Beast for a reason, and I'm betting for Grim he'd go all out monster if the need arose. I bet he'd never walk away from her. "Are you listening, shithead?!"

Dax lifts his gaze slowly, nonchalantly, and I see his need to let it fucking rip because he doesn't step back, and he sure as fuck doesn't back down. Tonight, he has a death wish. My throat closes up as York and Xeno step forward, backing up their best friend even with the knowledge that they could all be shot. Even Zayn shifts in his seat, ready to jump in. Their loyalty to one another cuts me deeper than I'd ever care to admit. I feel their loss acutely at this moment. The past three years without them have been hell.

"Back off, *dick*," Dax bites out.

"Dax," I whisper on an exhale of breath. "Don't."

The only person who seems to hear me is Grim. I feel her fingers rest on my wrist. A gentle touch that belies the firm look on her face. There's understanding in her touch, but also a warning. *Don't get involved*, it says. I'm not stupid enough to ignore it.

"Beast, stand down. His actions will be settled in the ring at a later date," Grim says to both men. A muscle in Beast's jaw twitches, it's the only sign he's struggling with Grim's demand. I half expect him to ignore her, but his nostrils flare as he takes in a sharp breath before stepping back.

"What do you have in mind?" Beast asks, a wicked smile curling up his lips as he looks at Grim with respect and very obvious love. It's potent and unashamedly there. He loves Grim and he doesn't give a fuck who knows it. There's a strength in that I admire.

"Seeing as you're intent on causing shit," Grim says to Dax who has now focused on her, "And are stupid enough to face off with Beast, then I'm suggesting a fight between the two of you. Three weeks today, here at the club. Loser owes the other a debt that can be cashed in at any time. That's if you're up for it?" Grim challenges Dax.

"Fuck!" York mutters, his concern evident. Owing a debt is not something to be taken lightly, I should know.

"Think about this," Xeno grinds out, his jaw tight as he places a hand on Dax's shoulder.

Dax shakes Xeno's hand off. "What's there to think about? You know I never back out of a fight. This *old man* is mine," Dax retorts, cocksure. My heart pounds in my throat at the thought of him fighting Beast. They might be evenly matched in size, but Beast doesn't look like he's ever been on the losing side of anything.

"With age comes wisdom, *son*, so I suggest you start training. I'm undefeated and I sure as fuck won't let some little upstart like you take my record," Beast counters with a smirk.

"That's settled then. Three weeks today you will fight. Tonight we talk business. I have matters I'd like to discuss with Mr Bernard," Grim says, motioning to Zayn who's still sitting at the table watching everything unfold. He hasn't lost his cool at the turn of events, but Jeb is practically salivating. I can see a slow smile spread beneath his mask as his calculating mind whirs with possibilities. Doing business with Grim must be something he's wanted for a while and I can't help but wonder what she has planned.

"I'm all ears," Zayn says, standing.

He approaches Grim, still playing the part, not even acknowledging me. I shouldn't be affected by his dismissiveness, but I am. My fingers curl into my palm as anger bubbles. I'm sure he expected Grim to chuck us all out, banning us from ever returning, but she hasn't and now he's taking the opportunity to do business. Beast looks at Grim, frowning, his confusion evident. Regardless, he makes his feelings known to Dax before losing the opportunity to do so.

"You disrespect Grim and her club rules one more time and I don't give a fuck how good a fighter you are in the cage or what pretty little girl has your back, you're dead. Understand?"

"Understood," Dax bites out, flashing a look at me that has my heart lurching.

Beside him, Xeno is scowling and York is watching me closely, his icy-blue eyes cold and unflinching. I flick my gaze away, not ready, or willing, to try and decipher what's going through their heads right now. I can't even begin to navigate through this fucked-up mess of an evening.

"Now that's settled, let's get on with business... Mr Bernard," Grim says tightly, indicating for Zayn to walk with her so they can discuss business elsewhere, away from prying eyes.

"One moment, if I may?" Zayn asks Grim respectfully, flicking his gaze to me.

Out of the corner of my eye I catch Grim watching me, waiting for me to give her a sign to intervene. I don't.

"Of course." Grim smiles tightly when I remain determined.

She steps away leaving me to face Zayn. It's only then, as a look passes between them both, that I realise Grim is fully aware that Zayn is playing Jeb. That she knows there is more to this than meets the eye, but I don't let myself think about what that means. Instead, I focus all my attention back on Zayn, zeroing in on just him and blocking everyone else out. I jerk my chin and straighten my spine, readying myself for the blow that I know is coming.

Zayn steps closer to me, his lips pressed into a tight line and his ebon eyes swimming with a thousand words left unspoken. I swallow hard, acutely aware that we're being watched by the rest of the Breakers, by Jeb, by Grim and Beast. I'm certain that most occupants of the warehouse are interested to see how things unfold too and I hate that I've lost control of the situation. Regardless, I wait for him to make the first move because right now I'm hanging on by a thread, the sheer force of my will keeping me standing upright and not collapsing into an exhausted heap. I tip my head back to look up at him as he towers over me. Beneath the mask, Zayn tenses, the red light from the skull casting his face in a demonic glow.

I feel small.

When I'd danced I'd felt tall in every sense of the word. I wasn't meek, I wasn't intimidated. I was powerful, strong, untouchable. Right now I'm just a girl who has nothing left to fight with. My energy is depleted, my will to fight dwindling. My proverbial bucket is empty.

I'm quivering with *everything*, because now that I've let my emotions out, there's no shoving them back in. There's nothing I can do to stop him, to stop *this*.

"Don't," I whisper. I *beg*, actually. There's no misinterpreting my plea. I don't want to be raped. I don't want him to hurt me that way, and I'm fully aware there's still a chance that might happen. Maybe not here, not now, but later when Grim can't step in to stop it, when I'm left alone with the Breakers and Jeb.

"You and I will take this up *later*." Zayn guts me with his harsh words and my throat tightens on a sob that I force back down into my curdling stomach.

"Please. No—" I respond in a shaky voice, but he cuts me off, stepping into my space and grasping the back of my head roughly.

"Later!" he growls, then kisses me hard. Hard enough to bruise my lips, hard enough to make me quake with fear. His fingers dig into my scalp, tugging on my hair so tightly my scalp prickles with the sharp pain. I whimper, my hands automatically pushing against his chest, but it doesn't stop him from wrapping a solid arm around my back. It doesn't stop him from sliding his whisky-coated tongue into my mouth and it doesn't stop him from pressing every inch of his body against mine, holding me close. He's hard, turned on, and I hate him for it. I hate him because a part of me, the part I've buried for the past three years, longs for him.

I've *longed* for this kiss.

But not like this.

A sob rises up my throat. Another time I would've responded differently, *passionately*.

But it's all I can do to stop the tears from falling and my heart from shattering into a million tiny pieces like a jewel bludgeoned with a hammer. The shards rip at my internal organs, cutting me up in a way I never knew was possible. I'm too weak to fight him off. Weak both physically and emotionally. So I let him kiss me. I stand stiff, unresponsive as he kisses me to prove some kind of point. His teeth clack against mine in anger. His tongue delves inside my mouth, stroking, searching, seeking out a response. God, I try so hard not to respond. I cling onto the hate because if I succumb, if I let him in, if I really lean into his touch like I've craved for so long, then I'm no better than him or any of these men and women who've allowed their weaknesses to take hold tonight.

Right here, right now. I'm making another point.

I don't want to be that girl who crumbles because of one kiss, no matter how talented the kisser, or how much her heart has longed for this moment.

I don't want to be that girl who forgives because the man she loves is kissing her with a passion that ignites all the things that are wrong between them, and burns them to the ground.

I never wanted our first kiss after all this time apart to be like this, to happen in a place like this. I've imagined every other possible scenario, but not *this*.

But just like Xeno did on the dancefloor in Rocks, Zayn takes, and I let him.

Just this once, I let him.

Eventually, he pulls back. Emotions rush beneath his gaze, too fast for me to decipher, to unravel in the moment. I'm drawn into his gaze, a dangerous vortex that spins with too much feeling. My breathing hitches, my eyes well with tears that I blink back fiercely because Zayn isn't looking at me with emptiness, with hate or anger.

He looks at me with longing, with fucking *hope*.

That look is the final straw, and my knees buckle again. They fucking buckle and internally I'm cursing myself for my physical weakness. Like a newborn foal, my legs wobble with exertion. Zayn hoists me up, steadies me. Worry replaces the hope in his gaze and with infinite care, he brushes his lips against my cheek and rests them against my ear, his body curving over mine as he crowds me. To anyone else watching us, this is the move of a dominant man, someone who's used to overpowering another. To everyone in this room bar the Breakers, this is one man taking ownership of someone deemed less powerful, weaker than he is. But I know better. The change is subtle, but unmistakable. When his fingers release their death grip on my hair, and he cups my head gently, his thumb rubbing over the spot that tingles still, I know that he's trying to break down the wall between us even though it's three years thick. I'm not certain I trust his motives, but I do feel the honesty in his actions and that gives me pause for thought. It gives me a little of my strength back.

"I'm sorry, Pen," Zayn whispers against my ear, his voice croaking with emotion, with a truth that crushes me because I hear *him*. I hear Zayn, my best friend, my first love. That kid who'd stood in the playground and watched me dance. That kid who taught me to trust.

"I'm sorry, Pen," he repeats.

Those three words are more than an apology, they're a door opening a crack, a route back in, a rickety bridge crossing a deep river of our tumultuous past. I want to question him, to dig deeper, but like always, outside factors prevent me from doing so. My fingers flex against his chest then curl into his shirt, the only sign that I've acknowledged his apology. We're balanced precariously. We're one wrong word, one wrong move away from slamming that door, from ripping that rickety bridge down.

"Mr Bernard," Grim prompts, her patience wearing thin.

My hands fall away and Zayn steps back, releasing me from his hold. "Take her home," he barks at York and Dax before glaring at Jeb and Xeno. "You two. Come with me."

"Yes, *Boss*," Xeno snaps, his eyes meeting mine.

I don't have the energy to shore up my defences. I let him see how tonight has ruined me and for the briefest of moments his gaze softens, he wobbles on his feet as though he wants to come to me, as though he wants to comfort me. But Jeb nudges his arm and the moment is gone, the walls stack back up.

With my feet rooted to the spot, my lips bruised and my heart thundering, I watch them walk away. Zayn is still pretending to be the leader of the Skins whilst the true leader gives me a look that tells me that this is far from over, that he's still the one who holds all the cards.

8

Pen

I silently follow York through the warehouse with Dax at my back, my feet are still bare and sore from dancing, my resolve to remain strong sagging with every step. I can't even bring myself to look at the gangs seated at the tables we pass by, though I'm aware of them watching us. I can barely see straight and if I don't get out into the fresh air soon, I might just pass out. That's why I don't notice Malik stepping towards me until it's too late.

"*Stopy Płomieniach*, it was a pleasure to meet you," he says, reaching for me.

"Back the fuck off," Dax growls, stepping up beside me, and cutting off his ability to touch me.

Malik laughs, dismissing Dax as though he's a mere trifling boy who has no power to do him any harm. That pisses me off, Dax too given his snarl. Dax and I might not be friends but that doesn't mean to say I like the idea of someone putting him down. It's a sore point for both of us having lived with parents who treated their children like shit.

"Mr Brov," York says, holding his hand out. "On behalf of the Skins, I'd like to extend the hand of friendship. We got off to a bad start."

"The fuck?!" Dax exclaims, taking the words right out of my mouth. We both glare at York who is now flanking my left side whilst Dax is on my right, half his body in front of mine. York doesn't pay us any attention, instead focusing on Malik.

"I see we have someone with manners. I respect that," Malik replies, canting his head at York and gripping his proffered hand in a firm shake before letting it go.

"*Manners*? *Respect*? You touched what isn't yours, motherfucker. Don't talk to me about respect!" Dax interjects. My heart sinks. I really, really don't have the energy for this.

"Careful, *chlopak*, you're playing with the real men now."

"You fucking cu—"

I can't help it, I reach for Dax, my fingers curling around his palm. He flinches at my touch, but it has the desired effect and his cuss falls short. Malik's bodyguards bristle at the insult, but Malik isn't perturbed. He smiles slowly, leisurely.

"I've been called many things to my face, *chlopak*, but a cunt actually isn't one of them. Though I am partial to one…" he winks at me, before smiling at Dax. My skin runs cold.

"You best move out of my way, *cunt*, because I ain't in the mood," Dax snarls, rising to the bait.

"Mr Brov, I think we should discuss business another time," York interjects firmly, flicking his gaze at me. "Without an audience." He makes a point at looking around the warehouse whilst I suck in a sharp breath at York's insinuation.

How dare he! How dare he talk about me like I'm a goddamn business transaction! Automatically I pull my fingers away from Dax, but he grabs them, squeezing tightly before rubbing his thumb over my knuckles. It's a reassuring hold, and it confuses me, but it works to deflate my indignation. I don't comment and I don't pull away.

Malik rips his gaze away from Dax and arches a brow at York. "I see not everyone is willing to protect this *piękna tancerka*? If she were mine—"

"We'll take this up at another time, *yes*?" York insists, folding his arms across his chest indicating with his body that this conversation is over.

"I look forward to hearing from you," Malik concedes, dropping his gaze, his cobalt eyes washing over me. "You are *exquisite*. I am a man who appreciates the beauty in all things. A dancer like you should be revered, treasured, *kept*."

With that he turns on his heel, his bodyguards following closely behind him and leaving me trembling in his wake. There's no doubt he's a certifiable madman. My psycho radar is going crazy right about now. Malik Brov is right up there with my brother in the world of cray-cray.

"Motherfucking, bastard, cunt!" Dax swears under his breath before gripping my hand and striding off. I have to jog to keep up with him. My feet ache with every step.

The second we step out into the darkened car park, Dax drops my hand as though burnt, rips off his mask and gloves and casts them aside. The cut above his brow weeps a little, blood trickling from the wound. His cheek is bruised and swollen, but he doesn't seem to notice. "Fucking joke these masks. You can all go and fuck yourselves if you think I'm wearing this bastard thing again," Dax adds darkly.

"Keep your fucking voice down and get Pen in the damn car before you get us all killed!" York seethes, turning on him.

"*Fuck off*! What was all that '*let's do business*' bullshit? Are you kidding me right now? We don't do business with men who are unhinged."

I can't help it. I laugh. Does he not realise who *he* fucking works for?

York rips off his mask, his white blonde hair sticking up in a sweaty mess as he shoves his hand against Dax's chest. "You don't need to fucking tell me who we're dealing with. *I* wasn't the one with a hand around the man's goddamn throat! Do you have a fucking death wish, you prick? You put us all in danger! I was just trying to de-escalate the situation."

Dax pushes York back. "Did you not see what he did? Did you not fucking see what he did to *Kid*?!" he bellows, a vein popping in his forehead as he points at me. The nervous laughter rising up my throat is swallowed back down as I draw in a breath. His old nickname for me makes my heart squeeze in pain. Did he just refer to me as Kid? What does that even mean? Was it a slip of the tongue? He hasn't called me that since returning.

"Dax...?" I question, my voice croaking.

"Get in the goddamn car!" he snaps at me, his lips pulling over his teeth in a feral snarl as he pulls a key fob from his pocket and presses a button. A dark grey Bentley parked not too far away from where we're standing, unlocks. Its headlights turn on, illuminating the three of us in a puddle of light.

"Don't talk to me like that!" I shout back.

"I said, get in the goddamn car!"

"Dax—" York starts, flicking his gaze between us. He pulls off his leather gloves too, discarding them and cracking his knuckles. Fuck, are they about to go head to head? They never fought like this when we were kids.

"Shut the fuck up, York." Dax snaps then glares at me. "Get in. NOW!"

"And what if I said screw you? What if I said, I'm done with tonight? I'm DONE!" I shout, unable to help myself. I'm tired, I'm hungry, I'm fucking emotionally drained to the point of collapse. I literally can't take anymore.

"I'd say get in the FUCKING CAR!" Dax roars, his face is red, and his eyes are flashing dangerously. I flinch as though slapped. He's never, *ever* spoken to me that way before. Not ever. I don't even recognise this man. My shoulders slump. Has he really changed that much in three years?

"Dax, keep your damn head and *chill the fuck out!*" York snaps. He's on edge too, that's clear enough from the sharp look he gives me, but it's tempered with the worry that flashes across his face. It's so brief that I'm unable to figure out if he's worried for me, or worried about the war Dax has brought down on their heads. Likely the latter.

"I won't *chill the fuck out,*" Dax mocks, "until we've got the fuck out of here." He glares at me, pointing at the Bentley. "For the last time, Pen. Get in the damn car! I've already stuck my neck out for you tonight."

"*Stuck your neck out for me*?" I blanch, fucking furious at the insinuation that this is all my fault. "Un-fucking-believable! Don't you dare blame this on me. I didn't ask for this. I didn't ask for *any* of this!" And I'm not just talking about tonight, I'm talking about everything. All of the bullshit that's happened between us. There have been so many times over the years that I've asked myself why I just didn't tell them what happened that night at Rocks, and I come up with the same answer over and over again.

I was a *kid*.

I was *scared*.

I made a choice in the moment because I thought it was the right thing to do, because I believed my brother when he said he would kill Lena, because I'd just seen Jeb shoot a man in the head. I turned my back on the Breakers because that was what I had to do to survive. Going over and over my decision won't change the fact it happened. It won't change the fact that they let me go.

Dax snorts. "Whatever."

"Arsehole." I growl, wincing as I step onto the gritty asphalt. A tiny stone pierces a blister on the ball of my left foot, and I drag in a pained breath through my teeth. "Fuck!"

Dax frowns, still glaring at me. "*What now?*"

My nostrils flare at his curtness. "What do you mean, *what now*? My *feet* hurt. If you hadn't noticed I'm not wearing any fucking shoes!" I snap back, matching his snippiness. Fuck him. I'm getting whiplash from his flip-flopping. "Perhaps I should've let you get shot."

"Pen, don't be a *bit*—" York warns.

"A *bitch?*" I narrow my eyes at him, barking out another laugh and ignoring the fact he looks beautifully dishevelled in his fitted suit, with his hair a mess and his eyes ablaze. Seeing him bare-chested lying on my bed is one thing, but dressed like this, like a suave, sophisticated, sexy *man*, is more than a little disconcerting. It's distracting and I hate it.

"Yes, a bitch!" he counters.

"Fuck you, York. How fucking dare you! I didn't see you stepping in at any point to help. You didn't do *anything*," I pant, throwing every last ounce of bitterness in my voice. It doesn't take a genius to figure out that I'm not just talking about this evening.

"What are you saying?" he snaps, knowing exactly what I'm talking about. I see it in his eyes. He knows. He fucking knows.

"You're good at reading me, York, at least you were once upon a time. So fucking read me," I challenge, glaring at him. Beside us Dax curses, he reaches for me, but I snatch my arm away. "Don't you dare touch me, Dax."

York keeps his gaze fixed on me and I let him do what he always did so well when we were kids. A second later, he tips his head back and lets out a strangled cry, before slamming his fist into the wall of the warehouse. The skin covering his knuckles split on impact, blood dripping from the wound, but he doesn't even seem to notice as he steps towards me. "Pen..."

"No. No! I can't do this!" I back away from them both, hobbling on my feet.

Dax looks down, a scowl pulling his brows together. "You're hurt," he states, blinking as though coming out of a trance.

"No shit, Sherlock," I retort, walking backwards awkwardly. Pain shoots up from the base of my feet. "God-fucking-damn-it," I curse under my breath, my head spinning with the pain, with hunger and disappointment.

"You're weak too. You haven't eaten in a while," Dax comments whilst stalking me. Behind him, York just stares, like he's stuck in a trance and can't quite believe what he's seeing. *Yeah, the truth hurts, arsehole.*

"Stay away!" I hiss.

Dax shakes his head. "Look at you, you're a fucking mess."

The thing is, I can't deny it. I *am* a mess. My dress has a sweat patch on both the front and back. There's a tear at the hem that opens over my upper thigh and shows off the strap of my knickers. My hair is sweaty and knotted from dancing. My feet, hands and shins are covered in blood from the cage floor and I know without looking that my mascara has smeared beneath my eyes.

I let out a hysterical laugh. "Well, this is what happens when you've literally got nothing left, no money to your name and no one who gives a shit about you. Mum washed her hands of me too now so it's not as if I can go home for a nice family meal cooked lovingly by my mother!" I scoff, shaking my head. "Ha! Who am I trying to kid? I was always one step away from starving. Who needs food anyway?"

"You still have Lena," York says gently, almost too quietly for me to hear.

My eyes snatch up, then narrow. "Leave her the fuck out of this!"

"Enough!" Dax shouts, and in two steps he's hauled me up into his arms, across his chest, and is striding across the car park towards the Bentley. Before I'm even able to blink he has me pinned between his chest and the car and is yanking open the passenger door. His hips are pressed against mine and his muscular thigh is shoved up against my crotch, pressing against my clit. I stiffen beneath him, willing him not to move and light up my body like a damn firework.

"I'm not a fucking rag doll that you can pick up and toss around at whim," I complain, my fingers curling into the material of his shirt to hold myself steady. His warm breath caresses my skin and he shifts slightly, the movement of his thigh hitting that spot I really fucking wished it wouldn't.

He scoffs. "No? Seems to me you're okay with being treated like a toy. Get in."

"A *toy*—?" *Motherfucker.*

"Get. In. Pen."

"I would if you'd actually let me go!"

Dax removes his thigh from between my legs and steps back just enough so I can squeeze out of his hold and get into the car. "Fucking finally!" he cries, slamming the door behind me.

A few seconds later, Dax is in the driver's seat and leaning over me. I press my body back into the chair, and turn my face away from him. He kind of tenses up at my reaction.

"Seatbelt," he snaps by way of explanation.

"I can do it myself," I whisper, but he makes a snorting sound and yanks at my seatbelt, clicking it in place before slamming back into his own seat. Anger radiates from him, making me tense up. He hasn't calmed down at all, and there's too much between us for me to even try to soothe him, let alone want to. I saved his life tonight. That's enough. "Where are we going?"

Dax doesn't reply, he simply jabs his finger on the button that locks the doors just as York tries the handle.

"What are you—" I begin, looking at the rage on York's face as he leans down and glares at us through the glass. He slaps his palm against the window, his icy-blue eyes sharp, unyielding. I jump.

"What the fuck, Dax? Open the fucking door!" York yells, slamming his fist on the roof of the car.

"Find your own way back, dickhead!" Dax jabs his finger on the button to start the ignition, puts the car in first then slams his foot on the gas. We fly out of the car park, grit, dust, and dirt churning up the air behind us. I twist in my seat, York is holding up his middle finger and even though I can't hear what he's saying, I know a string of expletives are flying out of his mouth.

"York looks pissed," I remark, turning back around, my

fingers digging into the plush leather seats as we speed through the gates exiting the compound.

"I don't give two fucks," he snarls. "Motherfucker overstepped. I'm done with the bullshit."

"The bullshit?" I query, wondering what that's supposed to mean.

"Yeah. I'm fucking done."

"Me too," I mutter. "Me too."

Half an hour of silence later, we draw up outside the Academy. With the engine still running, Dax presses his finger on the button to unlock the car doors.

"Home sweet home," he states, staring ahead, the glow from the streetlamp highlighting his features in stark, artificial light.

His jaw is the edge of a knife blade, and the muscle that ticks along it, a time bomb ready to go off. He might be dangerously handsome, but right now he's just dangerous. Any minute now, he's going to explode and a large part of me wants to provoke him, just to see what happens. The other part just wants to head inside, take a sleeping pill, and curl up into a ball where the events of tonight can be put aside for a few precious hours. The whole journey back he spoke not one word to me, just stared ahead and drove. Whatever he felt before at Grim's club when he stepped in and protected me from Malik Brov seems to have been forgotten. Right now he's back to hating me again.

"Why are we here?" I ask, unable to help myself. This is the last place I expected Dax to bring me. Jeb had plans for me tonight that started with rape and likely ended in something just as horrific. I doubt very much dropping me back home is what Jeb had intended for me.

"Because you *live* here."

"Yes, but why am I here tonight?"

"Zayn told me to take you home. I've done that. Now get out of the car, Pen. Go home," Dax orders.

"Yes, but Zayn isn't the one who asked me to bring an overnight bag, Jeb did, and Zayn isn't the one who ord—" I slam my mouth shut before I'm able to finish my sentence.

He snatches his eyes up to meet mine and they flare in anger before he twists in his seat and reaches for something behind him. "Here. One overnight bag delivered," he says, before shoving it into my arms.

"But how did—?"

His phone ringing interrupts my question. Reaching into his inside jacket pocket, Dax answers. "Yes?" he snaps, his scowl deepening.

I watch as he nods his head, his fingers tightening around the phone. He doesn't respond to whomever is on the other end but as every part of him stiffens, I know that whatever they're saying it can't be good. After another minute, the call ends and he chucks his mobile onto the dash.

"Fuck!" he shouts, slamming his palm against the steering wheel.

"What is it?" I ask.

"Doesn't matter. Just take the bag and go, Pen."

"But—" I protest.

Dax's head snaps around to look at me, warring emotions raging in his eyes. "Just. Fucking. Go!"

We stare at each other, our gazes clashing. Words are on the tip of my tongue. Dangerous words that won't do me or my sister any good if I were to let them spill free. Plenty are curse words but many more are the truth, and those are the ones I must hold onto at all costs because right now I *want* to tell him the truth. I *want* to set it free.

"Fine," I snap, unbuckling my seatbelt before reaching for the door handle and shoving open the door. Stepping out into the chill night air, I slam the car door behind me, hugging my bag against my chest. A beat later, Dax revs the engine and speeds off down the street without so much as a backward glance.

9

Pen

The first thing I do when I get inside my flat is ring my sister. She answers after the sixth ring, her voice sleepy.

"Who's this?" she asks.

"It's me, Pen," I say, sighing in relief just at the sound of her voice.

"What time is it? Are you okay?"

"Yeah, I'm fine. Just checking in—" I flick on the light switch in the bathroom and catch sight of my reflection. I look like shit. No, I look *broken*. I'm far from fine, but she doesn't need to know that. I've always protected her, shielded her from all the shit. Tonight's no different.

"Pen," she whines. "You told *me* off for calling you in the middle of the night. Not cool."

"Sorry, erm, is Mum home?"

"No. I mean she might be. I'm not there is all," she whispers into the mouthpiece.

"Where are you?" I ask trying to sound casual but failing.

"At a friend's house."

"Which friend?" I ask sharply.

"Stop stressing, Pen! I'm at Simone's house for the weekend seeing as you're so busy all the time." She hesitates a beat. "Sorry, I didn't mean that."

A long sigh escapes my lips. "I know you didn't."

"I'm fine. I miss you, that's all. Plus Simone's taking care of me."

"Good. That's good. Ring as soon as you wake up, okay?"

"Alright. Pen—"

"Yeah?"

"Are you sure you're okay?"

"Of course I am," I say brightly, hiding the wobble in my voice. "Love you, Lena."

"Love you too, Pen."

"Go to sleep, sis," I say gently. She clicks her tongue against her teeth in annoyance, but I end the call abruptly so she can't hear the sound of me falling apart on my bathroom floor.

Sometime later, I'm lying on my bed wrapped up in a towel with wet hair, dried tears on my cheeks and a painful kind of anger that verges on homicidal.

I want to kill Jeb.

I want to murder my brother.

I want to hurt the Breakers as much as they've hurt me, and yet...

Confusion wars inside my chest because tonight Dax stepped up. He stood between me and Malik Brov, *twice*. Zayn apologised, though I'm still uncertain for what or even if that brief moment of connection between us was even real. York had looked at me like he knew something was up, like he finally understood my pain and hated himself for it. Xeno... well, Xeno didn't do a damn thing, but the look he gave me, that spoke a thousand words. Just words I wasn't able to interpret. These thoughts sit like a grenade inside my chest. Someday soon the pin is going to be removed and I'll detonate. Maybe then I'll finally be at peace or at the very least, dead.

FOR THE REST of the weekend I hide out in my flat, living off the remains of my cheap food and waiting for the world to end. Clancy leaves me various text messages that I ignore. She even knocked on my door this morning, but I didn't have the energy to face her. It's Sunday afternoon now and I'm still trying to piece myself back together again. I'll have some grovelling to do with Clancy, but right now, I don't have the emotional energy to fake feeling okay when I'm not.

The only person I spoke to the whole weekend was Lena. I've been ringing her obsessively to the point of distraction and only relaxed when I found out she's going on a school trip tomorrow to the Isle of Wight for a week. I didn't ask where mum got the money to pay for such an expensive trip or acknowledge the jealousy I feel that she has. Money wasn't something we ever had much of, and even when mum did have some spare, she never used it to buy me things. I lived in hand-me-down clothes from our neighbours' children and survived on free school meals. Treats weren't something that were a part of my life, but none of that matters now. I'm just relieved that Lena's out of harm's way for the time being.

Now that it's past three in the afternoon, I've recovered enough to haul arse out of bed. I'm tempted to knock on Clancy's door, apologise, and hang out, but honestly, I'm still not ready to face anyone just yet. Physically, I'm stronger. My feet aren't as sore as they were, and my strength has returned enough for me to wrap them up and want to dance. But emotionally, mentally, I'm still on edge. Jeb has made no contact after that evening at Grim's club and I've no idea what he has planned for me. I've been waiting for the guillotine to fall because if there's something I know for certain, Jeb won't let this go. He'll come back tenfold with something heinous for me to do, or maybe he's just planning to kill me.

Needing to let off some steam, I dress in a pair of joggers and a loose t-shirt, pull on my trainers and grab my last bruised apple from my pathetically empty fruit bowl, and creep down to one of the studios. Once I dance, I'll feel better, at least I hope so anyway.

The hallway on the next floor down is quiet, peaceful, and I head into the nearest studio and hook up my mobile phone to the speaker system. Placing the apple on the table, to eat after I've finished, I remove my trainers and press play on *Elastic Heart* by Sia, and let the music wash over me.

I don't think beyond this moment.

I just move, running to the far wall.

Anger burns as I slam into the brick. My screwed up fists, smashing against the wall. Inside, all I can feel is this pent up energy, this rage needing release. If I don't find a way to ease it, I might just self-combust, and I can't afford to do that. I have to regain control, just like I did at Grim's club. Drawing in a deep, ragged breath, my feet glide lightly over the wooden boards as I spin and twist my way back to the mirror, stopping just before I crash into it. My chest heaves as I stare at myself, at the person I've become.

Fighting, always fighting.

Fighting to save Lena. Fighting against Jeb, my brother, the Breakers.

I feel exactly like the rubber band that Sia sings about. Right now I'm stretched thin.

I may have a thick skin but I'm fucking scarred from all the fighting. I might be able to take more than others. I might keep fighting back, but I'm only human and everyone has a breaking point, including me. Some days I'm strong, I'm fierce, and others I'm on the verge of breaking, my edges fraying. I can feel myself unravelling. This back and forth, this push and pull, the ups and downs, acting strong but feeling weak, it's taking its toll. I put up a front to the world, never really revealing who I truly am deep inside, even to the ones I love the most. But I did at Grim's club. That night, I fucking peeled back the thick skin I wear so well, and I let the Breakers see me.

Did it make a difference?

I'm not sure.

Does it even matter?

I don't know that either.

All I know right now is that I need to dance. Some people sing to let out their emotions, some people paint, some draw, some write, some play a musical instrument. I dance.

It's the only source of freedom I have left.

Flaring my nostrils, I draw in a deep breath then lift my fists and slam them against the mirror so hard it wobbles under my anger. "Let it all go, Pen," I say to myself fiercely, my reflection misting beneath my words. Pressing my forearms against the mirror, I drop my head between my shoulders and breathe in deeply, absorbing the music and Sia's lyrics until all I am is another outlet for emotion.

I'm no longer Penelope Scott.

I'm not Pen, Kid, Titch or Tiny.

I'm not someone with the weight of the world on my shoulders.

I'm not a girl fucked-up by dangerous men who want to hurt her.

I'm not a woman still in love with the Breakers.

I'm just an instrument of dance.

My body sways, as I clutch my head in my hands and stumble backwards on heavy feet. Pulling at my hair, I tip my head back and let out a silent scream, my body swaying in time to the music. It fills me up, it vibrates the air around me, the lyrics wash over my skin giving me the fuel I need to let it all out. I just go with it. This isn't a choreographed piece. This is me bleeding out. This is me trying to make sense of everything that's happened recently.

My hands fall away, and I jerk my body as though electrocuted. The reality of my situation and the events of Friday night finally sinking in. I drop to my knees, crawling across the shiny wooden floor before turning onto my back and slamming my hands and feet in time to the music, my feet push against the floor so that my body slides backwards. Sia's voice flows over me, and I absorb every damn word. I draw on it, using it to give me the nourishment I need to dance the way I must.

Arching my back, I lift myself up off the floor onto my hands and feet, then push up onto my hands, flipping upright in a back walkover that a gymnast would be proud of. Flinging my arms wide, I spin like a little girl who's carefree. I spin on my still sore feet trying to free myself of the pain and anger that's eating away at me and like Sia sings, I want my fucking life back. I want to live. I don't want to be afraid anymore.

I don't want to be afraid for my sister.

I don't want to be afraid for my life.

I don't want to be afraid of my feelings.

I want to live. I want to be free.

All these secrets, all this weight sits like rocks within my chest, dragging me down until it feels like I'm drowning. My body folds over and like a marionette doll, my fingers drag across the floor as though my strings have been severed.

But somehow I stand upright, just like the song. I bounce back. I keep fighting because vulnerability is a choice and I refuse to be a victim. I do what I do because I have to, not because I'm weak. With a heaving chest I run, leaping into the air, my legs kicking out in a split. I land and transition into a low spin, my right leg extended over the floor, the tips of my toes drawing an invisible circle over the floorboards before I put all my weight on my right foot and hands and tumble into a forward roll, pushing upright once more. My heart pounds inside my chest at the exertion, my skin flushes with heat and sweat beads on my forehead, but still I dance.

I dance to let go.

I dance to keep sane.

I dance even when Zayn steps into the studio.

I dance despite his presence.

Because of it.

I dance to show him that I can't be beaten.

That I *won't* be beaten.

No. Matter. What.

I might be pulled taut, I might be fraying at the edges, but I'm still here. I'm still fucking dancing. And even though I was brought to my knees in the cage at Grim's club, Jeb didn't break me. None of them did. I fought back. Just like I'm fighting back now.

Leaping into a spring jump, I extend my legs then land lightly, locking eyes with Zayn. My chest heaving as he watches me. My heart might be broken, it might bleed but it still beats.

It. Still. Fucking. Beats.

My fisted hand bashes against my chest, echoing my moves on Friday night. I'm *not* broken. I jerk my chin before throwing up my hands and stamping my feet. Anger oozes out of me like an invisible monster seeping into the wooden floors, edging its way towards Zayn. I can almost see the sharpened claws scratching across the wood.

"Pen, there are things I need to say, and you need to listen," Zayn demands, his words firm and unyielding even when he steps backwards, away from my pain like the coward that he is. Where's his apology now? Where's the sorrow in his gaze, the fucking empathy? I look into his pitch-black eyes and seethe when I see nothing but a fierce determination to hurt me even more. He'd get the same look in his eye when we were kids, when he was pissed off at something and wanted to vent, to hurt those closest to him because he knew we'd love him anyway. Today, I'm not feeling so generous.

"Just stop a moment," he continues, grinding his teeth.

My nostrils flare and my eyes narrow at his. "No!" I retort, refusing to let him control me, refusing to let him off that easy. Dancing like this is to help *me* cope. It's not my fault he's finding it too hard to stomach. He can stay and watch, or leave, either way I'm not stopping. With no more fucks left to give, I flip forward landing close to him then immediately spin away and out of his reach. I leap into the air in a scissor kick then drop to the floor into the splits before sweeping my legs out to the front and throwing my hands above my head. I lie on the floor, my back arching before dropping back down in time to the music as though my battered heart is desperate to burst free of my chest. It sure as fuck feels like it wants to. Sia continues to sing, her haunting voice floating over me, the lyrics to the song perfectly revealing how I feel. Squeezing my eyes shut, I force back the tears, needing a second to catch my breath, to shore up my defences. It's the worst thing I could've done because a beat later the air shifts above me and Zayn's warm breath wafts over my cheeks, his jacket brushing against my arms.

"Pen..." Zayn grinds out, his firm legs encasing my hips, his voice cracked and breaking. *Brittle.* "I need you to stop. I need you to listen..."

My pulse races as his body cages mine. his nearness creates an ocean of fear inside my chest and suddenly I feel like I'm losing the battle to stay afloat. Is he here to finish what he started? Is this the point when I completely lose my faith in the memory of the boy I loved more than life itself? My throat closes over as Zayn lowers himself over me, his warm breath feathering over my skin as his lips brush against mine. That delicate touch is too much, and a sudden, soul-searing anger rises up my chest.

No!

"No!" I repeat out loud. He doesn't get to invade my space like this. He doesn't get to be this close. He doesn't get to dominate me this way. He doesn't get to make me feel exposed, weak. He doesn't get to make me want him, despite it all.

Fuck this!

I snap my eyes open and glare up at him. Putting all my hurt into that one look. I imagine tiny little blades flicking from my eyes and into him. I imagine each one cutting him deep and causing him pain. I want to hurt him. I want to hurt them all. Every-fucking-one. He flinches, but he doesn't move.

"Fuck you!" I snarl, refusing to engage him further, willing to fight against this man I clearly don't fucking know. Lifting my hands, I push against his shoulders, shoving him upwards. He rears backwards and our eyes meet. His black orbs spark with fire, but rather than say anything he waits, his chest heaving as he looks down at me. I'm still on my back between his legs, but as Sia sings about hiding vulnerability, I flip onto my stomach, and use my forearms to pull myself out from between his legs, refusing to be vulnerable to him.

A warm hand wraps around my ankle, yanking me backwards and I slide against the floor as he drops back over me, his fingers wrap around my throat possessively, but his hold is gentle as he urges me upwards into a kneeling position.

"Listen to me, Pen," he growls, pulling me back against his body as I face away from him.

I'm ready to scream, to fucking elbow him in the stomach, to kick and scratch. I'm ready to fight, but then he presses his lips against my ear and whispers something that surprises me, that makes me question my sanity. "If you don't want to talk, then at least let me dance with you. Help me to feel again, Pen."

There's a desperation to his request. A heavy sadness, a *longing*. Am I imagining this? "What?" I whisper out, confused, taken aback. That's not what I thought this was.

"I need to *feel* like you do."

"No."

"It's been too long," he whispers into my ear. "I want to know I'm still capable."

"It hurts," I admit, meaning the pain between us, the deep ache I feel with his arms wrapped around me like this.

"I know."

"I can't—"

"Don't make me beg."

For a split second I consider turning him down, I consider

doing exactly that and making him beg, but as he drops his forehead onto my shoulder, his fingers stroking lovingly against my throat, I find that I can't.

I can't turn him down.

Instead, I raise my hand and tangle my fingers with his then push upwards, twisting on my foot, and pull him upright too. We lock gazes, our fingers gripping tightly. Zayn pulls me towards him with such force that instead of colliding with him and ruining the flow of music, I leap into his arms, my legs and arms wrapping around his body. He grunts, stumbling back slightly, then his arms come upwards as he holds me to him.

But I'm not ready to give in.

Not yet.

So I push back against his chest and drop my feet to the floor. His arms unravel from behind me and I run backwards away from him. Zayn chases me, throwing himself forward onto his knees so he slides across the floor and ends up at my feet. His chest heaves as he looks up at me his expression earnest, humble, as he begs me to forgive him without words.

And I want to do that. I want to do that so badly, but I need him to understand that I'm not a pushover, that he hurt me and that needs to be addressed.

He wants to feel, so he's going to feel.

I grab his throat.

My fingers dig into his skin as I pull him upright, and even though he towers over me, he allows me to squeeze just that little bit, submitting in a way I never thought he could.

Still holding onto him, I rise up onto the balls of my feet and clamp my knees together, bending them slightly. Moving my hips provocatively, I roll my body before him, close enough so that he can feel the whisper of me against him, but not close enough that my body is pressed against his. In a way, I suppose

I'm pushing his boundaries, daring him to claim me like he wanted to do at Grim's club, like I believe he still wants to now. Zayn's pulse beats erratically beneath my fingers, but a fierceness replaces the humility. He knocks my hand away then reaches for my waist, yanking me towards him, but I don't let him get purchase. I spin away, slipping out of his hold.

He chases me.

Rather, he *leaps* into the air in a barrel jump, his right leg kicking out as his arms spread wide, and he turns in the air, landing before me with a glint of iron in his stare. My mouth pops open, but I slam it shut. Zayn has just performed a move that I thought only Dax could pull off.

Where the fuck did that come from?

Even though Zayn is a hip-hop dancer at heart, he just moved with a fluidity that speaks of contemporary dance. I don't get to voice my question as he reaches for me, pulling me against him before placing his hand on my chest over my heart.

Without thinking about it, I raise my own, placing my palm over his shirt between the lapels of his jacket, and with only our palms touching each other, we move together. Zayn steps away from me, sliding his feet lightly over the floor. I mirror him. Chasing his every move.

I feel the heat of his body, the thump of his chest, the beat of his truth.

I see that honesty in the way he moves, in the sincerity of his stare, in every single step.

It upends me.

We dance, our hands moving away from each other's chest as we spin in unison, only to press back in the same place again. It's like we're two skaters dancing on ice as we slide over the floor, close, but not close enough. When he grabs my wrist with one hand and flips me around against him, my back to his chest, he groans again, his arms wrapping around me in a hug, his fingers finding my throat. For a moment we stand like this, his heart beating hard against my back. My tears clog my throat as he presses against it with the pad of his fingers. When his open mouth falls against my shoulder, his lips and tongue rubbing against the bare skin there, something inside opens up to him. *I* open myself to him.

"I hurt you," he mutters.

"Yes."

"But *you* hurt me too. You fucking hurt me too."

His hand slowly moves downwards, his fingers spread wide as he slides it between my breasts, resting it there over my frantic heart. Zayn bites my neck where it meets my shoulder, his teeth sinking in. Not hard enough to break the skin, but hard enough to make me suck in a jagged breath. The pain is pleasurable, especially when he licks over the same spot. Then he runs his lips up the side of my neck and latches onto my earlobe, biting it gently. I can't help myself; I moan. Goddamn him. With one hand wrapped around my waist, Zayn yanks me tighter against him, his hand working its way back up to my throat and cupping my chin as he stretches my head to the side and lavishes my neck with kisses. My toes curl, my core gushes with heat and my heart pounds erratically as he kisses and licks, bites, and teases. I've always had a sensitive neck and he fucking knows it.

By the time the song ends, I'm finding it hard to step away from him, but somehow I manage to do exactly that. Twisting on my feet, I stare at him, the distance between us vast even though in reality it's only a few feet.

"You may be the Breakers, but you will *not* break me," I say, my nostrils flaring as I echo Sia's words. It's a warning as much as it is the truth. I love him, but no matter how talented a dancer, a kisser, I won't let him break me.

I will not let *them* break me. Not now. Not ever.

Because I won't survive it again.

Zayn nods, his expression beaten, sad almost. "What if I told you that I don't want to?"

I bark out a laugh, my eyes narrowing on him and it's only then that I really see him. He's still wearing the same clothes from Friday night. My anger was too vivid, too in the moment to allow me to really see him.

But now I do.

I see the dark circles beneath his eyes.

I see the sorrow on his face.

I see something I hadn't before.

I see *him*. My best friend.

I see the boy I loved morphing into a man who's no longer a stranger.

Right here, right now, he's in front of me. There is no mask, no bravado, no distance. Just him, *just Zayn*, and my determination to hold onto the hate begins to crumble.

10

Pen

"What do you really want?" I ask heavily.

"To speak with you," he responds, stepping back towards me. His shoulders sag, exhaustion pulls at his features. As he moves, his jacket pulls apart and I see what I hadn't before. I see the dark stain of blood stark against his white shirt. "Zayn, what happened?" I ask, my eyes widening. He's hurt and even though anger lingers, even though there are things I want to say, that's all pushed aside for the moment.

"I'm okay," he replies, pulling his jacket closed hastily and buttoning it up. "It's just a scratch."

"That wasn't what I asked. What *happened*?"

Of course he doesn't answer. Instead, he lifts his hand to cup my cheek. "I'm sorry," he says, as his thumb brushes across my cheekbone. His night-time eyes are filled with a fucking galaxy of emotion, his secrets like shooting stars burning bright and too fast to grab hold of. I snap my head away, out of his hold. He's too close, too raw, too *emotional*.

"Stop."

"Pen. *I'm sorry*," he repeats, and I honestly don't know what to do with that. Does he want me to just forgive him because he's apologised? It would be so easy, so simple to do, and for the briefest of moments I consider doing just that. The thing is, we've never been simple. We've always been complicated, messy. Even when we were kids, our friendship was never straightforward. My love for the Breakers changed things. People say that true love should be simple, *easy*, but that isn't true, is it?

Love is chaotic, agonizing, complex.

It's like DNA, no one really knows the depths of its power or can unravel its mysteries. Love is just there, it's something that exists and we're all just a bunch of people either looking for love, are in love, or are heartbroken without it, *because* of it.

"For what, Zayn? What are you sorry for?" I whisper, because saying sorry isn't enough. It's too vague, too all encompassing. People say I'm sorry and expect it to be a sticking plaster for every sin they've ever committed. People say I'm sorry like it washes away the heinous things they've done. It doesn't. Zayn breathes out heavily, his stubbled jaw tight with stress.

"I didn't know what Jeb had planned. I'm sorry you were put in that situation. I'm sorry you were scared."

"*Bullshit*. I saw the look on your face. You wanted to screw me."

"No!"

"Don't fucking lie to me, Zayn. I saw the truth in your eyes that night."

Zayn presses his eyes shut briefly, and when he opens them

again, there's a determined look on his face. "Of course I want you, Pen, I can't deny that. Look at you, you're goddamn beautiful and fucking strong, and determined and unafraid. How could I possibly not want to fuck you? But not that way, not like that. I'm many things but I am *not* a goddamn rapist. Jeb was *wrong* to do what he did."

I bark out a laugh to hide my surprise and to deflect the fact my body is betraying me as I step closer towards him wanting more words, more truths. "Is he ever right?"

"I don't know. You tell me, Pen. You walked away from us to be with him. Has it been everything you hoped for?" he asks me, a sudden sarcasm and vitriol dripping from his tongue. I flinch as though slapped. Zayn's words hurt, but only because they're true. I did walk away from the Breakers to be with Jeb but not for the reason he thinks.

"And the others? What about them? Did they know what he had planned? That I was a fucking gift to be served up to you without any say or choice in the matter."

"Fuck, no! They didn't know."

"It doesn't matter though, does it? We're still enemies. I'm still on the outside looking in. I'm still the girl you all *hate*."

"I don't hate you, Pen."

I laugh bitterly. "You could've fooled me."

"Listen to me," he says fiercely. "I *don't* hate you. I never did. I was angry, hurt, fucking cut-up, but I never hated you. I want to understand. Tell me the truth."

"I—" I begin, but find I can't say anything without opening up a whole can of worms. He has a right to be angry, bitter. Then again, so do I. "It's not that simple—"

"Just fucking tell me, Pen. This is only as complicated as you make it. Put me out of my goddamn misery!" he growls, angry at me, at the situation, at *us*. "We could always talk, you and me. That was never a problem. What the fuck happened to change that? What you did came out of the left field. You blindsided us, Pen. We were happy. We fucking *loved* you." His hands come up once more and his fingers slide into my hair, tightening on the strands.

"I know you did—"

"Is that it? Is that all you can fucking say? *I know*. You don't fucking know. You don't fucking understand what that did to us," he shouts, his honesty taking wing on the back of anger. It flies around us with frenzied wings and sharpened claws.

"Of course I understand!" I shout back, yanking his hands away and backing off. "You don't think it hurt me to walk away? You think I haven't felt every minute of your absence all this time? You think I don't hurt, that it doesn't cut me up inside to know the boys I would do anything for never even questioned *why* I did what I did?" I'm panting now, shaking with adrenaline and the truth that is on the tip of my tongue. Zayn opens his mouth to speak, but I cut him off. "No! You don't get to come in here and throw down like this, not after Friday night, not after what happened. You don't get to pile on the guilt to make yourself feel better. You don't get to push me until I break. You don't get to hurt me like this anymore!"

Zayn blanches, regret replacing the righteous anger. "I'm sorry, okay? I'm sorry for what happened Friday night and everything before."

"No, it's not okay. None of what happened at Grim's club was okay. None of *this* is okay," I say pointing between us, wanting more than anything to turn back time and change what happened.

But I can't.

I can't change anything.

Our past is set in stone and our friendship is buried

beneath the soil of our distrust and the tears of our heartbreak. There's a whole fucking graveyard filled with the death of our friendship. I back away from Zayn, almost tripping over my own feet in my haste to get away. "I can't do this anymore. I fucking can't."

"Can't do what, Pen?" Zayn asks, crowding me. He forces me backwards until my back hits the wall. "I'm not letting this go," he says emphatically, grasping my head in his hands. His gaze searches mine like he's trying to uncover all my secrets with that one look. I can smell his expensive aftershave overshadowed a little by the metallic scent of blood and two days of wearing the same clothes. I don't hate it. I don't hate him.

How can I when I still love him despite it all?

"Fuck, Pen. Just talk to me. Give me something at least. Make me understand."

His breath is warm against my skin, his fingers tight against my scalp and his body flush against mine. I can't breathe with him so close to me, taking up my personal space with his presence. It's too fucking much. "There's nothing to tell."

"Pen, goddamn it, don't you dare shut down now. Give me something, anything. It's important."

"Why?"

"*Please*, Pen."

Our gazes clash, our breath mingles, and I get the distinct impression that Zayn isn't a man who pleads very often, that he doesn't beg for anything. I'm not sure if it's because he's showing a more vulnerable side, the absolute misery in his gaze —or the fact that I've missed his touch, *him*, so much—but I give him the only thing I can in the moment.

My kiss.

My lips smash against his as I grip hold of the lapels of his jacket and yank him close. I kiss him in anger and with love. I kiss him with fierceness and hurt. I kiss him with longing and loathing. This kiss isn't a white flag of truce. This kiss is meant to distract, to disarm. I can't give him the answers he seeks, but I can give him something to think about. After a beat, he kisses me back. He presses his body against mine, lifts me up beneath my thighs and traps me against the wall. His stubble scratches against my skin, but I don't care.

We kiss in a way that opens old wounds.

Our tongues mine the depths of our past, our hurt. Our kiss unearths our memories, hunting for the friendship we once shared, digging deep as our teeth clash and our tongues duel. There's no holding back with this kiss, and despite my intentions, I fall into it headfirst, searching for what we once had. Zayn's moans mingle with mine and the noises we make are nothing short of erotic. This kiss is filthy in the best possible way, it's wet and torrid and insanely hot. Instinctively, my legs tighten around Zayn's back, my core pressing against his lower abs. I jerk my hips, trying to ease the intense throb there but when he grunts in pain, I'm reminded of the wound to his torso and pull back sharply.

"Fuck, Zayn—" I say against his lips, but he shuts me up with his mouth, refusing to let reality settle back in and presses me harder against the wall, propping me up so that he can reach between us. His fingers slide beneath the waistband of my joggers and knickers, and his whole hand cups my mound. He just holds me there, the heel of his palm pressing against my clit that throbs beneath his hand. I don't push him away.

I *want* his touch.

I *want* his kiss.

I *want* his fucking attention.

On Friday I'd refused to lean into his kiss. It was a

conscious move on my part. To not give in that way. Today I kiss him not because I'm weak, but because I'm strong. I am the master of my own fate, my own decisions. I'm done feeling like I have no control, and I want that back. I want Zayn back. Rightly or wrongly, I crave him.

If sorry is a sticking plaster over the wound in my heart, then this kiss and his touch is a bandage. I feel it wrapping around the wound, stemming the flow of blood in an attempt to heal the pain. In the moment, nothing but the way he tastes, the way he feels, is important. I rock into his hand, pressing against his palm. I'm slick with heat, with want, with need, and as his finger rims my entrance lighting me up from the inside out, I weep for him, for *this*.

My pussy fucking cries out for his touch as tears slide down my cheeks. I cry with relief and with new beginnings. At least that's what I dare to hope.

"Pen," he laments as we both taste the saltiness of my tears. The sound of my name on his lips is different, it's reverent, *loving* in a way I haven't heard for three years. It sounds like grief, sorrow, pain, but also hope, joy and the start of something new.

As he rubs the pad of his thumb gently over my clit and kisses me with hunger, an orgasm builds at the base of my spine. Our tongues duel and his fingers rub against me expertly. I mewl into his mouth and he growls into mine, until the years apart fall away and we're just two best friends planting that first seed of love with touch and kisses and ecstasy. I can feel that promise, that *hope* growing inside of me. I can feel it pushing up against the dirt and the grime of our bad choices. I can feel it reaching for sunlight, for a chance to flourish, and despite everything, I let it, because what am I if not a girl desperate for this boy to love her again?

Zayn's finger hooks inside, pressing against that tender spot within me whilst his thumb circles my clit delicately. His tongue laps at my mouth, sucking my tongue into his and the groan he makes as I flood his hand makes me want to rip off his clothes and fuck him right here on the hardwood of the studio floor.

"Come, Pen," he growls against my mouth whilst his fingers fuck me into oblivion.

So I come.

I come on Zayn's hand, his fingers deep inside me.

I come with his chipped tooth biting into my bottom lip.

I come with a warmth in my heart that I haven't felt in a long, long time.

I come undone, and Zayn… Zayn holds me until I'm spent.

11

Zayn

I came here with a message from Jeb. I came here in search of Pen with his words burning on my tongue and his wrath bleeding from the wound on my chest.

I came here to destroy Pen.

Only she destroyed *me*.

Every step, every move, every twist, turn, and leap cut me deep. Far more than the two-inch slash to my chest. That's just a superficial wound in comparison, something I've become accustomed to, but seeing her like this, so raw, in pain, bleeding from her soul, that hurts me so much more.

It makes me view things differently. It makes me question *everything*.

Once again she cut me, just like she had Friday night at Grim's club.

Her power to wield her emotions and weaponize dance floors me.

She's incredible.

And she'll be the death of me. Of *us*.

I'm here to do a job. I'm here for our crew.

But Pen is a problem we hadn't foreseen.

Stupid.

Of course she would be here at the Academy. This place was always her dream, and despite every damn thing going against her, despite a mother who never supported her, she's made it happen anyway. She's grabbed her future by the balls, and I admire her for it even if in the beginning I'd believed that Jeb had pulled strings for her to be here. I can see now that wasn't the case. Why the fuck we didn't factor her into the equation is beyond me, and now we're all fucking struggling. The end goal doesn't seem so clear anymore.

Nothing is clear anymore.

Reluctantly, I release her from my hold and lower her to her feet. My hand is slick with her heat, with her release, and my cock is desperate for the same. But this moment isn't about me, it's about her. Pen.

My Pen.

She holds so many secrets. Secrets I need to unravel. I see them in her eyes. I tasted them on her tongue. I mourn for the time when we were open with one another, when she trusted me enough with her hurt and her pain. I want her to trust me again, but the second I give her the message from Jeb she will shore up her defences and harden herself to me.

I hate that.

I fucking *hate* that, but I have little choice.

Actually, who am I fucking kidding? I *do* have a choice. I could have told Jeb to take his message and shove it up his fucking arse, but I didn't. I played the game even when the prize wasn't so clear anymore. We've always had a goal in sight, and Pen was never part of that. Xeno never fails to remind us all of that fact over and over again. The fucking prick.

With flushed cheeks and the dignity of a queen, Pen looks at me, her gaze searching. "What do you want, Zayn?" she asks again. Her body is trembling and it's all I can do not to pull her back into my arms and hold her like I often did when we were kids. It takes monumental effort to keep my distance when all I want is to close the gap and end this fucking torment for good.

"Zayn, what do you want?" And I know she isn't talking about the here and now, she's asking about the future, about what's really in the depths of my fucked-up heart.

You.

God fucking damn it, I want you, Pen.

That's what I want. That's what we all want, even Xeno, if he would only just let himself acknowledge that. Of course, I don't give her the honest truth. Instead, I deliver the message from Jeb because that's what I *have* to do.

"I'm here to pass on a message. Jeb said that your dance, whilst entertaining, wasn't what he had in mind. That he hasn't forgotten your conversation and you'd be mindful not to piss him off again." I swallow hard, hating the way her gaze flashes with anger, then with fear. But more than that, I hate the fact that I still have her scent on my fingers whilst I deliver this message, that the connection we just shared, that her coming apart is tainted now. That it will always be tainted by him, by Jeb.

"And?" she asks.

"You no longer work at Rocks—"

"But I need the money..." she whispers after a beat, even though there's an acceptance in her gaze. She expected this, and for some reason that scores a deeper cut into my flesh than the knife wound that sits there now. She knew something like this was coming. Pen hasn't had it easy, but like with everything in her life, she handles it. The least I can do is the same. Drawing in a deep breath, I continue, loathing the fact that she's so obviously been struggling these past three years. She's thin, drawn, tired. She's barely hanging on and I'm a bastard for making this worse for her. We're *all* cocksuckers for making this harder for her.

"There's more, right?" She jerks her chin and squares her shoulders. I nod.

"Jeb said that you are too valuable to be working behind a bar. That your *skills* are required elsewhere." I try to hide my distaste, but fail. He'd talked about her like a commodity, like a piece of damn meat and that had angered me more than I thought it would. I've spent three years hardening my heart. Three years forgetting the girl I loved. It took me a long time to not think about her every second of every fucking day, wondering what she was doing with Jeb. Whether he was treating her well, whether he made her smile like we did, whether he loved her like I did, I *do*. I turned my pain into anger. I fucked other women, I cut people, *broke* them and didn't fucking blink, but a couple of weeks in her presence and I'm questioning everything I've become.

"Malik Brov…?" she croaks, swallowing hard.

"No! Not him. I made sure of that," I say fiercely. *No fucking way. Not that man. Not him.*

"What do you mean?" she snaps, confusion in her gaze.

"He offered a price for you, Pen, a high price that I paid for in blood, *my* blood."

"What are you saying? I don't understand."

I undo my jacket and point at the stain of my blood. I lied

when I said it's only a scratch. The wound had to be sewn up, a two inch gash that fucking stings like a bitch. It'll scar, just like all the rest. "Jeb cut me for disagreeing with him. I let him."

"Zayn, oh my god!" She reaches for me then, cupping my face this time and I swear to fuck my knees almost give out at the tenderness I see in her gaze.

"Don't do that. Don't pity me. That was *my* choice. I knew the consequences of disagreeing with him. I'm used to it."

"Used to it—?" Her hands fall away, and I see her connecting the dots. I'm scarred not just from the knife fights I've been in, but from the years of punishment I've had to endure at the hands of Jeb. Blood ties, blood binds, blood weeps. Anyone else would be dead for the insolence, this is nothing. He cuts me, I get to see another day.

It is what it is.

The Breakers don't know. They assume every cut is from a knife fight, and not me taking punishment for them, for any wrongdoing we make.

"So if not Malik, who?" she whispers.

"A deal was made with Grim," Zayn explains.

"Grim?" Pen bites out, anger flashing.

"Yes, you will perform in the cage at her club with the other…"

"*Strippers*?" she spits, her gaze narrowing on mine.

I nod tightly. Believe me, I fought against that decision too. I don't want her paraded like that, I fucking don't, but it was the lesser of two evils. Grim might be a tough bitch, but she has some morals at least. She won't let anyone touch Pen. She treats her girls well. She helped Asia and Eastern get out of a sticky situation with the King. Of course, she'd deny it. Grim hasn't got to where she is today by being an open book. She's secretive, private and an astute business woman. Beast is one of the handful of people on this planet that she truly trusts. Besides, whilst Grim gave Jeb the impression Pen would be stripping, there was a look in her eyes that told me that perhaps that isn't exactly what she has planned, and I hope to fuck I'm right about that.

"Grim might have a reputation that precedes her, but I don't believe she'd let anything happen to you—" I say, hating myself for even allowing this to happen.

"Fuck!"

Pen spins on her feet and strides over to the table, snatching up her mobile phone and the apple that sits there. It looks bruised and on the turn. I'd throw it away, but Pen clutches hold of it like it's the last thing she has left to eat. Looking at her, reading between the lines, it probably is. I stride over to her, and rest my hands gently on her shoulder. She flinches, but she doesn't pull away. Her head drops, and words fail me. I was always so good at finding the right thing to say. But now? Now I have nothing but hollow words that mean jack shit when all is said and done. After a beat, she lifts her head and locks gazes with me in the mirror opposite.

"I'll do it."

And even though she really doesn't have a choice in the matter, that Jeb will force her regardless, I can't help but ask myself why she's agreeing to it. It's a mystery I intend on getting to the bottom of, because if I've realised anything since returning it's this: my uncle has something over her, and I intend on finding out what. York and Dax are on the same wavelength as me, and after Friday night's fucking mess seem as invested in finding out what the fuck is going on. Being in Pen's orbit again is affecting them both and causing issues between us all and what we came here to do.

Xeno, however... Well, let's just say that he's being a dick.

He's determined to keep Pen at arm's length. He refuses to back down. He's single-minded in his goal. That's what's most important to him, and that fucking pisses me off because for a long time, it was the most important thing to me to. Not anymore.

"When do I start?" Pen eventually asks, turning to face me. I can see her mentally shaking herself. She used to do it a lot when we were kids. Pen would straighten her spine, raise her chin, and hold her shoulders back. Fierce, brave, fucking courageous.

Damn, I've missed her.

Ignoring the tightness in my throat, I dig into my jacket pocket and pull out Grim's card. Pen takes it, her eyes flicking to the black card with gold lettering. "Call Grim. She'll fill you in."

"Fill you in on what?" A bubbly voice asks. *Clancy.*

Fuck. I wanted more time alone with Pen. I growl under my breath. Don't get me wrong, I actually like Clancy, but her timing sucks. For a split second Pen stiffens as she struggles with how to answer. Then she flicks her gaze from me to Clancy behind us, and plasters a smile on her face. A beautiful, *fake*, smile.

"Hey girl," she grins, her face lighting up even when her eyes don't shine. I watch her tuck away the card into the pocket of her joggers.

"Hey girl? Don't you *hey girl* me!" Clancy exclaims, her words tempered by her laughter. "You've been ignoring me. I should be chucking your arse to the curb!"

"But you won't because you love me, right?" Pen asks, tipping her head to the side. There's a moment of apprehension in her gaze that only I can see before she steps around me, ending any further conversation between us. Not that I could say much with Clancy here anyway.

"Of course I love you! I know a good thing when I see it and I intend on keeping it close. Besides, I don't do easy," Clancy responds, her words clearly directed at me.

I grit my jaw, refusing to rise to the bait whilst simultaneously wondering what she knows. I flick my gaze to Pen, but she's well and truly shut-down. I see how it is.

"Well, I got shit to do," I say abruptly, twisting on my feet and striding to the door. Clancy gives me an incredulous look as I pass her by.

"Nice outfit," she smirks, her curiosity piqued.

Ignoring Clancy, I stop at the door and turn to face Pen. She meets my gaze with a steady look of her own. A few minutes ago I had my hand cupping her pussy and my tongue fucking her mouth. She'd fallen apart in my arms and opened herself to me, giving me a way in, but you wouldn't know it looking at her now. My ego takes a hit at her ability to shut off her emotions so well, but if she thinks this is over, she's got another thing coming.

Fuck that.

She's not shutting the door on me, not again. Now that I've opened her up a crack, I'm going to do anything I can to keep it that way. If Xeno has an issue with that, he can have a conversation with my fist. He's been begging for an excuse to fight. Right now I'm happy to indulge the bastard.

"We'll continue this conversation later," I say, brooking no arguments, because this isn't an invitation to talk, it's a promise.

One I intend on keeping.

12

Pen

"You sneaky bitch! What was *that* all about?" Clancy asks, her infectious smile like a tonic. It makes me feel like everything that's just happened between Zayn and me is normal, that I can make out with a guy and then dissect every single part of it with my friend. I've never had a female friendship like this, unless you include my sister, Lena, which I don't because there are just some things that I can't tell her. I look at Clancy, at the delight in her eyes and the sparkle in her green orbs, then sigh because what *can* I tell her?

"It's complicated."

She raises her brows and cocks out her hip. "Complicated? I bet. Stubble rash suits you."

Her laughter rings in my ears as I snatch my head around to look in the mirror. "Fuck," I mumble. Sure enough I have a stubble rash from my kiss with Zayn. I raise my fingers to my lips and cheeks. At least she hasn't noticed the slight puffiness of my eyes from the tears I shed. I don't want to have a conversation explaining that.

"How was it?"

"How was what?" I throw back, knowing perfectly well what she's asking.

She cocks her hip and raises her brow. "Playing tonsil tennis with Mr Hip-Hop Gangster, of course!"

Kissing Zayn was...

Fuck! It was everything I'd hoped it would be and now I'm reeling. "I—" I begin, then fumble. I've no idea what to say or do. I need time to unravel what's just happened. Clancy's smile drops as she reaches for my arm, squeezing it gently.

"Sorry. Listen, you don't have to tell me anything. I'm just here if you need me, okay? *Are* you okay?"

"I'm not sure," I say honestly.

She nods. "I thought you two weren't friends anymore?"

"We aren't."

Clancy raises a perfectly arched brow. "No?"

"No." I sound more certain than I feel.

"Pen. Forgive me. I'm not normally intrusive, I swear. It's just..." She cocks her head, her pretty red curls falling over her shoulder. "I've seen the way he looks at you. I've seen the way you look at him, at *all* of them. The tension is off the charts. It's hot-as-hell, fanny-fluttering, insanity. I could come just being in a room with you all."

I let out a broken laugh at that, my cheeks flushing at the memory of Zayn's hand cupping my pussy. Clancy is right, it was fanny-flutter inducing. I've not come like that in a long, long time, but instead of feeling fulfilled, I only feel his absence more keenly. Zayn wants to heal what's broken between us. I do too, but every way I turn I'm fucked. My brother wants information and I have to let them in then fuck them over to get it.

"I mean, all joking aside, you can't live like this. It's not healthy, Pen. Something's gotta give, and I'll be damned if it's you. Don't let them hurt you. Do you hear me?" she asks, her hands grabbing my shoulders before she pulls me into a hug.

My eyes fill with tears at her kindness, and it's all I can do to hold them back. But I'm Pen Scott and I'm strong. Instead, I hold onto her and whisper vehemently in her ear. "They won't break me. *Promise*."

"Good," she responds, pulling back. "They give you shit. I give them a shit-ton of trouble back."

This time I do laugh. She's so fiery, just like her hair. "What, all five feet, two inches of you are going up against the Breakers?"

"Well, if you can do it at no more than an inch taller than me, then so can I! We might be small, but we're fucking mighty, right?" I shake my head, rolling my eyes. "Right?" she insists.

"Right."

"Atta girl!" Clancy looks down at her wrist watch. "It's almost five. "Fancy a bite to eat?"

My stomach growls in agreement, but my wallet vehemently disagrees. I pull a face and raise my bruised apple.

"You're not serious?" she asks, unable to hide her disgust at my dinner. Frankly, I'm unable to hide my own disgust, but beggars can't be choosers. "Come on, Pen. Let's sort you out." Clancy puts her arm through mine and pulls me towards the studio door.

"I can't afford takeout, Clancy," I admit, my cheeks flushing with embarrassment. I don't even know if I'm going to get paid to work at Grim's club. I'm so fucked.

"Who said anything about a takeaway? *I'm* making you something to eat. It's nothing," she says, brushing away my concerns, but pride makes me argue.

"But—" I begin.

"I've got this," she repeats, brooking no arguments.

My stomach growls again, and this time I don't try and disagree. I follow her out of the studio and back up to her flat. Twenty minutes later I'm sitting on her bed eating a grilled cheese sandwich and slurping a cup of tea. Chewing on the last mouthful, I get up and pop our empty plates and mugs in the sink, washing them up. Clancy flicks through her phone, and clicks on a track in her Spotify playlist before placing the phone into her speakers. It's *Hideaway* by Kiesza, a lively song with a wicked beat that makes you want to clap your hands and stomp your feet, or in Clancy's case, tap dance.

She jumps up grinning, grabs her tap shoes, stuffs her feet into them and then starts to dance around me in the tiny space between where her bed lies and her kitchen ends. Her feet move like lightning, her tap steps in time with the deep club music, the tune harks back to 1990's dance. I fucking love it. I fucking love her infectious positivity.

"Come on, girl!" she shouts over the music, grinning crazily at me.

"We've just eaten!" I retort, laughing.

"What are you, my *mum*? Move your damn feet!" She dances over to her speakers and turns the music up until my ears are ringing with the sound.

I dance.

Wildly.

Freely.

With a full belly and friendship in my heart.

We jump up and down and wave our hands in the air like a bunch of ravers with no rhythm. She laughs.

I laugh.

We hug. We spin. We sing along to the song.

And I feel her friendship like a warm, comforting hug.

This girl's a keeper.

By the time the song's finished we're both lying on the bed, breathing hard and grinning. I feel a thousand times lighter. She turns her head to face mine, her pea-green eyes sparkling.

"Those boys are stupid for not seeing how amazing you are. I'm here, okay? I'm here when you need to talk, when you want to vent, when you want to dance like a drugged-up nineties raver." She giggles at that, and I smile back. We're totally on the same wavelength.

"Thank you," I mouth.

"So, how's your sister?" Clancy asks, propping herself up on her bent arm as she looks down at me, the music still blares out and I can barely hear her over the sound of some dubstep.

"A perfectly obnoxious teenager," I respond, not wanting to openly lie to her again. Guilt wraps around my heart. I told Clancy I was visiting Lena this weekend and the fact that I haven't doesn't sit well with me. I feel guilt for not seeing my sister and guilt for lying. I make a promise to go and see Lena as soon as she's back from her school trip to the Isle of Wight.

"Yeah, teenagers suck," Clancy responds grinning, giving me a funny look.

"What?"

"You know, strictly speaking I'm *still* a teenager..."

"Wait, what? How old are you?" I giggle.

"I'm nine*teen*, bitch. My birthday is in a couple of weeks."

Laughing, I sit up, pulling her up with me. "Well then, we got to make some plans, right?" My words run away with me before I've had time to really think about what I'm saying. I can't afford a night out, not to mention the fact I don't know what nights I'm supposed to be working for Grim… as a goddamn *stripper*. The thought of taking my clothes off for other people's pleasure pisses me the fuck off. I don't know Grim but after our brief chat, I thought I understood her, but clearly she's fucking me over too.

"Yesssssss, girl! We are going to partaaaayyyy!" Clancy exclaims, unaware of my inner turmoil. Her infectious excitement makes me smile despite my predicament. "I want to dance, I want to drink, I want to let loose, but most of all I want to find a nice man to fuck the rest of the night away with."

"Clancy—" I begin, about to be a party pooper again and explain I may have gotten ahead of myself, but I'm rudely interrupted by banging on her door.

"Who is it?" Clancy yells over the music, pulling an *'oh shit, we're in trouble, but I don't really give a fuck,'* face.

"Clancy, you little shit. No one wants to hear your crappy music! Turn it the fuck off!" Tiffany shouts through the door.

We look at each other again and burst out laughing. "Fuck you, Tiff!" Clancy shouts back. She swings her feet off the bed and strides over to her phone that's still attached to the speakers and turns the music up. Tiffany's curses are lost beneath the sound as we jump up and dance like ravers high on ecstasy once again. As she dances around the room without a care in the world and full of sunshine and smiles, I vow to myself that I'll make Clancy's birthday special somehow. It's the least I can do.

LATER THAT NIGHT, I pull out the card Zayn gave me with Grim's contact number on it. Sitting on my bed, I glance at my mobile phone. It's almost ten pm and normally I wouldn't be so rude to make a call this late, but fuck that. If Grim and Jeb can make a deal about me without my consent, she can take a call from me now.

Punching in the number, I wait for her to pick up. I don't have to wait long.

"Yes?" A gruff voice answers. It's Beast, not Grim.

"I'm calling to speak with Grim. It's Pen."

"Pen?"

"Yes, I was at Grim's club Friday night with the Skins. A *deal* was made," I say, unable to hide my disgust.

"Ah, *that* Pen. You caused a lot of shit. Quite the little badass mover, aren't you? Not to mention full of spunk." He chuckles, his gruff tone replaced with a warmth that surprises me.

"I didn't cause any shit. I was just dealing with the crap thrown at *me*," I reply, feeling more than a little prickly. I clamp my mouth shut, cursing myself for not being level-headed enough to realise I'm dealing with a man who'd sooner put a bullet in someone's brain than listen to attitude. Thankfully today he appears to be in a good mood.

"Grim, *Feet of Flames* is on the phone. She's cranky," he chuckles. I wince at the nickname, Grim must have told him what Malik Brov had called me. I swallow down my very *cranky* response as Beast passes the phone over to Grim.

"I'd wondered when you'd call," Grim says, conversationally.

I bite the inside of my cheek to prevent myself from going off on her. Despite what she said Friday night about ever needing a friend, she's already proven I can't fucking trust her.

"When do I start?" I simply say, my voice tight and filled with gravel.

"That's it? I'm surprised. I expected more of a reaction than that." Her voice is even, cool, and it pisses me off. I can't help it, I bite.

"What do you want me to say? Thanks for making a deal with the Skins without my fucking permission?" I respond angrily, my fingers wrapping tightly around my phone.

"Ah, there she is! Don't stop fighting, Pen. The minute you give up, they have you. Got it?"

"What are you talking about?" I retort, thrown by her response.

"I promised that you'd never be touched by any of the Skins whilst in my club, and I will keep that promise. Being a *performer* affords you that protection. The alternative would've been far, far worse. Jeb was willing to sell you off to Malik Brov. Zayn stopped that. He impressed me actually, the way he stood up for you."

"Wait, you know that Zayn was playing Jeb?"

Grim chuckles. "Yeah, I knew. Jeb has a lot of enemies. The bastard will willingly put his own flesh and blood in the line of fire to protect his arse. I knew it the moment he arrived that night. I played along until we were behind closed doors."

"I see."

"I'm not sure you do. Look, Pen. I don't know for definite how the fuck you got mixed up with the Skins, but I have a fair idea. No one who throws themselves in the line of fire does it without love. There's history between you and Dax, am I right?" I remain silent, not willing to give anything away. She's still a criminal after all. I don't know her. "Right?" she persists.

"We were friends once," I admit.

"Once?"

"We were kids. It's different now."

"Just you and Dax?" she pushes, seeking more.

"No, not just me and Dax. The others too. Xeno, York, Zayn. The Breakers…" I almost say *my Breakers*, but stop myself before I can.

She goes silent for a moment. "I won't profess to be an expert in relationships. Beast is the only man I've ever loved. I would die for him, as he would for me. That's the kind of relationship I know. But it wasn't always that way with him. We were enemies once."

"Why are you telling me this?" I ask, confused as to why she's opening up this way with me. We're strangers. She's some shit-hot, badass, criminal businesswoman and I'm a girl who can barely keep her head above water, just trying to survive in a world I never wanted to be a part of.

"Because, Pen, I see a little of me in you. I see the fight you wear like a badge of honour, and beneath it, I see the hurt…" her voice trails off as she swears under her voice. "Look, I'm gonna level with you. I have a vested interest in this. You get protection at my club. You get to dance—"

"Dance?" I scoff.

"Yes, dance."

"I have nothing against strippers, but that's not the kind of dance I want to perform."

"What? No!" Grim barks out a laugh. "*Jeb* might have agreed for you to be a stripper, but I only agreed for you to be a *performer*. If he's too thick as shit to understand the difference, then that's his problem, not mine. We shook on it, he can't break the deal now."

"What are you saying?"

"You're going to *dance*, Pen. There'll be no stripping for you.

Like everyone else Friday night, I was mesmerised. It's a rare feat to be able to command attention from a room full of violent gangsters without resorting to bloodshed or sex, but you did that. I want you dancing in my club. You are the best. I want the best."

"Wow," is all I can manage to say. I hadn't expected that. I thought I was fated to strip and bare my skin for a bunch of unruly bastards to salivate over. This was not what I was expecting.

"You will be paid a good wage. I treat my employees well. Does four hundred pound sound reasonable to you?"

"A month?" I question. It's less than what I was earning at Rocks, but I guess I could make it work. I only really need it to buy food and I can make do without all the fancy dance gear anyway.

Grim laughs. "No, Pen. I'm not Jeb. I actually appreciate my employees. Four hundred pound a weekend."

"A weekend?!" I blurt out, incredulous. "You sure I'm not stripping?"

"Positive. You dance at my club every Friday and Saturday night. You get to choose the songs. Dance solo, with other performers, whatever. I give you free rein. My girls have never danced as well as they did with you in the cage with them. If you want to use them in your performances, then go for it. If you want to bring in others, then do that too but I want to check them out first. I can't just let any old Tom, Dick or Harry into my club."

I swallow hard. Is she for real? This is too good to be true, surely. "Are you serious?"

"Never more serious in my life."

"So what does Jeb get in return...? I mean, it's none of my business, but I don't understand why you would make a deal with someone you said you hate in order to stop me from being sold to Malik Brov. Why would you do that?"

"Listen, Pen. I'm a successful businesswoman because I know how to spot a good opportunity. After your performance Friday, every damn crew were asking when you'd be dancing next. They come to my club to see a fight, to bet, to fuck, to get high and drink. But if I can get them in my club to watch you dance, then you can bet your arse I'm going to cash in on that."

"Right," I reply.

She sighs heavily. "I'm also a woman of my word, Pen. I made you a promise. I kept it."

"How much did you pay?" I ask, holding my breath. I appreciate what Grim has done, but just because she's allowing me to dance instead of strip, doesn't mean I'm not owned by her now, and if I know Jeb well enough, it definitely doesn't mean he's relinquished his ownership of me either. I'm not stupid.

"Believe it or not there are things that are way more valuable than printed paper and coins."

"Like what?"

"*Information*. Jeb wanted information. I gave it to him. Well, what he wanted to hear, anyway."

"What information? What do you mean by that?" I ask, realising I'm pushing my luck, but asking anyway. David's devil voice murmurs into my ear, reminding me that I'm still beholden to him too.

"And that really is none of your business," Grim responds, ending that thread of our conversation. "Look. I got you out of a sticky situation. You get to dance at my club, you get a level of protection being an employee of mine, and I get a new arm to my business. I've been looking for a way to make my club more upmarket."

"Fair enough," I respond, not really knowing what else to say.

"Don't get me wrong, I love a good, old-fashioned, vicious cage fight like anyone else, but there's nothing wrong with a bit of class thrown in too."

"Are you saying I'm classy?" I can't help but laugh, shaking my head at the bizarreness of this conversation.

"I guess I am. So, are you okay with my terms?"

"In all honesty, do I really have a choice?"

Grim snorts. "Well, no, but I'm trying to make this as palatable as possible. I might be a woman, but I'm not a cunt. Jeb is. I'm the lesser of two evils."

"I'm not sure that makes me feel any better. I've grown up knowing bad people. I've lived amongst the wolves my whole life, just because you didn't attack the moment we met doesn't mean I can trust you not to hurt me in the future."

"You're wise to keep your head, Pen. I admire that..." Her voice trails off as she mulls over what I've said. "Listen, you do right by me, I'll do right by you. That's the only guarantee I can give you."

I think for a moment. Grim is an unknown, but so far she's proven to be a woman of her word. At least while working for her, I'll be earning money doing something I love. Four hundred pounds for two nights of dancing is better than I could've hoped for. Drawing in a shaky breath, I nod my head. "Okay."

"Good. Your first performance will be in three weeks right after Dax's fight against Beast. I intend on getting the punters' blood pumping with violence and then woo them with your dance moves. I want you to show those motherfuckers what it truly means to be a performer."

Shit, Dax's fight with Beast, I'd almost forgotten about that.

"Is Beast really as fierce as he seems?" I ask, when really all I want to know is if he's capable of killing Dax.

"Yes, he is. He's every bit as monstrous in the cage as his name suggests."

"Fuck," I whisper.

"Fuck indeed. Beast won't hold back. He fights to win, every time. Dax is a great fighter, but he has no control. If he wants to survive Beast in the ring, he'll need to focus."

"I can't see him hurt," I admit.

"I get it, but there's no going back now. This is out of my hands. All I can assure you is that Beast won't kill him. That punishment is only reserved for his enemies. Dax hasn't stepped over that line. He just needs to be taught a lesson."

"That's not very reassuring."

"It wasn't supposed to be. I don't tolerate anyone abusing my rules. The only reason Dax wasn't shot was because of you. He's not lying in a morgue right now because you stepped in. That boy owes you his life, but I get the distinct impression he's too fucking stupid to realise that."

I sigh heavily. "Maybe you're right."

"Not maybe. Absolutely. You saved him. End of. Let's hope Beast knocks some sense into him."

Wincing, I don't respond to that. Instead I steer the conversation back to my new job. "So what time do I need to be at the club on my first night?"

"We open at nine. You'll be on at midnight, but I expect you to be there at seven. In fact, if you need to rehearse before then you're welcome to come any night of the week before. Just drop me a message and Beast will open up for you."

"Will I be dancing in the cage?"

"In the cage, around the cage, on the fucking table like you did Friday. I'll leave it up to you. If you want to work with the girls, let me know. I'll make sure they're available."

"Okay. I'll figure out a routine and let you know if I'll need them, or anyone else."

"Good. Talk soon," Grim says, cutting off my reply.

I flick off my phone and flop back onto my bed, my heart beating wildly. Part of me is excited about the prospect of being able to dance and earn money whilst I do what I love, but a bigger part is fucking terrified. Instead of getting away from this criminal world I've tried so hard to keep out of, I'm getting pulled further into its depths. I feel like I'm treading water in the ocean with a bunch of sharks circling me, just waiting for the moment when one of them attacks.

13

Pen

After a busy day of lessons, throwing myself into learning new dance techniques and avoiding the Breakers, I head up to my flat to change. Monday is the only day of the week when I don't share any lessons with them. Which is just as well, as I need to get my game face on ready for tonight's group practice. The show must go on, right? Madame Tuillard and D-Neath don't give a fuck if I've got issues with half of the dance crew and I need to show everyone I can be professional despite everything that's happening right now. Like Tuillard said, there are a hundred dancers willing to take my spot in a heartbeat and I refuse to fuck this up. I have to focus on the end of year show. I need something positive to hold onto in this mire of shit I'm wading through.

That show is my golden ticket. That's my future. My way out. It's my first step into a career in dance that I've always dreamed of and worked towards my whole life. Maybe I'm just being naïve believing that, but I have to hold onto something, right?

My stomach growls as I climb the stairs to my flat, reminding me that yet again I've eaten nothing for breakfast or lunch, and all that's keeping me going are two cups of cheap tea sweetened with sugar to give me a boost in energy that I lack these days. I've literally got ten pounds to my name and somehow that's got to keep me going until I start work at Grim's. I decide that my only option is to call my new boss and ask for an advance. It's not as if I can back out of my agreement with her, so she knows I'll be good for it. Stepping into my flat, I head into the main living area only to stop short when I see three shopping bags filled with food sitting on my kitchen counter.

"What the fuck?" I whisper, my mouth dropping open in shock.

Reaching for the first bag, I pull out three packets of pasta, several jars of sauces, bread, eggs, tea, coffee, and other essential items to make enough meals to last me until the end of the month. The next bag is filled with fruits and vegetables, and the third has snacks and crisps and all kinds of treats I've never been able to indulge in, making me squeal in delight. I pull out biscuits, bags of crisps and chocolate bars. It's all so wrong, but oh so right. I pick up a pack of chocolate biscuits and shove one in my mouth, moaning around the explosion of taste. My stomach gurgles, practically doing the jig as it relishes the sugary goodness I'm feeding it. I grab another biscuit, this time chewing on it slowly, rather than shoving it into my face, and take a good look at all the goodies. Relief floods my veins making me feel almost lightheaded, or maybe that's just the sudden rush of sugar.

"Clancy, you gorgeous wonderful woman." I laugh out

loud, not remotely cross that she's somehow snuck into my flat to leave me all this stuff. Not only is she an amazing friend, she's a freaking badass lockpicker to boot. Though I am beginning to worry about how easy it really is getting into my flat. I need to sort that shit out.

Noticing a piece of folded paper on the counter, I snatch it up grinning, but my growing smile freezes on my face when I recognise the handwriting. "Fuck," I whisper, placing the half-eaten biscuit on the counter and unfolding the note, my hands shaking.

Pen,
You will never go hungry again.
I've filled up your fridge too.
Eat first, then go look in your wardrobe.
Zayn.

NO WAY! No fucking way. My throat constricts. *Zayn* bought me all of this. I grip the counter to steady myself, blinking back the sudden rush of tears that prick my eyes. Ignoring his command to eat first, and with hope fluttering in my heart, I walk towards the wardrobe. Attached to the glass mirror is another note that I hadn't noticed when I entered.

This is the least I could do.
You deserve so much more, but this is a start.
Zayn.

I slide open my wardrobe and next to my clothes are a dozen hangers holding all sorts of dance gear. There are leggings, short and long-sleeved leotards, joggers, t-shirts, hoodies, even legwarmers. I flick through all of the items, my fingers running across the expensive dancewear. I've never owned anything as luxurious as these items. I'm used to hand-me-downs and second-hand clothes. I'm used to using what little spare money I have to buy from charity shops and cheap high street stores. All of this stuff is high-end dancewear that I've only ever dreamed of owning. It's overwhelming. My gaze follows my hand as I touch every item reverently, my fingers finally landing on a black suit bag that's been hung in the far corner of my wardrobe. There's another note pinned to it.

Malik might be a dick, but he was right about one thing.
You dance with passion, with fire. You fucking slay me.
I'd willingly burn up in your flames, and suffocate in your ashes, if it meant I could hold you close again. If it meant you'd let me in.
Zayn.

"Zayn," I whisper, needing him in a way I haven't allowed myself to in a long time. He was always so good with words. He always knew what to say.

I might still feel pain at the way things ended between us, but after Zayn's apology and our kiss I felt myself wanting to let him in. Even when he delivered Jeb's message, I couldn't hate him. He fought for me, protected me, and was cut by Jeb for his insolence. Now he's backing up his actions by taking care of me in another way. I don't know what this means for the rest of the Breakers, but at least Zayn's showing me he's not backing down, and that both fills me with happiness and dread because David's threat still hangs over me. He remains like a spectre in the night, a monster under the bed, a nightmare just waiting to happen. He taints everything, even this moment of happiness.

Taking a deep breath and pushing all thoughts of David aside, I unzip the bag, refusing to let him ruin this moment of joy that is so rare these days. Inside is an absolutely stunning dress, the top half is a dark-grey silk held up by delicate straps edged with lace. The bodice is lightly boned and fitted, but it's the skirt that takes my breath away. It's made up of layers of light, floaty, red, gold and orange tulle giving the effect of flames creeping up the dress.

Flames and ash, just like Zayn's note.

I've *never* owned anything as perfect as this.

Taking the dress out of the bag I hold it up against me and look in the mirror. I know without even having to try it on that it will fit. My fingers run over the material as I hug it against my body. A flush creeps beneath my skin as more tears swim in my eyes and I allow myself to believe that sometimes we *can* fix what's broken, that maybe hope is worth holding onto no matter how impossible a situation might seem.

Hanging the dress back up, my eyes trail to the bottom of the wardrobe and the dance shoes lined up there. I fall to my knees, picking up the ballet slippers, then the pointes. My fingers stroke over the silky material and I hug them to my chest before placing them back lovingly. My gaze falls to my ruined trainers and I yank them off my feet before picking up a pair of black dance sneakers and pulling them on. They fit like a glove. There is a pair of tap shoes too, as well as a couple of pairs of stretch canvas, half-sole shoes that will prevent the balls of my feet blistering when I dance. I won't have to constantly wrap my feet up now that I have these. Wonderment fills me at Zayn's generosity, his thoughtfulness, and his words.

My heart squeezes as my gaze settles on a pair of black, high-top, Adidas trainers with three white stripes up the side.

As a kid I'd hankered after a pair, often talking about the beauty of this particular trainer and how cool they were. I would go on and on about them to anyone who'd listen, mainly Zayn as he was into fashion as much as I was. Now here they are. With my throat thick with tears, I pull off the dance sneakers and grab the trainers. Tucked inside the left foot is another note and this time when I read it, there's nothing I can do to stop the tears from falling unbidden down my face.

Pen,
Do you remember how you used to talk about these trainers? Because I do. I remember everything. I remember wanting to be able to buy these for you, and I remember vowing that one day I would. These past few weeks I've been reminded of how it felt to be your friend and when we kissed in the studio yesterday, I remember how it felt to be loved by you. I told you it fucking hurt when you walked away, and it did. But I don't give a shit about any of that anymore. Do you hear me, Pen? I don't give a fuck what made you leave, only how to fix this distance between us.
I'm here when you're ready to talk.
I won't push you, but I'm not backing off either.
The others can do what they want.
You were mine first, so it's only right you're mine first again.
Zayn.

My tears blur the ink, and I swipe at my eyes roughly. It takes me another ten minutes of sitting on my arse in my hallway crying like a baby before I pull myself together and unpack the food Zayn bought for me. After scarfing down a pasta dish covered in a thick tomato sauce with mushrooms and bacon, I shower and change. Selecting a pair of knee length leggings from my new hoard, a black crop top and a loose green vest to wear over it, I pull on my dance sneakers and head across the hallway to Zayn's flat. There's only a few minutes until we all need to meet for practice down in Studio Two, and I wanted to thank him in private.

With nerves fluttering inside my belly, I knock on his door. A few erratic heartbeats later, it swings open. Zayn's talking softly into his mobile phone and his eyes smile at me whilst he continues to converse with whoever is on the other end of the line. He motions for me to enter, closing the door gently behind us as I step inside.

"It's been taken care of," Zayn says into the mouthpiece as I hover awkwardly in his hallway. I jump when he places his hand on the base of my spine and guides me into his main living area.

"Take a seat," he mutters to me. When I look from his unmade bed to the chair covered in clothes, he pulls an apologetic face and rushes over to the armchair in the corner of the room, gathers the clothes thrown over it and chucks them onto the still unmade bed. His room's a mess and it makes me smile inside. Zayn was never tidy. I guess some things haven't changed after all. Zayn scowls suddenly, clearly not happy with whatever's being said on the other end of the line.

"I told you, it's sorted. Speak to you later," he grits out, clearly pissed off. Flicking off the call, he chucks his mobile phone onto the bed.

"I came at a bad time..." I say, not sitting down. My hands absentmindedly run over my hips, my fingers reaching for the hem of my brand new top. Why am I so damn nervous?

"No! It's fine. Sit down, Pen. I'm glad you're here."

"Sure."

I sink down onto the armchair, flattening my sticky palms against my thighs. Zayn perches on the end of his bed and rests his elbows on his knees. He waits, watching me whilst my gaze roves over his bare arms and the tattoos that wind up them and disappear beneath his loose V-neck t-shirt. My gaze travels along his wide shoulders to the smattering of hair I can see peeping up behind the v of his t-shirt, then back down his arms to his hands dangling between his parted legs. I can feel heat bloom beneath my skin, remembering how his hand had cupped my mound, how his fingers had brought me to release. He coughs, covering a soft laugh as my gaze snaps up to meet his.

"Thank you," I blurt out.

"You're welcome, Pen." He gives me a lopsided smile, his chipped tooth peeking out at me from between his plump lips. My words get trapped in my throat and I have to mentally give myself a shake as Zayn takes the opportunity to admire the outfit he brought me. Well, at least I think that's what he's admiring, though the expression on his face tells me it might be more than that. "Everything fit okay?" he asks, his eyes lifting up.

"They do. They fit perfectly..." I falter at the look in his eyes. I don't see hate anymore. I see possibilities and a heavy dose of lust. "I don't know what to say."

"You don't have to say anything. Just accept the gifts. You deserve to be wearing the best gear. You're a star, Pen. You're a fucking phenomenal dancer..." He frowns, his plush lips pressing together in a hard line.

"What?" I whisper.

"Grim. The club. Did you speak with her?"

"Yes."

He nods tightly, a muscle jumping in his jaw. There's a sudden fierceness in his gaze and I realise he still thinks I'm going to be stripping at Grim's club. "I didn't want that for you, Pen. I swear to fuck, I didn't. I guess this was my way of trying to make up for it. *Fuck*!" he shouts suddenly. "I keep fucking going over and over it in my head. Was there something more I could've done? I don't want you bare for anyone. It twists me up inside knowing those fuckers will be watching you remove your clothes, knowing they'll see you fucking naked like that. It makes me want to kill a bastard. No. I'm going to sort it out. You ain't doing that shit."

"Wait! Calm down, Zayn, you've got it wrong. Grim wants me to *dance*, not strip," I say emphatically.

"What?"

"Grim doesn't want me to strip. She wants me to *dance*. I'll be starting the night of Dax's fight."

His shoulders drop, relief washing over his face. "Thank fuck," he exclaims.

"She's going to pay me a wage. A good one. I won't be needing any more handouts," I say without thinking. Zayn frowns, his mouth popping open to speak but I cut him off, cursing my stupid mouth for running away with itself. "That wasn't what I meant. I'm grateful for all the food, the clothes. I am. But everything I've ever been given—which, let's be honest, hasn't been much—comes with a caveat. My mum never did anything nice for me, but even when she passed on hand-me-down clothes or second-hand stuff it always came with a stipulation. To clean the flat from top to bottom until my fingers were raw from the bleach, to run errands. Even to grab her damn cigarettes because she was too lazy to get them from the convenience store herself. So, I can't help but wonder what you want in return," I say softly, holding my breath as I wait for him to disappoint me and hoping to God that he doesn't.

"Nothing but your friendship, and even then, only if you're willing to give it. I swear to you, Pen, I have no ulterior motive other than that."

"Are you certain? Because you seemed pretty keen on digging up the past yesterday."

"I can't deny that I want an explanation, Pen. That I deserve one, that we *all* do, but I'm not trying to buy your honesty or your truths. I understand that I need to earn your trust again, the old-fashioned way."

"Then I accept your gift for what it is, Zayn, and I'm willing to try." It takes everything in me not to throw myself at his feet and beg for forgiveness, but a little bit of fear and a whole shitload of pride holds me back.

"Good."

"But what about…"

"The others?" Zayn sighs, scraping a hand over his face. The shadows beneath his eyes might have lessened but the worry within them hasn't.

I nod. "Yes. How do they feel about it?"

"Honestly, I really don't give a fuck."

"Zayn, I don't want to get between you all—"

"I'm a grown man, as are those motherfuckers. They can do what they want, but it won't stop me from going after what *I* want, and I sure as fuck don't care what *he* wants."

"Xeno?" I question, knowing I'm right. "He'll never forgive me, will he?"

"Xeno has always been a hard arse, but these past few years have changed him, Pen."

I nod my head in understanding. These past three years have changed all of us. "What about York, Dax?"

"That's a conversation you need to have with them, but I will tell you this. When you walked away, Dax withdrew into himself more than ever and York lost his optimism, his enthusiasm for everything. It was fucked up. *We* were fucked-up for a long time," he says with brutal honesty.

"I'm sorry," I say, meaning it even though I know my apology won't change a thing, it won't negate what I did. There are so many wounds to heal, but it's not so easy a task to pick up where we left off. In fact, right now it seems like an impossible task given the situation I'm in. "I'm sorry I hurt you all."

"I can see that now, Pen. I can also see that something's eating away at you. York isn't the only one who can read you. He was just always better at it than me," he says, getting up as he looks intently at me, trying hard to see the secrets in my heart.

"Zayn—" I begin.

"It's okay. I meant what I said. I'm here when you want to talk." He walks towards me, wincing a little as he moves. The stitches must be bothering him still. I swallow down the bile rising up my throat. I can't believe Jeb cut him, has done it repeatedly over the years. I *hate* that man. I hate him so fucking much.

"You're in pain…"

"Not anymore I'm not," he says gruffly. "You look like you could use a hug."

My eyes flick downwards to his hand. I hesitate, wanting nothing more than to fall into his arms but David's words ring inside my head, reminding me once again that nothing will ever be easy or straightforward between us.

"You're going to befriend the Breakers once more. You're going to make them fall in love with you again, and you're going to find out every last secret Jeb is keeping from me. Then when the time is right, we are going to destroy them once and for all. I will stick to my side of the deal, so long as you stick to yours."

"Pen…?" Zayn questions, cocking his head to the side. He waits patiently, his hand held out. This is a peace offering, a chance to begin again and rightly or wrongly, I take it. I push David's words out of my head as Zayn pulls me against his chest and wraps his arms around me. "I've missed you so fucking much, Pen," he mutters into my ear.

"I've missed you too," I reply softly. He squeezes me tighter and I bury my nose in his neck, breathing him in and hoping to fuck I can find a way out of this mess before I hurt him all over again.

After a while, Zayn eases back and stares down at me. I recognise the look in his eyes, see the lust flaring in his obsidian orbs, and as much as I want to give into my own desire, we really don't have time for that now. I can't deny that I want to seal our tentative bond with more than a kiss, but I get the feeling that Xeno's petty enough to report back to Madame Tuillard if we're late to rehearsals. Besides, I need a little more time before I can give myself completely to Zayn like that. Sleeping with him is a huge leap, one I'm not quite ready for.

"Another time, perhaps?" he mumbles, reading my hesitation.

He leans down to press his lips against mine and I accept the softness of his mouth, revelling in the firm grip of his fingers as he grasps hold of me possessively.

"Hey, how did you get into my room exactly?" I ask when we finally head down to Studio Two.

Zayn laughs. "York isn't the only one who can pick a lock."

I shake my head in disbelief. So he knows about that then? "What the hell have you four been up to these past three years?" I ask. The question is light-hearted but the sudden change in atmosphere isn't. Zayn's smile drops.

"Nothing you'd approve of."

He holds my hand when silence descends over us. His

touch is reassuring but his words aren't. Do I really want to know who the Breakers have become? Do I really want to know why they're here at the Academy? Will the truth hurt more than all the secrets? Probably.

When we hit the bottom of the stairs, I reach for the door opening onto the first floor, but Zayn places his palm on the wood and steps close, trapping me.

"In time, I will answer any question you have, but don't ask me anything you don't want to know the *honest* answer to, okay?"

I nod. "Okay."

Zayn cups my cheeks in his palms then kisses me roughly. He pushes his hips against mine, pinning me beneath him. There's no doubting his arousal or mine when I moan into his mouth and his fingers tangle in my hair. We only part when both of our lips are bruised from the kiss and lust thunders beneath our skin.

14

Pen

I hear Tiffany's loud laughter before I even step into the studio. It tracks like sharpened nails down my spine. I fucking *hate* that bitch. It's like she's got a sixth sense of knowing when I'm close by and does everything in her power to piss me off.

"Xeno, you're too much," Tiffany simpers as I walk into the studio, Zayn stepping in behind me. Dotted around the room are the rest of the dancers. River and Clancy are talking quietly in the corner of the studio. Clancy gives me a huge grin, her gaze flicking to Zayn behind me. I can read her thoughts even without her having to say a word. '*Woah girl*,' and '*what the fuck? Spill*,' comes to mind. I try not to laugh. River gives me a wink and Sophie, Tiffany's side-bitch, looks me up and down, her gaze narrowing as she also notices how closely Zayn is standing behind me. I can feel his heat at my back, and I know my cheeks and lips must still be flushed from his kiss.

Dax and York haven't arrived yet, but that doesn't make me feel any better. I haven't seen either of them since Friday night. A sudden bout of nerves settle in my belly, but I resolutely ignore them. Instead, I funnel those nerves and turn them into hate aimed at Tiffany for being a clingy bitch.

"So, I've been working on a bachata routine. I'd love to show you what I've come up with after we finish tonight," Tiffany leers, her intention clear. She's wearing a skimpy dance outfit showing off her long, toned legs and tiny waist. I mean I'm not a big girl, but I do have curves in the places a woman should. "Perhaps you'd like to partner with me again," she adds, making sure to catch my gaze in the mirror.

"I'm going to deck a bitch," I mutter under my breath, stiffening when I see her place her hand on Xeno's arm, cocking her non-existent hip to the side. Xeno flicks his gaze at me briefly before giving Tiffany a sexy smile. His curly hair falls into his eyes as he lowers his gaze to meet hers, but I can tell by the way his shoulders stiffen that he's as affected by me as much as I am by him. The vibes I'm getting might be hate and distrust, but I'd prefer that over nothing at all. I can work with hate. At least he feels *something*, right?

"Sounds good," he replies, dropping his voice so he can whisper in her ear. Tiffany chuckles, then throws a pointed look over her shoulder directly at me like she's won some kind of battle. Well, fuck her. Fuck Xeno and his bullshit too.

"Perfect," she whispers sexily before twisting on her feet and sashaying over to her bag hanging up on the opposite wall. She makes a big deal about pulling out a bottle of water and wrapping her lips around it like she's sucking a fucking cock.

"You're late," Xeno snaps, drawing my attention back to him. He's pointedly glaring at Zayn standing behind me and even though I'm facing away from Zayn and can't see the expression on his face, I know there's a silent conversation going on, one that ramps up the tension in the room.

"I had something *important* to do," Zayn responds tightly, placing his hand on my lower back and guiding me further into the studio.

Xeno's gaze drops, noticing how Zayn's touching me, and his teeth grit. "Something more important than *this*?" Xeno questions, challenge in his gaze.

"Yes, something more important than *this*," Zayn throws back.

I dare not look at Clancy because I know she's putting two and two together and getting the exact right answer.

Xeno sneers, shaking his head in disgust. "You haven't forgotten what you're here for, have you?" he asks, and I get the distinct impression that he isn't talking about this particular rehearsal and the end of year show. No, he's talking about whatever it is that Jeb has them at the Academy for.

"Don't worry, I haven't forgotten why I'm here. I'm fully aware of what's at stake." With that, Zayn drops an arm around my shoulder, giving Xeno a proverbial *fuck-you* as he refuses to engage him further and guides us to an empty spot in the studio.

"You've got to be fucking kidding me. You're choosing that bitch?" Sophie growls under her breath, giving me daggers as we pass her by. Zayn pulls up sharp, and gives me a quick squeeze before rounding on her.

"What the fuck did you just say?" he seethes.

Sophie's eyes widen. "It was nothing."

Zayn cracks his knuckles menacingly, and whilst I don't think he'd ever hit a woman, Sophie doesn't know that. "I'm here to partner with you in our duet, to dance in this group for the end of year performance, but other than that I'm not fucking interested in you. *Got it?*" he sneers, and for a moment I see a glimpse of the man he's become in the three years we've been apart. There's a hardness in his eyes, a darkness that speaks of a violence not befitting the boy I loved or the man I'd always hoped he'd be.

Sophie blanches, her skin paling. "Fine. Got it," she mutters.

"Oh, and another thing," Zayn says, leaning in closer, his voice dropping so only Sophie and I can hear what he's saying. She shrinks into herself as his lip pulls up in a snarl. "If I hear you bad-mouthing Pen again you're gonna find out exactly what I'm capable of. Most of the rumours about me are false, but some of them are true. You don't want to find out which. Fuck with her, fuck with me. Understand?"

Sophie nods, gulping. "Understood."

Zayn stands upright, a warm smile plastered back on his face. "Perfect. Let's fucking get on with it, shall we?" he states, raising his voice so the rest of the room can hear. Zayn gives me a wink then strides to the front of the studio, ignoring Xeno who looks like he's about to combust.

"Where are Dax and York? We can't rehearse the group dance unless they're here too." Tiffany remarks as she folds her arms across her chest, looking one part annoyed and two parts wary. She might not have been able to hear clearly what Zayn just said to Sophie, but given the look on Sophie's face it's clear to everyone that what he did say wasn't a compliment. Internally, I'm fucking beaming, but rather than gloat, I simply start stretching. It feels good to know Zayn's got my back.

Real fucking good.

"They'll be here soon. In the meantime, warm the fuck up. Madame Tuillard and D-Neath will be dropping by at some point this evening. I need you all at your best," Xeno states gruffly, clearly not giving a shit that he's being more gangster than dance teacher this evening. He picks up his mobile that's attached to the speaker system and takes a moment to choose a track. His eyes meet mine for a brief moment before *Pillowtalk* by Zayn Malik begins to play. I can't help but think that he's trying to tell me something, or maybe this song is a message to Zayn seeing it's his namesake who's singing about reckless behaviour, paradise, and goddamn warzones. Zayn barks out a laugh and gives Xeno a dirty look, but he doesn't bite, refusing to engage. Xeno's lip curls up in a snarl, his anger snapping at my heels. He's amped up for a fight and it pisses me off. How fucking dare he try and push our buttons like this? What Zayn and I choose to do has fuck all to do with him. Xeno's made his feelings perfectly clear, but I won't put up with him trying to put a wedge between Zayn and me, not now that I've only just got him back.

"Problem, Pen?" Xeno asks.

"Yeah, you could say that," I retort.

Screw him. If he wants to have it out, he can fucking have it out. Friday night, I thought I saw something in his eyes, something close to empathy at least, but given his attitude today, I can see I was wrong. I move towards him, ready to go head-to-head and screw the consequences when Zayn takes a step in front of me, shaking his head. Not now, he tells me with his eyes.

Drawing in a deep breath through my nostrils, I unclench my fists and focus on Zayn.

"Fine," I snap.

It's not his fault Xeno's acting like a prick but I can't seem to help how Xeno makes me feel. I'm pissed off. Now might not be the right time to confront him, but soon Xeno and I will lock horns and I'll be fucked if I sit back and let him continue to walk all over me. No.

"What are you all fucking looking at?" Xeno barks out to the rest of the crew.

"Fuuuck," River whispers, not so softly that we aren't able to hear.

Xeno turns away from us all and grabs a clipboard resting on the table next to the music dock. I imagine it lists his ideas for our end of year show. Not that he's actually paying attention to it because I can see him watching Zayn warm up from his reflection in the mirror, a scowl on his beautiful face.

"What the fuck is going on?" River mumbles to Clancy as they start warming up next to me.

"I have no clue. Time of the month?" Clancy retorts under her breath, widening her eyes at River before pulling a face. He laughs and bends forward, placing the flat of his hands on the floor. Above him I meet Clancy's curious stare and silently thank her for not giving anything away. I mean, River isn't stupid, it's obvious that there's an issue between the three of us. Still, he doesn't know it has everything to do with our past and nothing to do with this end of year show. I'd like to keep it that way.

When Clancy's gaze shifts lower over my brand new dance clothes, a smile pulls up her lips. *Wow*, she mouths, flicking her gaze to Zayn and back to me, giving me one of her knowing looks. I cock my head, shrugging, knowing that I'm going to have to fill her in at least on a part of what's gone down between Zayn and I, considering we're now talking again. I'm not willing to share everything with Clancy just yet, when I'm not certain that Zayn and my tentative friendship is going to last given Xeno's so obviously against it. Then again, I should have more faith in Zayn, he's already shown me that he isn't that same kid who follows Xeno's orders like he always had when we were young. He's his own man.

Clancy shifts closer, leaning over to talk quietly enough that she's not overheard. "Girl, I think you've lit a fire beneath their arses," she says, covering her mouth to cover a snort.

"Seriously, you've no idea," I respond, thinking about Malik Brov's nickname for me and Zayn's letter. She's about to respond to that statement with another question when Dax and York enter the studio.

"Oh, shit. Here comes more trouble," Clancy mutters.

Refusing to look up, I concentrate on making sure I stretch in earnest and try not to focus on the heated glares between Zayn and the rest of the Breakers. The tension ramps up and I don't think there's a single person in the room that doesn't feel it. Eventually I give in, unable to stomach the tension I feel. I look over at Dax surreptitiously beneath my lashes. He's taken up an empty spot on the opposite side of the studio from me, his jaw is tight, his body tense. He doesn't look at anyone, instead he warms up robotically, moving stiffly. The muscles on his thick arms tense and flex beneath the material of his tight, long sleeved t-shirt. The cut in his eyebrow is scabbed over and the swelling to his cheek not as pronounced, but the dark bruise is obvious and I'm not the only one who notices. Tiffany and Sophie give each other a look, and I know they'll be gossiping the moment rehearsals are over. Screw them. They can talk all they like, so long as they don't try and comfort Dax, then we're good. Well, not good, but I won't have to kill a bitch.

I watch Dax closely, not in the least bit surprised by how stiff he is. He might have won the fight on Friday and beaten his opponent to a pulp, but that doesn't mean he hasn't suffered for it. I swallow hard, trying not to think about how Dax will fare after his fight against Beast. Dragging my gaze away from Dax, I focus on York who has ignored everyone and is talking to Xeno in hushed tones. Their heads are pressed together, and York seems to be hissing something under his breath. I see that Zayn is watching them closely too, and whilst he seems relaxed on the surface, I can tell he's far from it. I finish stretching out my spine and arm muscles and sit down on my arse. Spreading my legs wide, I lean over, placing my left hand on my right foot. I can feel the delicious pull of my hamstrings as I stretch them out, giving me the perfect opportunity to watch York and Xeno without being too obvious about it. A few moments later York catches me staring. He turns his back to me and reaches for the docking station to turn the music up. I sigh, resigning myself to the fact that this is going to be one awkward-as-fuck rehearsal.

Then again, what's new?

15

Pen

"Good work today, Pen," Sebastian says as I hand him my assignment later that week in my ballet lesson. Written work has never really been my thing, but it's actually been quite fun researching famous ballet dancers and then coming up with some choreography to tell their story. "So Luka Petrin, eh? Quite an interesting choice."

"He's an interesting man," I say with a shrug. "I mean, his dance career was epic and everything, but it was his off-stage antics that got me intrigued. He kinda disappeared off the face of the Earth after his wife's death."

"He was, indeed, an incredible dancer. One of the greats, actually. Though he's a prime example of how the fame side of dance can be a major downfall. Damn shame."

"What happened to him?" I ask.

Sebastian smiles at the other students, taking their written work and thanking them. He waits until they all file out of the studio before answering. "If you've done your research, I'm sure your assignment will tell me. He may have left the dance world behind because he was heartbroken over his wife's death but it was no secret the man was a serial philanderer with plenty of skeletons in his closet, I'm sure."

"Do you think that him sleeping around had something to do with her death?"

"Rumour has it she committed suicide. It was all very hush hush, but yes, I believe so."

"Wow."

"Either way, he left the ballet world behind. No one knows for sure what happened to him."

"So he dropped dance completely?"

"Yep. His career was destroyed by the media coverage following his wife's death. Being an incredible dancer with a fantastic career is the one thing we all hope for, but the fame? That's what kills the best dancers off in the end."

"Kill?"

"Their career, sweetie, not literally."

"Is that why you're here teaching? Didn't you want the fame?"

"At one point I did. I'm gay and, frankly, love the attention, but I'm also heavily into self-preservation. I don't want to live my life under the microscope. Take Madame Tuillard. She's suffered at the hands of the British press recently, especially since dating D-Neath."

"Really? I didn't realise."

"Don't you read the gossip magazines or hear the whispers?" Sebastian asks me.

"Err, no."

He laughs. "I love a bit of gossip…"

"No shit. So, she's dating an ex-criminal, what's the big deal? You can't help who you fall for."

"This is true, and whilst I totally get why she's into Duncan —the man is delicious, after all—I'm not entirely sure he's quite let go of his criminal tendencies."

"Should you really be voicing your concerns with me?" I ask, laughing a little inside. He really doesn't know the half of it, because the Breakers sure as shit aren't here to dance.

"No. I absolutely shouldn't. This conversation didn't happen, okay?" he winks, his eyes sparkling.

"You're such a gossip."

He waves his hand in the air, then gathers up all the assignments and his bag, and grins. "I can't help it, *comes with the territory*," he says, repeating the same phrase that I used when we first talked about me being judgemental of other ballet dancers.

"What, being gay, you mean?"

"No, sweetie, being a *Robinson*. My mother was the biggest curtain-twitcher on our estate. She knew everything about everyone. You couldn't take a shit without her knowing about it."

He laughs loudly and I can't help but join in.

"Right."

Sebastian's phone pings with a new message. "Damn, I completely forgot that I need to be at a meeting with Madame Tuillard in five minutes. We're discussing the end of year show. She wants to bring in some experts to help with the choreography."

"Doesn't she like what we're putting together?" I ask, bristling a little. It's not like we haven't been busting a gut in rehearsals lately or anything.

"Oh no, she loves it. But there's always room for improvement, no?"

I pull a face. "Have you seen what we've come up with? It's pretty fucking good."

"Good is wonderful, Pen. *Great* is what we're aiming for. There's no room for pride in dance. Don't take offence."

"I'll try not to," I mumble.

Sebastian pulls a face. "You wouldn't do me a favour, would you?"

"Sure."

"I need to grab a quick shower. Could you just let Madame Tuillard know that I'm running a little late?"

"Sure. Her office is on my way to my next dance class anyway."

"Fabulous!" he calls, rushing off with a little wave.

MADAME TUILLARD'S office is tucked down the end of a corridor just off the first floor. I've never had any need to go there, but remember where it's situated from orientation week. I lift my hand to knock on the door when I hear raised voices. The door has been left slightly ajar and I can see Madame Tuillard with her arms folded across her chest. She looks pissed off.

Uh-oh, lovers tiff.

I consider backing away slowly and letting Sebastian deal with being late, but something D-Neath says makes me pause.

"It's a solid plan, *mi cielo*. I've got this covered."

"Duncan, this is an establishment for *dance*. I have not built this place from the foundation up for it to be bulldozed by some man I've never met. No. You promised me that the

Academy would be kept out of this. We are already under scrutiny in the press. I do not need the police on my doorstep too."

"It's just for a short while. No one will know. It's a watertight plan," he cajoles. His voice is smooth, velvety, and I can see Madame Tuillard falling for his charm despite the tightness of her lips and the way her arms are crossed over her body. He leans in close, his finger running over her cheek and down to her jaw, where he lifts her chin, so she meets his gaze.

"I'm doing this for *us*," he says, his voice rough with intensity. He might sound and look sincere, but I've been around enough bullshitters to know when someone's getting played and it pisses me the fuck off. D-Neath is using her love for him to get what he wants. It makes my blood boil.

I knock on the door loudly, not bothering to wait for permission to enter. My sudden appearance has the desired effect and Madame Tuillard is shocked out of his spell. D-Neath, however, just steps back casually and smiles at me. He's a real pro at being a dick, that's for sure. He's just gone down in my estimation. I knew he was shady, the guy just got out of prison for fuck's sake, but I'd kinda hoped he'd turned a new leaf and was here because he loves dance. Then again, maybe I'm just fucking projecting. My thoughts immediately go to the Breakers and why *they're* here. This is all shady as fuck.

"Oh, shit, sorry to interrupt," I say, pulling a face and plastering on a sweet smile. "Sebastian asked me to deliver a message. He's running late for your meeting. He'll be here in ten."

Madame Tuillard seems to pull herself together and nods. "Thank you, Pen. I appreciate it."

"Sure," I fire back, looking between the two.

"Anything else?" D-Neath asks, raising his brows.

"Actually, yes," I state, stepping into the room. "Sebastian said you're bringing in some experts to help with the choreography for the end of year show. Is that correct?"

Madame Tuillard nods and D-Neath just glares at me. Screw him, this is a dance academy first, not some sideshow for his underhand dealings. "Yes, that's correct."

"Can I ask why? Do you not like what we've come up with?"

"This shouldn't come as a surprise, Pen. I told you all in your first week here that I would be bringing in the best of the best to help with this performance."

She's right, she did. "Yeah, but I thought..."

"You thought you were all so spectacular that you wouldn't need the help?" She laughs, shaking her head. "Arrogance isn't a good look on you."

"That isn't what I meant," I mumble, feeling entirely put in my place.

"That is not to say I'm not impressed by what you've all come up with so far, because I am. But this is *my* academy and how I choose to run it begins and ends with me," she says adamantly, and I can't help but think that her response was aimed more at D-Neath than it was at me. By the look on his face, D-Neath believes that too.

"Fair enough." I nod.

Madame Tuillard sits on the edge of her desk, cocking her head to the side as she studies me. "Mr Tyson was correct in teaming you up with Dax. He's a talented dancer, however..."

"However?"

"He came to me recently to request another partner for the duet. Can you tell me why that might be?"

"He did *what*?"

"Ah, so you're unaware. Well, I told him no anyway. You're

perfectly matched in my opinion. Whatever is going on between you two needs to be put aside for the performance, which I also told him. Keep your personal issues off the dance floor, understand?"

"Mi cielo—" D-Neath begins and we both look at him. Madame Tuillard's eyes narrow.

"*What*, Duncan?"

He glances between us, then shakes his head. "Nothing that can't wait."

Madame Tuillard looks furious, but she clearly doesn't want to have an argument in front of me. "Well, if that's all?" Madame Tuillard says, effectively dismissing me.

"Yep, that's all," I reply, plastering on a fake smile as I stride off down the hall in search of Dax, and wondering what the fuck the Breakers have got mixed up in.

16

Pen

Livid doesn't even cover it.

I'm fucking furious.

How dare Dax go behind my back like this. Is he really not man enough to tell me himself that he no longer wants to partner me? What's up with that shit? My fake smile drops from my face as I storm around the Academy in search of the man who once swore to protect me. I shove past students who are filing out of the building, no doubt heading home to their families to share a meal and talk about their day. A bitterness settles inside my stomach as I watch them all laughing and joking, not a care in the world.

All I've ever wanted was security, a family, a *home* filled with people who love me, who give a shit about what I've done during my day. Instead, I was given a mother who fucking looks at me like a piece of shit beneath her shoe and a brother who looks at me in a way no brother should ever look at his sister.

For a brief time, I *had* that family I longed for. The Breakers became my whole world and whilst Zayn has recently shown me that he's willing to start again, none of the others have. I know how close they all are, and I also know that Zayn's decision to fix what's broken between us isn't going to go down well. It will cause a wedge between them. Perhaps it already has if this bullshit is anything to go by.

"Well, if it isn't our very own *street rat*," Tiffany says, as I pass her by. She's so irrelevant to my life that I didn't even notice her until she stepped out in front of my path. She's with Sophie and another male student I don't recognise.

"Fuck off. I don't have time for your bullshit today," I retort, stepping to the side and walking around her, only to be yanked back when her bony fingers wrap around my upper arm.

"Now, now, don't be rude," she titters, gleefully. I don't know what's got up her nose, but she can fuck right off if she thinks I'm going to let her touch me without repercussions.

"Don't fucking touch me again!" I snarl, twisting on my feet and shoving her against the wall. Her eyes widen as a woosh of breath leaves her mouth from the force, but she recovers quickly.

A glimmer of amusement flashes in her gaze and a nasty smile spreads across her face. "I'm going to enjoy this," she smirks.

"Enjoy *what*?"

"Looks like you got dumped, *street rat*, and guess who's taking your place?"

Next to her, Sophie grins, and if I wasn't already about to knock one stupid bitch out, she'd be getting a Pen knuckle-sandwich too. Still might if she doesn't wipe that smile off of her face.

"Dumped?" My stomach rolls over and I pray to fucking God she's not talking about Zayn. We've kissed, we called a truce and I'm not naïve enough to think we're together like we once were, but still, the thought of any kind of rejection stings. I've never been a sensitive flower, but I'm not completely infallible, especially when it comes to the Breakers.

"Guess who's partnering with Dax now?" Her smile grows, and I have the sudden urge to stuff my fist down her throat and yank her nasty tongue out of her mouth. He better not have dropped me for this basic bitch. "Yep, that's right. *Me*. You're looking at Dax's new duet partner."

"Bullshit. Tuillard told me she declined Dax's request."

"Well, Madame Tuillard isn't the one who gave him the nod. D-Neath did, and we all know she's his bitch. Besides, why do you care? You never wanted him as your duet partner, so what's the big fucking deal anyway?"

"You're full of shit," I retort, knowing in my heart that she's telling the truth, but saying it anyway. I'll be damned if I give her the satisfaction of being right.

"Go ask him yourself. We've just finished rehearsing in Studio Five. He's all worked up from dancing with me. Nice and sweaty. I've never been partial to a man covered in that many tattoos, but I could be persuaded." She laughs, and Sophie smothers a smirk. The guy standing with them looks horrified. He should find some new friends. "A man that... *big*, has got to have a beautiful dick to match."

"You fucking bitch!" I shout, slamming my hand against the wall besides her head. She flinches, fear flashing across her face briefly before she hides it behind a nasty grin. She sure has a death wish, but I don't have time for her shit right now. I let her go with a shove, ignoring the pain racing up my arm and the vicious remarks that follow me down the hallway. She can go fuck herself. This is *not* happening.

The door to Studio Five slams open from the force of my anger, smashing against the wall. Dax is standing topless in the centre of the room, his gaze lifts slowly to meet mine. He doesn't say a word, so I say three for him.

"You fucking coward!" I shout, my chest heaving.

"It's done."

"That's it? That's fucking *it*! I get to hear from Tiffany that you've dropped me for her!" I laugh hysterically, too angry to even allow the tears to fall. They burn my eyes, but I blink them back. "You don't give me any say in the matter?"

"Did you?"

"*What*?"

"Did you give me, give *us* any say in the matter when *you* decided to walk away?"

"I—" My mouth pops open then slams shut because really, what the fuck can I say to that other than he's right? I didn't.

"Then don't expect the same consideration, Pen. We can't dance together. There's nothing more to say than that."

He watches me for a moment, and I take my fill of him. His chest is covered in a sheen of sweat just like Tiffany had said, highlighting his tattoos, darkening them. Dax is a beautiful man, quietly powerful, and when he dances... God, he's exquisite. It's little wonder all the girls want to get into his pants.

"Why?" I ask, hating the croak in my voice. Hating the vulnerability I can't seem to hide. I realise I have no right to feel this upset because as angry as I am, Tiffany was correct, I didn't want to dance with him. Except now that he's taken the decision out of my hands, I fucking hate the idea of him dancing with that bitch, with *anyone* else. Of all the four Breakers, dancing with Dax was like coming home.

He was my home.

"Does it matter?" He starts to stretch, pulling his arms up above his head so that the muscles on his chest and arms tighten then release as he drops them.

"It matters to me."

"Why? You didn't want to dance with me, Pen. You made that perfectly clear when we were paired up. Has that changed?" He pierces me with his eyes and the way he holds my gaze has my skin prickling with goosebumps. "Well?"

I look away, not able to tell him how I really feel. I *do* want to dance with him, so fucking much, but I'm too fucking proud, too fucked-up, too confused, too shit-scared to tell him how I feel.

"Yeah, that's what I thought," he says, misinterpreting my reaction. He walks over to where his stuff is sitting on the table and grabs hold of his mobile phone. When I don't leave, he glances over his shoulder at me. "Haven't you got somewhere to be?"

"No, actually, I haven't."

He nods, turning away from me and I take a seat on the bench that lines the wall, watching him as he puts on a t-shirt, the material pulling taut across his broad shoulders and back.

"Dax..."

"Yes, Pen?" His eyes meet mine in the reflection of the mirror.

"Why did you protect me from Malik Brov?"

He stiffens, his jaw clenching before he turns around slowly to face me. "Why did you save me from getting a bullet in the head?" he counters.

We stare at each other for long moments, long past the

point of it being comfortable. The truth is right there hanging in the air between us. Just one word that has both the power to bind people together and the power to rip them apart.

Love.

He waits. I falter.

Laughter shatters the tension in the air, preventing the truth from spilling from my lips. I swallow it down painfully and turn to find a group of kids walking into the studio, they can't be any more than thirteen or fourteen years old, and gather in the doorway nervously.

"*You're* our dance teacher?" a cheeky-looking boy with a flop of auburn hair asks, giving Dax a once-over. He has his arm casually slung over a girl's shoulder. Her large brown eyes widen as she takes Dax in. I notice a flicker of fear in her gaze.

"Looks that way."

The boy grins. "This is my girl, Olivia."

"Nice to meet you Olivia," Dax says. He glances over at me and I realise my mouth is hanging open in shock. I slam it shut. He's teaching kids how to dance. I'm stunned.

"And what should I call the rest of you?" Dax asks, waving them into the room.

"I'm Justin," the same boy with the cheeky smile says, introducing himself. His auburn hair falls into his eyes as he speaks. "This is Rafe, Tam, and his little brother, Sidney."

They all give Dax a nod of the head. I feel their wariness, but can sense their excitement too.

"Nice to meet you all. Shall we get started then?" Dax asks.

They enter the room and Justin—who I'm beginning to understand might be the leader of this little crew—clocks me gawping at them.

"Who's she?" he asks, jerking his chin towards me.

"That's Pen and she was just leaving," Dax says, fixing me with his stare.

"Actually, I thought I'd stay." I drag my gaze away from Dax and smile at the girl, Olivia. She smiles back, her body language relaxing a little. I don't blame her for her apprehension, Dax is intimidating at the best of times.

"If you're going to stay then you're going to need to take part. I won't have any slackers in my class," Dax challenges, lifting a brow.

"Fine by me."

Thirty minutes into the lesson, Dax has taught the kids some basic street dance steps and a quick routine. Like me, he has also established who in the group has the most natural talent and who needs an extra hand. He crooks his finger at Justin. "Up front," he says.

Justin steps forward with a cocky swagger. He winks at Olivia, who blushes. I notice how Tam, the kid with the beautiful smile and chin dimples, glances at her when he thinks no one's looking. Looks like Olivia's got herself another admirer. She catches his gaze and smiles back shyly.

"You're a good dancer. Got a lot of natural ability."

Justin grins, smirking. "Cheers."

"But you're not the best. Sidney, come on up."

Justin's jaw drops as the youngest boy in the group steps forward. He looks at least a year younger than the other boys, around twelve I'd say. Dax drops his large hand on Sidney's shoulder. "Wanna tell me how you learnt to dance?"

"YouTube," he replies quietly.

I can't help but smile.

"Like someone else I know." Dax glances at me and I feel my cheeks flush under his scrutiny. "Pen here has been dancing since she was a kid about your age, probably before that actually. She's one of the most talented dancers in the Academy. She started out learning to dance by watching YouTube videos then crafted her skill by dancing with her friends." He lets his gaze linger on me before looking away again.

"So are you saying we'll all become great dancers by watching YouTube? If I'd known that, I wouldn't have bothered coming here," Justin scoffs, obviously feeling a little salty for not being the best dancer in his crew.

"No, I'm saying that anyone can learn to dance if they really want it badly enough but ultimately, dance is just an expression of how you feel, and we all feel, right? Sidney here gave me the most emotion. That makes him the best dancer."

"Hear that, Sid, you're basically a pansy," Justin laughs, and Sidney's head drops, his face blushing furiously. No one else laughs and then it's Justin's turn to go red-faced. "What? Everyone knows Sid's *gay*."

"I'm not gay, arsehole," Sidney says fiercely, his fingers curling into his fists.

Dax scowls and I see his fingers squeeze hold of Sidney's shoulder gently in support. "It takes a small man to pick on a kid, but a bigger man to embrace his feelings," Dax says to Justin. "You, my friend, will never be as talented as Sidney here because you're afraid of your feelings. Putting someone else down to make you feel good about yourself ain't fucking cool. Apologise. Right the fuck now."

Justin's face turns an even deeper red. He glances at Olivia, presumably for support, but she's glaring at him too. "Sorry, man," he mutters.

"Good. If you're going to be in my dance lessons you listen to my advice, do as I say, and don't be a goddamn bully. Understand?" Dax growls.

"Got it," all the kids mutter in unison.

"Perfect."

"So, erm, do you dance with your feelings then?" Sidney asks, looking up at Dax, a frown on his face.

"What, you don't think I can?" he asks, chuckling.

"Well, you're kinda tough looking. I mean… Shit, no offence," Sidney mutters, his cheeks flaming.

"Dancing isn't just about following the steps. You need to dance with feeling."

The kids don't look particularly convinced and I can't help but step in. "Why not show them, Dax?" He locks gazes with me. "Show them that you're so much more than your appearance leads them to believe. Show them you have heart and integrity when you dance."

Show me. Show me the boy I loved is still within you.

He holds my gaze and I see his indecision, then he jerks his chin towards the bench. "Take a seat."

Dax sets up the music, then he moves to the centre of the studio and we all wait for him to begin.

17

Dax

All their eyes are on me, but all I can focus on is her.

Pen.

Kid.

She's challenging me. I see her. I get what this is.

When we were kids and shit got too much, she would challenge me to dance my feelings. To let them out. She was the only one who understood the damage I held inside. She knew what I needed to heal. Dancing gave me the ability to free myself of the ugliness I lived with daily. Her friendship gave me something positive to hold onto and her love... *Fuck*, her love made me feel so fucking big. I could rise above every punch and harsh word from my dad knowing that she loved me.

And that's why I can't fucking dance with her now.

I can't fucking do it.

Not after what happened at Grim's. Not after the fucking

hole she punched in my chest. I can't be close to her like that and not *want* her, *need* her. It's hard enough being in the same fucking studio as her, but to dance with her?

That's torture, plain and fucking simple.

I'm barely keeping my head straight around her and I need to do that. I fucking *have* to do that or everything we've worked towards will go to fucking shit.

Zayn has already caved, and York is on his way to saying *fuck it*. I can see it coming. I can see it in the way he looks at her, how he follows her with his eyes every time she's nearby. It's inevitable. And me? I need to stay the fuck away.

Xeno is the only one who's sticking to his word and holding his fucking nerve. That man has balls of fucking steel and a wall so thick around his heart it's impenetrable, but I saw how he reacted to Pen dancing at Grim's club and I sure as fuck saw how much he hated it when Malik kissed her. If I hadn't stepped in, Xeno would've, and then we would all have been fucked.

Jeb isn't a fool.

He challenged Xeno to kiss Pen at Rocks that night to see how he'd react. He set up that evening at Grim's to see how we'd deal with Zayn fucking Pen in front of us, in front of the whole damn warehouse.

He was testing us.

Skins before whores.

That's always been the Skins' mantra and Jeb has made it perfectly fucking clear that we are not to be distracted. We're here at the Academy for one thing and one thing only, and Pen is not part of the plan. Except now, Zayn has overstepped, and York is fucking crumbling. So it's up to Xeno and me to keep our fucking heads. The only reason Jeb hasn't chopped Zayn's dick off is because of the deal Zayn made with Grim that worked in his favour. That doesn't mean to say Jeb isn't keeping a close fucking eye on his nephew. Zayn is playing with fire and he fucking knows it.

Now here I am, doing the same damn thing.

Pen eyes me expectantly, her expression is impassive even when her eyes drink me in like she's gone without water for days. It sets me on edge.

But it's too late to back out now.

Fixing my gaze on the woman I loved then lost so spectacularly, I place my hands over my face and wait for the music to start. *Paralyzed* by NF begins to play over the loudspeaker and Pen sucks in an audible gasp. She recognises this song.

She should.

Because the first time I played this song to her was the same night my dad had beat me so badly I had two cracked ribs and a bruise covering the whole left side of my face. We were fifteen. That night, as she held me and cried the tears I couldn't, I knew without any doubt that I loved her, and I had vowed to myself that I would become a man worthy of this girl who held my heart in her hands.

But I let her down.

There's no getting away from genetics, I'm my father's son. Since she walked away I didn't fight the violence living within me. I became ruthless, cold, and dealt out punishment on Jeb's behalf with a brutality that would make Pen sick. That's all I've known these past three years, and now? Now, I don't know who the fuck I am anymore.

Slowly, I drag my fingers over my face and down my neck, echoing those tears I never shed and fix my gaze on Kid. I see tears welling in her eyes and they gut me. I wish I was capable of feeling like her, but like the song suggests, I'm fucking paralyzed. I don't know how to cry. I don't know how to let go of my bullshit past and the ghost of my dad. I don't know how to just be *me*. Dax the man, not the criminal, not the bully, not the monster.

Once upon a time I was the victim.

Now I'm the assailant.

But somehow I'm still both. I'm a dichotomy.

Which is just a fancy word for *fucked-up*. I'm fucked-up.

But when Kid looks at me the way she does, as though she's rubbed off the tattoos, pulled away the layers of skin, muscle and bone, and sees right into the very atoms of me, I begin to believe I'm *more*. I begin to believe that I'm capable of being more than a victim, more than an assailant, a criminal, a bully, a fucking monster.

I can be Dax.

I can be her Dark Angel.

I can be the boy she loved.

Sweeping out my left leg into a standing kick, I twist on the ball of my right foot then centre my weight on both feet and raise both arms up in the air, tipping my head back as NF begins to sing. For three years I've been numb, just like the song suggests. Now, I'm beginning to feel, and fuck, it hurts. It's painful, but still I dig deep, trying to hunt how I feel from deep inside. It's a mammoth fucking task because I'm used to burying my emotions. This time, however, I accept Pen's challenge and I burrow down, searching for the mess of feeling that clogs me up like cancer.

I find it.

My arms drop, I lift my head to look at Pen as my fist grips my t-shirt. Staggering towards her, I pull at the material gripped in my fist as though I'm being tugged in her direction by my heart.

And I am. I fucking am. My heart wants her so fucking bad.

But my head is waging a war against my heart.

I'm torn, and it's killing me.

Pen's mouth opens as she sucks in a shocked breath at the rawness of this moment. Her tiny hand lifts up to cover the choked sob I hear. Her pain pulls me up sharp and I stop a few feet from her, focusing on her and only her.

Do I listen to my heart or my head?

I don't know what the fuck to do.

Right now all I can do is dance.

My body takes over as I spin on my feet. Around and around I turn. I feel the emotion swirling within, the battle between my head and my heart is like a fucking tornado ready to rip me up.

I spin until I can't anymore

I drop to my knees, my clenched fist bashing against the floor, my chest heaving.

"Dax..." I hear her whisper, but it's like she's screaming my name. It's so fucking loud.

What the fuck does she want from me? Isn't this enough, doing this, bleeding out for her?

Then I catch her gaze and I see. This isn't enough. She wants more. She wants to dance with me. *She wants me.*

But fuck that.

No.

My head wins out.

The beat of the music changes and the rapping starts. That's when the anger comes.

That's when I really let it go.

Because fuck, I'm mad at her. I'm fucking *livid*.

My movements change from free-flowing to sharp, jerky

movements. I fall into my old hip-hop moves, focusing on the anger and the pain I feel. She *left* and I fucking turned into a monster. I turned into my father.

Those feelings of disgust and regret pour out of me now with every flip and every spin.

Every now and then I catch her expression and it's as though I'm physically beating her. She feels my anger like a punch to the gut. Well, she punched a fucking hole in my chest and ripped out my damn heart when she danced at Grim's club, so now she can experience what it feels like to be fucking slayed.

So I keep going.

I've not danced like this for years. Three years to be precise.

And fuck does it feel good.

I might have learnt choreography these past few weeks, but I haven't danced like *this*.

It's freeing.

All logical thought, all reason leaves me, and just like when I was a kid, I let it all out.

I purge my soul.

I feel.

I dance.

I move across the hardwood floor, until my veins are rushing with adrenaline and my muscles are screaming at me to stop. By the time I focus enough to be aware of my surroundings, all five kids are standing on their feet clapping and cheering, the song is long since finished and Pen… She's gone.

18

Pen

"Pen, can I come in?" Zayn asks, hovering on the threshold of the studio.

"Sure," I shrug, still feeling raw from last night. I challenged Dax to dance his feelings and he did that. Boy, did he fucking do that. I've just spent the last two hours trying to put together a routine for my first night at Grim's club and failing miserably. I thought it'd be a good enough distraction. I was wrong.

"How've you been?"

"Fine." I begin to pack away my belongings, not able to look at him. It's not his fault Dax ripped a hole in my chest, but he's here and Dax isn't, so he's getting the brunt of my hurt feelings.

"Want to talk about it?..."

I catch a glimpse of his expression in the reflection of the mirror and shake my head. "There's not much to talk about."

Zayn nods in understanding. Of course he knows what's up. Even if he wasn't friends with the Breakers he would have found out anyway. The whole Academy is talking about how I was replaced with Tiffany. It's no fucking secret. Clancy went off on one this morning, but I managed to get her to reel her neck in. I love that she's angry on my behalf, but it won't change a damn thing. Dax is as stubborn as they come. He won't change his mind on this.

"He said you were angry," Zayn states.

"Yeah, you could say that I had a few choice words for him."

"I bet. Put him in his place, did you? It's been a while since that's happened. I would've loved to be a fly on the wall."

"Not nearly as much as I wanted to. He kind of distracted me with his new students. I didn't know he was teaching too."

"Favour to Madame Tuillard. She gave him a spot at the Academy and in return he teaches a few local kids dance. He gets to be here, and she gets to look good. It's a win-win."

I raise my brows. "She seems very accommodating for you all. Wanna tell me what's up with that?" I ask, feeling the situation out. I'm still painfully aware of my brother's request, and so far I'm no closer to knowing why they're here.

"Want to tell me what's going on in your head right now?" he counters, cocking his head to the side.

I press my lips together and fold my arms across my chest. "Look, Zayn. I'm kind of busy," I say, feeling frustrated. He's not going to give me anything unless I do the same in return, and I *can't*.

"Busy doing what? Maybe I could help," he suggests.

"Actually, you know what, I'm done for the night," I say, grabbing my bag and swinging it over my shoulder. I walk towards him, but he blocks my exit, pressing his forearms against the doorframe.

"If that's the case then let's get out of here."

I raise my brows. "Are you asking me out on a date, Zayn?"

"Looks like it." He smirks, running a hand through his hair.

"Is that a good idea? What about the rest of the Breakers? What about Jeb?"

"This isn't about them. This is about *us*, Pen." He reaches for me, cupping my face in his hand. "Let me take you out. No strings attached. Just fun. Just us. Nothing more."

His sincerity takes me aback. I find myself agreeing before I've really had time to think about it. "Okay."

He smiles broadly, his hands dropping as he flashes his chipped tooth at me. There's a spark in his eyes I haven't seen since we were kids and it makes me feel all warm inside. It feels so easy to be in his orbit again. Natural, and honestly, that scares the shit out of me.

"So where are we going then?"

"To a speakeasy club in Shoreditch."

"A speakeasy? What century are we in exactly?" I laugh and he grins at my rhetorical question.

"The password is *diamonds*."

"Diamonds?"

"That's right."

"It's located on Brick Lane and only opened about two months ago. Entrance to the club is by invite only. The owners are particular about the clientele they invite into the club."

"That so?" I question, raising a brow. "Are they sure they know what they're doing inviting you then?"

He chuckles. "This is one of the most exclusive clubs in London owned by some very rich businessmen."

"Businessmen *you* happen to know." I raise my brows. "I thought you only rubbed shoulders with the criminals of this world."

"Who said they're not criminals?"

"Right."

"Are you up for it, Pen?"

"It's a school night."

"I promise to have you back in bed by midnight." He gives me a salacious grin that would've been creepy on anyone else but on him is sexy as fuck. "Well, what do you think? A few drinks with an old friend, maybe even a dance?" He cocks his head at me, his dark hair falling in his eyes. My stomach flip-flops as I feel that familiar pull between us.

"Sure, why the fuck not," I say, flippantly. What's the worst that could happen? David wants me to get close to the Breakers and Jeb was willing to sell me on to the highest fucking bidder so does he really give a shit if I go out on a date with his nephew?

"Good. I'll send a car to pick you up."

"You'll send a car? Aren't we getting the bus?" I joke, grinning. We spent a lot of time travelling on buses and jumping trains as kids. Happy times.

"I've moved up a little in the world since we were kids, Pen. No more buses for my girl."

"Your girl?" My stomach flips at that.

"That's right, *my* girl. Be ready at eight. I'll be waiting for you at the club."

"We're not going together?"

"I've got some business to handle beforehand."

"What business?"

"You open up to me. I open up to you," he reminds me,

before pressing a chaste kiss against my lips, then he strides off down the hallway leaving me with butterflies in my belly that I haven't felt since I was a kid.

THE GREY LEXUS—THAT Zayn arranged to collect me—pulls up outside a quieter section of Brick Lane, away from the main drag and the pubs and bars that dominate that end of the street.

"This is it?" I ask, eyeing the driver suspiciously. There's nothing but a betting shop, pawn shop and a thrift store. All of which appear to be closed, though there are lights on in the pawn shop that smacks as odd given the time of night.

"This is the address I was told to drop you off at. Is there a problem, Miss?" the driver asks me.

"No, I guess not. Thank you." I climb out of the car, slamming the door behind me. The driver pulls off, leaving me standing on the pavement nervously pulling at the hem of my dress. I wasn't sure what to wear, but thankfully Clancy was willing to lend me her black halter neck dress in exchange for fully unabridged details of my date with Zayn tonight. She wasn't impressed when I paired the dress with my trusty heeled biker boots but frankly it's comfort over impracticality any day.

"Well, now what?" I mumble, peering into the pawn shop. It's filled to the brim with all manner of items. There are musical instruments, cell phones and other electronics, antiques, collectables, jewellery and even bicycles lined up against one wall.

"Are you here to meet Mr Bernard?" A male voice asks me

from the shadow of a doorway between the thrift store and the pawn shop.

"Fuck!" I exclaim, jumping almost out of my skin as a tall man with a bald held and thick shoulders steps out into the streetlight. "Who the fuck are you?"

"I'm Ben. Are you Miss Scott?"

"Yes, that's right," I say, giving him a once-over. He's dressed exactly like an upmarket bouncer would be in a smart suit and shiny shoes.

"Just this way," he says, opening the door to the pawn shop. A bell tinkles overhead and an attractive blonde woman, wearing a tight fitting silver dress, stands up from behind a counter at the back of the store as I enter.

"Shit, I didn't see you there," I say, holding my hand over my heart.

"Good evening, what are you looking to purchase this evening?" she asks me when I reach her.

"Purchase?" I look around the store. "Are you for real?"

"Yes." She taps her long manicured nails on the glass cabinet in front of her and I'm drawn to what's sparkling beneath her fingers. Diamonds. Well, in this case I reckon they're nothing more than cubic zirconia, still, I understand her well enough. "What are you looking to purchase this evening?" she asks again.

"Diamonds?"

She smiles, her red painted lips pulling wide over her straight white teeth. "Welcome to *Jewels*. Through here, please," she says, her hand disappearing beneath the cabinet. A second later a door marked *storeroom* swings open and I'm stepping into the entrance of a club with a topless man and a scantily clad woman dancing on two platforms on either side of a reception area where a perfectly coiffed gentleman stands.

There's marble flooring beneath my feet and chandeliers hanging from the ceiling. A wide circular staircase leads upwards and there's a floor to ceiling red curtain pulled closed directly opposite me. The deep sound of a familiar voice singing draws my attention towards whatever lies beyond the curtain. "Is that Rag'n'Bone Man?" I ask no one in particular.

"Indeed it is," the man standing behind the reception desk answers. He's handsome in a silver fox kind of way. "My name is Jasper. May I take your name please?"

"Holy fuck," I mumble under my breath, catching my reflection in the mirror behind Jasper. I look as far out of my comfort zone as I feel. Shit, maybe I should have worn Clancy's Louboutin stilettos. Too fucking late now. I roll my shoulders and run my fingers through my hair. If I can handle myself in a club full of criminals, then I can deal with the type of clientele that must attend an exclusive club like this. This is a club for the rich and likely famous, a far cry from the street kids and criminals that attend Rocks or Grim's club.

"Miss, your name?" Jasper repeats.

"Pen."

"Pen…?"

"Oh, you want my full name. It's Pen Scott," I tell him, biting down on my inner cheek.

"Ah, yes, Mr Bernard has been expecting you. Please follow me," he says, stepping out from behind the desk and walking towards the curtain. He pulls it aside with a smile, revealing another large room filled with people dining at tables with cut glass champagne glasses and sparkling silverware. In front of the dozen or so tables is a dance floor, and behind that a stage upon which Rag'n'Bone Man aka Rory Graham sits. He's currently singing *Human* and I swear to fuck the hair on my arms rises at the velvet smoothness of his sexy-arse voice.

Zayn wasn't kidding when he said that this was an exclusive club if they've got Rory Graham singing here tonight. He's one of my favourite artists and I'm a little starstruck, honestly.

"This way please," Jasper says, weaving through the tables until we reach the one closest to the stage. Rory looks over at us passing through the other diners and smiles. Fortunately for me, I maintain a modicum of decorum and smile shyly back, my cheeks blazing when he winks.

Just wait until Clancy hears about this, she'll shit a brick.

"Impressed?"

Too distracted by Rory, I bump into Zayn as he stands up from his seat at the table. He grins widely at me, looking suave in a beautifully cut grey suit and black shirt. His hair is slicked back and he's cleanly shaven. My mouth drops open then closes again as I take my fill of him. He's so beautiful.

"This place is insane," I say, smiling at Jasper who pulls out my chair for me. Zayn grins, sitting down beside me.

"It's pretty cool, isn't it?" he agrees.

"What would you like to drink, Miss Scott?" Jasper asks, beckoning over a waiter who seems to appear out of nowhere.

"Erm—"

"Pen would like a glass of the finest champagne you have," Zayn says for me. He gives me a look asking if that's okay.

"Sure, that'd be great," I offer, not really minding what I drink so long as it takes the edge off my nerves. I'm feeling well out of my comfort zone. I'm sure I just spotted Adele sitting in the far corner of the club chatting to some guy. If she gets up and sings, I might just have a coronary.

"Perfect," Jasper responds with a nod to the waiter who leaves to get my order. "I have taken the liberty of requesting the rump steak, Sir. Chef ordered it in especially."

"Good choice, Jasper, thank you." Zayn gives him a quick smile and a nod of the head and Jasper gets the hint, leaving us to talk in private.

"So you know some pretty cool people," I say, focusing my attention back on Zayn who sits back in his seat and smiles languidly. He looks relaxed, real relaxed, like he owns the place. It only makes me more intrigued as to how a kid from a Hackney estate who spent most of his time getting into trouble, ended up being friends with people rich enough to own such an establishment.

"I know a lot of people, Pen, but not one of them is as special to me as you are." His gaze softens, and I don't know if it's the soft lighting, the sensual atmosphere, or the sound of Rag'n'Bone Man singing, but I swear to fuck actual stars shine in Zayn's night-time eyes.

He reaches for me, his fingers wrapping around my hand.

"Very suave," I say, smiling ruefully. My heartbeat kicks up a notch and those butterflies in my tummy take flight.

Zayn cocks his head to the side and I'm acutely aware of his thumb tracing over my knuckles in such a way that my clit throbs. I need to keep a lid on my reaction to him, because this kind of attention and sincerity is doing stupid things to my libido and stripping me of that common sense and self-preservation that keeps me so level-headed.

"I didn't bring you here to impress you, Pen. I brought you here because you deserve to be treated like a fucking queen. I want you to eat good food, drink expensive champagne, enjoy the best fucking singers, and dance because you want to, not because you've been forced to."

He winces at that, and I still see the guilt he holds over what happened at Grim's club. It softens me further towards him. We might've bridged the distance between us already, but there's still a ways to go.

"Thank you," I reply, locking gazes with him.

Our conversation is interrupted by the waiter who brings me my champagne. I thank him and take a sip, needing the alcohol to settle my nerves. The taste is delicious, and the bubbles fizz on my tongue as I swallow. "Wow, this isn't like that cheap shit you can buy at the supermarket," I say.

"Nope, it certainly isn't cheap at fifty pound a glass."

"*What?!*" I hiss, almost spitting out the expensive mouthful. I swallow it down, not wanting to waste it.

Zayn laughs, his whole face lighting up in amusement. "Relax, Pen, I've got this covered. Only the best for my girl, remember?"

"You're insane."

"Only for you," he whispers, dragging the pad of his thumb over my bottom lip gently.

He leans in, replacing his thumb with his lips as his hand slides around the back of my head and cups my neck. I open up to him, meeting his tongue with mine. His fingers curl into my hair as he kisses me deeply and I can taste whisky on his tongue. Something about the fiery flavour makes my knees weak just as much as his kiss does. We kiss for long minutes, only to pull away when a gentle cough interrupts us.

"Apologies, Sir. Your food is ready," the waiter explains. I look up at him and give a weak smile, knowing my cheeks are flushing just as much as his.

"Thank you," Zayn responds, moving back reluctantly.

For the rest of the evening, we eat, we talk about everyday things and whilst I learn nothing about why Zayn and the Breakers are at the Academy, I get an insight into the man Zayn is today, and I like him. *A lot.* When Rag'n'Bone starts to sing *Skin* my own skin covers in goosebumps. The man is an exceptional singer, his voice melodious, deep, touching.

Zayn stands taking my hand. "Dance with me? Let me do it right this time."

"It wasn't wrong, Zayn," I reply, because what happened in the studio between us might've been painful, but it was far from wrong.

"I want to dance with you, Pen. Fuck, there are a lot of things I want from you but right now, right this second, I want to dance with you. Dax is a fool, but I'm not. I want you back and I won't lie about that to myself or anyone else."

"What about Jeb?" I whisper. He might've loaned me to Grim, but he still owns me. Zayn might not know the full story behind our relationship—if you can call it that—but he's still playing with fire even being here with me. Jeb doesn't take kindly to his toys being played with by anyone else.

"Jeb isn't going to be a problem…" he says with certainty. I frown, not understanding what he means by that. Jeb has always been *the* problem, alongside my brother. "Just don't think about it tonight, okay? Just dance with me, Pen. *Please.*"

"Okay," I agree.

The moment we step onto the dancefloor, Zayn's arms wrap around my back. He tugs me towards him, a sexy smile pulling up his lips then he lowers his head and kisses me gently.

"Dancing with you is a gift, Pen. Loving you an inevitability," he whispers against my lips before tucking my head against his chest and moving with me to the sensual beat of the music.

Later that night I fell asleep beneath the covers of my bed thinking about the boy who grew up into a man that's attentive, warm, respectful. Zayn made no move to seduce me. We returned to the Academy, kissed on the threshold of my flat and then went to our separate beds. Did I want to sleep with him? Yes, of course I did, and I know he wanted it too, but tonight wasn't about that. Tonight was about starting again. It was about reconnecting. It was about friendship and, ultimately, it was about trust.

19

Pen

"So, girl. You and Mr Hip-Hop, eh?" Clancy asks me in tap class the following day.

She's tying up her shoes and grinning up at me as I sit on the bench beside her, waiting for our teacher, Sasha, to start the lesson. She's a brilliant tap dancer, no more than ten years older than us and hot as fuck. Seriously, if I wasn't into men, then I'd be into her. Tall, with an hourglass figure, shapely legs, and dark cocoa skin. She has rhythm, soul, boundless energy, and endless patience. A perfect combination for dancing and teaching tap.

I watch, distractedly, as she chats with York on the opposite side of the studio. He's giving her one of his smiles that he used to share in abundance with me growing up, but hasn't thrown my way since we clapped eyes on each other again. It's clear that she's taken a liking to York, which doesn't surprise me in the least because he's hands down the best tap dancer at the school bar Clancy, who gives him a run for his money on a daily basis.

"Pen, are you seriously going to avoid the subject?" Clancy presses with a cheeky smile. When I don't answer immediately, she sits upright and nudges me with her shoulder. "Like, I held off asking you about it the moment you snuck back into the Academy last night—"

"Wait, were you spying on us?" I laugh, shaking my head.

"What can I say, I was going to the laundry room and saw you snogging each other's faces off." She shrugs, giggling.

"You were going to the laundry room at midnight?"

"Yup, sure fire way to piss off Tiffany, given her flat is right next door to it. Nothing like a washing machine to keep someone up at night."

"You're brilliant, do you know that?"

"She fucking deserves it for what she's done to you. Fucking bitch. I don't know how you didn't punch her lights out. I still can, if you want. Dax too. Just say the word."

"Seriously, it's fine," I say, shaking my head.

"Anyway, stop avoiding the subject. I can't contain my curiosity a moment longer. I mean, you don't have to tell me all the gory details about your date or anything but, you know, just the fun ones." She wiggles her eyebrows and I groan, realising I need to give her something or she'll never leave me alone.

"It's new, okay. We've called a truce—"

"What does that mean? Friends or friends that fuck?" she interrupts with a gleeful expression.

"*Friends*," I reply adamantly, pissed that my cheeks are flaring and giving away what my heart so desperately wants, even when I can't completely admit that to myself. "We're taking things slow."

"I'll put that down as a *friends that might be fucking soon* then?"

"Oh, shut up," I respond, shoving her lightly.

She giggles, then stands and proceeds to perform a quick ball-heel shuffle sequence that boggles my mind at how fast she can move her feet. I grin up at her as she pulls a crazy face and flings her arms out wildly. I can't help but laugh.

"You know you're a crazy bitch, right?" I say when she finally stops moving.

"Me?" she questions, pressing her finger into her chest, then cocking her head to the side. "Yep. It's why you love me."

"You're right, it is," I agree, laughing as she pulls me upright and into a hug.

"All joking aside, just be careful, okay? I like your heart and I don't want it broken," she says, squeezing me a little tighter before letting me go. I see the sincerity and concern in her eyes, and it warms me up from the inside out. What she doesn't realise is that my heart has been in pieces for three years, now a part of it is slowly being stitched back together.

"I will, you don't need to worry. I know what I'm doing," I say, sounding more convinced than I am. Truth is, I'm wading through a quagmire of emotions and memories so thick that I'm not sure how to just be in the moment. Not to mention, I'm on edge waiting for my brother to call, or Jeb to rear his ugly head again at any moment. This truce with Zayn not only serves to remind me of what I've missed these past three years and why, but also that whilst I may have Zayn back, I don't have the rest of the Breakers. They all hold a piece of my heart and I'm resigned to the fact that it will never beat properly again unless we fix what's broken which, let's face it, isn't going to happen. Xeno still hates me, and apart from my confrontation with Dax the other night, he and York have been avoiding me as much as I've been avoiding them. Not to mention the small fact my brother's a fucking psycho and determined to murder anyone I hold dear if I don't do what he wants.

"Come on, girl. Let's tap all that frustration out, yeah?" Clancy says, snapping me out of my dark thoughts.

"Yeah, let's do this," I nod, following her and finding a spot at the back of the class and as far away from York as I can get.

After a good ten minutes warm-up that has my blood pumping and has relieved some of my pent up anxiety, Sasha asks us to fan out in a circle, leaving a wide open space in the middle of the studio.

"Right, ladies and gents, I'm going to do something a little different today. Most of you here already have many years' experience in performing tap, and I've now gotten a good hold of your ability. So, I wanted to explore a little more. I want to see your improvisation skills. Every single one of you can follow choreography, but tap is so much more than just a sequence of steps and noise. It can be as emotive and as deeply powerful as any of the other disciplines if performed with enough intent."

She smiles then and moves into the centre of the circle we've made and begins to tap in a way that wows me, proving her point. Like everyone else in the studio, I'm stunned by her quick footwork, but it's her ability to tell a story through her steps that impresses me the most. Dance has always been about expression to me, and for a long time I assumed that tap could only really express happiness just like Fred Astaire in his movies. It's why I was drawn more to hip-hop and contemporary as a kid, because with those two dances in particular I felt able to express my anger and pain the most clearly. I've learnt over the years, however, that tap dance isn't always an expression of joy, that there's a lot more depth to the dance than that.

Sasha moves over the wooden boards with lightning speed interspersed with moments of clarity and intentional delay. She's telling a story, and she's doing it all with a smile plastered on her face that, in my opinion, juxtaposes what she's trying to express with her feet. This dance isn't a happy one. It's one of frustration and anger. Someone must've pissed her off royally to influence her dance this way.

"Can anyone tell me what they *felt* when watching me dance just now?" she asks the room. If it sounds like a trick question, that's probably because it is. She's trying to catch people out with that same smile plastered on her pretty face. I keep my thoughts to myself though because I'm not as certain of myself in this dance lesson as I am in my others.

"Anyone?" she presses.

"I felt anger," York finally says, pinning his gaze on Sasha.

"Good." She nods. "What else?"

"Frustration," I blurt out, cutting off Clancy before she can say the same. She looks at me and winks.

"Excellent. The expression on my face gave you one picture," she says, plastering that same pretty smile back on again, "but my steps were telling the *truth*. That's the heart of tap dance. Its truth is always in the *steps*." She points to her feet and does a quick sequence that speaks of joy even though her face is a blank mask. "See, I'm *happy* you got it even when that might not appear to be the case."

"I like this woman," Clancy says, leaning in close. "I might have a girl crush."

Smiling, I look about the room. "Yeah, you and about twenty other people."

My gaze falls onto York who is looking at Sasha like she's

all his dreams come true. I see the admiration in his eyes and interest that has my heart bottoming out. They look good together, his pale skin against her beautiful, silky chocolate shade. Like Ying and Yang. I'm sure they'd make beautiful babies. Jealousy raises its ugly head and I bite down on the inside of my cheek. It's one thing giving Clancy his attention when practising their duet, but quite another when he's looking at Sasha the way he is. I trust Clancy not to overstep, but Sasha has no reason to stay away. York is beautiful, talented, and whilst he might be her student, that won't prevent him from making a move. York has always been the type of guy to flagrantly ignore rules. He's also the type of guy to get everyone else to break them too.

"Okay, so this is what we're going to do. I'm going to play a randomly selected song and then tap one of you on the shoulder. If I've picked you, you need to move into the circle and start improvising," Sasha explains. "I want you to show whatever emotion the song makes you feel in your *steps*, regardless of what mask you wear on your face. Let's see how well you interpret the music and how well you express those emotions."

"So we interpret the music with an emotion and funnel that into our steps, but try not to show that on our face?" one of the other students asks, wanting to clarify.

"Exactly that, but to make it more challenging, I'm going to select another person to dance too. That person will need to counter, or complement, whatever emotion is portrayed in your partner's steps with an interpretation of your own. Once the song is finished, I'll play another and choose two more people to dance together. We'll do that until you've all had a chance to dance."

"Kind of like a hip-hop battle?" a guy with short, spiky

green hair and a ring in his nose asks. I think his name is Amos, but I can't be certain.

"Yes, in a way," Sasha agrees, "But rather than a battle where there can only be one winner, I want *cohesion* by the end of the song. Now, let's see how you fare."

Sasha pulls out her mobile phone and chooses a song I don't recognise but has an up-tempo beat. She selects Clancy first who steps into the circle and wows us all with her ridiculous talent. It's clear that joy is the emotion she's chosen to express in her dance steps despite the cross look on her face. Her feet move lightly, and her steps are suffused with happiness, *bliss*. The way she dances reminds me of a kid on Christmas morning. I see the excitement, the wonderment and, of course, joy. When Sasha taps on Amos's shoulder, he counters Clancy's steps with deep digs and heavy shuffles of his feet. He stomps over the floor, stepping into her space even though he has a smile plastered to his face. Eventually, the pair start to dance in time together, mashing up the joy Clancy is expert at showing and the misery Amos displays. By the time the song ends they're both panting with the effort, but grinning widely. We all start clapping. They're a tough act to follow.

"Excellent work," Sasha says, beaming.

For the next thirty minutes she moves around the circle pairing up dancers. My heart hammers in my chest with every selection she makes and every time I think she's going to choose me, she doesn't. When the penultimate pair have been chosen and begin to dance, I zone out knowing that the only person left for me to be paired up with is York.

"*Damn*, girl," Clancy mutters as York's ice-blue eyes meet mine over the pair dancing in the circle between us. She reaches for me, her fingers wrapping around my wrist in solidarity. I swallow hard. I'm not ready for this.

I'm not fucking ready.

A broad smile pulls across York's face as Sasha asks him to step into the centre of the circle. That smile doesn't reach his eyes and is as much of a mask as the one I'm wearing now. When she motions for me to come forward, I do so with heavy steps. Sasha chooses a new song, and as *Running up that Hill* by Kate Bush begins to play, York's smile slips. For the briefest second I see the hate in his eyes before his features fix into a blank mask that matches my own. As the familiar beat begins to play, York starts to dance. It's blatantly obvious the emotion he's trying to portray and even if I hadn't caught the look in his eyes, I would've understood him well enough.

20

York

I can't help myself.
I thought I'd got a lid on my emotions around her.
I fucking haven't.
And by the brief flash of pain in Pen's eyes, she thinks all this hate I feel is aimed at her.
It isn't.
It's aimed at *me*.
I fucking hate myself.
I hate myself for watching Pen unravel her soul and cut herself open at Grim's club and not doing anything to stop it.
I hate that it wasn't me who climbed into the cage and fucking choked Malik Brov for putting his hands and lips on her.
I hate that I let her believe I would ever consider making a deal with the bastard.

I hate that I didn't chase after her, that I didn't check in with her at any point this past week to see if she was okay.

I hate that Zayn did, that he was the first to chip at the walls encasing her heart.

I hate that I'm still torn when it comes to her.

I hate that nothing is clear as it was, that I don't know what the fuck to do.

But mostly, I hate that she's here now hurting again, because I can't seem to get over my fucking self and really tell her how I feel.

So I let my steps do the talking. I leave my face a blank mask, because even though I've always been able to read Pen's expression to see her innermost thoughts, Pen's gift is not just expressing herself through dance, but reading us in the same way. I dropped dance the moment she left us, refusing to open myself up to anyone like that again. I didn't want anyone else to be able to read me.

Just her.

Just Pen.

Just Titch.

Coming back here was a means to an end. We have a goal, an end in sight. That's it. That's all. Except now it's so much more than that. Now, I'm faced with Pen on a daily basis and reminded of all the things I want. That I never stopped wanting.

And I hate myself for that too.

Kate Bush sings about being hurt by someone unintentionally, reflecting my growing thoughts about Pen's decision to walk away and how none of us acted. Pen hurt me. I hurt her. We were fucking blown apart from the events of that night three years ago and all that pain was echoed once more in the way she danced at Grim's club.

Now I'm an open wound. A goddamn mess.

Slamming my feet on the floor, I let my emotion seep into the boards. My steps speak for themselves. I don't think my feet have ever moved this fast or with such intention. Pen watches me, struggling to hide the emotion on her face as I move around her in a circle, slamming my feet against the boards, ripping up all the rules of tap and making this dance my bitch. She flinches with every step, her jaw tightening, her eyes glassy.

Both of us are oblivious to the other dancers in the room.

There is only *us*.

There has only ever been us.

And I fucking hate that she walked away from what we had.

I hate that I let her. That *we* let her.

Kate Bush's words fuel my ire, they move my feet. I *should've* run after her. I *should've* done something. She was right to be angry at me. I saw the disappointment in her eyes after we left Grim's club. I felt the accusation, her hurt, because it was warranted. I did nothing that night, just like I did nothing to stop her walking away three years ago.

I let my anger, my jealousy, my disappointment and hate rule me at Rocks. I was a kid who'd never loved anyone before Pen, nor since. She broke us all and I wasn't man enough to do anything about it at the time. Every one of us had felt that hurt before when other girls had used us to get to Jeb, but we never loved them like we loved Pen. So I was selfish in my anguish. I wallowed in it for months, then I threw myself into doing shitty things because hurting other people made me numb. I didn't want to feel anything. But I'm different now. Things have changed. Something's gotta give because she's the Ginger to my Fred, always has been and it's time I'm honest with myself, with her. Fuck hiding. Fuck hating. Fuck Xeno and his goddamn inability to see sense. Fuck Jeb.

Fuck *him* most of all.

There are no words to describe my next steps, only feeling. I move through all the usual tap sequences, but none of them are enough to really portray all that I'm feeling. So, I do what Pen did Friday night. I push the boundaries, I do it for her, for Titch.

My girl.

Our girl.

I rip open my fucking chest and let her see the mess she made of my heart.

Pen's jaw tightens as she watches me, and this time instead of showing me every last emotion like she did on Friday, she holds onto that beautiful mask she's an expert at wearing these days and begins to move instead. Like mine, her steps begin angry too, and we counter each other. Two people head to head, like boxers in a ring. Opponents. Enemies. Adversaries.

Every step is a punch to my gut, an uppercut to my chin, a slam to my cheek.

Anger fills her once more, just like it had at Grim's club and I'm reminded of the way she'd bent over in front of Zayn, how her perfect, rounded arse and pussy had been on display for him. I had to will myself not to get up and snatch her away from the fucker and knock him out. I've never been jealous of my friends and their relationship with Pen when we were kids. We all loved each other, we *wanted* to share the most precious thing to us, at least in the end we had. But that night, I both wanted her and wanted to protect her from my best friend. I thought he was going to hurt her, but he didn't get a chance. She didn't need me to step in because she fought for herself.

My girl. My fighter. My Titch.

Pen is a warrior. She's *courageous* and worth a million times more than any of our sorry arses. She lambasted us, blasted us apart and not one of us has been the same since that night. Even Xeno, who's still trying to deny he feels anything for Pen. The motherfucker refuses to acknowledge what he feels. He lied to my face when I confronted him. He said that he didn't give a shit about Pen, but I know different because you can't kid a kidder, and this kidder is done kidding himself.

Right now, as Pen dances before me, I let her see what I truly *feel* in my steps as I read her own. For someone with no formal training in tap, she's amazing. I mean, I've had no formal training either but my absolute love for tap as a kid made me determined to get every step perfect. There have only ever been two obsessions in my life. I'm dancing one of them and looking at the other. I might have given up dance when Pen walked away, but being back here with her has changed shit. Call it muscle memory, but I've easily fallen back into dancing again as though I never stopped. Coming back, being here at Stardom Academy, seeing Pen again has revived my heart in a way that scares the shit out of me. I'm a great dancer, yes, but only because of her, because of Pen. She brings out the best in me, always has.

For the briefest of moments I look over at Sasha who's watching me closely. I've been training with her in private since starting here, and whilst I appreciate her assistance, and admire her talent, I'm not interested in her in quite the way she's interested in me. There's no doubt that her little display earlier was for me. She's pissed that I turned her down and by the end of this dance, I think she'll understand just who it is that occupies my heart and soul.

Titch.

I can admit that now.

A loud crack of Pen's toe-cap hitting the board forces my attention back to her, back to the only woman who's ever ruled my heart. Her moves match mine, mirroring me, or at least she tries to, and her tenacity to keep up with my steps does something to me. In dance she's never afraid to push past her limits, to make mistakes and learn from them. She was always the beating heart of the Breakers, and I'm reminded of that right here, right now. My steps falter, and the anger falls away as I allow myself to feel something other than hate.

She notices.

And her footwork changes too, her steps altering, becoming heavy, delayed, sombre.

Tap isn't her first love and she trips a little over her feet trying to transition from a complicated sequence of steps through to a shuffle ball change. Correcting herself, she moves into a cramp stomp to the left then switches to a bombershay ending in a low foot slide, bowing to me. My throat fucking squeezes alongside my bloody heart.

She's saying *sorry*. Emphatically, with her body, her whole fucking soul.

Her face might not be giving anything away, but there's no denying her steps or the meaning behind them. So I do the same because *I* can't deny my feelings a fucking second longer.

Stepping into her space, my right foot reaches between her open stance and I tap a softer sequence that has me leaning into her. It's not easy to express softness in tap like it is for other dances, but it is possible. Leaning in, Pen's close enough that I can draw in her scent, that intoxicating mix that I've never been able to identify but is so perfectly, unashamedly *her*. It's like a drug. Heady, enthralling. It makes my stupid cock twitch in my pants. It makes me want to fucking kiss her, right here, right now, in front of everyone. Pen's eyes meet mine and a million emotions are portrayed in them. She has opened up and has allowed me to see right into the complexities of her.

She's the defiant little girl beneath that oak tree, bruised and battered but never beaten.

She's the woman with secrets that weigh her down, but will not end her.

She's the dancer that inspires passion in others.

She's her. She's Titch.

And just like that, I'm a goner.

Hook, line, and fucking sinker.

She's captured me like a fish on a goddamn rod and there's nothing I can do about it.

I'm hers again. There's no doubt in my mind. There's no fear, no pain, no anger, no fucking question. I'm hers if she'll have me.

The music stops abruptly, snapping us both out of the moment and into the room once more. Neither of us make a move to walk away. We simply stand facing each other, our chests heaving, our breaths mingling. Sweat trickles down my back, sticking my t-shirt to my skin. The air vibrates with tension and the rest of the dancers remain silent as though they too understand the significance of this moment.

I lean towards Pen, my eyes closing as I press my cheek against her own, my shoulders drop, my arms reaching for her, my fingers digging into the skin of her back as I crush her to my chest.

"Titch," I breathe against her ear.

"York," she mutters back.

Her name is worshipful on my tongue, my name a mixture of relief and hope—but also fear—on hers. The fear worries me. I've seen too much of it in her as of late and I need to know the source. I was blinkered before, telling myself I didn't care. But I do. I fucking do.

Zayn was right. He said out loud what we've *all* been thinking. Pen might have betrayed us. She might have walked away, but there's more to it than that.

Much, much more, and we were too fucking stupid not to see it.

My grip tightens, and I feel her arms close around me as a deep sigh releases from her chest.

"Well, thank you both. What an intelligent display of hate versus love. Two sides of the same coin. However, that's it for today," Sasha interrupts, her voice sharp. "We can pick this up in the next lesson."

Around us the other dancers begin to murmur, but none of them walk away, too enthralled by what's happening between me and Pen. They want to see what happens next, just as much as I want to experience it.

Not able to help myself, I press my lips against her ear, revelling in the way her body shivers in my arms. I should pull away, but I don't. My lips drag over her cheek before resting against the corner of her mouth. She doesn't move, in fact her fingers grip hold of me tighter and I can't help it, a smile pulls at my lips.

She wants me as much as I want her. Zayn might have got to her first just like when we were kids, but I was the one who brought her into the fold. I was the one who found her beneath that oak tree. I'd known from the moment she slipped her hands into mine that she would be ours. I didn't fucking hesitate then, and I refuse to do so now.

With that memory swirling inside my head, I kiss her roughly, hungrily. She gasps, her lips parting with the sound, her body pressing harder against mine as I grasp the back of her neck and tug at the strands of hair there. She whimpers, her tongue stroking against mine and I take that as an open invitation to continue. So I do. I kiss her desperately, not giving a shit who's in the room with us. Not caring about the surprised laughter or the shocked gasps.

Not giving two single fucks.

My tongue laps into her mouth as I haul her against my chest, lifting her off the floor. She might still be the same height as she was when we were teenagers, but fuck she's all woman now. I want to explore every sexy, curvy, inch of her.

"My Titch," I mutter against her mouth.

"I think you should take this somewhere else," Sasha interrupts, but I barely hear her over the rushing and pulsing of blood in my ears. Pen, however, pushes against my chest and unlocks her lips from mine.

"York, we should go," she whispers, her cheeks suffused with heat, and not just from our kiss.

Pressing a kiss against her forehead, I lower her to the floor, but keep an arm latched around her shoulder so that she's still pressed against me to hide my erection as much as her embarrassment.

Locking my gaze with Sasha, I nod. "Yeah, and I was thinking we could practice some more."

"York!" Pen hisses, pressing her forehead against my chest and groaning.

"This is my studio, and just like the rest of the students have, I'd like you both to leave."

"That might be an issue…" I allow my voice to trail off and my gaze lower to where Pen's so tightly pressed up against me.

Sasha shakes her head, rolling her eyes. "Fucking horny teenagers," she grouses, giving me the death-glare over Pen's head.

"I'm not a teenager," I counter, smirking. She wouldn't have made a pass at me if I was, and she fucking knows it.

"Then stop acting like one. Now, get out of my studio and be thankful that I'm so impressed by your interpretation skills today that I've decided not to chuck you both out of my class for good."

Pen turns in my arms, her cheeks suffused with pink. I can't help it. I grind my dick against her back, silently telling her that I'm all man now. She chokes on a laugh and the sound of joy in her voice, however brief, makes me harder. I've dreamt about that sound for years.

"I apologise, it won't happen again," she says.

"Hmm," Sasha responds, flicking her gaze up to mine.

"I wouldn't count on that." I smirk again, winking at Sasha who rolls her eyes.

"Fucking children," she mutters, before turning her back on us both.

Taking that as our final cue to get the fuck out of her studio, I grab Pen's hand, and pull her along the hallway, ignoring the stares and whispered comments of the other students we pass by. Clancy's standing by the doorway that leads up to the stairwell of our flats. She sees us coming and with a huge grin plastered across her face, pushes the door open.

"Don't do anything I wouldn't do," she grins, winking at Pen.

21

Pen

York pulls me into his flat, slamming the door behind us. Within seconds he's pushing me up against his door, his hips grinding against mine. His kisses are frenzied, passionate and my head is swimming with the way he's making me feel.

Hot, needy, desperate, *mindless*.

I can't think straight. Goddamn him.

"I want to fuck you until we both see stars. Maybe I'll light up just like the vampire dude you always loved so much in those books—" he states between kisses.

"York," I mutter against his mouth, needing a moment's breathing space as his words settle in my bones like a permanent tattoo. The fact that he wants me so bad and remembers my infatuation with a certain series of books makes me smile inside, despite my stupid brain trying to put a stop to what's happening. My fingers rise up his chest and I push against him, despite my clit throbbing with need. "York, I need a second."

He bites his lip, his ice-blue eyes heated, but he pulls back, one hand still pressed against the door beside my head, the other running through his hair. "Shit, okay."

"I just think we need to talk or something," I say a little helplessly, realising that's probably the last thing we should be doing. Then again, the alternative is fucking and as much as my body wants that, I need to just reel myself in a little. Back when I was kid and realised I was in love with him, with all the Breakers, all I wanted to do was kiss them, fuck them. It's all I thought about. I was plagued with fantasies just like this where York would kiss me like the girls he brought back to Jackson Street, with the same kind of intensity, and here I am pushing him away.

"Yes, right. Fuck."

He pushes off the door, adjusting himself with a rueful smile. My gaze flicks to his erection pressing against his joggers, and I bite the inside of my cheek to stop myself from grinning and to remind myself that pain comes hand in hand with the Breakers just as much as pleasure. *Keep your head, Pen.*

"Come in," he says awkwardly, a little bit of the boy I knew peeping out from beneath the chiselled jaw and dirty mouth he wears so well now.

I follow him into his flat, which has the same layout as mine. The only difference is that his flat is tidy. The room's spotless, actually. My gaze falls to his arse and the swagger of his walk. It makes me smile inside. He was always *jaunty*. It used to piss him off when I referred to him that way. Being jaunty isn't cool, but it certainly suits him.

"Sit down," he says, pointing to his bed.

"Thanks."

York hovers in the kitchen, giving me space as I run my palms over the smooth cotton of his bedsheet and flick my gaze around his flat trying to avoid eye contact. I need to get my shit together. I need to keep my head. Seriously though, there's always been something about York's eyes that make me weak. It's not just the unusual, piercing colour, but the way he watches me so closely, like I'm the only thing that matters to him.

"Want a drink or something? I've got a Coke?"

"No Amaretto Sour?"

"Beer perhaps…" he grins, with a shrug. "Still your favourite drink then?"

"A Coke is fine."

York nods and grabs me a cold can from the fridge, our fingers grazing as he passes it to me. "So…" he begins, looking down at me.

"So…?" My eyes drop from his to the can. I pull back the tab and take a gulp, wanting to press the coldness against my cheek to prevent the flush I feel creeping over my skin.

"You wanted to talk… *or something*? Isn't that what you said?"

Heaving out a sigh, I lift my gaze to meet his. We look at each other for long moments. When York takes the can of Coke from me and places it on the floor, my breath hitches. Taking my hands, he kneels, his thumbs running over my knuckles as he looks at me. Actually, as he *stares*. It's unnerving, but beautifully erotic. My clit throbs some more.

"What is it with you boys getting on your knees for me?" I blurt out, remembering how Zayn had done the same in the studio.

"Ah man, he fucking didn't…" York smiles, but it doesn't reach his eyes, and it has me questioning what's changed.

When we were kids, there was never any jealousy between them when it came to me. Well, not enough to cause a wedge, anyway. We just worked. Xeno was the only one who made it difficult, until he finally came around that night at Rocks. I try not to wonder what would've happened if my brother hadn't threatened me, if I hadn't walked in on Jeb. Where would we be now? Would we still be together? Would we be happy? Or had Xeno been right all along?

"What's the deal with you guys?" I ask, pushing thoughts of that night aside. It's an open question that can be answered a multitude of ways. I'm interested to see which way he takes this.

"The deal? We're still the Breakers."

"That so? Still breaking things then?"

York heaves a sigh. "We've done a lot of fucked-up shit."

"Because of me?"

"In the beginning, yeah, we used you as an excuse. Then all the fucked-up things we did couldn't be put on a girl we didn't know anymore. That was all on us." He drops his forehead to our clasped hands, resting his head there for a moment. I draw one hand away and start stroking his hair. He kind of sighs, his shoulders dropping.

"Do I want to know what you did?"

He shakes his head. "No, Pen, you don't."

"Titch," I say, my fingers tightening around the strands.

"Titch," he mutters, his hands travelling up my thighs and around my hips. My legs part allowing him to slide between them, and my hands grasp his head, pulling against the strands of his white-blonde hair until he's face-to-face with me once more.

"Are you still that boy I remember?"

"Are you still that girl?" he counters, closing his eyes briefly as I cup his face in my palm.

"No," I whisper.

"I'm not that boy either," he admits.

"What do we do?"

"We start over, Titch."

"I'm not sure that's possible—"

"It's fucking possible." I frown, but he leans in and kisses me roughly. "It's fucking possible," he repeats, gripping my face tightly in his hands. "You, Titch, aren't slipping away again. I won't fucking allow it."

"And what if it doesn't matter? What if you've got no control over what happens between us? What if this is out of my hands? What then?"

York's gaze flashes with a fire hot enough to burn. "Then I kill the fucker that's standing between us."

"What if he kills you first?" I whisper, my throat tight. These words are the closest I've got to the truth of what happened that night at Rocks. I swallow hard, willing him to understand that I've never been a master of my own fate, not when I'm owned by Jeb, by my brother. Not when I'm trapped.

"Not gonna happen. I'm a motherfucking vampire, remember? They can't die." His lip lifts up in a half-smile, reminding me of that boy standing under the streetlamp outside of number 15 Jackson Street.

"Everyone has a weakness, including you. What if I'm that weakness, York? What then?"

York shakes his head. "You were never our weakness. You were always our strength."

"Until I wasn't. Until I walked away."

"Then don't walk away again, Titch. Don't fucking walk away."

"I want to stay—" I mutter.

His fingers tighten in my hair, his lips brushing against my mouth. "I *want* you to stay. Now, tomorrow, forever, Titch."

"I can't promise you forever, York. No matter how much I want to do that. I can only promise you this moment. That's all I can give you right now."

"Then I'll take that. I'll take the now, and we'll bench the future until we can figure this mess out."

He brushes the tip of his nose against the bridge of mine. Then kisses my mouth sweetly, tenderly, with a softness that makes my heart ache and my toes curl in my trainers.

"Titch," he mutters against my mouth.

"Yes?" I respond breathily as his lips graze over my chin, my cheek, my forehead, my ear, my throat.

"Can I tickle your pickle?"

My responding laughter has him grinning against my throat, his tongue lapping at my pulse which is throbbing in time with another part of my anatomy. "I thought you'd never ask."

With one last intense kiss, York pulls me to my feet and into the bathroom. Grasping my hips he lifts me up and positions me on the vanity unit. "Don't move," he says.

I'm too worked up to respond, instead I watch him as he turns on the shower, before yanking off his t-shirt in that sexy way only men seem able to do by grabbing behind his head and pulling. My eyes drop to the beautiful tattoo that decorates his chest and arms.

"This is the tree we met under, isn't it?"

He nods, stepping towards me. Taking my hand, he places it on his chest. "It took a week of trips to the tattooist to finish this. I relished the pain," he sighs. "I hated you for a long, long time, Titch."

"I know," I mutter, as my fingers trail over the trunk and up across the branches that extend over his upper chest, shoulders, and biceps. York's skin erupts in goosebumps at my touch, and his cock jerks beneath his joggers.

"But I never, *ever*, stopped loving you. Even if I can only admit that to myself now."

My gaze lifts to meet his and the truth of his confession is right there in his eyes. "Why didn't you stop me?" I ask softly. It's a dangerous question, but I can't seem to help myself from asking it.

"Stupidity, mainly. Anger. Teenage pride. Hurt. Take your pick."

"We were kids…" My gaze drops, my chin falling to my chest. "*I* was a kid."

"You were. We were. But we aren't those kids anymore, are we?"

"No, we aren't."

"We're *more —*" York lifts my chin with his finger and presses his hot mouth against mine, his tongue searching, probing. I respond, helpless against his ministrations as he presses up against me. I can feel his cock rubbing against my core as my legs wrap around his arse, and my fingers tug at the shorter strands of hair at the nape of his neck. York grasps me to him, his hand on my lower back as he encourages me to grind against his length before ripping his mouth away from mine, one hand cupping the back of my head. His eyes gleam as he stares down his nose at me, his hot breath coming in short pants.

"If it hasn't escaped your notice, we're *men* now, Titch. *Capable* men. Some would even say we're dangerous, violent, and they'd be right. We might have been teenagers blinded by pain once upon a time, but it's different now. I'm just sorry it's taken me so long to see what was right in front of my face. Zayn's filled me in on everything he suspects. We're on the same wavelength. I need you to know that."

"York, I can't—"

"You can't talk to us right now. You're not sure if you can trust us. I know that too, but I also know this. If you tell me what's in there," he says, bringing his finger up to tap my temple gently, "And you open up here," he adds, resting his palm over my beating heart, "then I swear to you, Titch, we'll make this right."

"*We?*" I ask, my heart thumping, my pulse rushing in my ears. "Because I know that isn't true."

York sighs, scraping a hand through his hair. "I'm working on that."

"It's just like when we were kids," I mutter.

"Titch. You're wrong, it's *nothing* like when we were kids."

"Dax refuses to even look at me."

"Dax took it the hardest when you left. He'll come around. I know him."

"And Xeno? He certainly doesn't like that Zayn and I have reconnected. Once he finds out about us—"

"I love Xeno like a brother," York says, cutting me off, "But I sure as fuck don't take orders from him."

"No, is that because you take orders from Jeb?"

York grits his jaw tightly, and I can hear his teeth grinding together. "I did."

"And now?"

"And now things have changed."

"Why are you here, York?" I ask, my eyes searching his.

For a long time he doesn't answer, and I realise it's because he doesn't know whether to trust me either.

"I tell you what, we'll make a deal. Today, we bench this talk. Today, we forget about everything in our past and just concentrate on the here and now. Be in the present with me, Titch. Can you do that?" He cups my face, his thumbs pressing into my cheekbones as he watches me.

"Yes, I—"

York doesn't let me finish my sentence. Instead, he smashes his lips against mine and tugs me in for a kiss that silences all my reservations and turns my insides into mush. This boy—no, this *man*, can kiss. The gentle sweep of his lips against mine has gone, replaced instead with a single-minded determination to get me off.

Within seconds our clothing is nothing but a pile on the bathroom floor and we're standing naked in front of each other. York grins down at me, the most beautiful, dazzling smile pulling up his lips. I reach up and yank on the flop of hair in his eyes just like I used to do so much growing up. His grin widens.

"Zayn may have got to you first, but right here and now, you're mine, Titch. You're mine."

22

Pen

Taking my hand, York guides me into the shower cubicle, the warm water cascading over him and plastering his hair against his head. He swipes a hand over his face, pushing his hair up in an adorable mess before easing me under the spray. The water cascades over my body, running in rivulets down my heated skin that flames even more when his fingers follow the flow. He looks down at me, water dripping from his nose and chin as he cups my breast in his hand, squeezing gently. I gasp when he thumbs my nipple, rolling the pad over and over my erect nub.

"You know Zayn and I haven't…"

"Fucked…?"

"Yeah."

His hand stills on my breast as he watches me closely. "I didn't think he had it in him to hold back once he made his mind up about you. Guy was a loose cannon after that night at Grim's club.."

"I needed time," I admit.

"And yet you're standing naked in a shower with me?" He grins again, his hand stroking over my clavicle and between my breasts as he presses me up against the shower wall. He's looking smug as fuck.

"Looks that way."

"So what are we gonna do about it?" York asks, his gaze falling to my breasts and then lower to the neatly trimmed strip of hair covering my mound. I don't answer, knowing this is a rhetorical question. "Oh, yeah. I'm gonna tickle your pickle… with my *tongue*."

My breath catches as he drops before me and presses his nose against my mound, breathing in deep. I look down at him, at his broad shoulders and the length of his strong back. My fingers tangle in his wet hair as I grasp hold of him. This escalated fast.

"Titch, I've dreamed about this moment so many fucking times," he says, looking up at me, his ice-blue eyes sharp with desire, his warm breath caressing my sensitive skin. "I don't wanna stop, but if that's what you want…"

"Don't stop," I breathe out, wanting to take a leaf out of his book. "Let's be in the now. I'm sick of thinking about the future."

York nods his head once, the lust billowing off him as he runs his hands up the backs of my legs. Grasping my arse, he lifts my right leg, hooking it over his shoulder. "I'm gonna savour every fucking second of this, Titch," he states, then his hungry mouth latches onto my clit, sucking it into his mouth.

I jerk against him as sensation explodes outwards. I've never been kissed this way before, let alone fucked by someone's mouth. *Jesus Christ.* If I had any sensible thought left in me, it's gone now, dissolved under his expert lips.

"Fuuuuck!"

"Damn!" he echoes, his needy voice vibrating against my core. "You taste as sweet as I imagined you would, Titch."

York ducks lower, lifting his ice-blue eyes to look up at me. I see so much lust in them and that makes me wetter, hotter. I damn near come just by the glazed look in his eyes. With his gaze still locked with mine, he licks me tenderly from my arse, around my core and up to my clit, then back again. Up and down he licks me all the while muttering dirty words that make me weak.

"Beautiful... Pussy... Mine... I love... fucking your pretty... little cunt... with my... tongue."

My legs begin to tremble, but he holds me steady with every sweep of his tongue, his hands grasp my arse, yanking me against his face as he devours me. I swear to fuck, I'm nothing but a ball of sensation. Every nerve ending alights under his expert mouth.

"York!" I cry out, my head rolling against the tiles, my fingers yanking his hair as my hips jerk against his mouth.

A deep chuckle reverberates through his body into mine only adding to the sensation, heightening it. With my shoulders pressed against the cool tile and the water raining over us both, York slides his tongue straight into my dripping core, alternating with feather light licks around my entrance, to deep dips into my channel. My eyes roll back in my head as I clamp his head to me, making noises I didn't know I was capable of.

And he loves every second of it.

The sounds he makes turn me on, and I can't get enough of looking down at him eating me out. Fuck, I spent hours in my youth watching pornos with scenes just like this, and just like then I'm turned on beyond belief. Every part of me is on fire.

I'm both weak and coiled tight.

But this, this is so much better than a porno. It's my fantasy come true.

"Titch, I'm gonna make you come so hard," he growls, pressing his thumb against my clit as he pulls away briefly, and slides his finger slowly into my core, watching every nuance on my face as he does. "You're so fucking tight. I could come right now myself just thinking about slipping my cock inside of you."

"Oh, God."

"No, Titch. Say *my* name."

"Please."

"Say *my* name, Titch," he repeats. "I wanna hear it release from your beautiful fucking mouth."

"York," I pant, smiling inside at his possessive tone. I had no idea.

"That's much, *much* better."

He grins evilly, his pupils blown wide with lust. There's nothing but a tiny ring of ice-blue around the black as he looks up at me and I look down at him. My core leaks all over his hand as his finger slides in and out, in and out. Not once does he take his eyes off of mine.

"Please," I hush out.

"Please what, Titch?"

"Please make me come."

"With fucking pleasure," he growls before removing his thumb, hooking his finger deep inside of me and assaulting my clit with the flat of his tongue.

He's relentless.

Expert in his attention.

He's a fucking *god* at this.

And me, I'm at his mercy.

My legs begin to shake in earnest now as though my body knows what's about to happen and isn't ready for the onslaught of such pleasure. I feel the orgasm building in my core as my muscles tighten around his finger. Up and up I go, rising high with the impending orgasm. I let myself ride the wave, moaning with the intensity of pleasure building inside of me. That waves crests and my spine stiffens, my hips jerk against York's face.

"Look at me, Titch!" York orders against my core.

My head snaps down as my eyes meet his. The fire in them is unmistakable and a wicked smile lifts up his lips as he lifts my other leg around his shoulders and his finger presses against that secret spot inside of me.

"Come on my face. Now!" he orders, sucking both my clit and my pussy lips into his mouth.

I come.

Fuck, do I come.

Apart.

Screaming York's name.

My whole body shudders.

I clench around him.

My thighs clamp around his head.

My core weeps.

My opening spasms as he pulls his finger free and replaces it with his tongue.

He laps at me, swallowing down my cum.

He holds me up until I'm spent.

As my orgasm ebbs away, he lowers me gently to the floor on shaky legs.

"Do you know what you do to me, Titch? Do you know what you've done?" he mumbles against my skin as he climbs up slowly, kissing every inch of me as he does so. He kisses my hip bones. His lips slide across my abdomen. He tongues my belly button, the tip swirling there, imitating how he tongued my pussy. He runs his teeth against the underside of my rib cage. His hands grasp my tits, squeezing tightly, before he pinches my nipples and his mouth closes over one then the other.

I moan, still riding the tail-end of my orgasm.

"What do I do to you, York?" I ask breathlessly as my fingers tangle in his hair, and my chest heaves. I feel weak. Satiated. *Loved*. I always assumed this kind of sexual act is all about lust, but what he just did, that was so much more than that.

"You make me want to be a better man. I was blinded for too long. Now I can see fucking clearly."

Pinning his forearms against the tiles either side of my head he presses his hips against mine, his rock hard cock pressing against my stomach. He leans his forehead against mine, and brushes his lips against my mouth, his tongue parting them gently. I can taste myself on his lips and fire lights within me once again. My hands rove over his skin, clasping his muscular back, his firm arse, before I slide my hand between us and fist his cock. He groans into my mouth as I palm his dick up and down.

"Jesus Christ," he groans.

"Not Jesus, just me, just Titch," I reply, smiling against his mouth as he bites down on my bottom lip when the pad of my thumb runs over his slit. I trace the thick vein that runs from the base of his cock to the tip.

"Fuck, Titch," he groans, his teeth pulling on my lip before he releases it with a pop and drops his head back under the flow of water. I watch in awe as his Adam's apple bobs up and down and I cup his balls, massaging them gently. His nipples peak, and I can't help it, I capture one in my mouth, sucking on the point. A rumble vibrates up his throat, and his dick grows in my hand. He's bigger than I remember.

"Your turn," I say, a smile creeping over my face as my teeth scrape over the skin of his chest, and my tongue traces the branches of his tattoo. I pump his dick and massage his balls until he's panting, his lips parting with every breath.

"You're killing me, Titch," he grinds out, cupping the back of my neck as he guides my lips back to his nipple, evidently loving the sensation just as much as I enjoy pleasuring him this way.

My lips slide across his chest and capture his other nipple which I lick and tease, all the while pumping him in my hand. He groans, his hands sliding over my hair, my neck, and my shoulders. I feel the slight pressure from his hands, and I know exactly what he wants because I have every intention of giving it to him.

Slowly, I move downwards, kissing my way across his abs and down his happy trail. On my knees, I squeeze him a little tighter, forcing him to focus his attention on me. It's the perfect view as my eyes lift up from the head of his stunning cock, to his glorious chest before finally resting on his beautiful face as he looks down at me. His hair has fallen forward, and a river of water runs from the end as he reaches for my face, his fingers smoothing over my cheek.

"Is this where you tickle my pickle?" he asks roughly, swallowing hard.

I grin, then ever so softly lick the bulbous head of his cock keeping my gaze pinned on him. I've never sucked anyone off before, but I've watched enough pornos to get a good idea of what to do. With a confidence I didn't know I possessed, my lips close over the tip of his cock, my tongue swirling around the ridge. His taste explodes on my tongue, and there's a hint of something salty that makes me groan around him. There's no questioning his excitement.

"Fuck!" York exclaims, bringing his other hand down so that he can cup my face firmly and guide me lower onto his cock. I adjust my position and take him further into my mouth as his fingers curl into my hair. With my hand twisting up and down the base of his cock, I take him in as far as I can, then draw back to suck on the head of his cock gently before repeating the action over again. Unlike the pornos I've watched, he doesn't fuck my mouth until I gag, he simply guides me, allowing me to establish my own rhythm. He thickens in my mouth and when his legs begin to shake and his arse tightens with each gentle thrust, I know he's going to come.

"Titch, I'm gonna come now, baby," he croaks out and with one last jerk of his hips, his hot cum spurts into the back of my throat. I swallow his seed down, licking and sucking until he's spent, my clit throbbing just like the vein beneath his silky skin.

Afterward, York and I wash each other silently. Our hands smoothing over each other gently. There's a kind of peacefulness that falls over us both. We're satiated, yes, but this is more than two people getting off.

This is healing.

I feel it in his touch as he washes me, and see it in his eyes as he looks down at me. York gets erect again, but he doesn't make any move to take it further, and in a way I'm grateful. It's been too easy to get lost in him. Stepping out of the shower, I wrap my body up in a towel, watching him closely. He seems distracted, and a little bead of worry begins to grow bigger inside my chest.

"What is it?" I ask, cocking my head to the side.

"We're still in the now, okay. It can wait. I'll give you a minute to get dressed," he says, pressing a lingering kiss against my forehead before stepping out into the hallway and closing the door behind him.

Concentrating on the task at hand, I dry myself and pull on my clothes. I've no idea what time it is, but given how long I've been with York I know I've missed Xeno's lesson. He's going to be angry... Honestly, he can stand in line. What's one more pissed off man to add to the long list?

Running a hand through my wet hair in an attempt to get the tangles out, I hear a loud knock on the front door. Whoever's on the other side isn't feeling particularly patient.

"Hold up, I'm coming!" York shouts, striding past me in just a pair of slacks as I open the bathroom door and step out into the hallway.

Xeno is standing in the doorway.

Oh, fuck.

It's too late to go back into the bathroom as his eyes find mine. Xeno scowls, and my skin heats at the glare he's giving me, but I remain steady, refusing to apologise for what's happened. Xeno rips his gaze from me to York, and I see his fists clenching. There's no doubt what we've been up to seeing as we're both sporting wet hair, flushed cheeks, and swollen lips. Not to mention York is bare-chested and looking at me with a heavy dose of lust, still sporting a semi from our intimate moment in the shower.

"What?" York asks, leaning against the wall casually. He folds his arms over his chest and waits.

Xeno's lip curls up into a snarl as he gives York a death

glare. "You *know* fucking what," he says, before turning his attention to me. "What the fuck are you doing here?"

"Don't speak to her like that," York says, a warning note in his voice.

Xeno's head snaps back to York. "Are you for real?"

York pinches his arm. "Pretty fucking sure I'm not a statue."

"Look," I say, interrupting. "Clearly you're angry, but honestly, I really don't give a fuck."

"Come again—" Xeno snaps.

"I said, I don't give a fuck. I've long since stopped caring about what you think, Xeno. I'm here with York. In fact, I was just in the shower with him, and last night I was on a date with Zayn. I kissed him too, though I think you know that already, right? Isn't that why you're here now to try and control what's happening between York and me? Did you get to Dax already, is that why he dropped me for Tiffany?"

"The fuck!" he snaps, anger blazing in his eyes. "You've no fucking idea what you're talking about."

"Time to go, Xeno," York says, placing the flat of his palm on Xeno's chest, giving him an intense look that seems to stop him in his tracks. He slams his mouth shut on whatever bullshit he was about to spew. "Go, Xeno."

"*Jeb* needs to see us tonight. He wants to meet us at Rocks, ten o'clock sharp."

"Got it." York nods tightly, a brief flash of concern crossing his face.

"York?" I question.

"It'll be fine, Titch. Don't sweat it," he replies. His casual response only worries me more. He focuses his attention back on Xeno. "Is there anything else?"

Xeno snarls, his top lip literally pulling up over his teeth then his eyes snap back to mine. "You need to catch up with what you missed. I want to see you in my studio at eight. Don't be late," he orders.

I should tell him to go fuck himself, but I don't. Whatever he has planned isn't a bachata lesson, and like a train wreck waiting to happen, I know there's no point in putting off the inevitable.

"Fine, *Teach*," I respond, refusing to feel intimidated. "Will Tiffany be in attendance like the last time? She seems more than willing to assist you. Though, honestly, I thought you had better taste." I bark out a laugh, unable to help myself.

"This isn't a fucking joke. I thought being here meant something to you. Instead, you're *fucking* around," he spits, looking at me with disgust.

"One, why do you even give a shit, and two, I'm not *fucking* around," I retort angrily, understanding his insinuation and hating it.

He snorts. "Whatever you need to tell yourself, Pen. Does Zayn know about this?" he asks, and my cheeks flush. Fuck him for making me feel like what I just shared with York was wrong. I've not had a chance to discuss what's happening between York and me with Zayn and vice versa. It's a conversation we all need to have, but fuck Xeno for shoving my apparent lack of transparency in my face.

"Fuck you, Xeno," I snap.

"That's enough, dickhead," York snaps, placing his arm around my waist and pulling me into his side. "Go cool the fuck off. Titch will see you later, and the rest of us will see you at the club."

York doesn't bother to wait for Xeno to respond, he simply slams the door in his face and pulls me into his arms.

"What a prick," I mutter.

York presses a kiss against the top of my head. "I'm sorry Xeno's being such a dick. He's angry because he doesn't know how to unravel how he feels about you. He's hurting, Pen. He cares. I know he fucking does," York says, making me wonder who he's trying to convince more, me or himself.

I push back against his chest and look up at him. "I should go."

York nods, his arms falling to his side. He knows as well as I do that the moment between us is gone. We both have a lot of thinking to do. York can pretend that what Xeno says doesn't matter, but I know him, and it does.

"I'll talk with him—"

"Don't trouble yourself," I say. "If Xeno has something to say to me, he can do that all by himself."

As I let myself into my flat, I can't help but wonder who's the bigger liar of the two, York because he believes Xeno cares, or Xeno because he's adamant he doesn't.

Closing my door behind me, I lean against the wood and close my eyes, my brother's words once again ringing in my head.

"You're going to make them fall in love with you again... Then when the time is right, we are going to destroy them once and for all."

Who's the liar now?

23

Pen

It's ten minutes past eight, and I'm purposely late. Screw Xeno and his demands. He's being an arsehole. How dare he say I'm *fucking around*? We all knew he was talking about me reconnecting with Zayn and York, rather than not taking my position at the Academy seriously. It makes me wonder if that's what he thought of me when we were kids. Deep down, did he genuinely believe that I was a slut wanting to be with them all by refusing to choose?

I *couldn't* choose because I loved them equally.

I fucking loved *him*.

Heaving a sigh, I decide that I won't let him get under my skin anymore tonight. He's taken up residence in my thoughts for too long already today. I'm going to get this torture over with and then drink myself into oblivion with Clancy straight after. It's her birthday next Sunday and I've got a plan that I hope she'll enjoy.

Pushing open the stairwell door onto the third floor, the Academy is quiet, and the hall dark save for a light on in Xeno's studio at the end of the corridor. All the students have gone home, and the rest of the scholarship students are either in their flats or out for the evening. I saw Tiffany and Sophie heading out about half an hour ago dressed to impress. I might not like the pair, but I have to admit, they have style. No doubt they're heading back to The Pink Albatross. It is Friday night after all, and those who can afford to go more than once, do. Rather them than me. I won't ever return there, not when I know Jeb owns that place. It does make me wonder about D-Neath though, given that's supposed to be *his* club. Actually, I've been wondering about the whole reason the Breakers are here and am now convinced it has everything to do with D-Neath and the plans I overheard him talking about with Madam Tuillard.

As I walk towards Xeno's studio, I brush my hands over my skin tight black jeans, benching those thoughts for now. My brother is going to call soon, it's been a while since we spoke and I'm going to have to have *something* to tell him.

My phone vibrates for the hundredth time in the last half hour and I reach into my back pocket of my jeans, pulling it out. I shake my head, clicking on the message from Clancy.

Clancy: Don't forget. Drinks. My flat. 9pm. River's coming. Want me to invite York and Zayn?

Clancy ends the message with a wink emoji, and I roll my eyes. She's been bugging me all afternoon about what happened between York and me earlier today. I was hoping to have her to myself tonight so I can share, but she's invited River over to her place so any convo about the boys will have to wait. I like River, he's a cool guy, so I don't begrudge her their friendship. Besides, I couldn't think of anything worse than sitting in her flat between York and Zayn whilst River and Clancy watch us like some kind of side-show. Not that they'd go anyway even if they were invited.

Clancy: So…?

Me: Ha Ha! Nope.

I can see the three bubbles moving as she types a response.

Clancy: If you want to spend the night with them I won't be offended. Gotta admit, I've always wondered what a ménage á trois would be like.

She follows it up with a wink emoji, drool emoji and two eggplants.

Me: Sod off Clancy.

Clancy: Seriously, girl. I don't mind.

Me: I want to spend time with you. Besides, I have an idea for your birthday. I wanna chat to you about it.

Clancy: Oh yay! Atta girl!

Me: See you at nine.

The three bubbles move again, but I shove my mobile

phone back in the pocket of my black jeans and ignore the vibrations of a new message. It's probably just a string of emojis anyway. The girl's fixated with the damn things. Sometimes she sends me text message after text message filled with emojis that I have to decode. It's just as well really because *all* of them are rude. She's a saucy minx, that's for sure. I've no doubt she'd enjoy a ménage á trois. Knowing her, she's already experienced one. My thoughts stray to the memory of York and Dax when we were younger. Fairly sure Clancy would enjoy *that* memory just as much as I do. To this day, I'm not sure if Xeno has any idea what happened that night. I doubt it.

Reaching the studio, I take a deep, steadying breath and ready myself for Xeno's attitude, then push open the door, repeating the same mantra in my head.

It's just a dance lesson. I'm just catching up with what I missed. It doesn't mean anything.

I've been telling myself those lies over and over again. Whatever Xeno has planned for me, I'm not stupid enough to believe it's catching up on what I missed today.

"You're late," he snaps, meeting my gaze in the reflection of the mirror. Moody fucker.

"This look takes time, you know," I sass back, doing a little twirl on my heeled biker boots that are totally inappropriate for a dance lesson. It was another purposeful move on my part. Being small isn't something I enjoy for the most part. These boots give me at least another three inches. I don't feel so *Tiny* in them. Xeno turns to face me, leaning his arse against the edge of the table which he also grips with his hands a bit too firmly in my opinion. His heated gaze roves over me slowly, and even though I'm feeling more than a little uncomfortable under his scrutiny, I sure as fuck don't let it show. Instead, I cock my head, allowing my hair to fall over my shoulder.

"Didn't know you liked Black Sabbath," he says, commenting on my top.

"Why would you? We're not friends. I'm not sure we ever really were," I say, stepping towards him. It pains me to say that, but his insult earlier hurt, and ever the petty bitch, I want to hurt him back. So sue me.

He nods, pushing upwards off the table, a strange look on his face. For a beat he just stares at me then seems to make a decision. Picking up a chair from beside the table he strides to the centre of the room, dropping it down so that it's facing the mirror. "Take a seat, Pen," he says, tapping the back of the chair.

"I thought you wanted me to catch up on what I missed out on today. If that's not the case, then I have better things to do."

"That was the original plan, but given you're refusing to take me or my classes seriously, I've decided to switch shit up. *Sit down*, Pen."

"Why?" I ask, suddenly feeling nervous. There's a knot of anxiety in my chest that has gotten more twisted every second that I've been in the room with him. He's always made me feel on edge. Even as kids, I was always that bit more nervous around him than the others, and I hate that after all this time it still feels the same way. Back when I was a kid it was because he never quite opened up to me in the same way as Dax, York and Zayn did. He always held back that little bit of himself, and I never quite felt good enough, like he didn't trust me enough, or even like me enough to fully open himself up to me. Now, he's even more closed off. He's a stranger, and that hurts. He's also an arsehole, and that makes me feel a tiny bit better. It's easier to dislike an arsehole.

"Just sit." He turns his back on me and picks up his mobile phone flicking through it, completely oblivious to my current indecision.

I should walk away. I should tell him to go fuck himself right now. I don't because when it comes to Xeno, I've never been able to say no. It's that little girl in me who still craves his approval, his acceptance. He was the last piece to our puzzle that never allowed himself to fit, and when he did, it was too fucking late. It pisses me off that he seems to know that and is using my weakness against me. Then again, walking out of here wouldn't be any better either. So, I remove my phone from the back pocket of my very tight jeans, and sit, resting it on my lap.

Xeno strides over to the door, locking it, then reaches for the hem of his t-shirt and pulls it off, chucking it on the floor. He flexes his neck, rocking his head from side-to-side like he's about to step into the ring and fight. I swallow hard, hiding my surprise and prickling of fear behind bravado. It worked for me as a kid, it'll work for me now.

"What's this? Some kind of pissing contest, Xeno. Are you jealous and needing to make a point? I thought you had no interest in me, but here you are getting naked?" I reel off. What the fuck is he doing? More to the point, why is he so damn hot? I will my cheeks not to flush. I do *not* want him to know how much he turns me on despite his cuntish attitude.

We are not friends, and we sure as fuck aren't lovers.

He smirks. "I find I can dance better unencumbered," he says, sounding ridiculous.

Unencumbered? Did he swallow a damn dictionary tonight? "It means not having any *burden*."

"I know what it means, Xeno. Out of the five of us, it was me who actually bothered going to school the most. What're you gonna do next, grab a dictionary and start *lambasting* me with words? I'm a street kid, and whilst sticks and stones may break my bones, names sure as fuck won't hurt me."

"No, that's not what's gonna happen tonight." He smiles evilly, like the hottest fucking devil who knows he's as beautiful as much as he's dangerous. I grit my jaw, my gaze roving over his body as he circles me, all predatory.

"You know if you wanted to fuck me, perhaps you should've taken your chance at Grim's club. Oh, wait, Jeb didn't give you permission to *rape* me like he did Zayn..." I snarl.

"And yet two days later, you let Zayn fuck you with his fingers because of a few sweet words and smooth moves in the studio," he bites back, sneering.

"Number one, *fuck you*, and number two, how the fuck do you know what happened?" I move to stand, but he rushes forward, and places his hands on the backrest, lowering his gaze to meet mine, his lips pulling up over his teeth.

"Number one," he retorts, mimicking me, "I'm the one who holds the Breakers together so I make it my business to know what's going on and number two, you should lock the fucking door to the studio if you want some privacy!"

"You piece of shit," I snap, my cheeks roaring with heat at the thought he had watched Zayn and me, just like he did when we were kids. What is he, some kind of voyeur?

"I gotta give him credit. He's smooth, real fucking smooth."

"Fuck you!" I flinch looking away, not able to hold his stare. My eyes catch on something glinting at his neck. It's the same necklace Zayn gave me that night at Rocks. It was their birthday gift to me.

"That's my necklace," I say, reaching for it, but Xeno captures my wrist, preventing me from touching it.

"No, it's not. This is *mine*. The Breakers are my brothers, Pen, and I will do *anything* to protect them."

"I'm not a threat," I lie, because the truth is, I am and Xeno knows it.

"That's where you're wrong. You threaten *everything* and I'll be damned if I watch them fall for you again only for you to break their fucking hearts. You need to stay the fuck away from them." With that Xeno steps back, lifts his head and says, "Play track twenty-two."

I recognise the track immediately. It's *You Broke Me First* by Tate McRae. The singer is a few years younger than me and is a dancer as well. I remember watching her on some American dance show. Girl's got talent.

She's edgy. Current. Cool.

The song begins to play, and for the whole first verse Xeno just fucking stares at me like some goddamn creeper. As she sings, the words feel too raw, too specific to our situation. I grab my phone and stand but Xeno steps forward once again and I drop to my seat.

"You will sit there, and you will watch *me* dance this time, Pen." There's a steeliness to his gaze, a coldness that makes me swallow hard. When did he get so fucking cruel? I must've asked that question out loud because he laughs bitterly, stepping away from me. "I told you before. I'm no longer that boy you knew." Then he flips backwards, lifting so high in the air that I forget for a moment to hate him and only watch in astonishment as he performs a series of tumbles that are damn near perfect.

Xeno's head snaps up, and he pins me with his glittering green eyes. His chest heaves, and if the words to the song weren't a big enough clue to how he's feeling, the expression on his face doesn't leave any room for misunderstandings.

Then he dances.

Not bachata.

Not hip-hop.

But *lyrical*. He dances to express the words of the song and every damn move he makes is like a knife gutting my stomach. York was correct. He *is* hurting, and it's painful to watch.

But that doesn't make this right.

I danced the way I did to prevent myself from getting raped.

He's dancing to hurt me.

With every step he rips up the friendship we had as kids and leaves it in tatters across the studio floor. With every jerk of his torso, and snap of his limbs, he shreds my heart.

The tears come this time, and there's nothing I can do to stop them.

If Xeno notices my tears, it doesn't prevent him from sliding the knife in further.

He glares at me, every sinew and muscle taut and angry as he dances. There's no softness to his movements, there's no empathy in his gaze, no understanding.

Just anger. Raw, painful anger.

He thinks *I've* got a nerve wanting to reconnect. He doesn't believe I deserve them. Well, fuck him.

On the other side of the studio, Xeno drops his head, his shoulders stiffening as he breathes heavily. My stomach tightens, and my heart squeezes painfully. He's so fucking lost in his anger, and I hate it. Why can't he let it go? Why can't he allow himself to see past his own pain?

"Xeno..."

His head snaps back up at the sound of my voice and his eyes narrow.

Fuck.

Xeno sprints towards me, all that anger and pain forcing his legs to move, then he throws his legs out in front of him and slides across the floor. I stiffen, waiting for the moment of impact, but his feet meet the front chair legs and he pushes me across the floor a few feet from the force. My heart hammers inside my chest as he looks up at me from his position on the floor.

"Xeno, stop," I whisper.

My voice comes out weak, and I hate that. It doesn't reflect how I feel inside. I'm angry, livid, and so utterly heartbroken. Swallowing hard, I wipe at the tears on my face and maintain his gaze. I want him to know that I hurt just as much as he does, that he doesn't get exclusive rights to pain.

He shakes his head and grits his jaw then pushes upwards onto his feet and continues to dance. Every step is as angry as the last. By the time he's finished, I'm as heartbroken as I was that night at Rocks when I walked away.

"Now you know how *I* feel," he grinds out, striding towards me, a light sheen of sweat covering his skin. "Get out of my studio, Pen."

But I can't seem to move. Instead, my gaze drops from his eyes to the tattoo on his right arm that I've seen from a distance but haven't looked at closely before now. There's an anatomical drawing of a heart surrounded by a diamond shape. Three of the points have circles and the lowest point merges with the bottom of the shattered heart, broken pieces falling into a coin with large cracks running through it.

A *penny*.

I reach for it, my fingers stroking over the shattered heart, and resting on the coin. Beneath the Queen's head is a name.

Tiny.

"Xeno?" I question, looking up to meet his gaze once more.

"You broke me first," he accuses, echoing the title of the song.

24

Pen

We gaze at each other as a fist wraps itself around my stomach and squeezes hard. My heart fucking aches for him. It aches for me, for all of us. I see the loss of what could've been right there in his eyes before he blinks it away furiously, refusing to acknowledge that feeling.

"We broke each other, Xeno. You chose the Skins long before I ever chose Jeb," I counter sadly.

Xeno scoffs, stepping back and away from me like I'm some kind of bad smell or poisonous creature he can't be within a few metres of. The tiny moment of softness in his eyes is gone, snatched away once more by his furious need to *hate*.

"What did he promise you, Pen? Was it riches? Was it a guaranteed place here at the Academy? Did he promise you that all your dreams would come true, huh?"

"No, it wasn't like that." I wrap my fingers around my phone and grit my jaw, standing. The chair scrapes over the wooden floor as I do. I'm still not tall enough to match him in height, but my heeled boots give me an extra few inches. I straighten my spine and raise my jaw in defiance. Angry that he could think so little of me.

"No? Did he *fuck* you good then? Was that it? Did he fuck you better than the four of us would, given half the chance? Did he take your fucking virginity, Pen? Or did he loan you out as some kind of whore? Did you *let* him?"

The sound of my hand slapping his face rings out before I've even realised what I've done. His head snaps around, the sting of my slap is a bright red mark against his cheek. My chest heaves as more angry tears burn my eyes. "How fucking *dare* you!"

"That's more like it. That's the girl I knew," he says, pinning me with his green eyes that are like two broken bottles glinting in the sunlight. "Where the fuck did she go?"

"What?" I snap, barely holding on.

"That night. Where did that girl go, Pen? Who the fuck was that person who sat at our table and fucking broke us? Who the fuck was she? Because she sure as fuck wasn't the girl we knew. She *wasn't* Tiny."

"I didn't go anywhere," I say, looking away from the intensity of his stare, my throat closing over, unbearable pain lancing through my chest.

"You walked the fuck away, Pen! Just like all the other girls who fucking used us to get to *him*," he spits.

"Who?" I ask.

"Jeb! Who the fuck do you think? All those girls we trusted over the years. Every last one of them used us, used the Breakers to get to him. We thought you were different. We believed you when you said you loved us!" he shouts.

"I—" I begin but slam my mouth shut. I didn't know that. I

just assumed the boys dumped them, not the other way around. My chest is heaving, fucking tears well behind my eyes but I blink them back. I will not cry. I fucking won't.

"Was it his status? The allure of the big-dicked gangster."

"No," I shake my head, but he doesn't appear to be listening.

"You said *we* were the ones you wanted, and when we gave you that, you fucking shat on us."

"You *were* the ones I wanted," I say, but even to my own ears it sounds feeble. Not that Xeno hears me. He's too lost to his rant.

"We were a fucking family, Pen. You fucked us up. You fucked *me* up!" he roars, gripping hold of my upper arms. "Look at me. Look at what I've become!"

And I do look. I do see what he's become, and it makes me feel nauseous. He really has changed, but he doesn't get to pin that on me and use me as an excuse.

No. No fucking way.

"I'm not responsible for how you choose to behave, Xeno. Yes, I walked. Yes, I broke your hearts, but I haven't seen you for three goddamn years. I didn't make you into this person. You did that all by yourself," I say, swiping at the tears rolling down my face. "You don't get to blame me for that. You don't get to blame me for everything *you've* done in *his* name whilst we've been apart. So don't you dare accuse me of breaking us first when I lost all four of you to Jeb way before that night." I shove my hands against his chest as hard as I can, and he stumbles backwards. Shock and sadness replaces the self-righteous anger and pain.

I don't hang around. I'm done with him.

I'm fucking done.

He reaches the door just before I do, and I almost collide into his body. "We are not fucking done," he growls.

"Get the fuck out of my way, Xeno!" I'm shaking so much that my teeth are chattering. "I'm not doing this with you. You wanted me to leave, so I'm leaving."

"I've changed my damn mind. We're doing this right the fuck now."

I glare at him, my heart pounding loudly. Everything hurts.

He's hurting.

I'm hurting.

But neither of us can take the leap to end the torment.

"What the fuck do you want from me, Xeno?" I shout, livid now.

"I want the damn truth!" he roars back.

I blink, stepping away from him, from his red-hot wrath. For a moment we just stare at one another and I swear I see guilt flash across his gaze before he hardens his heart again.

"Pen—" he growls.

"Fine. You want the truth. You've fucking got it," I bite back, striding over to the sound system and plugging in my mobile phone. Yanking off my shoes, I flick through to find the perfect track, hit play, then walk into the middle of the room.

Xeno watches me warily, his jaw tight, his arms folded across his chest as he leans back against the door. His bare chest is covered in a sheen of sweat, the taut muscles of his abs pronounced against his skin.

The piano intro begins and as soon Jorja Smith starts to sing *Let Me Down*, Xeno's chest heaves. He draws in a deep, shuddering breath, knowing this song just as well as I do. Good, then he'll get the meaning well enough. When this song released, the Breakers had been gone a year. I'd still been a heartbroken, lonely mess and this song hit me hard. Nothing's changed.

It still hits me hard, I'm still a broken mess.

Fixing my gaze on Xeno, I tip my head back and bend backwards, raising my hands in the air as I do. My right foot draws a circle in front of me as I pull upright and push forward onto the ball of my foot, drawing my left leg behind me in a kick that crosses my body. I land unsteadily, the emotion of the song, the burning fire in Xeno's eyes and the confrontation between us still coursing through my blood. My steps falter just like my shattered heart.

Jorja Smith sings about being let down, and I feel her words as if they're my own. Pulling myself upright on unsteady legs, I grasp my face, swiping at the wetness on my cheeks with the back of my hand. I hold his gaze, refusing to look away, refusing to back down or hide my feelings. My mask was ripped from me that night at Grim's club and I haven't quite been able to put it back on again. It doesn't fit anymore.

Xeno slams his fist against the door, his veins popping beneath the skin of his forearms. I know he gets it.

He understands what I'm trying to say.

He let me down.

They all did.

Just like I let them down.

It's all such a fucking mess.

When Stormzy starts to sing, I kick up my leg in a vertical hold before slamming it back down.

I let go.

Jerking my body so that my hips go left whilst my torso goes right, I fling out my arms, my hair lashing around my head like a damn whip as I spin, using Xeno as my spot so I don't get dizzy. Grabbing my left wrist in my right hand, I yank myself towards Xeno, my finger pointing at my wrist as though a watch ticks there. Stormzy sings about squandering time, about missing precious moments. The lyrics echo the resentment I feel inside.

Three long years.

Three years to make mistakes.

To harden our hearts.

To shore up our defences.

Wasted time.

Squandered.

God, I've fucking missed him.

I hold my arms out to Xeno, my fingers splayed as I reach for the boy I loved, to the man I'm angry with now. For all his bitter and hateful words, I still love him. I don't think I'll ever stop. Why is love so fucking painful? Why does it have the power to bring us to our knees?

Our eyes meet, and he glares at me, but still he refuses to let the hurt go. His mouth presses into a hard line and he knocks his head back against the door, slamming his eyes shut.

Fucking stubborn bastard.

I scoff, spinning away then ducking low. Sweeping my leg out before I lean on my right hand and flick into a walkover. When I look back over at him, he's staring at me, his body vibrating with tension. I walk towards him slowly, fully aware of the frantic beat of my heart and the desperate need to hold him. Stopping a few feet away I draw in a deep breath then jerk my chin up with my knuckles. Jorja's words flow over me. Reminding me of the girl who was never quite sure if I was good enough for him.

Those same insecurities that plagued me over the years when we were friends flood me now. They twist me up with self-loathing, with guilt, with hurt. They wrap around me as I try to shake them off, as I throw my arms and legs out and spin away from him in a series of open split leaps.

No.

I *was* good enough.

Xeno *pushed* me away when we were kids.

He *made* me fucking choose.

He *watched* me walk away, and never questioned it.

He *saw* me fucking bleed out my soul when I danced at Grim's club and it did nothing but make him question my intentions. Xeno doesn't trust me and he can't fucking bear to see me reconnect with his brothers.

He's *let me down* in the worst possible way.

But at least I'm willing to *try*, despite everything against us.

At least I'm willing to look past the damn graveyard of our friendship and attempt at building bridges.

Xeno's a motherfucking coward.

I stop dancing and pull up straight, forcing my shoulders back. Striding over to my shoes, I snatch them up and abruptly end the song, then grab my mobile phone. He tracks my every move as I walk towards him, lighting my skin with his wrath.

"You're not going anywhere," he snarls, gripping hold of my arm as I reach for the door handle.

"This is over," I say softly. He barks out a laugh. There's a wildness in his eyes that scares me, that flips a switch inside my chest. I *will not* let him hurt me. If he dares to fucking touch me, I will fight. "What are you going to do, Xeno? Prove to me how much of a big bad gangster you are, huh? Are you going to *hurt* me, is that it? Is that what you do for Jeb, Xeno? Do you hurt people and get off on it? Is that why you're here? To hurt me, to keep me in line for Jeb, or are you this mad because York and Zayn aren't following your rules anymore, that they're making their own minds up? Are you pissed because they're choosing *me*, just like I warned you they might when we were kids?"

Xeno's eyes widen, my words somehow hitting their mark, and it makes me wonder how close to the truth I really am. I don't have to wonder for long.

"Yes, I've hurt people, Pen. I've done it in Jeb's name, in the Skins' name and I fucking loathe myself for it. I'm ashamed of the man I've become, and it eats me up inside, but do you know what I'm *not* ashamed of?" he asks, his fingers squeezing tightly to the point of pain.

"What, Xeno?" I hush out.

"I'm not ashamed of the fact that I did it to protect *them*. To protect my brothers. Everything I do is for Zayn, York, and Dax. That is what *love* is, Pen. Not walking away, not turning your back on people you care about when it gets too hard." He's panting now, his body shaking with feeling and I let out a sad laugh.

"I know everything about protecting the ones you love," I say softly, gutted that he thinks so very little of me. His eyes flash with pain, then confusion, and I reach up to cup his cheek, tempering his painful grip with a soft touch of my own. He flinches, but he doesn't pull away. "Because that's what I did too. That's what *I* did, Xeno. You were just too angry to see it. You're *still* too angry to see it." My hand drops from his face, and this time he doesn't prevent me from leaving. This time he lets me go.

Ten minutes later, with a face covered in make-up to hide the blotchiness of my skin, I plaster on a fake smile and sip some cheap white wine whilst Clancy and River try to entertain me with their drunken banter. It's just as well we're drinking because it's easier to pretend that your heart isn't a bloody mess when alcohol numbs the pain.

25

Pen

Lena grins, throwing her arms around my shoulders and squeezing me tightly. "Pen, I've missed you!"

"I've missed you too," I laugh, guiding her to the booth and away from all the prying eyes.

This is our favourite café in Hackney and most of the locals come here too. Pietro, the owner, makes the most amazing cakes and the best hot chocolate in London. We don't often get to come here, but now that I've got enough food to last me until my first payday, I figured I could spend my remaining tenner on a couple of hot chocolates and a slice of chocolate cake to share between us. I've still not quite recovered from the killer hangover from Friday night with Clancy and River, and I need a sugar hit, stat. I spent most of Saturday in bed avoiding everyone, but feel considerably better today. I seem to be good at burying my head in the sand when the need arises. Not that I needed to hide, given I haven't seen *any* of the Breakers since

Friday. I've tried not to think too much about what they were meeting Jeb for or what they've been up to since. I figure if shit went down, I would've found out about it by now.

"I've loads to tell you about the school trip. Who knew the Isle of Wight could be so much fun! I thought only old people lived there."

I laugh, capturing the attention of Pietro with a wave and a smile. He comes over to take our order. Once he's returned to the counter, I turn my attention back to Lena. "So, you enjoyed yourself then?"

"It was so good! I shared a room with Simone and Laura. We snuck some booze into our suitcases and got pissed every night. It was such a laugh."

"Lena, you could've gotten caught!"

"Yeah, but we didn't. Besides, we weren't the only ones who did it. What's the headteacher gonna do, suspend all the students for doing the same thing? They'd have no one left in the year." She giggles, rolling her eyes.

"It was supposed to be an informative trip. You were supposed to be learning shit, Lena, not getting drunk every night."

"I *was* learning shit. I learnt that local boys are all pussies and don't like being dared. I also learnt that Teddy Smith in our year has a nine inch cock, and that he likes his balls being tickled when he's getting sucked off."

"What?! You're fourteen, Lena!" I hiss, shocked at the thought. "Who the fuck is Teddy Smith?"

Her grin blows wide and she starts laughing. When she's finally calmed down, she swipes at the tears falling from her eyes and shakes her head. "Seriously, Pen, your face! Oh my god! *I* didn't give him a blowjob, that was *Simone*. Besides, I'm almost fifteen."

I blow out a breath, shaking my head at her. "I'm not even sure that's any better. She's your best friend and also *fourteen*."

"Seriously, don't tell me *you* were any better behaved at our age. You hung out with the Breakers and everyone knows they're manwhores. Come on, you must've gotten up to shit with them."

"They were my *friends*, Lena. It wasn't like that between us." At least not at fourteen, but she doesn't need to know that.

She gives me a 'yeah right,' look and shakes her head. She's way sassier than I ever was at her age. I'm not sure that's a good thing either. Sassy can get you into a whole heap of shit.

"Want my advice?" I ask.

"Nope, but I know you'll give it to me anyway," she says, waving her hand in the air as Pietro comes back with our order. We both thank him and wait for him to return to his other customers before picking up our conversation.

"You should keep away from boys; they're nothing but trouble and no giving blowjobs until you're at least twenty-five."

Lena pulls a face. "Why do *I* have to be the good one? You didn't keep away from the Breakers, and you're seriously telling me you've never given a man a blowy."

My cheeks flush with the memory of me on my knees in the shower with York. Thankfully, Lena's way too interested in devouring the slice of chocolate cake to notice.

"I did keep away from the Breakers... eventually," I say, batting away her comment. "Besides, you need to learn from my mistakes and make better choices than I did. Just because Simone is happy to give someone a blowy, doesn't mean you should. You need to be *good*," I say sternly.

"Being good is boring, I'd rather be like you."

"What's that supposed to mean?"

"You know, I want to be *cool*. Hanging out with the bad boys, getting up to stuff I shouldn't. I want to have fun, Pen. Like you did when you hung out with the Breakers."

"Firstly, being cool doesn't equal getting up to no good, and the Breakers weren't *bad boys* just misunderstood. Plus, I'd rather you not blow some kid, and get an education. I want you to make something of yourself, okay?"

"And you're *not* making something of yourself? Come on, Pen. You're, like, living your dream. You're a *dancer*. All my friends want to be like you."

"I've managed to get into the Academy, yes, but that's no guarantee of a future in dance. I'm fully aware of that fact."

"Urgh, have a little faith in yourself. Jeez, mum really did a number on you, didn't she?"

"That's not what this is about. I'm *realistic*. I've got nothing to fall back on should my whole dream go to shit, Lena. I went to school, but I didn't really try. Don't be me. Don't make the same mistake. Have a back-up plan."

"Yeah, yeah, okay," she replies, doing a good job at eating all of the chocolate cake. I don't mind, the hot chocolate is enough of a sugar hit for me anyway.

"So, how's mum?" I ask, feeling like it's something I have to say because truthfully, I really don't care how she is, I only care in relation to how she's looking after Lena.

"She's mum," Lena responds, shrugging.

"What does that mean?"

Lena pulls a face.

"Lena!" I warn. "What are you hiding?"

"She forgot to come pick me up Friday afternoon when I got back from my trip. It was so embarrassing waiting for her long after everyone else went home. Eventually Miss Spratt felt sorry for me and offered to drop me home. I had to make an excuse about her being caught up at work. She was passed out on the sofa when I got in. I think she had one glass too many."

"That irresponsible bitch!" I growl. "Why didn't you call me? I would've come got you."

"It was cool, honestly. Besides, I didn't want you to get into trouble having to leave a lesson to come get me. I don't want to get in the way of your dream."

"Lena," I say, leaning over the table to grab her hand in mine. "You're my top priority. Always. No matter what."

Lena gives me a half smile, the little dimple in her left cheek showing. "Yeah, but I shouldn't be. That's mum's job. You're not my mum, Pen. She is."

"I'm well aware of that and I don't care. I'm here for you. Next time something goes wrong, you call me, okay?"

"But—"

"You call me," I insist.

Lena nods, and I see the weight she's been carrying lift from her shoulders. Guilt attacks me. I hate leaving her alone with our mum. I'd always been the buffer between Lena and my mum's addiction and nasty behaviour. Now Lena has to face it on her own, and it guts me.

"I can deal with it. You had to."

"But that's the whole point. No one should have to deal with that shit."

"Yeah, I know," she sighs. "But I swear, Pen. I can handle Mum. I just give her some painkillers and put her to bed if she's semi-sober. Otherwise, I let her sleep it off. It's no big deal."

Anger boils inside my chest. Lena's a kid. She shouldn't have to deal with this. I can't stand it. "Maybe I can find a flat or something. You could move in with me..." I voice out loud, trying to find a solution to the problem

"Pen, I *know* you don't have the money for that."

"I'm starting a new job in a couple of weeks—"

"Wait, what? You didn't say! So you're not working at Rocks anymore?"

"Nope, and my new employer pays better too. If I can save for a couple of months, I could get a deposit together for a cheap rental somewhere. Like a studio flat or something. If mum's getting worse I can't risk leaving you with her. It's not safe."

"No, Pen. I know you see me as a kid, but I'm not a baby. I swear I can handle it. Save your money and then maybe when you've finished the scholarship at the Academy and have an amazing job in a West End show we can talk about this again."

"Lena—"

"I can handle Mum." She gives me a determined look. It's the look of a kid who's had to grow up too fast. It's the look of a kid who's already jaded by the world, and I fucking hate it.

"I don't like this, not one bit, Lena," I say, swiping a hand over my face. "Promise me you'll call the second anything goes wrong. I mean it. If you need me, I don't care what time of day or night it is. You call, understand?"

"I understand. Besides, I spend most of my time at Laura's or Simone's house so it's cool."

"Don't their parents mind?"

"Nah, believe it or not teenage girls are always in each other's houses. It's totally normal. Not everyone was bestfriends with a bunch of boys like you."

"Okay, well good. As long as they don't start sniffing about. The last thing we need is social services asking questions."

"Chill, okay? It's all good. I'm gonna stay at Laura's for a couple of nights anyhow. I'm meeting her today." She gives me a smile then looks at her watch, wincing.

"What?"

"I gotta go…"

"Go where?"

"I told you, to Laura's house," Lena says slowly. "Me and the girls are doing this TikTok thing… We've got this whole new idea we think will get us a load of followers. I said I'd hang with them." She screws up her nose, looking two parts cute and one part guilty.

"So long as this new idea doesn't involve anything illegal," I warn, giving her my best big-sister glare.

"No, I swear. It's all good fun. Promise."

"Fine! Go, be with your friends. Have *fun*, don't get into trouble, and ring me later, 'kay?"

She grins. "Are you sure? I could arrange to meet them in another hour or so?"

"Nah. It's all good. I've got to choreograph a new routine anyway. It's no biggie. Come on, let's hug it out. I'll walk you to the bus stop."

A FEW HOURS LATER, I'm just putting the finishing touches on my choreography that I've been working on for my first performance at Grim's club when my phone starts ringing. With sweat dripping down my spine, I pick it up.

It's my brother.

Fuck.

Bile rises in my throat, but I swallow it down. I need to remain calm.

"David."

"Hey, *Sis*, it's so good to hear from you... Oh, wait. You've not bothered to call me at all. What the fuck's up with that?"

"I've been busy doing what you asked," I reply, holding my voice steady even when I'm fucking trembling.

"Is that so? Want to tell me what you've found out?"

Curling my fingers into my palm enough that my nails dig into my skin, I take a deep breath. The only thing I can tell him is what I overheard between Madame Tuillard and D-Neath. It's not much, but at least I'm not betraying the Breakers. "D-Neath wants to use the Academy for something nefarious. I haven't been able to find out exactly what just yet, but Madame Tuillard isn't happy about it. In fact she refused—"

"And?" he demands, his voice cool.

"And that's it. That's all I have."

"ARE YOU FUCKING KIDDING ME, PENELOPE!" he roars into the phone so loud that I have to pull it away from my ear. Anger like this would've earned me a punch to the face. Thank God he's still living on the other side of the world.

"I'm trying, okay?" I plead.

"Not fucking hard enough!"

"D-Neath just got out of prison after a stint inside for drug racketeering. I think maybe he's taken up that line of work again."

"No fucking shit, Sherlock," David says with a heavy dose of sarcasm. "Listen very carefully, I want to know what the fuck he's up to, and I want to know if the Breakers and Jeb are in on it. Which, given the fact they're conveniently at the Academy, is a no fucking brainer."

"It's not as easy as that—"

"No? Just use your *charms*, Penelope. Fuck one of them. Hell, fuck *all* of them at once," he sneers. By the tone of his voice he isn't happy with the idea, and it's not because he's coming from a position of brotherly concern. Nope, his unhappiness is based more in jealousy than anything else. My stomach twists. He's *sick*.

"I'm trying, David. It's complicated."

"Fuck complicated. Do as you're goddamn told! You do not want to test me, *whore*!"

I flinch at his words, my whole body shaking with fear. I hate him so fucking much.

"I need a little more time. Please, David. I'll find out what you want to know. I *promise*." Pleading has never worked before, and I don't expect it to now, but it's all I have. "She's your little sister…" I whisper, unable to comprehend how he could even think about hurting her, let alone follow through on the threat.

"You think that matters to me?"

"What about Mum? You care about her, at least. I know you do. If you hurt Lena, it will kill her."

David laughs like I've said the funniest thing and it makes my skin crawl. He's evil. Pure and simple. "The only thing that woman was good for was giving birth to me. She's a waste of fucking space."

"David—"

"You don't need me to remind you what's at stake, do you, Penelope?"

"No. I understand," I manage to bite out.

"Good. I'll be waiting because, believe me, my patience is wearing thin. Don't fucking disappoint me."

"I won't." My voice is barely above a whisper as I try to hold onto my tears.

"You have until the end of the month, Penelope. If you don't tell me what the fuck is going on by then, she's *dead*," he warns, ending the call with that threat ringing in my ears.

26

Pen

I've spent the best part of the last of couple days in fucking turmoil over David's threats, backing off from the Breakers when I should've been getting closer to them. I've not been complacent though. I've tried to find out more about what Jeb and D-Neath are up to by feeling out the other students. If D-Neath is back to his old tricks and selling drugs, then it stands to reason he'll start right where he has a willing market. I'm no criminal, but that seems the most logical step. The Academy is full of students who live and breathe a life of dance and everything that goes with it. I'm not saying they're all drug addicts, but it's not a secret that some dancers use drugs to keep them going when their natural energy is depleted. Fuck, some just do it for fun. It's not as if I haven't considered it myself.

But so far, nothing. We all know that Madame Tuillard has a zero tolerance policy for any drug taking. If she finds out a student is using, they're out. No second chances. Which makes me laugh, given her choice of a fucking boyfriend.

It's all so fucked up.

It's midweek now, and tonight we have another rehearsal for our end of year performance. This time we're working on the duets. I wasn't the only one who got fucked over when Dax dumped me for Tiffany. River was dropped too. Naturally, we're now paired up, and whilst I think River's a fantastic dancer he just isn't Dax. We don't share the same connection.

I feel sick, just thinking about it. I can't bear to see that bitch all over Dax. I'm not sure I'll survive the torture. Dax has avoided me at every opportunity, and knowing he doesn't want to partner with me twists my gut, but at least I've had this performance for Grim to concentrate on. Dancing might help me to express my emotions, but it also helps me to think. I'm fully aware that I need to get my shit together, which is part of the reason I called Grim and asked to meet with her under the proviso that I need to teach the strippers, I mean *dancers*, the choreography I've come up with. Of course, that's not the only reason I'm here at her club today. What I'm about to ask is a risk, but one I have to take. I don't have any other choice.

"It's good to see you again," Grim says, eying me from behind her desk. "I've been looking forward to seeing what you've come up with for your first performance."

I nod, chewing on the inside of my cheek.

"She was quiet as a mouse on the drive over too," Beast says to Grim, concern crossing his features as he props himself up against the wall. "Not her usual cranky-arse self."

"Is that right? What's on your mind, Pen?" Grim asks, turning her attention to me.

"Thanks for picking me up," I mutter, my mouth going dry

as I try to make small talk. Not quite ready for the big question.

"I was in the area," Beast shrugs. "Besides, Grim said I should pick you up, and what she says goes. I don't argue with the boss."

"So, do you want to tell us what this is about? I can see this is more than you giving us a preview of your dance. By the way, the girls are waiting for you outside. They're excited to get started. I don't think I've ever seen them as enthusiastic about anything else before," Grim says, pushing back her seat and lifting her foot up onto the edge of the desk. She narrows her eyes at me as though trying to figure out if I'm going to try and fuck her over. I'm not. I just need her help.

"You once said that if I ever needed a friend that I should call—"

Beast's eyebrows shoot up, but if he has any opinion on the matter, he keeps it to himself.

"That's right, I did."

"Were you serious?"

"Yes." There's no hesitation in her response.

I blow out a breath, fixing my gaze on hers. "Okay then."

"What do you need?" Grim asks, getting straight to the point.

Jeb and David *dead*, preferably. Though, of course I don't say that out loud.

"Spit it out, Pen," Beast prompts, giving me a grin to show he's not being an arsehole. I'm beginning to get the impression that he's more kind-hearted than his appearance and reputation dictates.

"I need a friend. I need a friend like you."

"What else have you got yourself mixed up in?" Beast asks, his eyebrows shooting up.

What else? He makes it sound like I'm some kind of magnet for trouble… Then again, I suppose I am. I scowl at him and he chuckles.

"A friend like me?" Grim tips her head to the side, showing off her pretty neck tattoo, the roses rise up her shoulder and wrap around her throat.

"Someone who has a reputation, and contacts…" I explain.

"I see, so if you think I can help, why the hesitation?" she asks.

I can feel myself trembling, coming here is a huge risk. Asking this woman for help, an even bigger one, but I don't know what else to do. The Breakers work for Jeb and despite everything York and Zayn have said, I still don't know if I can trust them completely. I want to. God knows I do, but they're still part of the Skins' crew and after Xeno warned me off them, I have very few options but to stay away until I can at least secure Lena's safety. At least Grim has shown me she's got some principles that I can agree with. She doesn't let anyone touch her girls and she fiercely protects what she loves: her business and her man. She's already told me she dislikes Jeb and she's given me a job at her club that comes with her protection. It's more than I could've asked for, but I'm hoping she'll extend that protection to my little sister too.

"It's complicated. I don't know who to trust."

"Yet here you are," Grim says, studying me.

"Here I am…" I chew on my lip, my heart fucking racing. If I'm wrong about Grim this could be it for me. David will kill Lena. Jeb will kill me. Heck, Grim could decide I'm too much of a fucking problem and kill me herself.

"Do you trust me?" she asks, and isn't that the million dollar question? Trust is easily breakable. I should know. Yet, just like Grim said, here I am. I'm trusting my gut and hoping to fuck I'm not wrong.

"You didn't have to do what you did—giving me a job here. I know you said that me dancing at your club is good for business, but I also know there are tons of dancers out there who are just as good as I am. I also know that you could easily have agreed to Jeb's terms and forced me to strip. You didn't. I figured you had your own personal reasons for hiring me that wasn't just to do with business. Besides, you did say if I ever needed a friend… I didn't peg you for a liar."

"Uh-oh, looks like you're getting a name for yourself, Grim. Is the clock ticking, my love? Are you getting maternal in your old age? Because, babe, you know I'm up for helping with that." Beast chuckles and she shoots him a dark look that has him slamming his mouth shut. It doesn't stop the amusement in his eyes though. There's no hiding that.

"Fuck off, Beast! I'm not fucking old, I'm twenty-six, you piece of shit, and if I wanted a baby, I sure as fuck would choose a better sperm donor than you," she snarls.

"Fuck, love, my goddamn heart." Beast places his huge hand over his heart and feigns heartbreak. Grim growls at him.

"Go on, Pen," she snaps, focusing back on me.

"Maybe this was a mistake. Forget I said anything. I'll figure something else out," I say, moving to stand.

Grim lets out a laboured breath. "Sit the hell down, Pen." She waits for me to settle back in the seat, then picks up a cigarette and lights it before blowing out a plume of smoke. "I'm a woman of my word, and despite how much this conversation seems to amuse this arsehole here, I meant what I said. Though I can see you still have reservations about me. I can understand that. I don't trust easy either, but here's the thing, Pen, you *can* trust me.

"I want to. I need to," I admit.

"I'm going to call Ford and get Asia on the line," she says suddenly.

"Asia?" I question, my mouth dropping open. "As in *graffiti* Asia? You know her?"

"Seems like we both do," Grim says, dialing a number on the phone and pressing the loudspeaker.

I sit back in my chair, frowning. How does Grim know Asia and, more to the point, why is she ringing her now?

"What's up?" a deep male voice answers after a couple of rings.

"Hey, Ford, how's shit going down in the back arse of beyond?" Grim says, her smile a genuine one.

"Oh you know, so-so. The little rugrats are keeping us busy. You good?" he asks, his voice holding a pinch of concern. Grim's eyes soften, and I detect love there. Wow. I don't know who this dude is to Grim, but he clearly means something to her.

"Of course I am. Never better. I'm gonna call you back later to chat properly, but right now I need to speak to Asia… girly shit."

"Girly shit? Is Beast treating you well?" Ford's voice darkens and Beast laughs.

"You bet I am, you cheeky little shit. You ain't too far away that I can't come down there and beat your arse for insinuating that I'm not treating my queen with utmost care."

"Never doubted it, mate. Just gotta check. You know how it is."

"Yeah, yeah, shithead," Beast retorts.

"Okay, enough of the bromance. Can I speak with Asia a sec?" Grim asks.

"Sure thing."

The line goes quiet for a moment before Asia picks up. "Hey, Grim. What can I do for you?"

I've never met Asia in person, even though we grew up in the same borough, but I've heard a lot about her over the years and have admired her artwork from afar. It was bullshit when she got sent to a reform school for her graffiti art a couple of years ago. The girl should be adored and admired like Banksy, not put away for her art. Then again, like me, she's just another street kid viewed as a nuisance rather than seen for her talent. That's just how it is for us. There were rumours about her links to the King, another criminal who lorded it over the London criminal scene, but then Asia seemed to fall off the face of the earth about a year ago. No one knows for sure what went down, but the King's death and her disappearance are more than a little coincidental in my opinion. I'm curious as to how Grim knows her though.

"I've got someone with me who's a little unsure whether she can trust me. I figured my friend here would've heard of you given you grew up in the same area, and I was right. Wanna back me up?"

Asia laughs, but there's caution in her voice. I don't blame her. She obviously disappeared for a reason. I could be anyone. "Who is this someone?"

Grim looks over at me and nods, giving me the go ahead to speak. "My name's Pen. You once did some artwork as a gift for me. I used to hang out with the Breakers," I say, hoping she'll remember that Christmas when the boys asked her to do some graffiti on the basement wall in number 15 Jackson Street.

"Pen? Shit, yeah, I remember that. Those boys were into you, girl. Pretty sweet gift."

I laugh, but it comes out strained. "I never got a chance to thank you. It was a beautiful piece."

"Well, cheers..."

"So, now that you've been introduced, I want to put Pen's mind at rest. She isn't sure she can trust me, and I don't blame her hesitation—"

"Look, we don't know each other, Pen, but I can tell you this. You *can* trust Grim," Asia interrupts without hesitation. "This woman is one badass bitch you don't want to get on the wrong side of, but if you remain on her good side then you're set up. Let's just say she had my back when I needed it the most. She helped me and my family. I owe her my life. Whatever it is that's going on with you, if she can help, she will."

Grim looks up at me, her eyes meeting mine. "Is that good enough?" she asks.

I nod. "Yeah, it is. Thanks, Asia..."

"No problems. Grim is one of the best, and I love her like a sister, but don't tell her I told you that, okay?"

"Okay," I nod, even though she can't see me and flick my eyes to Grim whose cheeks are now a soft pink. She coughs and rubs at her face.

"Well, Asia, give those boys a kiss from me," Grim says, eliciting a growl from Beast. She looks at him. "Not *Asia's* boys, the other two cuties," Grim reassures him, shaking her head.

Asia laughs. "Still the alpha arsehole, Beast?"

"You got it in one, sweetheart," Beast replies, chuckling.

"Well, it's been good to speak to you all, but I gotta go. My two *little* boys need their lunch and the big boys need my attention."

"How the fuck do you keep them all in line, Asia?" Grim asks chuckling, shaking her head.

"Oh, it's easy when you know how. Looking after my brothers is a breeze. Having four boyfriends ain't so hard either."

"Sounds like it'd be just the opposite," Beast says, laughing at his own joke. Grim rolls her eyes.

"Ha ha," Asia retorts, but we can all hear the smile in her voice.

So the rumours were true then? Asia did get away from Oceanside with more than one boy in tow. Listening to her laughing and talking about having a relationship with four men like it's the most natural thing in the world makes me feel better. That might not be something I can ever see happening for me now, given how Xeno and Dax feel about me, but I don't feel so bad about ever wanting it, now that I know other people live the same way and make it work.

"You two should come visit sometime. I know Ford would love to see you, though he'd never admit to that," Asia says, and we can all hear a male voice in the background cursing. "See, he loves you. Don't you, Ford?"

I can hear him groan, and Asia giggles. Their easy way with each other makes me long for my Breakers. We were like that once, knowing what buttons to press to get a rise out of each other, but doing it out of love and affection not unkindness. I miss it.

Beast chuckles and Grim smiles. "Talk soon," she says, before clicking on a button to end the call. She levels me with her gaze. "So, wanna tell me what the fuck is up?"

27

Pen

I nod. If Asia can trust her, then I figure I can too. It's time to put my pride aside. I need help. I need a friend, and whilst once upon a time the first people I would've gone to were the Breakers, right now I can't risk trusting them without figuring out if they really are on my side. Well, two of them at least. My heart squeezes painfully. Zayn and York have made their feelings known even if they haven't opened up about anything else, but Xeno unleashed his pain on me and told me in no uncertain terms to stay the fuck away from them. I don't think he'll ever come around, and Dax? Dax has made it easy and stayed away from me, refusing to even acknowledge my existence when we pass in the hallways at the Academy.

"Pen?" Grim prompts.

"I have a little sister, Lena," I begin, drawing in a deep breath. Grim frowns, flicking her gaze to Beast then back to me. "Her life is being threatened, and I need to protect her at all costs. I'm asking for your help to do that. Whatever I earn here at the club, I will use to pay towards her protection. I'll work more nights, every night if I have to, to cover the cost. But I need eyes on her at all times. I need her life protected."

"Well, shit," Beast says. "What little cunt is threatening your sister? Just give me a name and I'll sort this."

Grim holds her hand up, immediately silencing Beast. "This isn't some two-bit street kid with a bad attitude threatening her, is it?" she asks me.

"No. Do you think I'd come here asking for your help if it was? I might be a dancer, but I've grown up fighting my own battles. I can deal with some stupid *roadman*."

Grim nods. "I don't doubt that. So, who *are* we dealing with?"

My fingers curl around the pad of my seat and I lock gazes with Grim. "I can't tell you that."

"What do you mean, you can't tell us? Listen, Pen, we need to know who we're dealing with if we're gonna agree to protect your sister," Beast states, shaking his head like he thinks I'm a lunatic for even suggesting it.

"I can't tell you because I don't know who it will be…"

"So your kid sister's got a hit on her head? Why? What the actual fuck is this? Who uses kids as a tool to threaten—" Beast snaps, his tirade cut short by Grim.

"Jeb?! That motherfucker."

"He's threatened my sister's life, yes. But it isn't him I'm most worried about, not since you stepped in. I don't think he'll do anything to Lena now that you've hired me." I give her a half-smile that doesn't meet my eyes because whilst I hope that's true, I really have no fucking idea whether I'm right. Jeb only does things that suit him. Right now, me dancing for Grim fits into whatever little plan he has. When that stops being beneficial to him, all bets are off.

Grim looks at Beast, a whole conversation passing between them both. It must feel good to know someone so deeply that just one look can convey a whole conversation. It used to be like that for me and the Breakers. I really want that back.

"Who's the other person?" Grim presses. I swallow hard. Fear keeping me mute. Am I doing the right thing? "Who else, Pen?"

"My brother."

"Your fucking *brother*," Beast repeats, incredulous.

"Yes. My brother runs Jeb's drug business in Mexico. He's threatened Lena's life and will kill her if I don't find out what Jeb and the Breakers are doing at the Academy."

"Fuck me." Beast whistles.

"He'll kill my little sister if I don't betray the men I love. Whatever they're up to, David hasn't been kept in the loop. He's pissed off and when he's like that, he'll act out. I can't risk him hurting my sister," I choke out, my chin wobbles and tears prick my eyes. But I don't cry, instead I grit my jaw knowing that I have to be strong, though it's getting harder and harder these days.

"Your brother sounds like one twisted fuck."

I met Beast's gaze. "He is."

"And you didn't consider asking the Breakers for their help?" Grim asks.

"How can I when they still work for one of the men who's threatened my sister's life?"

Grim raises her brows. "You think they'd actually hurt your sister?"

"No. I don't." I sigh heavily, swiping a hand over my face.

"At least, I don't think they'd hurt Lena, but they're different now. I'm not sure I know who they are anymore."

"You can't trust them?" Beast asks, more of a question than a statement.

"I want to, but Xeno hates me, Dax has avoided me since I danced here last—"

"After what you did for him? I knew I should've shot the little shit," Beast exclaims, a long list of expletives erupting from his mouth. "Give me the word, Pen, and I'll beat his arse to a pulp in our upcoming fight. I'll put him in hospital for being such a fucking dick."

"*Please*, don't," I say.

Beast's lip curls. "That prick doesn't deserve you. What a fucking selfish little cu—"

Grim holds her hand up, quietening Beast's tirade.

"And the other two? Zayn, York?"

"We've got closer again this past week or so, and they want me to tell them what's up, but how can I do that? How can I do that knowing who they work for? Jeb is Zayn's uncle, for fuck's sake. Besides, I don't want to put them in the line of fire either. Jeb will *kill* them if he thinks they've turned their back on him, but not before my brother gets to them first. David hates the Breakers. Always has."

"This is a complicated situation you've got yourself in," Grim remarks, picking up another cigarette and lighting it. I watch her take a few deep inhalations, the smoke she blows out clogging the air between us. "You get close to them and find out what they know, betraying their trust. You stay away and find out nothing, and your sister winds up dead."

"That's about the sum of it," I say. Grim nods, glancing over at Beast who pulls a face. It's actually quite comical and I would laugh at his expression if I didn't feel like fucking crying. "I can't hurt them again. They'd never forgive me. But I can't let David hurt my sister either. So here I am. If I can ensure my sister's protected, then I can figure the rest out somehow."

"Sounds like you're stuck between a rock and a hard place," Beast remarks, stating the obvious.

"Yeah," I laugh bitterly. "You could say that."

Grim taps her fingers on the table, staring at me. She screws up her nose, thinking before she stubs out her cigarette in the ashtray on her table. "I'll put her under surveillance, stat. I'll make sure my best men guard her, Pen."

"Should I warn her…? I don't want to scare her. I've always kept her shielded from David. She doesn't know anything about this."

"My men are professionals. She'll have no idea. Believe me when I say it, Pen. No fucker will get close enough to touch a hair on her head. I give you my word, she'll be safe," Grim says, giving Beast a meaningful look.

"Text Grim a photo of your sister. I'll get things moving," he states, striding towards the door. "We got this covered."

My shoulders drop, relief flooding through me as I do what he asks and send through a photo of Lena to Grim's phone. "Thank you. I don't know what to say." I can feel the tears welling again and I choke them back, hiding them beneath a cough. I've really no idea why she's helping me, but right now I don't care. Lena will be safe, and I can figure the other shit out later.

"We'll protect your sister until Jeb and your brother are dealt with," Grim says, picking up her mobile phone and tapping a message out as the door closes behind Beast. Her brows pull together in a frown at the very quick response.

"What do you mean, until they're dealt with?" I ask, my gaze flicking to her mobile.

She doesn't answer me right away, instead she taps another message out, then places her mobile on the table. "Just business," she explains, nodding towards her phone. I don't question her further because it's really none of mine.

"What are you planning on doing?" I ask, a shiver tracking down my spine.

"I told you I dislike Jeb. He's been on my shit list for some time, Pen. Your brother just got added. No motherfucker threatens a child's life and gets away with it. As far as I'm concerned, they're already dead."

There's a fierceness in Grim's gaze that comes from a place of experience. It makes me wonder what happened in her past to make her feel this way. She's a part of this world that exists like a secret society beneath the mundane everyday life and yet it seems to me that it's not something she really likes or wants to be a part of, for that matter.

"Can I ask you something, Grim?"

"Sure."

"Why do you do what you do when half the people you invite into your club are arseholes just like Jeb and David?"

"First of all, they might be criminals but not all of them use kids to do their dirty work. There are some—just a few, granted—who can be trusted not to do that kind of shit. Secondly, it's all I know. This is the world I grew up in, Pen."

"Why didn't you get out?"

She laughs. "Because I didn't want to."

"But I thought—"

"You thought that I was some kind of secret church-going prissy bitch because I have a few morals? Believe me, I'm not. I make a good living doing what I do. I met the man I love right here in this club and I live a good life, an exciting one. I like the power and the lifestyle that being *Grim* affords me. Don't mistake my kindness for weakness."

"I don't. I'm just trying to understand."

"Then don't. The only person who understands who I am and what I'm about is Beast."

I nod, remaining quiet, thoughtful. "Look, Pen, just because I happen to like my life it doesn't mean to say I'm happy about how some of these arseholes run their businesses. I'm not down with kids being used or threatened as part of someone's business plan. Adults can make their own choices. Kids for the most part, can't. I take umbrage to a child being coerced into doing something they don't want to do. I also hate fucking pricks who threaten a kid's life. That's a hard fucking no from me. Hence why I'm helping you."

"Whatever it costs to protect my sister, I'll pay you back, every single penny. I swear it," I say, because I know that what I've asked for doesn't come for free. There's always a favour owed or a debt to be paid. I came here willingly knowing that.

She levels me with her stare. "I don't want your money, Pen."

My gut turns over, I was expecting something like this. She's not as respected as she is in the criminal underworld for being a Mother Theresa wannabe who helps kids. There's the other side to Grim, one I've only scratched the surface of. Whatever her reasons for helping me, I know there's more to it than she's willing to say right now.

"No? What do you want?"

"When the time comes, I'll be sure to let you know."

"Sounds ominous." I swallow hard, and grit my teeth.

"I'm not like Jeb or your brother, Pen. I won't be asking

anything of you that you wouldn't be willing to do. You're going to need to trust me on this."

So, that's what I do. I put my trust in Grim and Beast. Let's just hope I've not made another mistake that will bite me on the arse later or worse still, get me killed.

28

Pen

After spending the rest of the afternoon teaching the *girls* —as Grim refers to them—the choreography, Beast gives me a lift back to the Academy. He puts on some jazz music and spends most of the journey humming along to some tune I've never heard before. If ever a dude was a motherfucking contradiction, it's this man. A small smile pulls up my lips.

"What?" he asks, flicking his gaze to me.

"Nothing." I shake my head and look out of the window, biting down on my grin. I'm not sure if I'm feeling a little hysterical after today's meeting with Grim and the epic fucking rehearsal that followed, or if I'm genuinely this comfortable in Beast's presence.

"Seriously, what?"

"You're kinda odd, you know that?"

"*Odd?*" he barks out a laugh, chuckling at my observation of him. "I've been called far worse things in my time. I didn't get this name for nothing."

"Yeah, I bet." I fall silent, not sure what to say to that. It's certainly an *odd* feeling being driven around by the man everyone calls the Beast. His name fits his appearance, that's for sure. I mean, he's good looking and all, but there's this wild quality about him. From what I observed at Grim's club, he's as well respected and *feared* as much as Grim is. Yet, there's this whole other side to him that somehow I'm getting to see. I'm not sure whether I should be flattered or scared. Knowing too much about someone isn't always a good thing. David being a case in point.

"So, now that you feel comfortable enough to insult me, sweetheart, wanna tell me how you managed to get a bunch of strippers to dance the way they did this afternoon? Of course, none of them held a fucking candle to you. Don't tell Grim I said this, but damn have you got some moves." He grins widely, winking, then laughs when I blush at his compliment.

"That's easy. Stripping is a form of dance—"

Beast barks out a laugh at that, but when he catches my scowl, shuts up. "Fierce little thing, aren't you?" he mutters, shaking his head. "Fuck, I'm a sucker for a feisty girl."

"Don't let Grim hear you say that," I respond, realising how flirty that sounds. I cringe inside.

"I'm not coming onto you, Pen, if that's what you're thinking. There's only one woman for me. Grim got hold of my balls a long time ago and hasn't let go."

"Sounds painful," I deadpan, holding in the giggle I feel inside. This really is a surreal conversation.

"Fuck, no. Best thing I ever did was let her in. She could drag me into Hell by the balls, and I wouldn't fucking complain. In fact, the woman regularly holds me by the bollocks. She does this thing where she—"

"Okaaaay," I cut in, doing a timeout with my hands. "That's way too much information, big guy."

He chuckles. "Fine. Back to the strippers."

"*Dancers*," I correct him. "They may strip for a living, but those girls are dancers. No doubt about that. I think they proved that today."

"Sure as fuck did. Grim was impressed."

"She should be. It's easy to pass someone over based on what you think you know. Strippers equals hookers, right? Isn't that what everyone assumes?"

"But you saw something different?"

"Yeah, I did. To be able to strip and appear sensual yet not sleazy, isn't easy. They might reveal their bodies for a living, but they dance whilst doing it. Most people just see tits and arse. They think sex because they're incapable of seeing anything else. But I see rhythm, control, *expression*. All key skills for dancing. It wasn't hard to teach them because I already had so much to work with."

"The girls certainly took a shine to you. Never seen them so enamoured. They've been in the business for a long time. Jaded, is the word I'd use. But you brought out the best in them. That's pretty fucking impressive, I'd say. The punters ain't gonna know what hit 'em."

"I appreciate you saying that."

Beast glances over at me and nods. "I gotta admit, when Grim told me she was bringing you in as a performer at the club, that she was gonna give you access to the girls and full artistic control, I was sceptical. Then again, Grim is never wrong when it comes to business matters. Not only did she see an opportunity, she saw something in you. Grim relies on her gut in everything she does. She was right about this, about you. You're certainly something."

"Thanks," I mutter, not used to receiving compliments, especially not from a big, tatted criminal who has a reputation for fucking people up both in and outside the cage.

"Honestly, Tales has been needing a facelift for some time. Looks like you're gonna be the person to give it one. I've no doubt you'll be the star of the club."

"*Tales*?" I question.

"Yeah, it ain't called Grim's Club, though most people refer to it that way these days. *Tales* is the official club name. Always has been."

"I like that... *Tales*," I say, sounding it out.

"Yep, tales you win, heads you lose. The fighters of Tales never lose," Beast reels off like some kind of mantra.

"Is that right?"

"Our fighters are the best of the best. I trained most of them myself. Grim's father started this business many years ago. She became Queen of Tales when he died and made it more than just an underground fight club. Grim is smart. Much smarter than my sorry arse. It took me a long fucking time to realise just what a woman she is."

"What happened to her dad?"

Beast scowls, his face darkening, and I see a real glimpse of the man whose name precedes him. "That, sweetheart, is not a story I'm willing to tell."

"Fair enough," I reply, not my business anyway.

"Well, here you are, Pen," Beast says, as he pulls up outside the Academy a couple of minutes later. He's parked on a double yellow line on a busy London road and doesn't give a shit.

"You'll get a ticket." I point out the parking attendant

striding towards us with the look of glee on his face. Beast laughs loudly, his whole body vibrating with humour.

"Oh, fuck. You really do kill me." He rolls down his window and pokes his head out. The second the parking attendant sees him, the smug look on his face drops and he turns on his feet and walks the other way. "Yeah, that's what I thought," Beast shouts after him before turning back to face me. He winks.

I laugh, shaking my head. "Perks of being the Beast, yeah?"

"You could say that. I've maimed people for less than a parking ticket, Pen," he says it with humour, but I know it's the truth, and it reminds me just who I'm sitting next to. That sobers me a little. Beast must sense my change in mood because he puts the car in park and turns to face me.

"Look, I'm gonna be straight with you. What you're mixed up in is next level shit, but you're a smart woman, and you made the right move today. I ain't gonna lie and tell you that everything's gonna work out okay because I ain't fucking God. I'm not all-knowing or all-seeing but I will tell you this. Grim will *always* back the ones she thinks are worth it, and believe me, she doesn't do that very often. She's offered you a lifeline and expects loyalty in return. Don't fuck her over, okay?"

It's a warning, and one I understand completely. "I don't intend to."

"Good. You got my number now, so call me direct if you need a lift to the club at any point. I don't mind chauffeuring you about. You're cute as fuck, and I mean that in a completely platonic way."

I laugh. "Yeah, I know…" My voice trails off and I gnaw at my lip.

"What?"

"The fight with Dax. Could you —"

"Nope. No fucking way. That kid needs to learn a lesson. Don't worry, I won't hurt him… *that* much. Now, sod off. I got shit to do."

"PEN SCOTT, you've got some explaining to do, girl," Clancy states, greeting me as I enter the atrium. She's looking over my shoulder trying to capture a glimpse of Beast. "Who the fuck was that hunk-a-chunk, and where the fuck have you been? York and Zayn were barely holding onto their heads in class just now. I swear they're like two pack dogs, and just as territorial. They clearly don't like not knowing where you are."

"I had something I needed to do…" I say, realising how lame that sounds. Clancy's covered for me again and I owe her a proper explanation, not some vague bullshit that I've fed her.

"Hmm, like your text said." Clancy narrows her eyes at me. "Was that *something* more important than your dream? 'Coz honestly, Pen, you're on shaky ground. Madame Tuillard wasn't impressed."

"Shit."

"Yeah, she decided to drop in on the lesson. Tonight she's coming to watch each of us rehearse our duet…" Clancy winces.

"Well, she's gonna be even more pissed then, because River and I aren't gelling all that well."

"He's glad to be dancing with you, Pen. He fucking hates Tiffany."

"Yeah, me fucking too… But it's not the same dancing with River." I sigh heavily. I'll get my own back on that bitch when I've dealt with more pressing matters. "So, what did you tell Madame Tuillard?"

"I said you had a family emergency and had to go home to see your mum."

I puff out my cheeks and blow out a steady breath. "Thank you."

"Don't thank me yet because I gave York and Zayn your number. I figured you might answer their text messages given you were ignoring mine."

"Messages, what messages?" I ask, pulling out my mobile phone. "Battery's dead. I'm so sorry. I need to charge it up."

"You need to *fess up*, you mean," Clancy retorts, folding her arms across her chest and acting all indignant. "I know how much being here means to you, Pen, but skipping class is a sure-fire way to get thrown out on your arse. I figured that whatever you needed to do was important, and was happy to cover for you, only then I see you having flirty banter with that hot-as-fuck dude and I'm like, *so she's bunked class to shag that delectable man-mountain*. I mean, I don't blame you, but couldn't it have waited until after the class was finished?"

"It's not like that..."

"It better not be," a familiar voice states from behind me.

Zayn. Shit.

Clancy's eyes widen as her gaze flicks to Zayn over my shoulder. "Should I give you two... ah, no, *three*, a minute? Hey, York," she smiles sweetly, lifting her hand in the air and wiggling her fingers. She's loving this a little too much. I guess karma's a bitch. Clancy covered for me and I left her hanging. Not cool. I need to explain, to make it up to her. Only now I've got to deal with York and Zayn first.

Fuck, this is all I need.

"No, it's fine, Clancy, you don't need—"

"Actually, we'd appreciate that. Catch you at rehearsals later, yeah?" York offers, effectively dismissing her.

"Sure thing, partner." Clancy gives him a cheeky salute, then leans in to hug me, whispering in my ear. "You best give me the lowdown later, or I'm gonna break into your flat and open up a tin of tuna chunks and leave it in your knicker drawer." Then she kisses me on the cheek and saunters off, cackling. If she wasn't my friend, I'd worry she was being serious about her threat to make my underwear smell like dead fish.

"Tuna chunks? Fucking gross," I mutter.

Clancy hears and throws me a wink over her shoulder. "Better than prawns *and* tuna!" she says, disappearing through a door leading to the canteen, leaving me to face Zayn and York on my own. *Perfect.*

"You've been avoiding us, Pen," Zayn remarks when I finally turn around to face him.

"I have." There's no point denying it when it's true.

"Care to elaborate?"

Zayn's pissed off but trying to downplay it by appearing calm. York, however, isn't doing so well at hiding his anger. He looks dangerously close to combusting.

"Have you forgotten my new job? I was rehearsing with the girls for my first performance."

"What, and suddenly Beast is your fucking chauffeur?" York snaps, his voice getting louder. Jealousy crackles within his glacier eyes and it surprises me. I've never seen York like this.

I look about the atrium that's milling with students, some of whom are now watching us. The rumour mill has been doing overtime and lately we've been the centre of attention. I don't want to add any more fuel to the already burning fire. I've quickly come to realise that the students who go here are nothing but a bunch of gossips with nothing better to do than talk about other people's lives because theirs are clearly fucking boring.

"Not here."

"*My* place then," York states, before spinning on his feet and heading towards the staircase that leads up to our flats.

We ascend in silence, York leading the way and Zayn bringing up the rear like he's worried I'm going to run if he doesn't keep his eyes on me. Truth be known, I feel like a piece of shit keeping away from them both, especially since we've reconnected, but with Xeno's warning and David's threat what else should I have done? At least now that I know Lena's going to be safe, I can relax a little bit. Maybe even explore what's happening between us. It feels real, and yet I have so many insecurities that are fucking with my head that it makes me question everything.

"So, you've been at Grim's club?" Zayn asks, the second we step into York's flat.

"That's right. I really don't know what the big fucking deal is," I reply, feeling defensive. I sit down on York's bed whilst the two of them glare at me like I've actually spent the time fucking Beast rather than rehearsing. "It's my job now, remember?"

Zayn takes the bottle of beer York offers him and swigs back a mouthful. "I'm well aware, Pen."

"So why the anger? I had a routine to go through with Grim's dancers. I can't do that here at the Academy."

"Because, Titch, you were dropped off by *Beast*," York says, opening his own bottle of beer and taking a glug. He eyes me down the long neck of the bottle, fuming.

"And?" I cross my arms over my chest and raise a brow. Yes, we might've reconnected, but at no point did I agree to them being overbearing bastards. I'm not down with that. They don't get to come back in my life after three years and dictate who I do and who I do not get into fucking cars with.

"*And* Beast doesn't do that shit. Ever," York grits out between his teeth.

"What, give someone a lift in his car?" I roll my eyes. "You both need to dial it back a notch. I might've longed for this kind of alpha, chest-beating bullshit as a kid, but I'm different now and I'm perfectly capable of accepting a lift in a man's car without it having to mean I'm *fucking* them. Besides, have you forgotten who Beast's girlfriend is? You two are crazy if you think I'd mess around with him. Grim would have me killed." That's one man I will never fucking touch with a barge pole. "Besides, there's something called *girl code*, not to mention the fact that I don't fucking want *him*," I shout.

They both blink at my outrage. York places his bottle of beer on the counter and sits down on the bed next to me. "Who do you want, Pen?" he asks softly.

I laugh bitterly, unable to hide the stress in my voice. "Who do you think, York? I'm not the kind of girl to jump into bed with just any man who shows me the least bit of interest."

"Wait, you two have slept together?" Zayn asks, looking between us both. His eyes narrow at York and he downs his beer in one long glug.

"And if we had?" I retort, feeling my hackles raise.

"Then I guess York is better at this wooing shit than I am..." Zayn's voice trails off as I glare at him.

"*Wooing shit*? Is that what this has been about, Zayn, getting in my fucking pants?" I narrow my eyes at him, then glare at York who winces. "Oh, I get it. This is another one of your games, isn't it? Well, fuck you both!"

Standing I stride towards the door, but a firm hand grips my wrist and yanks me back around. "No, this isn't a game,

Pen. Fuck, that came out all wrong," Zayn says, looking at me intently, an apology in his eyes.

"Way to go, bro," York mutters, shaking his head.

I look between them, not knowing what to think. Then I figure I may as well give them a little bit of honesty because what the fuck else have I got left to lose? "The only men I want are *my* Breakers. It's only *ever* been you four," I say, trying to pull my hand free. Zayn's grip just tightens. He steps closer, his free hand running up my arm and cupping the back of my neck.

"That was a cuntish thing to say, Pen. I'm sorry. I wouldn't care if you had slept with York, though, admittedly, it might hurt my pride just a little," he smiles tentatively. "See, here's the thing. All I've thought about is you for the last three damn years. I denied ever wanting you. I lied to myself, but now that I've got you back, I'm a little fucking territorial over who gets to spend time with my—"

"*Our*," York corrects.

"Our girl," Zayn continues. "Seeing Beast put a smile on your face did something to me. It fucking scrambled my brain. I apologise." He looks at me beseechingly. "I'm sorry, Pen."

"That's better, you fucking muppet," York states, getting to his feet and joining us. He stands behind me and wraps his arms around my waist, pulling me back against him then drops a kiss on the top of my head.

"Don't call me a muppet, you prick. You were about to blow a gasket seeing Pen with Beast. Don't pretend to be all chivalrous now."

York grumbles, but he doesn't deny it.

"I'm just trying to work through this," I say quietly.

"This as in us, or as in what you're keeping secret?" Zayn asks tentatively.

"Both," I admit.

He nods, glancing at York above my head. "Pen, I know you feel like you can't trust us. Fuck, it hurts like a motherfucker that you feel you can't, but I get it. I *understand*." Zayn's thumb rubs over my knuckles soothingly, and York's arms tighten around my waist in comfort, but it isn't enough.

"You don't get it, Zayn. I so desperately want to tell you what's going on, I really fucking do, but how can I when not all of you are on board? This isn't just about you and York, it's about Dax and Xeno, too. It's about everything that happened between us three years ago. It's not something I can share if half of the Breakers refuse to even look at me, let alone try to fix what's broken. Fuck, I shouldn't even be saying this."

My shoulders drop and my head falls back against York's chest as I shut my eyes against the sting of tears threatening to fall. Today, I secured my sister's safety, but what about my heart? Because that's still broken, and it still fucking bleeds.

"Pen—" Zayn whispers, his voice filled with empathy that only makes my heart break more.

"I don't know how to do this anymore," I admit, fucking exhausted from trying to hold it all together. It's like trying to make a castle out of sand. Every time I think I've made something strong enough to withstand the elements, a huge waves comes along and fucking washes it away. "This is so much bigger than I can handle."

"Then share your burden, Titch. We can help."

"It's not as simple as that. I just…"

"You need Xeno and Dax too," York mutters against my hair, his lips pressing kisses to the top of my head.

"I need *all* of you. I always have. This was never just about me," I say, trying to make them understand.

Zayn cups my face. "We're going to fix this, Pen. If it

means me beating the shit out of my two best friends to make them see sense, then I will. I'll fucking do it."

That makes me smile, a tiny laugh escaping my lips at the absurdity of it. "It's a nice thought, but we all know Dax would make mincemeat out of you, and Xeno will take the beating and still not budge."

York chuckles. "You're not wrong there, Titch."

"I don't fucking care. Someone needs to knock some sense into them," Zayn says adamantly.

"Beast thinks so too," I say, biting on my lip when Zayn's eyes flash with jealousy. "I asked him to go easy on Dax…"

"Is he going to?" York asks, and I swear I feel him smiling against my head.

"No."

"Good. Stubborn fucker might finally meet his match."

"Oh God, this is all my fault." I turn in York's arms, my fingers curling around the material of his top as fear grips my throat. The thought of Dax coming to harm makes me feel physically sick. Beast might have promised not to kill Dax in their fight, but I'm fully aware of what's at stake. Beast has a reputation to uphold, and Dax has his pride to keep intact.

"Hey, Dax can hold his own," York says, trying to reassure me. He grips my shoulders and bends down to look me in the eyes. "Dax can hold his own. He'll be okay."

"You don't know that."

"Believe me, Titch. I *know* that."

I untangle myself from York's hold and step away from them both, needing a moment to breathe. I've come so close to just spewing my guts and telling them both everything, and I need a second to gather my thoughts. "I need to get ready for our rehearsal. River and I need to practice before Madame Tuillard stops by. I should go…"

They both look at me like that's the last thing they want me to do, but I think they also understand that I'm done with this discussion for today. Zayn nods tightly, and York swipes a hand through his hair. They're both as tense as I feel.

"Pen, I promise you that I will do everything I can to persuade Dax and Xeno to come around. No, fuck that, I *will* get them to come around, but you have to promise me something in return..." Zayn says.

"And what's that?"

"When that time comes—and believe me it *will*—you have to tell us *everything*. No more secrets. No more half-truths. No more lies," he says.

I nod in agreement.

"Atta girl," Zayn grins, his relief like a tonic. I have no right to feel hope, but I do, within his smile and York's grin, I do.

29

Pen

"River, Pen, thank you. I appreciate you working together on such short notice," Madame Tuillard says, giving us a false smile that doesn't meet her eyes.

She looks royally pissed off. I don't blame her. Separately, River and I are great dancers, but together? Not so fucking much. It's blatantly clear we don't fit. He's a beautiful dancer, and I'm so much better at ballet than I ever was, but there's no chemistry between us.

She knows it, and so do the rest of us.

Xeno would too if he actually fucking bothered to turn up to the rehearsal. Fuck knows where he is, but Madame Tuillard hasn't even questioned the fact he's not here. So either she already knows why he's missing or doesn't care. Across the other side of the studio, York and Zayn are talking in quiet whispers, glancing over at me every now and then. Hopefully they're discussing how to persuade Dax to take me back as his dance partner because seriously, this is fucking ridiculous. Dax doesn't fit with Tiffany any more than I do with River.

Regardless of that very obvious fact, Dax is apparently riveted by Tiffany as she prattles on about something to him and Sophie. He avoided eye contact with me the whole evening. Even when I was dancing with River, he kept his gaze fixed firmly on the dancefloor. He certainly hasn't had the balls to look me in the eyes at any point so far this evening. I never took him for a coward. Maybe I really don't know him at all.

"We got this, Pen," River says, wrapping a friendly arm around my shoulder as we take a seat on the bench. He's been so enthusiastic, and has worked hard every time we've gotten together to practice, but he's got to know that this isn't working. Then again, he never wanted to dance with Tiffany, so I guess dancing with me is a welcome relief. I don't fucking blame him. No one in their right mind wants to dance with that bitch. I glance over at Dax, and he grins at Tiffany when she places her hand on his bicep. Pressing my eyes shut, I draw in a deep breath. *Keep your head, Pen.*

Clancy plonks herself down between me and River, giving me a nudge. "Hey, you're doing great. That was wicked," she says, lying through her teeth. I roll my head to the side and meet her gaze. "It was—" she protests under her breath when I raise my brows at her.

"We just need to rehearse some more," River says from behind Clancy. He looks so hopeful that all I can do is smile.

"Sure, I can do that."

"Dax and Tiffany. You're up next," Madame Tuillard says, looking at Dax and cocking a brow.

"Fuck," I mutter under my breath. I'd rather rip my own eyes out with a rusty spoon than watch them dance together. Clancy grabs my hand, giving it a supportive squeeze.

"Duncan, given you felt so strongly about allowing these two to dance together I think it's only right that you actually pay attention when they do." Madame Tuillard folds her arms across her chest, and glares at D-Neath. He looks up from his mobile phone, distracted. Fucking arsehole couldn't give two shits about the end of year performance. If he did, he would've said no to Dax's request. By the look on Madame Tuillard's face, she's beginning to understand that too.

"Of course," he grins, giving her his best, most dazzling smile. Then his phone rings, and his smile drops when he looks at the caller ID.

"Duncan—" she warns.

"I apologise," he replies insincerely, "I need to take this call; it's business." He gets up and strides from the room, leaving her bristling with anger.

"She needs to throw his arse to the curb," Clancy says under her breath. "The guy's a dicknugget."

"I couldn't agree more."

"I wonder who's on the phone…" she muses, her Clancy-radar going off. I swear, my best friend should've been a cop or something because she sure has a knack at sniffing out trouble.

"I've no idea, and I really don't give a shit," I lie. Truth is, I'm wondering that too. "Do you think Tuillard would mind if I took a quick five-minute toilet break? I really don't want to have to sit through watching Dax and Tiffany dance together." I mean, it's not a complete lie, I *don't* want to have to watch those two dance together, but I need a reason to leave the studio so I can go spy on D-Neath.

"Right now, I think she feels so guilty about allowing D-Neath to override her decision that she'll let you do just about anything," Clancy says.

Dax and Tiffany walk into the centre of the studio, and

Tiffany flashes me a grin. I stand abruptly, refusing to look at either of them. "Madame Tuillard, would you mind if I—"

"Go," she waves me away before I've even had a chance to finish my sentence.

"Thank you, I won't be long. I just need to use the toilet."

I don't look at York or Zayn as I make a quick exit, though I'm fully aware of them watching me. Jogging down the empty hallway, I pass the ladies toilet, following the sound of D-Neath's voice. I find him standing at the far end of the hallway, far enough away to not be overheard by anyone. He's looking out of the window onto the street below. Tucking myself at the end of a row of lockers nearby, I listen.

"That's only a couple of months away. I'm not ready to accept the shipment yet. I need to fix up my end first, ensure it's watertight." he says, annoyance clear in his voice. Whoever's on the other end must be pissed off at his response because he tones down the attitude a little after that. "I just need a little more time to smooth everything out my end. There are a lot of things that need to be put in place to ensure this runs efficiently, that's all. I've got this. Trust me, you did the right thing coming to me." There's a few seconds of D-Neath listening to someone clearly giving him shit, then he clicks off the call. "Fuck!" he snaps, slamming his fist against the wall.

"Everything alright, Duncan?"

"Motherfuck!" I hiss under my breath, too busy listening in on D-Neath's conversation that I almost jump out of my skin when Xeno steps out of a door on the other side of the corridor. He glances my way, but doesn't let on to D-Neath that I'm hiding here.

Fuck. Fuck. Fuck. Fuck.

"Yeah, I'm good. Just some business that needs sorting.

What's up with you though, man? We ain't had a chance to catch up lately. Is everything cool?"

"Aside from one of the female students having a bit of an unhealthy obsession with me, I'm good." Xeno side-eyes me again, and I see something close to amusement flash across his face.

"Is that so?" D-Neath laughs.

"Yep, *tiny* little thing. She pops up every now and then like some creepy fucking stalker."

D-Neath laughs, and I scowl. I'm not his damn stalker, the big-headed, egotistical bastard.

"She hot?"

"She's not really my type. Though I've heard on the grapevine she's pretty free with her lovin', if you know what I mean."

My jaw grits and I swear to fuck the grinding of my teeth is loud enough to give me away.

"You know the students here are all perfectly legal... Maybe you should try out the goods before you pass her up." D-Neath laughs and Xeno smiles.

"Nah, I'm not into second-hand goods."

Second-hand goods?! The fucking prick. I clench my fist, glaring daggers at Xeno. His lip quivers with amusement. If I didn't have to keep myself hidden, I'd be slapping the smile off his stupid fucking face.

"Fair enough. Well, I'd better get back to rehearsals, otherwise my woman will chop my bollocks off. I'm already in her bad books."

"Yeah? Maybe I can help with that. That thing we discussed the other day, you got a minute to go over the details?"

D-Neath pauses for a moment. "You know what, now

might be the perfect time. Might give the Missus time to calm the fuck down."

"That bad?"

D-Neath scoffs, and it makes my blood boil at the dismissive sound. "She's pissed that I gave Dax the go ahead to change dance partners. I don't see what the big fucking deal is anyway. Pretty sure the leggy ballet dancer is a way better match than that short, snappy bitch."

Short, snappy bitch? What an arsehole.

"Pen," Xeno grunts.

"What?"

"Her name's *Pen*." He's glaring at D-Neath now, and his reaction throws me because just a minute ago he was talking smack about me too. I stare at him, trying to figure out what's going on in his head, but he keeps his gaze fixed firmly on D-Neath.

"Yeah, that's the one. She caught your eye or something?" D-Neath asks, chuckling.

He steps towards Xeno, and my heart nearly fucking bursts out of my chest as I press my back up against the locker. If D-Neath realises I've been standing here listening to his conversation, I'm in big fucking trouble.

"Come on, let's talk shop. You know me, haven't got time for that shit." Xeno grins, dropping the angry glare and wrapping his arm around D-Neath's shoulder. He steers him into the room he just stepped out of. I breathe out a sigh of relief, and as the door closes Xeno's green eyes meet mine.

"Go," he mouths, flicking his gaze along the corridor.

I nod my head, not needing to be told twice. It's only when I reach the studio that I realise, despite his bullshit digs, Xeno just covered for me when he could just as easily have thrown me under the bus. The question is why?

"So, Pen, you're gonna need to spill. I'm so done waiting to hear all the juicy details," Clancy side-eyes me during lunch at the local park the following day. I'm eating a cheese and tomato sandwich brought from home whilst she's digging into a Greek Salad courtesy of the local deli. "Those boys were about to burst a blood vessel yesterday. Who was that dude you were with?"

I place my half-eaten sandwich on my lap and gulp back a mouthful of water. "That was Beast."

"Beast? As in Beauty and the Beast?"

"As in, *I'm going to fuck you up in a cage, Beast*. He's a fighter at Tales, an underground fight club owned by a woman named Grim who happens to be Beast's girlfriend."

"Okaaay, and why in the fuck were you with him? Are you sleeping with him? Fuck, you are, aren't you? I was totally right."

"I'm not fucking him, Clancy," I say, rolling my eyes. "Girl, seriously, that is not a man I would want to fuck, let alone fuck with. Not to mention his girlfriend, Grim, is not someone you'd want to cross."

"Grim?" She wrinkles her nose at the name.

"Yep."

"Right, well shit. Then why were you in the car with him and why were York and Zayn so fucking pissed about it?"

"I've got a new job at Grim's club. I'm no longer working at Rocks."

"At her *fight* club? What are you, a ring girl?"

"Nope. I'm going to be dancing at the club. Grim has hired me to dance with her other... *dancers*." I refuse to call them strippers, not because I dislike the term but because in my eyes they are dancers.

"In a fight club?" Clancy looks confused. I mean, if the shoe were on the other foot I would be too.

"Yep. She's trying to broaden out into a different kind of entertainment. Balance the fighting with dancing."

"Well, shit. How did you get that gig? More to the point, why the fuck haven't you told me about this before now? You're such a secret squirrel." She grins, nudging me with her shoulder to show me there are no hard feelings.

"Zayn, he put in a good word," I lie.

"Then why was he so pissed about you being in the car with Beast?"

"A misunderstanding, mainly, but also because Dax is fighting Beast at Tales. On my first night on the job, actually. Dax and Beast don't get on... *At all*." I pull a face.

"Shut the front door!" Clancy chokes on her salad. "Dax is going head-to-head with that *beast* of a man in an underground fight club! Will it be filled with criminals?"

"Yeah, lots of them."

"Well, shit. I'm gonna need front row tickets. Bitch, I can't believe you didn't tell me about this sooner! This is gold!" she laughs gleefully. "Give me a badass gangster any fucking day."

"Clancy, they're dangerous people."

"I know. Such a fucking turn-on."

"I knew I shouldn't have told you a damn thing," I say, shaking my head.

"Fuck that. Now, what have I got to do to get tickets?"

"It's invite only, Clancy."

"So, invite me!" She grins widely.

"I work there. I don't have that kind of sway."

"Figure it out because I'm coming, preferably on some badass gangster's cock!"

"Oh, sweet Jesus."

Clancy bursts out laughing, and I can't help but smile. Despite that, there isn't a chance in hell I'm getting her tickets to attend. I do not need another person I care about mixed up in that world.

No. Fucking. Way.

"So, your birthday. I never got a chance to tell you what I had planned..." I begin, grinning in earnest now, but my grin fades when she winces, pulling a face.

"About that..."

"What?"

"I know you said you had something cool planned, and I really, really appreciate it, but I was kind of hoping we could check out this new club in the West End..."

"A new club in the West End...?" I repeat.

"Yeah. It sounds really fucking cool. My dad knows the owner. He can get me, you, and River in for free, all expenses paid as my birthday treat. You only get to leave the teenage years behind once, right? I figured we all deserved this."

"Sure, of course." I shrug off the stupid feeling of unworthiness and plaster a smile on my face. Clancy grimaces and slings her arm around my shoulder.

"Oh God, I'm so sorry, Pen. I'm such a bitch for even suggesting we do something else. Let's do what you had planned."

She looks so disappointed that I shake off my feelings of inadequacy and put them to the side. To be honest, what I had planned was shit anyway. A homemade curry, a few bottles of wine and turning one of the studios at the Academy into a private club for three wasn't exactly what she had in mind.

"Fuck, seriously. My plan was shit in comparison. I can't believe I even thought it was a good idea."

"You sure?"

"Yep," I nod my head. "I'm absolutely positive. A night out all expenses paid sounds fucking perfect actually. I could use the chance to let my hair down."

She grins, squeezing me tightly in a hug before smacking a kiss on my cheek. "What would I do without you, eh?"

"Probably end up in some dodgy swing club in a sleazy part of town, no doubt." I wink, teasing her. She cocks her head then sucks on her fork provocatively.

"Yeah, you're damn right, and I'd fucking enjoy it too."

"You're intolerable, do you know that?" I giggle. "Such a saucy, little minx."

"Pot, kettle, black," she retorts winking, and my cheeks flush. "By the way, don't think I've forgotten about your little smoochy-smoochy session with York, girl."

"There's me thinking it'd slipped your mind," I joke.

"See, what I *really* want to know is if he can make you come without touching you? Are the rumours true, Pen Scott?" she asks, putting on a serious interviewing voice and holding her fork up as a pretend microphone.

"A lady never tells."

"Because we all know that's a skill that no man has had, *ever*. Though those vibrations are something else, I'll give him that."

I burst out laughing, shoving her on the arm. "He really does tap that floor hard, doesn't he?"

"More like tap that ass."

We burst into a fit of giggles, and it feels really good to just hang out with Clancy and laugh like this. It's been a while since I've felt relaxed enough to do that.

"So, what *did* you have planned for my birthday?" she asks a few minutes later as we head back to the Academy. I tell her about my shitty plan and we both end up laughing hysterically. "Oh God, Pen. I love you, girl, I really, really do. We'll do the curry night another time, yeah?"

"Yeah," I reply, linking arms with her.

As we walk up the steps of the Academy, I hold onto this moment of happiness knowing that these days they're few and far between.

30

Pen

The following week things at the Academy go relatively smoothly. Beast keeps me informed about Lena, and so far no one's attempted to kill her. However, there have been a few horny teenagers who've got too close and been given a boot up the arse. I couldn't help but chuckle when Lena complained about her lack of pulling powers on the phone to me last night. Little does she know that there are two very capable men scaring off potential suitors. Good. She needs to concentrate on her studies anyway. She'll totally thank me for it later.

York, Zayn and I hang out when we can. Being together again is still all so new, and since our talk last week, they've both backed off a little in the touchy-feely department. It's not that I don't want their kisses and their attention that way, because I really fucking do, but we're trying to build our trust and friendship, and right now being intimate has taken a backseat to that.

"So, erm, how's Dax and Xeno?" I ask tentatively, taking a sip of my coffee and peering at them both from behind my rather large coffee mug. It's Thursday morning, and we're sharing a table in the canteen grabbing a drink before lessons start for the day. I'm shattered from a week long dose of rehearsals for the end of year performance and really fucking exhausting dance classes. This week Madame Tuillard seems to have turned up the heat beneath all our teachers, and every lesson has been full on, sweat-dripping, muscle-shaking torture. I love it though. "Guys?" I prompt when they don't answer right away.

York glances at Zayn then pulls a face. "Dax is being a stubborn bastard, and Xeno is being... *difficult*."

I sigh. "Yeah, I get it."

Zayn reaches across the table and grabs my hand. "They'll come around, Pen."

"Who's *coming*?" Clancy asks, her eyes bright and her grin wide as she and River slide onto the bench next to me. This girl's got a one track mind.

"We were just talking about—"

"*Coming* to Chastity Nightclub with us tomorrow night?" she interrupts, looking at me and smiling broadly. Is she asking them to join us or just fucking with them? She finds it highly amusing when they go all alpha possessive, and loves to wind them up at every possible opportunity. Clancy knows that us going clubbing without them is a sure-fire way to do that.

"You're going clubbing tomorrow?" Zayn asks, looking between the three of us. I see a flicker of possessiveness flash across his eyes before he covers it up with a smile. Part of me is turned on by his jealous streak, the other part is appalled. I'm all for girl power and I've never been one for letting a man tell me what I can and can't do. Though, seeing he cares enough to feel jealous does something to me.

"It's Clancy's birthday—" I explain.

"Count us in then!" York grins widely, raising an eyebrow at Clancy and daring her to object.

"Sure thing, partner, though don't expect me to get you into the VIP area too. You'll just have to use your charms. River, Pen and I already have a nice spot waiting for us."

"Is that so?" York asks, staring at me with raised brows.

"Yup," River confirms, grinning. Urgh, he and Clancy are a nightmare. "Clancy tells me it's a themed club. Better get your leathers, whips, and handcuffs ready, Pen."

"Wait, what?!" I snap, narrowing my eyes at them both. They better be pulling my leg. I am not going to some dodgy sex club. Then I remember Clancy's dad is paying for our night out, and I relax. There's no way he'd be up for covering the cost for us to go to a sex club.

"Don't worry, River. I'll make sure I come prepared," I say, playing along.

Both York and Zayn make a kind of growling noise that has Clancy and River cackling and my lip twitching with mirth.

"Hey, girl. I'm gonna need you to bring the leash too..." Clancy gives me a quick peck on the cheek then grabs River and runs. Oh my god, she really does love to stir up shit. I shake my head at her as she walks away. She just throws me a kiss over her shoulder. "Love you," she mouths.

"What?" I ask when I finally make eye contact with York and Zayn.

"Chastity Nightclub, eh?" York asks, cocking his head and dragging his thumb over his bottom lip. Why the fuck is that so sexy? Is there some secret club where boys go to learn sexy stuff like this or do they just go on TikTok and pick up all the lip biting, hair stroking, and eyebrow arching intense shit from there? I take another mouthful of coffee for something to do, because all of a sudden the air has got thick with sexual tension.

"Uh huh, she's turning twenty and wanted to do something fun."

"*Fun*? I've heard about that nightclub," Zayn says, toying with his own mug of coffee as he runs his finger around the rim. He smiles, baring his hot as fuck chipped tooth at me. In fact, they're both looking at me so intently that my cheeks start to heat.

"It's no big deal, just a few drinks and dancing the night away. You *should* come."

"Oh, Titch, you really don't know, do you?"

"Know what?"

"It *is* a sex club."

Zayn grins, looking at York as they both stand. "I'll bring the handcuffs, you wanna bring your truncheon?"

"What?" I practically spit out my coffee at the look of pure lust in their eyes, not to mention amusement.

"Catch you later, Titch. You better *come* prepared."

"Wait…"

"Pen, you're in for a treat." Zayn winks and they both walk off with stupid grins on their faces, leaving me feeling way too breathless for first thing in the morning. I snatch up my mobile phone from my table and tap out a quick message.

Me: Clancy, I'm going to murder you!!!

In response she sends me a stream of laughing emojis, followed by an eggplant and a purple smiling devil face.

Me: Seriously, your dad got you VIP treatment at a fucking sex club?!

Clancy: My dad is very liberal. Besides, it's not a sex club per se. They just make use of some very hot, naked dancers and private rooms for, erm... chatting in. Promise it's just dancing and drinking... Unless of course...

"Oh, my fucking God," I mutter, and I'm not sure if I'm imagining it, but I swear I can hear Clancy laughing from the other side of the Academy.

LATER THAT NIGHT I wake up from a nightmare where Lena is lying lifeless on her bed, deep purple marks ringing her throat. A sob escapes my throat as the remnants of the dream still try to persuade me it was real, but I force myself to rationalise what is and isn't true.

Lena is safe.
She has guards watching over her every minute of the day.
She. Is. Safe.
Despite that, I send a quick message to Beast, not expecting an answer but getting one anyway.

Beast: Lena is good. Sleep.

It's past two in the morning and I already know that sleep isn't going to come. So I get dressed and head down to one of the studios to dance off my restlessness. At night, the Academy is vastly different to the hustle and bustle of a busy day. The corridors are dark and filled with hidden corners where predators could lie in wait. I know feeling this creeped out is just the after effect of my dream still trying to convince me that there's danger around every turn, so I do my best to ignore the feeling that I'm not the only one sneaking through the halls at night.

Heading into Studio Three, the automatic lights flicker on overhead and I place my mobile in the dock, turning on the music and keeping the sound level low. I stretch through one song, easing out the knots in my muscles, then begin to move to the beat of the next song.

It's *I Can't Make You Love Me* sung by Teddy Swims.

This damn song perfectly suits my mood.

Unrequited love. A broken heart. Loss. Heartache.

It's all wrapped up in this song. A song I've listened to on repeat countless times.

I might have a glimmer of hope knowing that Zayn and York are willing to work through our feelings, but my heart has always been equally divided up into four pieces. Each part belongs to one of the Breakers. I know it won't ever beat fully again without them all.

And that just isn't going to happen. I feel the truth of that knowledge like a bludgeon to my heart, it smashes through my chest forcing my knees to the floor.

My head falls forward, my fingertips sliding over the dusty wooden floorboards as tears clog my throat. For a moment, I just allow the music to wash over me, and I'm reminded of Xeno's cutting words and Dax's dance. Two men, two pieces of my heart who refuse to let me back in.

I don't blame them.

I hurt them.

I deserve this pain.

Pressing my palms to the floor, I lift my body slightly and

slide my feet outwards slowly into a side split before sweeping them together in front of me. Teddy sings about unrequited love, about not being able to force someone when it comes to love, and that sob in my throat breaks free. I capture it in my hand, cupping my fingers over it as though it's a living, breathing thing.

I suppose it is in a way.

Over the years my pain has become its own entity, growing within me, suffocating me as it became this monstrous thing. I don't want to feel that way anymore.

I don't want to hurt. I don't want to hate. I don't want to be afraid.

Climbing slowly to my feet, I kick out into a spin. Above me, my cupped hands hold onto that ball of pain I've kept buried inside of me. For a long time no one could see it.

I kept it hidden from my sister to protect her.

I kept it hidden from my mother to protect myself.

I kept it hidden from Jeb and my brother to show strength when inside I was breaking.

I kept it hidden from the Breakers to ensure their safety.

Moving across the floor, I dance with my pain held in my hands, wanting so badly to let it go. Every step I take, every turn and leap is edged with a sadness that tries hard to break me.

But something else happens too.

A sense of understanding.

I need to set my pain free and the only way I'm going to be able to do that is by sharing the truth.

I need to tell the Breakers what happened that night.

I need to tell them the truth and let the chips fall where they may.

Then and only then will I be free.

And maybe, just maybe they'll be set free too.

With that thought in my heart, I open my palms and let the pain go.

I set it free.

Gathering my phone, I leave the studio and walk slowly back to my flat, unaware that someone else had watched my dance, unaware that they'd captured my pain and made it their own.

31

Pen

"Girl, you look fucking HOT!" Clancy grins as I slide into the cab beside her and River. She's wearing a skin tight, hot pink PVC mini-dress and platform heels in deep orange to match her hair. Around her neck is a studded dog collar, and her eyes are lined with neon pink liner. Beside her, River is wearing black hot pants that leave nothing to the imagination and a white tank that's see through and shows off his nipple bar. It takes everything in me not to stare at it. Who knew?

"You two went all out," I reply, feeling woefully underdressed.

Don't get me wrong, I'm all for people exploring their sexuality and dressing to impress, but I've never been comfortable in anything more than jeans and t-shirts. This outfit I'm wearing is well out of my comfort zone as it is.

"And you look understatedly beautiful. Seriously, Pen, if York and Zayn don't drag you into one of those side rooms tonight to fuck your brains out, then there's something seriously fucking wrong with them."

My cheeks flame and the cab driver coughs. River and Clancy just laugh. Pulling at the hem of my mid-thigh satin shorts, and wrapping my denim jacket tighter around my body I settle in for the ride. I can't believe I let Clancy persuade me to wear black stockings and a suspender belt over the top of my shorts. That paired with a fitted and boned black bustier and killer heels, I'm feeling about as comfortable as a pig at a slaughterhouse.

Twenty minutes later we're inside the club, and I've just downed a second glass of champagne courtesy of Clancy's *liberal dad* and wishing I'd kept my denim jacket on.

"Girlllll, this place is full of hotties. I don't even know where to look first," Clancy says, grinning widely. She's in her element, and honestly her vivaciousness is a joy to watch. She's a girl who knows what she wants and doesn't give a fuck about what anyone else thinks. She epitomises female sexual freedom and girl power. I love her for it.

"I don't know either." I laugh nervously, side-eying the beautiful black woman dancing in a cage hanging over the dance floor. She's naked bar a tiny pair of G-string knickers. Not only is she stunning, she also has some sick dance moves that I file away to try out myself when I get back to the Academy.

"Look at River go!" Clancy points to our friend who is currently sandwiched between a beautiful beefcake of a man with arm muscles bigger than my thighs and a woman that looks like a bloody catwalk model with her willowy figure. When the woman starts kissing River's neck, I snap my gaze away. Clancy, however, is salivating, unable to take her eyes off the trio.

"River did not tell me he swung both ways, the secretive fuck."

"You like him?" I ask, noticing the flare of jealousy across her features.

She flicks her gaze to meet mine. "Yeah. I do."

"Then, go get him, tiger." I wink.

She doesn't need to be told twice.

I watch as she strides onto the dancefloor, her hips swaying provocatively. The sensual lighting and the sultry music all adding to her sex appeal. Clancy is hot with a capital H.

When she reaches the trio, she taps the woman on the shoulder and whispers something in her ear. The woman smiles and steps away, allowing Clancy to take her place. River is currently tongue-fucking the man, but when Clancy grips his hips and hooks her leg over his waist, grinding against his arse, River pulls back, and turns his head to the side. There's a moment of surprise when he looks down at her, but then he smiles and grasps her thigh, before flipping around to face her.

When they start to kiss, I drag my gaze away and look about the club. Apart from the half-naked dancers and hidden rooms to the side of the dancefloor, this is like any other exclusive club and not nearly as shocking as I was expecting it to be. If there is a lot of sex going on, it's not in your face, that's for sure.

Lifting my hand, I motion for the barman and request another glass of champagne. He passes me the delicious drink and I knock it back in one long gulp, then I start to sway my hips to the beat of the song that starts to play. It's *Dance With A Stranger* by Sam Smith.

"I love this song," I say to no one in particular.

With alcohol running through my veins and music flooding my senses, I stride into the centre of the dance floor and dance like no one's watching. Heat from the crowd permeates my skin, which is soon flushing with warmth. Around me people are dancing closely, grinding their hips into one another. There's a lot of kissing going on, but rather than feel embarrassed to be dancing on my own, I embrace it. Across the dancefloor I notice River, Clancy, and the couple he was dancing with enter a side room. Clancy hesitates on the threshold of the door and turns looking through the crowd. When she spots me she gives me a small smile and a wave. I nod.

"I'm okay. Go!" I mouth.

She winks then closes the door behind her.

Pulling out my mobile I fire off a quick message.

Me: Have fun. I'll make my own way home.

She sends back a smiling emoji with several hearts.

Throwing my arms up in the air, I close my eyes and sway my hips from side to side, feeling tipsy and carefree. When hands wrap around my waist, and a warm kiss drops to my naked shoulder, I stiffen momentarily.

"Relax, Titch. It's just me," York says, his voice gravelly and filled with undeniable lust.

I twist my head to the side, arching my neck back to look up at him. He grins, his ice-blue eyes pop even more than they usually do.

"Hey, are you wearing eyeliner?" I whisper, biting on my lip. Fuck, that's sexy.

"Nail polish too. I'm funnelling my inner metrosexual self. Like it?" He lowers his lips to meet mine, pressing a sultry kiss against my mouth. His white blond hair is luminous in the UV light and his eyes sparkle with promises.

"I love it," I smile.

York licks his lips, then grinds his hips against my back, moving at a slow tempo as his hands slide up over my thighs and hips. He takes in a sharp breath when he feels my suspender belt.

"Fuck me, is that what I think it is?"

I smile, biting my lip at his groan. "Yes." Reaching behind me, my fingertips brush against his hips. "Is that leather?"

"Sure is, Titch. Feels fucking good, doesn't it?" His fingers curl into my hips as he brushes his teeth over the shell of my ear. I can feel his thickening cock digging into my lower back, the soft material of his leather trousers rubbing against the space between my bustier and silky shorts.

"Where's Zayn?" I whisper.

"He'll be here in a minute, Titch," York responds before spinning me in his arms.

Holding onto me, he drops me backwards in a dip. The beat of the music thumps in time to my heart and clit as York bends over me and slides his hand down my neck between my breasts, then smooths over my stomach before lifting me back up. We grind against one another, dry humping to the beat of the music. He grows harder, and I grow wetter. Somewhere between the entrance and the dancefloor, I left behind my inhibitions and it feels so fucking good.

"Fuck, Titch. This is dangerous," he mutters before lowering his mouth to mine and licking the seam of my lips. When he grasps my chin, pushes my head to the side and runs an open-mouthed kiss down my throat, my heartrate kicks up a notch.

"What are you doing?" I pant breathlessly.

"Tonight, I'm fulfilling all your fantasies."

Then he bites me. I nearly come in my knickers.

With my core throbbing and the skin on my neck stinging from his bruising bite, York spins me back around, one large palm cupping my throat, the other resting over my pubic bone, his middle finger tantalisingly close to my clit.

"Looks like we've got an audience," York mutters, the tenor of his voice dropping with a growl. I follow his gaze and can see Xeno standing on the other side of the dance floor, he's talking to Dax who alternates between staring at us both like he wants to commit murder and then looking back at Xeno with a scowl.

"What are they doing here?" I ask, perplexed.

"Zayn might've dropped a hint that you'd be here tonight."

"And they came?"

"Looks that way."

"Why?"

"This is a sex club, Titch, and *you're* in it."

"I'm not even sure what that's supposed to mean…"

York smiles into my neck, running his lips over the bare skin of my shoulder as my chest heaves under his ministrations. "Sometimes all anyone needs is a little push…"

Across the dancefloor, Zayn joins Xeno and Dax. He glances at me and smiles. Xeno notices and grasps hold of Zayn's arm and whispers into his ear all the while looking directly at me. Even from over the other side of the club I can feel his hate. It burns as hot as York's kisses against my skin. Well, fuck him. He didn't have to come here tonight.

I hold his stare until he looks away. Zayn snatches his arm back and says something back to Xeno. If I were a betting woman I would guess he's telling him to fuck right off. I feel momentarily guilty for getting between them before I give myself a stern talking to. They're grown men, they can handle their own shit.

My eyes flick to Dax who is, once again, staring at me, and I know he's fighting with himself. I can see his indecision and the need in his eyes. God, I miss him.

Fuck it, in for a penny, in for a pound, right?

York must be able to read my thoughts because he lowers his mouth to my ear and says, "Let's give him something to think about, shall we?"

York's hand slides lower and his finger settles over the top of my silky shorts, rubbing against my clit. I allow my head to fall back against York's chest, and my eyelids to fall to half-mast as I let out a low moan. From where he's standing, Dax won't be able to hear me over the music, but there's no mistaking what's happening. He'd have to be blind not to notice.

"I'm going to slide my finger between your pussy lips now, Titch. Let's see how your *Dark Angel* deals with that..."

"You know about—?" My question is cut off as York shifts my silk shorts to the side and does exactly what he said he would do. I draw in a shocked breath, my body shuddering at the blissful intrusion. Fuck. I'm so turned on.

"So fucking wet," York murmurs, running his lips over my bare skin.

Across the other side of the club, Dax visibly shakes, his hands curling into fists. "Motherfucker!" he roars so loudly that most of the clubbers surrounding us turn to look at them, which is just as well because York is finger-fucking me in full view and I'm moaning and flushed and turned on as all fuck. I might be a dancer, but I'm not an exhibitionist, not usually anyway. Tonight, however, I seem to have left all fucks at the door of this establishment.

Dax storms off, successfully interrupting Xeno and Zayn's argument with his hissy fit. They both turn their attention back to us, and like a heat-seeking missile, Xeno's gaze drops to York's hand between my legs. I swear to fuck, any minute now he's going to burst that very angry-looking vein on his forehead. Zayn lifts his lips in a slow smile, then raises his gaze to York above me and cants his head to the side.

"We'll finish this later, Titch," York promises, removing his finger and lifting it to his lips, sucking my juices free.

Fuck, that's sexy.

Turning me in his arms, York jerks me against his body and cups the back of my head. He slides his hand over my arse cheek and hitches up my leg so he can grind against me. "Look at you, Titch. I don't know how the fuck they can keep away," he says, watching me intently before lowering his head again and kissing me until I'm a breathless, molten mess.

32

Dax

"Motherfucker!" I roar load enough that the whole fucking club turns to stare.

Even Xeno and Zayn stop arguing like a couple of bitches.

Fuck this bullshit.

Fuck them all.

Fuck.

Fuck.

FUCK!

Twisting on my feet, I storm off to the bar and demand a triple shot of bourbon. The barman doesn't even ask for payment, must be the look of sheer fucking murder in my eyes.

I'm going to strangle that motherfucking cunt, York.

Then I'm going to tan Pen's backside until she's fucking raw.

This is not how shit's going down.

I will not be provoked. Not by my fucking best mates.

Not fucking happening.

"Another," I roar at the barman, who is already waiting with the bottle. I knock that back, relishing the burn. When my heart rate has dropped to a more reasonable level, I stalk back the way I came. Only the motherfuckers have gone.

All of them, *including* Xeno.

33

Pen

Xeno grips my hand tightly and pulls me through the crowd behind him. My cheeks are flushed from York's kisses, but it's Xeno's urgency that has my heart racing.

"This way," he demands. His voice is strained, angry. I try to pull my arm out of his hold, but he just yanks harder.

"Let me go!" I hiss, slamming the flat of my hand against his bicep.

"Don't fucking test me, Pen!"

When we reach one of the rooms situated off of the dancefloor, he kicks it open with his foot. The room is dimly lit and there's nothing in the space but a loveseat against one wall, a cabinet against the other and a weird cross thing with silver hoops at either end, a rope threaded through it. He yanks me inside the room and my stupid heel on Clancy's shoe snaps, pitching me forward. Shit. She'll murder me. These are her favourites.

"Sit the fuck down!" he roars, pointing to the loveseat as he shoves me away from him. I stumble on unsteady legs, only to be held upright by two strong hands.

"What the fuck, Xeno?!" Zayn shouts, steadying me on my feet as York comes barrelling into the room behind him. He takes two steps towards Xeno, then punches him in the face. Xeno stumbles back from the force, but he corrects himself quickly and within a couple of steps has his forehead pressing against York's. He's vibrating with anger, but he doesn't fight back. For a few seconds they remain head to head, their nostrils flaring.

"Come on then. Fucking give it to me!" Xeno taunts, a nasty sneer on his face.

York pushes against his chest. "DO NOT FUCKING TOUCH HER LIKE THAT AGAIN!" he yells.

"What the fuck is happening here?"

I whip my head around and watch Dax enter the room. He's so huge, he practically fills the whole doorway. Xeno and York don't acknowledge him, and Zayn's gaze remains fixed on his bestfriends going head to head. I catch Dax's eye as he steps slowly into the room and closes the door behind him, locking it. There's a glimmer of something in his eyes that has me swallowing hard.

Fuck. It's just me and them.

"Isn't this what you wanted, motherfucker? To push me to act and now that I have, you don't fucking like it? Well, fuck you and your damn games, York," Xeno snarls back, blind rage making him seethe.

"I've been pushing you to open your motherfucking eyes! To see what's right in front of your stubborn arse face. She doesn't know anything. Can't you see that? Can't you fucking see that she's a goddamn victim in all of this?"

Xeno's gaze flicks to me, and I can only stare open-mouthed, trying to wrap my head around what the fuck's happening. What don't I know anything about? What does he mean by victim? What do they think they know?

"Stop fucking talking, York," Xeno warns, focusing back on me as Zayn's arms tighten around my waist. "Pen here has a habit of listening in on conversations she shouldn't."

"Screw you, Xeno. I didn't ask to be dragged into this room," I snap, but it comes out choked.

"Listen, Pen—" Xeno starts but Zayn cuts him off this time.

"No, shithead. You need to listen for once. You're so fucking blinded by your anger and the betrayal you still feel that you can't see this for what it is. I never took you for a fool, but fuck, man, you're the biggest fool there is."

"Get her out of here. Right the fuck now!" Xeno shouts.

No one moves.

It's like a damn standoff, and I've had it. I've fucking had it.

The silence is deafening until music begins to play into the room. The haunting voice of Jacob Lee singing *Demons* fills the space. It couldn't be a more perfect song. The beat of the drum echoes the pounding beat of my heart and the throbbing tension surrounding us. This song has a dangerous side to it, a darkness that sits right in the pit of your stomach. It's sensual, but edged in threat. Like the blunt edge of a knife running over bare skin, or the coarseness of a rope wrapped around your wrists, just like the one hanging from the cross.

Making a split second decision, I kick off my shoes, shrug out of Zayn's hold, and walk slowly over to the rope, swaying my hips to the beat of the music.

Picking up the end of the rope, I grasp it in my hand and step slowly backwards letting it unravel onto the floor. With my back to the Breakers, I spread my legs, drop my head backwards and raise my hands up in the air, the length of rope dangling from my clasped fingers. Holding onto the end of the rope with one hand, I curl my other hand around the thickness, then widen my arms slowly before snapping the rope taut above my head.

My heart pounds so loudly that it rivals the beat of the song. My body trembles with what I'm doing, but I have to get them to understand. Feeling like this, so fucking caught up in this mess is like a rope around our necks. We need to sever it. We need to be free from all this bullshit between us. Lifting my leg, I wrap it around the section of rope hanging from my hands, then spin to face my Breakers.

Jacob Lee sings about internal demons, about secrets and betrayal. His words are the darkness that throbs between us all, the pain and the anguish. The bass vibrates up through the floorboards, every beat echoing my thrashing heart as I lower the rope over my shoulders, so it hangs around me like a necklace.

I see anger. I see desire. I see hurt. I see lust.

I feel those same emotions. They rise up within me as my hips begin to sway sensually.

Right here, right now. This is our story. These are our demons. This is our dance.

It's a risk, baring myself to these men so intimately like this. I'm locked in a room with them in a sex club. Two of them want to fuck me and the other two want me to feel the same pain they feel. Yet I don't feel fear, only a desperate need to fix what's broken.

I keep moving my body like a snake charmed by the music. Sliding the back of my hands up the side of my neck, I lift my hair up, then allow it to fall back down as I bite my lip provocatively. My hands twirl in the air above me, and I relish the way my Breakers watch me so intently that I feel as though every inch of my skin is on fire. Bringing my hands back down, I slide them over my breasts, following the curve of my waist and hips.

Xeno's eyes blaze with anger.

Dax's body is tense with hurt.

York's mouth parts in desire.

And Zayn, he steps towards me with lust billowing between us.

Placing a kiss on my shoulder blade, he lifts the rope over my head and holds it out in front of me.

"Arms up, Pen," he murmurs into my ear.

I raise them into the air once more as he wraps the rope around my waist, unravelling it from my leg at the same time. As he pulls, the rough material chafes against my leg, damaging my stockings and running between my legs. It makes me gasp with shock as the rope passes over my mound, rough against my clit. When the whole length of rope is wrapped around my middle tightly, he hands me the end, steps to my side then places his palm on the middle of my chest.

"You fucking slay me," he says, leaning in for a kiss before wrapping his arm around my back, and tipping me backwards.

With my feet pressed against the floor and my knees bent at an angle, Zayn looks over at York and nods, inviting him to join in. York doesn't hesitate. He crouches behind me, holding me beneath my shoulders, supporting me so that Zayn can stand up. With my core muscles locked tight, my thighs pressed together, and my feet flat on the floor, Zayn takes the rope from me and tugs. With perfect timing, York flips me around, the momentum of Zayn's tug and the force of York's hands helping me twist over until I land on my hands and knees. I lift my head to look up at York, flicking my hair and arching my back suggestively. I feel the material of my silk shorts riding up my arse cheeks, the roundness of my arse on display to Dax and Xeno, and I love it.

Swinging my hips, I crawl towards York who smiles down at me as I kneel before him. His fingers stroke down my face then rest beneath my chin. He urges me upwards, and I climb to my feet slowly. With one hand on my arse and the other cupping my face, he yanks me towards him and kisses me roughly, his tongue spearing my lips on a groan.

"Let those motherfuckers watch. Let them see what they're missing," York says against my mouth harshly. He squeezes my arse, bruising me with his touch. I fucking moan, not caring how I sound as he kisses me. At this moment, York owns me. He plunders my mouth, he grasps my arse, he grinds against me. It's a powerful, intoxicating kiss.

"My turn," Zayn growls.

There's a tug at my waist, and I break the kiss as Zayn pulls on the end of the rope forcing me away from York. I turn with the momentum, rising onto the balls of my feet as he unravels me. Zayn captures me on the last turn, grasping my elbow and sliding his leg between mine roughly. His thigh hits my clit, and I can't help but grind against his firm muscle as he lowers me backwards and slides his lips against my throat, but York is not to be outdone. From my upside down position I watch him spin on his feet, drop to his knees and grab hold of the rope, before spinning back upwards in a corkscrew turn. He places the rope around my neck and as Zayn lifts me back up it tightens slightly.

"York!" Dax warns, but I know York means me no harm. If anything, this turns me on, to be at their mercy like this, to be able to trust them not to hurt me.

At Grim's club, my choice was taken away, but right here, right now, I want this.

My fingers curl around the rope as Zayn kisses me, his thigh grinding against my sensitive clit, setting me alight. "Zayn," I mutter against his mouth. My husky voice, needy. I need him. I need *them*.

"Pen, fuck…" York cups my arse from behind, the rope loosening around my neck, more like a necklace than a noose. Grabbing my arm, he jerks me away from Zayn, twisting me around before lifting me off the floor and stepping backwards, the rope still dangling from my throat.

He kisses me again. Hard. His teeth clacking against mine, his hands cupping my face, his hard cock pressing against my stomach. I reach down between us, my hand rubbing York's cock over the soft leather.

"Enough!"

I feel a sharp tug, and my eyes widen suddenly as my fingers fly to my throat. The rope tightens around my neck and I'm ripped away from York, only to stumble backwards into a hard chest. A firm arm wraps around my waist tightly.

"Stop this now!" Xeno growls into my ear, anger vibrating up through his body. But it isn't just anger. I can feel his passion pressing against my lower back. He's turned on and he fucking hates it.

"You want me," I whisper, pushing him, testing his strength as I grind my arse back against him and push the rope off my neck. It falls to the floor at our feet.

"No!" he roars, pushing me away, ending the moment with anger and denial. If he meant to hurt me, he succeeded. Tears prick my eyes in humiliation as Zayn rushes forward, picking me up from the floor. He spins us around to face Xeno, rage suffusing his features. Fear spikes in my chest. Why did I push them? What have I done?

"Fuck you, Xeno. You prick! Man the fuck up and admit how you feel about Pen. Stop pushing her away when we all know you want her just as badly as the rest of us."

"You've no fucking idea what you're talking about, Zayn. Shut the fuck up!" he counters, his fingers curling into fists.

"No. I won't. I'm calling this a motherfucking intervention of Breaker proportions. The time is now," Zayn throws back.

"Zayn, don't. Please. I don't want this. I shouldn't have—" I whisper. I don't want anyone to be forced into admitting how they feel about me, good or bad, and by the look on Xeno's face, it's bad. Really, really bad.

But Zayn doesn't seem to hear me. Instead, he turns me in his arms and clasps my face in his hands. His obsidian eyes gleaming with passion and determination. "If he isn't man enough to say how he feels, then fuck him. I am."

"Zayn—" I start, but he cuts me off.

"Three years ago you walked away with Jeb. You fucking broke my heart, Pen. I fell to pieces and Xeno, he held me together. He held *us* together. We vowed from that moment on, that no matter what, the Breakers would come first. Always. We vowed to look out for each other, protect each other. No matter what. But Xeno forgot one fundamental thing. We all forgot."

"And what was that?" I ask, my voice barely above a whisper.

"You, Pen. We forgot that you were a Breaker too. From the moment you stepped into the basement of Jackson Street, you became one of us. You became our beating fucking heart, and I refuse to let those two fuckers forget that," he says, jabbing a finger at them both. "You were always ours, Pen. You were always mine, and I refuse to deny what my heart wants. I don't give a fuck what's at stake."

Zayn doesn't give me time to respond, he just crashes his mouth against mine and kisses me like a desperate man. He kisses me like the floodgates have been opened wide and the past three years of loss, hurt and anger are nothing but painful memories that no longer belong to us anymore.

Our kiss is interrupted by slow clapping. Zayn jerks away, leaving me breathless and wired. I have to blink back the fog of lust in order to concentrate on just keeping upright. This is all too fucking much.

"Nice speech, Zayn. Never thought you'd turn into such a pussy-whipped bitch."

That's all it takes to fan the flames of Zayn's anger. He runs at Xeno, tackling him to the ground, his fists meeting Xeno's face, the sound of his aggression echoing around the room. Xeno doesn't fight back, he just fucking lies there and takes every punch to his head.

"Stop it!" I shout, launching myself at them, but York steps in my way and grasps me around the waist before I can break the fight up.

"No, Titch. Let them fight this out. It's been a long time coming."

I struggle against his hold, flinching with every punch that lands with a loud smack.

"Don't fight over me!" I scream and Xeno snaps.

Roaring loudly, he flips Zayn over and straddles him, landing a hard punch against Zayn's mouth that throws his head to the side and splits his lip. Blood spurts out from the cut, and I lose it completely.

"Stop!" I scream, but they don't hear me. They don't fucking hear me. York yanks me backwards, but still I struggle.

"This needs to happen, Titch."

"No, York, it doesn't. It doesn't!" I turn to look at Dax who is watching the fight with a blank expression. "Please, Dax, stop this. Stop this insanity!"

Dax meets my gaze and grits his jaw.

Now I'm the one who snaps.

I scream.

Loudly. Piercingly.

I scream in frustration. I scream with every last bit of hurt. I scream until I'm fucking hoarse.

My fists beat at York's arms and he holds me tighter. I don't stop. I don't hear the words York is saying in my ear. I hear nothing but the unravelling of my soul.

I let out all my anger. I let out every last drop of hate for Jeb and my brother for causing this, for leading us to this point. I scream and scream until finally my anguish gets their attention.

Xeno's raised fist stops mid-air, as if his own rage has been tempered by mine. He snaps his head around, looking at me over his shoulder. A rivulet of blood runs down his temple and over his cheek from a split in his eyebrow as he breathes heavily. Beneath him, Zayn's eyes widen with concern, his anger draining away with every second that passes. I sag in York's hold.

"Stop it. Just stop it. I'm not worth this. I'm not worth it."

I'm sobbing now, huge tears track down my cheeks and I can't fucking stop them.

I can't.

If this uncorking of my emotions makes me weak, then so fucking be it.

"Titch," York laments, his arms easing from around my waist. I push his arms away, stumbling out of his hold.

"No. Enough," I retort, backing away from him.

Zayn pushes Xeno off him and scrambles to his feet towards me. His shirt is ripped and blood runs over his teeth and chin from the split to his lip. "Pen, come here," he begins, but I stumble backwards, holding my hands up.

"No. Don't!" I swipe at my tears, trying to get my head together. "I can't see you do this to each other. I can't. I'm sorry. Fuck, I'm so sorry for hurting you all. I never meant for any of this. I never meant to break you like this."

Behind Zayn, Xeno swipes at the blood trickling down his cheek. His shirt is torn, his hair a wild mess but it's the emotion in his eyes and the words he speaks that cut me the deepest. "But you did break us," he accuses softly. "You broke me."

This time there's no malice there, just the truth. Just the cold, hard, heart-breaking truth and just like in the cage at Grim's, I'm forced to my knees with the weight of everything wrong between us and all that I want to fix.

"Kid..." Dax steps forward and I drag my gaze away from Xeno to him. His eyes soften as he crouches before me and swipes at my tears gently. "Get up, baby."

"I need to tell you. I need to tell you why—"

"Not here. Not like this, Kid," he says, cutting me off. "Get up. This isn't you. This isn't our girl. Stand up!" he demands, and I see the fierceness in his gaze, the love.

I see it. I feel it.

So I climb to my feet. I grit my jaw and force strength back into my heart.

"That's my girl," Dax says, wrapping his arm around my shoulders as he hauls me to his side before he glares at his bestfriends. "I should've trusted what's left of my goddamn fucking heart, but instead I listened to you, Xeno. Not anymore. You three need to sort your goddamn shit out, and you, motherfucker," he says, pointing at Xeno, "Need to take a long hard look at yourself. I'm done with this. Whatever happened, Kid doesn't deserve to be on her knees for us, for any-fucking-one. I'm taking her home. Right the fuck now. Don't come back until you've dealt with your shit!"

And just like when we were kids, Dax swoops in, protecting me once again.

34

Pen

After sending a text to Clancy and River telling them that I've left the club, I sit in silence looking blindly out of the window as Dax drives us both back to the Academy. Well, at least that's what I thought he was doing. Only when we pull into an underground car park filled with expensive cars, all gleaming and shining, do I realise we're not at the Academy at all.

"Where are we?" I ask as Dax pulls into an empty bay with the number 605 painted in yellow on the concrete wall in front. There are three empty bays next to it all marked with the same number.

"Come with me and I'll show you," Dax replies, stepping out of the car. I watch as he walks around the bonnet and opens the door for me. "Come with me, Kid."

"Tell me where I am first," I reply, my head still fucked up from everything that went on in the club. I feel like I've been hit by a freight train. My head is spinning with all the emotional punches I received tonight. I feel vulnerable, uncertain.

"Pen, this is our home. The *Breakers'* home."

"Your *home*?"

"Yes, come with me. *Please*?" He asks, framing his request like a question.

"Okay," I say, taking his proffered hand, too exhausted to question him. His warm fingers curl around mine and I step out of the way whilst he closes the car door, locking it with a click of a button.

Beneath my feet the concrete floor is cold, and I wince, shifting from foot to foot. Dax takes one look at my shoeless feet, and just like he did when we left the club, lifts me up into his arms and cradles me to his chest. My initial reaction is to stiffen in his hold, but as his familiar scent washes over me I find myself relaxing against him, my head leaning against his shoulder. With me held aloft in his arms, Dax walks over to the elevator and presses a button to open the doors. They slide apart and he hits the button for the sixth floor.

"I can walk now," I murmur, as he steps out into the hallway from the lift with me still in his arms.

"Nah, I got you," he says, stopping only when we reach apartment 605. "The key to open the door is in my inside jacket pocket… Could you grab it?" He keeps his gaze fixed on the door, and when I cast my gaze down it's because the top of my bustier has slid lower. I adjust myself, wriggling in his arms a little.

"You could just put me down and open the door yourself," I suggest.

"No." Now his eyes clash with mine, and I swallow hard at the determination I see swimming in the grey-green depths of them. He was always my protector. Always. He seems to be reverting back to that role tonight and a large part of me likes it. *Wants* it. *Needs* it, actually.

"Fine," I mumble, sliding my hand between his shirt and jacket, trying not to pay attention to the way his heart is thumping beneath my hand, or the firmness of his pecs beneath my fingers.

Twisting slightly in his arms, I manage to pinch the credit card style key between my finger and thumb, then wave it over the lock. A green light flickers on, and the door swings into a large open plan living space with floor to ceiling windows that look over the city spread out below us. A grey L-shaped couch is set off to one side, with a large flatscreen TV attached to the white wall directly opposite it. To the left of the room is a flashy white kitchen with a large island and four black bar stools placed around it. Dax strides into the room, with me still in his arms. I'm acutely aware of how Dax's fingers are digging into my bare flesh as he clutches me against his chest. It's like he's afraid of dropping me, even though that isn't possible, given his strength and size.

"*This* is your place?" I ask incredulously as he lowers me gently to the floor.

"Yes. We bought it six months ago." He moves towards the kitchen and starts making tea. I perch on one of the bar stools and watch him closely.

"We?"

"The Breakers, of course."

"Where exactly are we?" I ask, hiding my shock behind another question. I wasn't exactly paying attention in the car, too lost in my own thoughts to notice what part of London we were heading into.

"Islington."

"Is this an apartment in one of the new developments?" I ask, recognising some of the landscape through the huge window. It might be dark but there's no mistaking those familiar buildings.

"Yes."

"Fuck," I mutter, having no other words to say. I can't even begin to think how much this place cost to buy. "But why have you all been staying at the Academy if you've got this place?"

"Not all of us. Xeno and I live here whilst York and Zayn stay there."

"Why? Why not all live here, together?" I press, not understanding.

"For reasons I can't go into just yet…" he says, shutting down my line of questioning. I frown, but leave it at that.

"Here," he says, passing me a cup of tea. "You still like two sugars?"

"I do," I answer softly, watching as he slides over a dish of sugar across the counter towards me. I drop two heaped spoonfuls into my tea and stir before taking a sip. We sit in awkward silence drinking our tea.

The truth sits between us, the proverbial elephant in the room. "Dax, I owe you an explanation—"

He shakes his head. "No. When the others come home, then we can talk. Are you hungry?"

"Sure, I could eat," I say.

He pulls out his mobile phone and scrolls through his list of contacts before hitting dial. "I'll order in, you're welcome to go change into something more comfortable. You can borrow something of mine… My room's the last door on the left," he says a little awkwardly, nodding towards a door on the far side of the apartment, past the L-shaped sofa.

"Actually, that'd be good. Thanks," I mutter, following his instructions.

I find his bedroom at the end of a long hallway. There are five other doors situated off the hallway too, all of them closed. I'm curious to look inside but refrain. Dax's bedroom is dominated by a large king-sized bed situated in the centre of the room. A built-in, mirrored wardrobe runs across one wall, and a chest-of-drawers is situated beneath a large window that looks out over the city, providing a pretty backdrop of twinkling lights against the night sky.

"I haven't had a chance to put my stamp on it yet," Dax explains, making me jump. He's standing in the doorway, his forearms pressed against the frame as he watches me.

"It's lovely," I reply, but he's right, there's none of Dax's personality in this room. There are no knick-knacks on display, nothing to personalise the space. It's empty. Yet, when I look up at Dax, his expression is full. It's full of *everything*. He's not hiding behind a hoodie and a cap now like he used to do so often when we were kids.

"Dax, I—" I begin, gulping down the rock lodged in my throat.

"I've ordered us pizza. You're welcome to use the shower," he says, as he walks towards me. "You've got mascara all down your face..." Dax reaches for me, his thumb running over my cheeks.

"What's happening?" I whisper as he moves closer and closer, nothing but longing in his gaze. It's the wrong thing to say because he suddenly realises what he's doing and seems to shake himself.

"I'll wait for the food delivery. You should find something to wear in the chest-of-drawers. I'll be waiting for you in the kitchen, okay?"

He shucks off his jacket before discarding it on the back of a chair, then kicks off his trainers and strides from the room without a backward glance. I can't help but notice how his jeans and t-shirt hug his muscles in all the right places, or how his tattoos wind up the back of his neck reaching the base of his skull, in thick, dark lines. He's such a big man, so much bigger than the boy I remember, overwhelming in so many ways.

Over the past few weeks, Dax has done everything in his power to ignore me, to shut me out, but tonight something has changed. I see it in his actions, hear it in his words and feel it in his touch. He may still be fighting that right now, but he can't deny it. Neither can I. I let out a whoosh of breath and step into the bathroom. Right now, I need to get clean, and I need to eat. I have to focus on the simple things so that I can deal with the complicated things later.

Stepping into the bathroom, which is as immaculately kept and as perfectly decorated as the bedroom, I strip off my clothes. This whole apartment reeks of the kind of luxury I've never experienced before, and I can't help but wonder what kind of dark deeds the Breakers have had to commit to be able to afford to live in such a place. It's exactly how I imagine a posh hotel to be decorated, with neutral colours and rose gold accents. There's a sensual vibe to the décor that appeals to me and the life I've always dreamed of, *longed* for.

And out of nowhere that realisation is like a sucker-punch to my stomach.

Tears spring from my eyes as I turn on the shower and step beneath the spray. Fat droplets fall unbidden down my cheeks mingling with the water that flows down the drain. My body shakes with emotion as the tears keep coming and I have to stuff my fist into my mouth to stop the sobs from escaping. The flat of my hand slams against the shower wall as I double over and cry for all the things that might've been. Right here, naked, and vulnerable inside the Breakers' home, I let all the agony out.

I let it all out, and on the back of my tears, I realise something fundamental. Whilst I've been struggling, living in a dingy council flat with my bitch of a mother, trying to take care of my baby sister and trying to make ends meet, the Breakers have slept in clean sheets, in warm clothes, with food in their bellies and friendship in their hearts. They've had each other throughout it all, and whilst I might've had my sister, it hasn't been easy. I've not been able to relax once in the past three years. I've just kept going. Looking after Lena, dealing with my mother's shit, my brother's threats and Jeb's demands all the while striving for something better, something more. I've done it all. I've carried all that stress.

On. My. Fucking. Own.

That *hurts*.

But I cry for more than my own selfish pain. I cry for them, for my Breakers, because there's no soul in this flat. This isn't a home. It's a place to lie their heads, it's the culmination of all the bad decisions they made and all the pain they've caused in Jeb's name, and I hate it. I hate that they fought each other this evening. I hate that my actions pushed them to that point. I did exactly what Xeno said.

I broke them.

Now it's my job to fix them. Fix us.

Stripping naked and washing away the events of tonight won't rid me of that feeling of guilt.

Only the truth will. That knowledge gives me the strength to force back my tears and to stand upright. Sniffing loudly, I swipe at my eyes, washing away the mascara, and scrub my body clean. I wash my hair thoroughly before stepping out of the shower to dry myself off on a beautifully soft towel. It's like being wrapped up in a luxurious fur coat sprayed with expensive perfume. These towels haven't been washed with cheap detergent like my mother is prone to use, but even though I'm surrounded by luxury, opulence, richness, all of it is soulless. There's no heart. This isn't a home.

Sighing heavily, I head back into the bedroom and search through the drawers. I find a black t-shirt and a pair of grey joggers with a tie-waist that I'm able to fasten to stop them from falling down. Both items of clothing swamp me, but I don't give it a second thought. I'm not here to impress Dax, or any of them. I don't care what I look like.

Twenty minutes later, with my fingers working out the tangles in my hair, I head back into the main living area to find Dax with his back to me, dishing out slices of pizza. I stop dead in my tracks. My body sways, my stomach churns, and my mouth waters not just for the delicious smelling food, but for Dax.

Dax the man, not the boy.

Dax with the wide shoulders and slim waist.

Dax with his strong muscular arms.

Dax with his beautifully detailed tattoos.

Dax who's removed his t-shirt and has bared his skin to me.

I watch him move gracefully, my throat drying as he twists on his feet lightly, placing plates onto the kitchen island. His eyes snap up as he notices me standing there gawking at him, and for a moment the only hunger I feel is for *him*, my Dax, my Dark Angel.

35

Dax

Jesus fucking Christ.

What the fuck was I thinking bringing her back here?

I tense under her scrutiny, my fucking heart beating like a drum and my cock stirring with dirty thoughts. I press my hips against the counter, trying to tame my bastard dick as I dish out the pizza. Now is not the time for that. But seriously, how can she look so damn beautiful and so fucking terrifying at the same time? Seeing her barefaced, with wet hair and dressed in my clothes does stupid things to me. I thought she looked fucking stunning in that sexy little outfit and those damn heels, but this woman before me. This is the woman who turns me on, who makes my fucking stomach drop out, my heart miss a beat, and my cock ramrod straight.

And when she dances… Fuck. There's nothing like it. No one stirs me up quite the way she does. No fucking one. She's an enigma. This tiny woman, so easily squashable, and yet so fucking strong. She's a damn warrior and I've *missed* her. I've fucking missed everything about her.

"Sit. Eat," I snap, fully aware that I'm acting like a dickhead but I'm unable to help myself.

She flinches at the harshness of my voice, and I already feel the apology rising up my throat.

I grit my jaw as she approaches, pushing the plate laden with food across the table. I take a seat opposite her, not knowing what the fuck to say. I've never been a big talker, but that's only because I don't feel the need to chat shit with anyone, except her. I *want* to talk with her. Xeno swore us off Pen, said she wasn't part of the plan. But fuck him and his demands. I listened to him for far too long. Fuck, if I'm being brutally honest with myself, I wanted to take her in my arms the second I saw her on the dancefloor at Rocks.

"Eat," I persist. We can talk once she's filled her stomach and got some colour back in her cheeks.

"Why?" she asks, looking between the slices of pizza and back at me.

I notice her hands are shaking. I see the heartache in her eyes, and it angers me. Jeb's a prick. He hasn't taken care of her. No one's taken care of her. My fist screws up into a ball, and it takes all my control not to fucking hit something. My cock softens at the thought. Now that I've acknowledged to myself what I've known all along since returning — that she's in trouble — I can't turn my back on her. I won't. My cock and its wayward thoughts will have to chill the fuck out.

"Why eat? Because you're stick thin, Kid…" I pause as she looks at me strangely. York might have always been able to read her the best, but there was no mistaking her emotions or her words tonight. Nothing is as it seems, and I feel like a cunt for only just wising up. "You need to eat," I repeat, "So I bought you food. Don't read too much into it."

"That isn't what I meant. I appreciate the food, but why take care of me like this now? Only a few days ago you wanted nothing to do with me. You dropped me for Tiffany. You've avoided me at every turn, Dax."

"Eat, Pen," I grind out. She might be able to flay herself open, but it's not so easy for me. I need a fucking moment to gather my thoughts. To explain.

For the next ten minutes, we eat our meal in silence until she's full. When her plate is empty and she lets out a tiny burp that makes her cheeks flush with embarrassment, I grab a bottle of water from the fridge and a packet of painkillers from the cupboard and slide both across the counter to her. She raises her brow at the painkillers.

"I figured you might have a headache," I mumble lamely. Damn, I have a headache from all the shit that's gone down tonight.

"Thanks," she says softly, popping a pill before unscrewing the cap on the bottle of water and taking a long swig, washing it down.

"You've still got some sauce on your—" I say, my voice trailing off as her face pinks up.

"Shit," she mumbles, swiping at her chin and sucking the sauce into her mouth from her finger. There's still a small droplet sitting on the corner of her lips and with my half-eaten food forgotten, I skirt around the island and stop in front of her. Automatically she turns to face me with her knees pressed together, and her small hands resting on her thighs.

"What?" she whispers. "Did I miss some?" Her tongue slides along her bottom lip as she catches the droplet just at the same moment my finger reaches it. The tip of her tongue presses against my finger, and we both stiffen. Her eyes widen, her pupils enlarging at that faintest of touches.

"Right there," I say, my voice hoarse, my stupid fucking dick jumping in my pants.

She withdraws her tongue, her gaze focused on me. I don't think she's actually breathing. I know I'm fucking not, but I can't seem to remove my finger from her lip. In fact, my whole hand cups her cheek, my thumb replacing the spot where my finger was, whilst her eyes flash with both confusion and *hope*.

I see that hope, and it makes my fucking heart break and my head fill with questions.

She belongs to Jeb, and yet she's looking at me like she used to when we were kids. She's looking at me like she's mine, like she's always been mine. and I don't know what to do with that.

Actually, that's bullshit.

I know exactly what I want to do. I want to pick her up in my arms, carry her back into my bedroom and fucking *love* her like I've wanted to do for years now. Fuck the consequences. Fuck everything.

I contemplate doing just that when she reaches up and grasps my wrist, as though to pull my hand away. Her breathing is coming in short, sharp breaths as her fingers tighten around my wrist. My thumb rubs across her bottom lip, making the pinkness turn a deeper shade from my bruising touch. I imagine biting that lip, making it bleed like she made me bleed when she walked away from us. That moment when she told us we were over is branded in my soul. I've never felt pain like it. It hurt. It still fucking hurts.

"Don't," she mutters, her lips parting on a breath, but it's a half-hearted demand. There's no conviction behind it. She's worn out, beat down, and I hate that.

"Pen—" I step closer, disobeying her as my fingers slide into her hair, and I grasp hold of her a little too tightly. "I just want to—" *comfort you, hold you, be there for you.* Fuck, I need to man up. I need to say what I really feel, but it's hard, so fucking hard. There's too much distance between us and I'm not good with words. York and Zayn were always better at this part. They always knew what to say. "Fuck!" I curse, annoyed with myself.

Her warm breaths puff over my bare chest, and her eyes lock onto the angel tattoo sitting right over my heart. She raises her hand, her brows pulling together in a frown as she runs her fingers gently over the tattoo.

"When did you get this?" she asks, her voice so soft, I have to strain to hear, not to mention the fact that I'm fucking distracted by her touch.

"Not long after—" I sigh heavily. *Come on, Dax, man the fuck up.* "I got it not long after that night. I wanted a reminder of what I loved, and what I fucking lost. Back then, I wanted to look in the mirror and be reminded of the pain you caused so I wouldn't be weak and seek you out. I got this tattoo as a warning to never, ever let you into my heart again."

Pen's hand falls away, and I can see tears glistening on the edges of her lashes as her gaze bores a hole right through my chest.

"I'm sorry…"

"Pen, listen —" But I can't get the words out. My heart is still fucking bruised, and my words are caught in my throat at all the hurt between us. So much fucking hurt. There's no hiding the feelings bubbling within us both, within *me*.

"I'm done with men using me," she finally whispers out. It's a random declaration but the truth in her words cuts me deep, slicing right through my skin. I need to get to the bottom of that statement because it's heavy with secrets, but when I tip her head up so I can get a real good look at her, I know that she's on the cusp of blurting everything out and I owe it to my brothers to wait for their return. They need to hear what she has to say, and I'll be damned if I make her say it more than once, given how much it's killing her.

"You should sleep," I say, loosening my grip and stepping back, my hand falling away. "We can all talk when you've rested."

"Dax, I —" There's a sadness to her tone and I want to pick her up and fucking hold her. It takes all my effort not to snatch her up into my arms and crush her against my chest.

"Sleep, Pen. Take my room. You need to rest. You're exhausted."

Her gaze locks with mine and in that moment, I see *her*. I really see her.

My Kid. My beautiful fucking girl.

There's nothing else in her gaze but honesty and this sad kind of loneliness that fucks me up in the worst possible way. I don't need to fight in a cage to feel pain, I just need to look into her eyes.

"Dax," she chokes, stepping off the stool. She seems to wobble on her feet. I swallow hard, my whole body vibrating with need for her. I can't fucking help it. I hold my arms open, needing her. Needing this.

Fuck everything.

"Kid, come here," I croak, my own throat closing up with emotion. This time she doesn't hesitate. She walks straight into my open arms, slamming into my chest as she wraps her arms tightly around my waist.

"I missed you so, *so* much, Dax," she whispers, her fingers digging into my skin, her cheek pressing against my chest right where my tattoo sits over my crazy, out of control heart. I hold her close, cupping her head and pulling her against me tightly. I don't ever want to let go. Not ever.

So I don't.

I hold her tightly as she sobs quietly in my arms, and every tear she sheds, every fucking sob that rips out of her mouth breaks down every last shred of resentment and anger I hold inside. It falls away. All of it. All of the years of wondering why she turned her back on me, on *us*, is shredded. Pen rarely cries. She was always so fucking strong. But I have a feeling, since we've returned, that's all she's done. Right here, right now, she falls apart in my arms, and I've never felt so fucking small in my life.

I've done this to her.

We've done this to her.

We came back into her life and pushed her, treated her like shit, like she meant nothing when all the while she meant every damn thing. No, she *means* everything. And if Xeno can't fucking see it, then screw him.

My instincts kick in. My need to protect her like I did when we were kids takes over, and I slide my hands down her back, cupping her arse as I lift her up. She doesn't protest, she simply wraps her legs around my waist, her hands sliding over my chest as she buries her face in the crook of my neck. I feel her lips brush against my shoulder, and my heart fucking collapses into a bleeding pulpy mess in my chest, whilst my cock thinks the circus has come to town. I snarl internally. This isn't about that. I won't break this truce by taking advantage of her in such a vulnerable state, no matter how much I want to rip my clothes from her body and sink into her until there's only us.

Without saying a word, I carry her back to my room,

kicking the door shut behind me, and lay her on my bed. She unravels herself from around me and lies down, her red-rimmed eyes staring up at me as I hover over her, my knees trapping her thighs, my forearms resting on either side of her head.

We don't talk. This moment between us is too huge for words, too momentous. If I could dance with her now, I would. If she wasn't so emotionally drained, I would take her into my arms and show her with my steps exactly how I feel. I'd make her understand that I never stopped loving her even when I convinced myself that I did.

But we have time for that.

Right now she needs to trust me again. She needs to know that from this fucking moment onwards, no matter the cost, I'm on her side.

"Dax, will you just hold me?"

My chest heaves as she looks at me with haunted eyes that make me want to kill everyone who ever hurt her, including my best friends, including myself. I nod, lowering down on arms that fucking tremble from holding back. She's the only woman who's ever made me feel weak and fucking invincible at the same time. My Kid. *Fucking mine.*

There's nothing more that I want to do than sink myself inside of her, to love her the way I want to, the way I need to. Instead, I press my lips against her forehead and squeeze my eyes shut. My fingers curl around the bedding as I force myself to hold back. To wait.

It's a fucking herculean task and dragging my lips away from her is painful, but I do it. I lie down beside her, my finger capturing a tear that rolls down her cheek whilst she resolutely looks up at the ceiling. I see her drawing strength from deep inside. I see her shoring up her reserves, replenishing the empty well within that the events of this evening have stolen from her. Tomorrow, when we're rested, we can talk. Until then, I intend on holding her all fucking night long, but first my apology. Words aren't enough, but for now they're all I have.

"I'm sorry, Kid. I'm so fucking sorry for it all."

"I'm sorry too," she replies, then turns on her side and pulls her legs up to her chest, hugging herself close. It's a closed position, and one that is self-comforting, but screw that. She needs to know I'm here, that I've got her back, so despite my bastard cock growing harder, I wrap my arm around her waist, and curl myself around her body, spooning her.

Before long, her muscles relax, her eyes close, and she falls fast asleep, snoring gently in my arms. Not long after, I hear the front door open, and York cursing my name. I don't move.

He can come find us. Nothing has the power to drag me away from Kid right now, nothing.

When York pushes open my bedroom door and sees Kid wrapped up in my arms, I expect a mouthful of cusses, threats to my life. Instead, he meets my gaze, relief washing over his features.

"Where are Zayn and Xeno?" I ask, keeping my voice low.

"Doing what you asked." York flicks his gaze at Kid, his freakish eyes flashing with something I recognise only too well. *Protectiveness*.

"Yeah?" I snort.

"Yeah. So rest up, bro, cuz that shit's gonna blow up soon, and you need to be ready for it," he says.

"Is that so?"

He nods, his fingers wrapping around the doorframe as his gaze trails over Kid. "I'm heading back out to join them, don't expect us back anytime soon. It's gonna be a long fucking weekend—" he says, then hesitates.

"What?"

"When we're done, we have things to discuss. Just make sure Pen is still here when we get back. Don't let her out of your sight."

"And what about Xeno?"

York puffs out a breath, shaking his head. I see the worry in his eyes, and it churns my stomach. "You need me?" I ask, hoping to fuck he doesn't.

York shakes his head, gritting his jaw. "Right now we need you to take care of Titch. We'll figure the rest out later," he says, then quietly closes the door behind him.

36

Pen

Turning over in bed, I swipe at my eyes, feeling the first rays of dawn warming my skin through the glass. Groaning, I sit up, feeling disorientated for a moment. It takes me a few seconds for everything to fall back into place, and my stomach turns over.

Uneasiness settles in my stomach, and I reach out my hand, pressing against the spot where Dax had lain down next to me. The bed sheets feel cool, indicating that he left a while ago. I can't help but wonder whether he stayed the night holding me, or if he left the moment I fell asleep. I force myself not to think too much about the fact he's no longer here. There's still so much left unsaid. As much as I want to fix us, I know that might not be a possibility given everything standing in our way.

The Breakers' bond is solid. It was forged before they accepted me into their crew, and it remained strong long after I walked away. The fact of the matter is there's still too much bad blood between us all. Dax might have stepped in last night to stop it spiralling out of control, but in the stark light of day can we really get over everything that's passed between us? The honest answer is that I don't know, and the only way I'm going to find out is to have that talk with all of them.

I need to be brave.

The thing is, what do I say? I still have no idea how I'm going to deal with this situation. I'm still beholden to Jeb, to David. My sister's life is still under threat, nothing's changed in that respect, and I'd be a fool to believe that the Breakers will suddenly come to my rescue. They still work for Jeb, after all. They've taken a blood oath, have sworn to put the crew first. What phrase had my brother loved to throw back in my face as often as he could…?

Skins before whores. Yeah, that was it.

Heaving a sigh, I slide towards the edge of the bed. I'm not sure exactly what the time is, but it can't be much past six am. That means I've only really had four or five hours of sleep. My throat feels dry and my tongue furry, so I head into the bathroom and squeeze some toothpaste onto my finger, rubbing it over my teeth then rinse my mouth with water. I wish I had my toothbrush with me, but beggars can't be choosers.

"Come on, Pen. You can do this," I say to my reflection, gathering my courage. Striding out of the bathroom and across the bedroom, I step out into the hallway and head towards the main living area.

"Dax?" I call, half expecting him to pop up from behind the kitchen counter, topless, just like he did last night. When he doesn't appear, I twist on my feet and head back the way I came.

"Dax?"

I try the next three doors, peering into more bedrooms. All of them are similarly decorated without any personal touches and none of them have been slept in. One room has a few more items dotted about, and I recognise Xeno's jacket thrown over the back of a chair and a couple of pairs of trainers left discarded by the wardrobe.

"Hello?" I say, my heart pounding in my chest.

When I reach the last door, which must be a spare bedroom or a bathroom, I can hear the faint sound of music start to play from behind it. "Dax, are you in there?" I ask, knocking on the thick wood. When there's no answer, I push open the door, stopping dead in my tracks when I'm faced with Dax.

He's dancing… to *Halo* by Beyoncé… in nothing but a pair of knee-length, grey jersey shorts. His skin is slick with a sheen of sweat and every inch of him is covered in tattoos, right down to his bare feet; they wind up his legs and creep beneath his shorts. He's a walking painting, a work of art. My eyes drink him in greedily, grazing over every inch of him, from his chiselled abs, to his powerful thighs and strong calf muscles. He has arms almost as thick as my thighs, defined, strong. I remember how it felt to be wrapped up in them last night and my stomach tightens.

My beautiful, damaged Dax. My Dark Angel.

I swallow, my heart bruising the inside of my ribcage, it's beating so damn hard.

Fuck.

Dax is so engrossed in his movements that he doesn't notice me straightaway, so I slip inside the studio, gently shutting the door behind me. The space is a little bit larger than Dax's bedroom and en-suite bathroom combined, and is roomy enough for the Breakers to dance in together.

Though right now the space doesn't feel big enough for

what I'm witnessing, because Dax takes up the whole damn studio with his presence. He's like a goddamn hurricane trapped inside a glass jar. Any minute now the full impact of his passion is going to hit me. I already feel my skin tingling and my body swaying to his movements. He flies across the floor dipping and turning, producing leg kicks, spins and arm flares that leave me breathless. There's so much power behind his moves and he lifts off the ground with ease.

It's magic.

Pure fucking magic.

His muscles ripple as he moves, tightening and flexing as he dances. The expression on his face is filled both with longing and pain, but there's also relief. He's lost to the music, to his movements. This is Lyrical dancing. He's dancing to illustrate the music, the words specifically. Every beat of the song, all the words Beyoncé sings are expressed through his movements and I understand what this is.

I *get* it.

When he leaps into the air, performing a grand jeté, his powerful legs splitting wide, I let out a gasp of astonishment. He moves with a lightness that's insane given his bulk, and lands like a ballerina with grace and control.

I'm itching to join him, to mould my body to his and just let everything go. But this isn't about me, this is about him, and as the words of the song wash over me, I understand that this is Dax's way of truly opening up. He's expressing himself the only way he knows how, the only way he can, and I *feel* it. I open my heart, and I accept everything he has to give as he flips backwards, tumbling like a gymnast. I accept this gift as he extends his body, as he moves with intention, with feeling. I accept his story because this is exactly what this is. This is Dax baring his soul to me. This, right here, is brutal honesty. This is *his* story.

And, fuck, is he stunning.

So fucking beautiful.

Dax has always been an expressive dancer, but I've never seen him dance like this. I can't seem to breathe as he twists and turns, his body moving fluidly, with precision and purpose.

What I'm seeing is intense, passionate, and as Beyoncé's haunting voice sounds out over the speaker system I find myself transfixed, because right here and now Dax shows me the true depths of his heart.

He. Floors. Me.

He transforms, telling me his story step by agonising, heart-breaking, step. He shows me the loneliness he felt as a child, the walls he built to protect himself from his parents, and I let out a strangled cry as he falls to his knees, curls over and clasps the back of his head as though protecting himself from the ghost of his father, from the punches and the kicks, from the harsh words and the hate. He never really talked about what happened to him when we were kids, though we all knew only too well just how bad his home life was. The bruises, the stiffness in the way he used to hold himself. The way he hid beneath his caps and hoodies. The rage that would take him over when it all got too much. We knew, we saw, and we did our best to help him, to heal him with friendship and love.

But that kind of abuse, that kind of betrayal and hurt, it never leaves you. It stays with you. It's a black stain, a curse that haunts your dreams. It drags you down, takes hold of you until the only way to cope with the pain is to either turn it in on yourself or on someone else. Violence from a parent, from someone who's supposed to love you, it leaves a lasting wound that never, *ever* heals. I know that. I *understand*.

Dax covers his head, his body visibly shaking as he reaches up with one arm, his hand opening and closing to the beat of the music. This is the boy he was. The beaten and bruised kid, begging for it to stop. This is the child who had nothing until he had the Breakers, until he had me. The guilt I feel in this moment is like a stranglehold around my throat, because I walked away from him, from the rare, precious gift of his love. Stuffing my hand over my mouth, I force the sob back down because Dax never cries, *never*. At this moment I want to be there for him, to be his strength when he finally lets it all go, because I feel it coming. That glass jar is about to shatter and all that he is will rain down over me. I need to catch him when he falls.

But right now he needs me to see, to *understand*, and not get lost in my own emotions.

So that's what I do.

I *see* him, and like last night when I opened myself up to the Breakers, he does the same now.

It's a gift. A messy, glorious, complicated gift that I accept wholeheartedly.

Dax slams his fists onto the floor in time to the beat of the song, then lifts his head and pins me with his stare. Our gazes clash and I feel *everything*. All the damage inside of him comes tumbling out in that one look. I watch him crawl towards me, hauling himself forward on his forearms in time to the beat, dragging his legs behind him as he slams his fists onto the wooden boards.

Thump.

Thump.

Thump.

Thump.

Then he slowly rises, pushing up on his hands and knees,

climbing to his feet. He unfurls, transforming from a broken boy to a fearless man. He stands tall, strong, *proud*, leaving behind that beaten down boy. With a heaving chest, Dax jerks his chin, grits his jaw, then flings his arms wide, tipping his head back.

Beyonce sings about walls crashing down and with every beat of the song, he stamps his feet on the floor, his fists clenched, his arms held out to his sides. I watch him in awe as he squashes the brutality of his childhood beneath his feet, letting it go with every step.

"Dax," I lament, my feet moving towards him of their own accord. Like a magnetic force, I feel the pull, and I can't seem to stop myself. I don't want to.

With glistening eyes, Dax offers me the hand of friendship just like he did when I met him that first time in the basement of Jackson Street, just like that boy—a complete stranger—who let me rest my head on his shoulder, who gave me comfort.

"Kid," he croaks out, his fingers flexing, his gaze focused and fierce on mine. A single tear slides down his cheek, but I don't see weakness.

I see strength.

I see the man I've loved most of my life letting go of all the shit. He's showing me the power of forgiveness. He forgives me for hurting him, for leaving him.

That one single tear eviscerates his past hurts and bad decisions, just like it eviscerates mine.

It's time to heal.

I don't hesitate, I *run*, leaping into his arms.

37

Pen

We come together without words.

We come together with walls crumbling, with pain ebbing away.

We come together with heat, with longing.

We come together with *love*...

Heart-wrenching, soul-squeezing, gut-punching, pussy-trembling love.

I'm not sure who kisses who first but the power behind our kiss is like two atomic bombs detonating against each other. It's fierce. It's full of fire and passion and desperation.

Our bodies smash together.

Our teeth clack.

Our tongues dance.

Our lips bruise.

Our fingers grip and squeeze, stroke, and scratch.

We claw at one another, and Dax bites down on my bottom

lip, making me draw in a sharp breath as the metallic taste of blood mixes with our saliva. But I don't stop kissing him. I grind into him, my pussy pressed up against his hard abs as I moan with desperate wanting. We're frenzied, charged with an unstoppable desire to rip away any remaining walls between us. It's been three years of longing, of yearning, of loneliness and grief.

"Kid, fuck," he mumbles against my mouth as his large hands grasp my arse and squeeze.

"Please," I moan, my core slick.

Wanton, wet, willing.

I don't care how much we've hurt each other. I don't care that there are still things we need to talk about, to iron out. I don't care about anything other than this moment right now.

Right now, it's just us.

In this moment, only healing matters. I want this.

Today, I choose Dax, and that makes me feel powerful.

My legs tighten around Dax's waist as his hand slides up and over my hips, lifting my t-shirt in a frantic tug. I break our kiss, trusting him to hold me up as I rip off my t-shirt and bare myself to him. His gaze drops from my face to the flushed skin of my chest and the peaked points of my nipples. I arch my back telling him what I want. What I *need*.

Nothing else exists.

Only us, right here, in this moment, now.

"You're so fucking beautiful," he grinds out, lowering me backwards, his large palm supporting my back as he folds over me in a move that is asking me to trust him.

I arch my spine, my head dropping back between my shoulders and Dax squats down, balancing my arse on his firm thighs whilst his hand slides down the middle of my chest. It takes strength to keep me held like this, balanced this way, but

Dax does it with ease as he kisses a hot trail over my skin. "I've thought of nothing else but the way your skin tastes, your pussy tastes," he grinds out as his mouth clamps around my nipple. I moan as the wet heat of his tongue laps at me, drawing my already sensitive bud into the vacuum of his mouth. He sucks, and I squirm against him, sensation zapping from my nipple clamped between his teeth, to my pussy. Heat blooms between my legs, and my clit spasms, needing release.

"Dax. Oh, fuck!"

The desperation in my voice forces Dax to let go of my nipple. He lifts me upright, folding his arms around my back, his fingers gripping the back of my neck as he kisses me, blindly walking across the room until my back hits the wall. He traps me there, his body pressed against mine as he cups my face, his fingers digging into my scalp.

"Do you know how many nights I've dreamed of this, Kid? How many times I've hated myself for letting you go without a fight, then hating you because you fucking walked away with *him*. There were so many times I fisted my cock and came with anger in my heart and rage in my blood, all the while thinking of you. Do you understand how much we've fucking hungered for you, how lost we've all become? Do you understand that I won't allow you to hurt me again? This is your only warning, Kid. I'm taking a leap of faith, not for loving you like this, but for trusting that you won't break me again. I won't survive it. Do. You. Understand. Me?"

I clasp his face in my hands and press my forehead against his. "Yes. Yes, I understand."

And I do. I understand the momentousness of what's happening. That there's no going back now that we've opened up this way.

"Will you be honest with us? Will you tell us what the fuck

happened?" he asks, his thumbs brushing against my cheekbones.

I nod my head once. It's time to let it out. It's time to trust again. "I can't do this on my own anymore," I admit.

"Then you won't. Whatever this is, I'll be there. I'll protect you," he says fiercely, before pressing himself into me and kissing me like he wants to work his way beneath my skin, like there's no other place he wants to be, like this is it for him. I gasp as he grasps both my breasts in his large hands roughly, not to hurt me but because he can't seem to control himself. The sound of my surprise is enough to make him pull back, to hesitate. Our gazes clash and the depth of feeling I see within his grey-green eyes startles me.

"I had no intention… I didn't plan this… You can tell me to stop, and I'll fucking stop, Kid. I might die from blue balls, but I'll stop." He lets out a small laugh and his body trembles with the sheer force of his will as he holds back. I shake my head fiercely.

"Don't you dare stop! Don't you dare stop loving me!" I cry, my fingers curling into his shoulders and the heels of my feet pressing into his rock hard arse as I force him tighter against me.

"Never. I never stopped. I loved you even when I hated you. Oh, Kid. Fuck! I need to be inside you!"

"Yes. Oh God, yes!" I respond, writhing against him. Needing him as much as he needs me. His lips find my collarbone, as his hand slides upwards over my neck and rests against my cheek, twisting my head to the side.

"I'm going to taste every inch of you," he says, licking across my shoulder and up my neck, biting on my earlobe before kissing the tender spot beneath my ear. "I've missed your scent. You smell like summer heat and starry nights. You smell like *home*."

His mouth finds mine in a glorious, wet, passionate kiss. I match his pace, my tongue duelling with his, my pussy grinding against him.

We're not tender.

We're not gentle.

This isn't us slowly coming together. This is three years of distance, of want and longing and hurt colliding in one explosive, chaotic, beautiful mess.

That's us. A beautiful mess, and I don't want it any other way, even though there's a voice in the back of my head, a tiny, miniscule voice warning me that sleeping with him might hurt. It reminds me I've only had sex once before. But the rest of me, the woman who is starving for Dax, tells her to sit back and enjoy the fucking ride.

"Please, Dax, I need you now," I say, breathlessly.

"Condom," Dax grinds out, and with me still in his arms he opens the door to the studio and strides across the hallway and into his bedroom. He frees me from his hold, practically chucking me on the bed in his haste. I giggle, feeling lighthearted, happy, as he yanks open his bedside drawer with such force that it falls to the ground, spilling its contents. I watch him grab a foil condom packet and then in one move, he yanks off his shorts almost falling over in his haste.

"Hey, be careful," I laugh, joy bubbling inside me like champagne bubbles in a glass. But laughter dies on my lips as I see his huge cock bobbing in front of us. It's as big as I remember, and I bite my lip, aggravating Dax's bite from earlier.

"Fuck, I need to up my game," he says, looking at the mess on the floor.

"Your game is pretty good," I quip, flicking my gaze between the blush-red head of his cock and his face.

"Oh, Kid, you've no idea what I'm going to do to you."

Leaning over, Dax grabs the bottom of my joggers and whips them from my body in one quick tug, leaving me bare and naked before him. His eyes drop to my shaved pussy, and his mouth pops open with a groan.

"I want to taste you," he says, dropping to his knees at the edge of the bed, his hands reaching up and grabbing my ankles as he yanks me towards him. I let out a screech, laughter bursting from my lips. "Tell me no one has tasted you like this. Tell me this pussy's never been fucked with a tongue," Dax asks between kisses and licks up my inner thigh.

"York—" I breathe, not wanting to lie to him. He catches the worry in my face and curses. "Well then, I'm gonna have to erase that motherfucker's lips from your cunt. If it was anyone else, I might've committed murder."

"Please, don't. I love him too…" I whisper. Dax locks gazes with me and smiles.

"Kid, we don't deserve you," he says, as I wriggle beneath him, my hands sneaking down towards my clit. I need to ease the ache there.

"No!" he snaps, and my hands fall away at his abruptness. "This is all on me. I'm going to make you come, Kid. *Me.*"

"Okay," I whimper.

"Good," he grinds out, lifting my legs over his broad shoulders as his hands slide under my thighs and grip onto my hip bones. He hovers over my pussy, his warm breath teasing. I jerk upright onto my elbows, watching him look at my slit. It's the hottest thing I've ever fucking seen. This big, tattooed man, my Dax, my Dark Angel looking at me like I'm some kind of exotic meal he can't wait to taste. His tattooed hands and fingers grip hold of my creamy skin, his fingers leaving indents from holding on so tight.

"Jesus," I mumble, words failing me. Dax smiles, his eyes flicking up.

"So fucking pretty, so pink, so wet, so *mine*. I'm going to taste you now," he warns, then he lowers his mouth and licks me from my dripping hole to my clit in one firm stroke. I fall back onto the bed, moaning at the sensation. Just like our kisses he tastes me with purpose, his tongue sliding over every inch of my pussy, his tongue flat against my clit, his lips sucking my outer labia into his mouth. He sucks, he licks, he buries his face between my legs and eats me out, burying his nose in my pussy until I worry he can't fucking breathe. But he doesn't let up and my thighs clamp around his head as a groan comes from deep inside my throat. I reach for him, my hands grasping his head. I grind against his face. I'm so wet that the lower half of his face is covered in my juices, but he doesn't seem to care. When his hand reaches down, and his thumb presses against my clit, circling it expertly, I come hard. There's no warning, no build up, just a clit orgasm that spreads out across my body until I'm crying out and thrashing beneath him. Dax pins me down, not letting up, and I feel my opening spasming beneath him, my internal walls tightening then loosening, desperate for something to hold onto. I push against his face, wanting to be filled with his tongue, his cock, his fingers. Right the fuck now.

"Touch me!" I beg, not caring how desperate I sound.

Understanding what I need, Dax slides a finger inside of me, and I cry out, my pussy clenching around him.

"You're so damn tight. Fuck," he grinds out, moving his finger in and out before he rubs against that spot inside. I jerk against his hand, Dax's finger lighting a fire beneath the dying embers of my orgasm.

"Oh fucking yes," I pant.

I hear Dax's laughter as though it's down the end of a very long tunnel. My chest heaves and my eyes roll into the back of my head as I ride his hand, chasing another orgasm that's way more intense than the first. His finger curls inside of me, and when he slides another finger into my opening, I relish the slight burn. I whimper as he rises upwards onto his feet, his fingers still inside me as he hunches over, looking down at me.

"Have you fucked before, Kid?" he asks, a serious expression on his face. There's an edge of jealousy in his gaze that must be reflected back in mine because he grins, his thumb pressing on my sensitive clit. There's no way a man like Dax has stayed faithful to my memory. He had every right to sleep with women whilst we were apart, but that doesn't mean I have to like it. "I'm not a virgin," he says, his voice smooth, low, apologetic almost. "I wasn't a virgin when we met that first time, and I know that it wouldn't be fair to expect you to be one either, though it fucking kills me to know another man has taken your virginity when it should've been one of us."

My cheeks flush for a different reason this time, because I'm not experienced. I slept with that one man, and it was awful. It's been a long time since that fuck-up of an evening.

"Kid?" he asks, his fingers penetrating deeper, hitting that spot that makes my eyes roll back in my head. I wonder how on earth he expects me to answer him when he's fingering me the way he is. "Kid?" he persists, rubbing on that spot. "Tell me."

"Once before... It wasn't particularly good," I admit, my words tumbling out of my mouth in a breathy rush.

Dax scowls. "Then I'm gonna fuck you until you forget

your first time, until all you remember is this. *Us*. I'm gonna make sure you enjoy every last second of it. Okay?"

My response is ripped from my lips in a deep-throated moan as Dax finger-fucks me, the concentration on his face is sinful as he stirs up another orgasm, one that builds deep inside my womb and circles outwards. I thrust my hips upwards to meet his hand, my eyes snapping downwards to watch as the muscles in his forearms flex. I see the large veins bob beneath his tattooed skin, and I reach for his arm, running my fingers over his skin, clamping on his wrist, and urging him to go harder, faster.

"I got you, Kid," he grinds out and with his hand still between my legs, he lowers himself beside me, his thick thigh resting on mine whilst his foot slides down my other leg nudging me wider. I bend my knee, lifting my leg to the side and opening up for him. "That's it, spread your legs for me." His voice is a sexy rumble as he brushes his lips against my ear, his teeth capturing my lobe, nipping me gently as he strokes my internal walls. "You lying here beside me like this... Spread open for me like this. Fuck, I feel like a king. I feel like the richest man in the world. You, my Kid, our Pen, our lucky penny."

I turn my face to look at him, his pupils are blown wide in lust, and his face is flushed as his movements get steadily quicker. I reach up to him, clasping the back of his head, urging him to kiss me deeply. He doesn't hesitate. His thumb presses on my clit, rubbing it in such a way that has my toes curling and my fingers gripping hold of the bedsheets.

"Kid—" he says against my lips, pulling back slightly.

"Yes—?" I bite down on my lip, holding onto the cry that's ready to rip out of my throat.

Dipping deeper inside me, he crooks his fingers and rubs

on that special spot quickly, over and over again, his hand jerking. "I want you to come."

His words split me apart and I detonate around his hand, my internal walls squeezing his fingers in an orgasmic grip. If it was his cock, I've no doubt I'd wring him dry. Dax groans, and when my orgasm ebbs away, he gently pulls his fingers out of me before sliding them into his mouth, a savage look on his face.

"If I hurt you, tell me. If I go too hard, too fast, tell me. If you want me to stop, tell me. I want this to be good for you," he says, seriously.

"That's sweet, Dax, but honestly I don't want slow. I want to feel you. I want to know I'm yours."

Another sexy growl rumbles up his throat as he climbs on top of me and smashes his mouth against mine, his tongue sweeping inside my mouth erotically. I can taste myself on his lips and it makes me hunger for more. When he trails his mouth lower, his teeth scraping over my cheek, my collarbone, my nipples, I groan and moan, not recognising the sounds coming out of my mouth. Kneeling, he reaches behind my head, grabbing the condom and tears open the foil wrapper with his teeth, rolling it over his considerable length before shifting over me. I'm not that experienced in the male anatomy, but I know he's large. At a guess, he's a good ten inches, and wide. I stare at his dick, at the long vein on the underside, and swallow hard. Fuck, I've no idea if that's even going to fit. Dax gently nudges my legs apart with his knees, and grasps his cock in his hand, rubbing the tip along my slit.

"I'll take care of you, okay?"

I nod, not able to talk as he lowers himself over me, the tip of his cock resting against my entrance. His forearms cage my head, and his fingers curl into my hair as he looks at me intently. Slowly, he pushes into me, only stopping when the head of his cock is sheathed.

"Damn, you're so tight!" he exclaims, trembling as he holds back. The veins in his neck stand prominently beneath his skin, and I lift myself up to meet him, my mouth pressing against them.

Dax sinks into me, inch by glorious inch until I'm full. He settles above me, breathing hard and allowing me to adjust to his size. I'm slick with need, and when he begins to move agonisingly slowly, I slide my tongue up his neck and lick the shell of his ear.

"Fuck me like you mean it, Dax," I say, breathily.

So he does.

Dax pulls out and slams into me in one harsh movement. A scream rips out of my throat at the sharp sting of him impaling himself balls deep inside of me, only for that pain to ebb away with every thrust afterwards.

Dax fucks me.

He doesn't hesitate.

His hips piston.

His cock rams into me.

And I lift my pelvis up to meet every harsh thrust.

This is pleasure and pain.

This is a clawing, roaring, shredding of inhibitions, of our pasts.

This is us battering down every last blockade between us, smashing through three years of loss, of anger and pain.

This is coming together in the most basic and raw way.

I groan, gasping for air, suffocating in his kiss, revelling in his hurricane that churns us both up into nothing but eddying emotion. Thick, full, potent.

"Fuck, Kid."

The bed creaks beneath us as Dax shifts his position, flipping my leg across my body so that I'm half turned away from him. He grasps my hips, leans over, and fucks me harder, slamming into me. The new position means that he's deeper inside me, and I tighten around him, accepting every inch as another orgasm gathers strength. It rushes upwards and out of my centre, a tsunami that blinds me momentarily and snatches my breath. With his fingers tangled in my hair, his lips pressed against mine, and his cock buried deep inside of me, Dax comes. He comes with jerking limbs and rolling eyes, and a roar that explodes out of his throat as my pussy tightens around him and milks him of every last drop of cum.

38

Pen

It's Sunday morning, and I've spent the weekend in bed with Dax. We've fucked, we've danced together in the studio, we've talked, we've healed each other. I've asked about the others, but he just told me they needed time to deal with their shit and left it at that. I haven't pressed him for any more information, and he hasn't offered up any more of an explanation than that. Right now he's cooking me breakfast. On the side table, my phone beeps and I pick it up, opening the text message.

Clancy: Babe, I've spent the whole weekend in bed. River has skills for daaaaayyyyssss.

She follows up her message with a string of emojis that I can't even begin to decipher right now. Though I'm gathering from the copious amounts of egg plants and lips that they've had a lot of fun.

Me: *Too much information. I hope your dad doesn't know what you got up to this weekend. I still can't believe he was cool with all of that.*

Clancy: Babe, my dad would shit a brick if he knew. Friday night was on me. I knew you wouldn't come if you thought I'd paid for it all. Don't kill me.

Me: *Clancy!!!*

Clancy: Sorry Babe, got 2 go. River's waking up.

Shaking my head, I place my mobile phone on the side table. "Should've known, the sneaky bitch," I grumble.

"Who's a sneaky bitch?" Dax asks, peering around the door into the bedroom, the delicious smell of sizzling bacon drifting into the room.

"Clancy fibbed to me about something. It's all cool though. I still love her."

"Good, I like Clancy. Has she been a good friend to you?"

"Yeah, yeah she has." I climb out of bed and pull on Dax's t-shirt and joggers. He stares at me hungrily the whole time. He's insatiable and my cheeks blush at what we've shared. Talk about making up for lost time. "Don't look at me like that, Dax. I still haven't recovered from the several orgasms you gave me last night, not to mention the day before."

"Is that so?" he cocks his brow, a self-satisfied smirk pulling up his lips. "So, tell me, did York and Zayn give you as many orgasms? Coz you bet your arse I'm making a mental tally. Those boys better up their game."

I pick up a pillow from the bed and throw it at him. It bounces off the wall, completely missing him. He laughs loudly and the sound warms my heart. When he pops his head back into the room, he's grinning.

"Come on, let's eat," he says, pushing the door open and offering his hand.

When we step into the living area, I'm confronted with three very exhausted men. I stiffen, my mouth suddenly going dry. Xeno is sitting on the coffee table, his head in his hands, Zayn is on the sofa and York is frying up the bacon in the kitchen.

"It's okay, Kid," Dax says, trying to reassure me. "They might look like shit, but they're good now. I swear it. Any more trouble, and they'll have me to deal with," he warns them, tugging on my hand. He leads me to the sofa, positioning me next to Zayn who immediately wraps his arm around my shoulder and pulls me close, pressing a kiss to my head.

"Hey, Pen," he says softly, gravel in his voice. He sounds exhausted.

Dax settles on the other side of me and rests his hand on my leg. I glance at York, who takes the pan off the heat and sets the bacon aside. He joins us, pressing a kiss against my head before sitting down. He doesn't say a word. None of them do. They wait, and I realise after a moment that they're not waiting for me to speak, but for Xeno to face us all. The fact that he still can't do that fucking hurts.

When a long drawn out silence begins to make us all feel uncomfortable and Zayn mutters something cutting under his breath, I realise it's me who has to make the first move. I have to bridge the chasm between us. I don't know what's gone on between the three of them, but judging by the heavy bags under Zayn and York's eyes, it's been a long weekend. They've all changed clothes, so I imagine they've been at the Academy this whole time. Xeno being here now is a huge step, and I need to pull up my big girl pants and tell them the truth.

It's time.

Drawing in a deep breath, I slide out from between Zayn and Dax and kneel in front of Xeno.

"Will you look at me?" I question softly. Reaching for him, my fingers press against his knees gently. He flinches but I refuse to be put off. "Please. I need to tell you something important."

"Jesus, man, just let it go, Xeno. Fucking look at Pen," Zayn says in frustration, but still he refuses. I won't let that deter me. This is the barrier my decision to walk away from them put up between the two of us. It's up to me to break it down.

"The first thing you need to know is that I *love* you. All of you. I never, ever stopped," I say fiercely, my fingers wrapping around his jean-clad knees. I look over at my boys sitting on the sofa and smile through the cracks in my voice. It feels good to say that out loud, to mean that. "Walking away from you all was the single hardest thing I ever had to do. You have to know I wouldn't have done it if I had a choice."

"Fuck," Dax utters, but I return my attention back to Xeno.

If I was the beating heart of our fivesome, then he was the glue. Without him we won't stick, no matter how much we want to. My fingers slide up Xeno's arms, and I cup my hands over his. He has his palms resting over his eyes and his fingers curling into his hair. I wrap my fingers gently around his hands and pull them away from his face.

"Please, just look at me," I beg.

He lifts his gaze slowly to meet mine, and I draw in a deep breath at the utter despair I see reflected back at me. The split in his brow is scabbed over, but he still has bruising around his cheek and there are bags beneath his eyes that tell me he hasn't slept much these past couple of days.

"Why didn't you have a choice, Pen?" Xeno asks. His voice is dangerously low, and I'm not immune to the murderous edge I hear within it. Holding his hands in mine, and gently rubbing my thumbs across his fingers, avoiding the bruised and split knuckles, I tell him.

"Because I had to protect Lena. I had to protect you all."

"Fucking *what*!" Dax exclaims, but I refuse to look at him. I might lose my nerve if I do.

"Do you remember after the battle at Rocks, after we won, I went missing for a while?"

"You were with *Jeb*." Xeno spits his name out like poison, and for a moment he turns his head away, not able to look at me.

"Not at first. That was *after*..." I swallow hard, forcing myself to get the words out. "Before that point, my brother had a few things he wanted to tell me." Xeno's head whips back around to face me. His eyes narrow into slits.

"*What* did he have to say to you?"

"My brother gave me an ultimatum. Walk away from you all or see Lena dead."

"THAT MOTHERFUCKER!" Dax roars, and I flinch.

Out of the corner of my eye, I see Zayn grip Dax's arm. "Be calm," he says.

I look over at York and he nods, encouraging me to go on.

"David admitted he had—" I have to swallow the bile burning in my throat at the memory of his words. "He admitted that he had feelings for me. He was *jealous* of you all. He blamed me for his sickness."

"That perverted fuck!" Zayn snarls.

"David said he would kill Lena if I didn't walk away from you. You have to understand that I couldn't let him hurt my little sister."

"Why the fuck didn't you say anything, Pen? Why?!" Xeno exclaims, sitting upright. He glares at me.

"I was scared..." I blink back the tears I feel pricking at my eyes as Xeno stands and starts pacing back and forth.

"We could've done something. We could've helped! You have to know that, right?"

He pulls at his hair and I stand too, watching him as I hug myself. "I *couldn't*. That wasn't the only nightmare I lived through that night."

"What do you mean?" Xeno snaps, cutting me in half with his emerald gaze.

"After David's threat, I somehow ended up walking in on Jeb getting his cock sucked by some random dude."

"Jesus fucking Christ. This just keeps getting better," Dax says from behind us.

"Jeb has kept his sexual preferences hidden for years. I don't know why he's so fucking worried about it, but when I walked in on him, I knew I'd seen something I shouldn't have. I ran, but he caught up with me—"

"What the fuck did he do to you, Pen?" Zayn asks, this time it's him who's unable to control his anger. He gets to his feet, anger blazing across his face.

"He took me to a room and shot the man who was supposed to be keeping watch whilst he was getting sucked-off. He blew his brains out."

They're all silent for a moment, shock rendering them

speechless. "He fucking blew his brains out because I saw something I shouldn't have."

"And then?" Xeno finally asks.

"He considered shooting me too." I laugh bitterly at the memory. "Instead, he said that if I could keep his secret, then he would let me go. He would let me be with you all…"

"But you couldn't do that, could you?" York asks gently, knowingly.

I shake my head sadly. "How could I, York? David would've killed Lena if I did."

York sighs. "So you asked Jeb a favour in return, right?"

I nod. His gaze flicks to Xeno behind me before settling back on me. There's so much regret there, it would break my heart if it wasn't so thoroughly shattered already.

"I did. I asked him to send David far away. I begged him to help me because I knew that no matter what, he'd hurt my sister if he remained here. I couldn't put her in danger. I couldn't risk it."

"That's why Jeb sent David to Mexico," Dax states, finally understanding.

"Oh, I'm more than positive now that he was going to do that anyway," I say bitterly. "Jeb sent David away as a *favour* to me so long as I gave him something in return."

"And what was that?" Zayn questions, his jaw gritting roughly.

"To be *his*. Or at least pretend to be. I had to break up with you. I had to break your hearts, work for him at Rocks, and wait for the day when he'd need to call in the debt I owed. He said if I didn't do that then my life and my sister's life were forfeit."

I sit down heavily, my arse hitting the hardwood of the coffee table. "Part of that debt was to let Zayn fuck me at

Grim's that night so that he could still pretend he was straight. I don't know what else he has planned for me because he hasn't tried to contact me since," I say softly.

"Motherfucking cunt! He won't get a chance to plan any-fucking-thing because I'm going to murder the bastard." Zayn snarls fiercely, his black eyes snapping with fury.

"*You* will do nothing, Zayn. Fucking hear me?" Xeno snaps before focusing back on me. "So what's changed, Pen? If you were so afraid of what might happen to Lena, why are you telling us all this now?"

"Because I have help."

"From who?!" he demands, stepping towards me. I don't like the look on his face, not one bit.

"Grim. She's got two of her men watching over Lena for me."

"Fuck, Pen!" York exclaims. "You should've come to us first."

"Xeno made it clear that I should stay away from you all. I didn't have anyone else to turn to."

"God-fucking-damn-it!" York grits out, glaring at Xeno. "Your stubbornness has put her in danger again!"

Xeno flinches but says nothing in response to that. "But why did you need to turn to them at all? You could've just kept away from us like David wanted," Xeno asks and there's a tremor to his voice that I don't understand. A crack, like he's shredding the walls encasing his heart in a way that is dangerous for all of us. I swallow hard. This is the last truth I have to share. I owe it to them to be completely honest.

"David heard about you returning. He knows you're at the Academy for Jeb. He's pissed that he's been left out of the loop of whatever you're up to and asked me to find out what's going on. I have until the end of the month or Lena's dead. That's why I went to Grim. At least she's safe from harm until I can figure out what to do about this fucking mess."

Xeno's eyes hardened. "How?"

"What?"

"*How* would you find out what's going on?"

I swallow hard, the words sticking in my throat. I look at Dax, at York and Zayn, then back at Xeno. "By making you fall in love with me again, by finding out your secrets and breaking your trust. That's how," I whisper.

The room falls silent, then like a hurricane ripping through the front room, Xeno strides over to the kitchen, tears open a cabinet door and starts throwing the contents onto the floor. Plates crash against the tiles, shattering on impact, shards of bone china scattering across the floor. We all watch as Xeno rips open cupboard after cupboard and drags the contents out. He roars, smashing plates, throwing pans, even the utensils' drawer gets pulled out and upended on the floor. When he starts punching at the wall with an aggression that scares me, Dax grabs my hand tightly in his, tugging me backwards and away from him.

"We should go," Dax says.

"No!" I protest, "He's going to seriously hurt himself. Please, Dax, make him stop."

My voice seems to register in Xeno's head because his hands fall to the side and he turns to face me. "Take her back to the Academy—" he grits out tremulously.

"Xeno, please, let's work through this." I step forward towards him, but York steps in my path and shakes his head.

"No, Titch. He needs time."

"Come on, man," Zayn says, resting his hand on Xeno's arm and looking at me with an apology in his gaze, but Xeno smacks it away.

"Don't!" he snarls, turning his attention back to Dax and completely ignoring me. "She can't be around me. Take her back to the Academy. Right the fuck now."

"Xeno, don't do this…" I rub at my chest, feeling his pain as though it's my own. I wanted so badly to believe that by telling them the truth we'd be able to start over, to start again, but I was wrong. I was so fucking wrong, and it hurts.

"We should go," Dax says, drawing me away from the trio.

"I can't leave him like this," I plead, fixing my gaze on Xeno. He can't even look at me.

"JUST LEAVE!" Xeno roars, and when Dax wraps his arm around me and lifts me off the floor, I have no choice but to go with him.

39

Pen

It's been almost a week since I spilled my guts to the Breakers.

Almost a week since Xeno lost his shit and told me to leave.

Almost a week since Xeno left town.

He's gone.

Not a word to the rest of the Breakers. Not a word to Madame Tuillard or D-Neath. He just upped and fucking left. I guess I'm not the only one capable of walking away without an explanation. Perhaps this is karma. Perhaps this is just what I deserved.

Or maybe he's just a fucking coward.

York, Dax, and Zayn are trying their best to hold everything together, but every day that passes without word is a day too many. They're worried. *I'm* worried, but if the rest of the Breakers can carry on regardless, then so can I. Right now I have to put all thoughts of Xeno out of my mind if I'm going to get through my first performance at Tales and secure my sister's safety. Grim might have agreed to keep Lena safe, but I'm not testing my theory that Lena's protection would stop the second I didn't perform. She has a business to run first and foremost. Me not dancing because I'm fucked up by recent events isn't going to wash. So here I am. In twenty minutes, Dax will be fighting Beast in the cage, and at midnight, I will be performing with the girls. We just need to get through tonight then figure out where to go from here.

"How are you doing, Pen? Nervous?" Grim asks me as she steps into my changing room. She's wearing her usual uniform of leather trousers and black shirt, and she's holding onto a bottle of whisky with one hand and two cut glasses with the other. "Need a bit of Dutch courage?" she asks me, dropping the glasses on the vanity unit in front of me and filling them both up with a double shot.

I take the proffered glass, knocking back the liquid in one fiery gulp. "Thanks, I needed that," I reply, pulling my floor length dressing gown tighter around my waist. Beneath it I'm wearing my outfit for my performance later, but I don't want anyone to see it until I'm ready to dance.

"I thought you might." She cocks her head to the side, watching me.

"What?"

"It's a busy night. The warehouse is packed—"

"That's good, right?" I ask, not understanding the concern that flits across her face.

"Yes, good for business, sure."

"But…"

"The Collector is back."

"Malik Brov is here tonight?"

"Yes. He paid a lot of money to be seated closest to the cage."

"Fucking great," I grumble. Couldn't she at least have barred him entry? I really don't need another goddamn nutcase on my back. Then again, Grim doesn't owe me shit. It's me who owes her, so I guess I'm going to have to just suck it up.

"The Skins are here too, including what's left of your Breakers."

I flinch at that. "News travels fast then, I take it…"

She nods tightly. Of course she knows Xeno's gone. Grim makes it her business to know everything, after all.

"Perfect." I swallow heavily.

This is the first time I've laid eyes on Jeb since that night here three weeks ago. Am I comfortable with the fact that Zayn and York are sitting with him? No, of course not, I hate it, but I'm also aware that getting out of the Skins only happens when you're dead and I don't want my Breakers dead. So here we are.

"I'm giving you a heads up because I didn't want you to be surprised. Don't worry, my men will have eyes on *both* of them all night. You're safe, Pen," she says, trying to reassure me.

I laugh. I can't help it. "Safe? I don't think I'll ever feel safe."

Grim grits her jaw in understanding. "You just go out there and dance. Do your thing and let us worry about the rest, okay?"

I frown. "Us?"

"Yeah, me and Beast. He likes you, Pen, and my man barely likes anyone."

"Does he like me enough to go easy on Dax?"

Grim laughs. "Nope."

"Good, because I don't want any special treatment," Dax

says as he enters the room wearing the same boxing shorts as he had the last time he fought here. My gaze lingers on the red skull motif emblazoned on the shorts and my stomach churns. He nods at Grim. "Evening."

She gives him a curt nod. "Well, I guess that's my cue to leave. You're up in fifteen, Dax. Make this quick."

"Got it." When Grim leaves, Dax kicks his foot against the door, shutting it, before pulling me into his arms. "She likes you," he mutters against my hair as I press my cheek against his bare chest.

"I'm her employee. I think that's as far as her liking me goes."

"It's more than that."

"Yeah? If she liked me so much, why has she allowed Malik Brov in here tonight? The guy wanted to *buy* me, Dax," I point out, looking up at him.

"That motherfucker's here tonight?"

"Yes. As if I haven't already got two crazies to worry about. Now I have to worry about that arsehole too."

"Nothing will happen, okay? Jeb already made a deal with Grim. He can't back out on that. You're safe," he repeats, echoing Grim's words.

"I don't feel safe, Dax." It hurts me to say that to him, standing here wrapped up in his arms, but it's the truth.

"I swear to you, Pen. We won't let anything happen to you." He pulls back and rests his forehead against mine. "I would rather die than see you taken from us again."

"Don't say things like that, Dax. Not when you're about to go into the cage with Beast."

He smiles at me. "You think I'm going to lose, don't you?"

"I think you're going to get very badly hurt."

"Have a little faith, Pen."

I frown, and he presses a gentle kiss against the crease between my brows. "Do you know how many times I wished I could turn back time, Dax? How often I've thought about making a different choice? I should've gone to the police. I should've told you back then what happened. Maybe Xeno was right, maybe together we could've dealt with my brother. Now look at us. Xeno has gone AWOL, you're about to go head-to-head with Beast, York and Zayn are out there sitting at a table with *Jeb*, and you're still part of his crew. You're still Skins."

"You can't change what's happened, Kid, but you gotta trust me on this. We're gonna make this right. I promise you."

"How? How can you possibly make this right? Xeno's gone, and my brother will be ringing me at the end of the month regardless. I know Grim and Beast have made a promise to protect Lena, but can anyone actually tell me that she's going to be one-hundred percent safe?"

"Believe me when I say, no motherfucker is getting anywhere near Lena. The rest? We'll figure it out. It *will* be okay."

Outside a bell rings telling us both that Dax's fight will be starting in five minutes. He hugs me close. "You gonna come out and watch?"

I shake my head. "I don't think I can," I murmur.

"I'll see you back here in twenty then."

"Twenty minutes? You're that confident you're going to win?"

"Yeah, Kid. I'm that confident." He gives me another lingering kiss on the lips then leaves.

THE FIGHT IS over in thirty-five minutes.

Beast wins.

"I want you at my gym, Dax. You've got potential," Beast says as he lowers a beaten and bruised Dax onto a chair in my dressing room.

"What have you done to him?" I screech, glaring at Beast before dropping onto my knees before Dax. His face is literally covered in blood, and his left eye and right cheek are swelling fast. "You fucking arsehole!" I shout, pressing the sleeve of my white towelling robe against his cheek. Blood blooms. Beast just smirks.

"I told you I wouldn't hold back, but I didn't kill the shithead. Just knocked him out briefly," he says, shrugging. I get a sick sense of satisfaction when he follows that statement up with a wince of his own. Arsehole.

"You knocked him out? We need to get him to hospital to check for a concussion!" I say, still dabbing at Dax's bloody face.

He gives me a weak smile. "I'm good, Kid."

"Beast, look at him!" I snarl, not liking how unfocused Dax's eyes are.

"Don't sweat it, sweetheart. We have a guy on hand who can check him out. Besides, he was only out for a minute. It's just as well he went down. Fucker wouldn't have stopped otherwise. I've got a reputation to maintain, you know."

"Un-fucking-believable!" I grit out. "Go fucking get this guy then!"

"Kid," Dax warns. He understands Beast has a reputation and is worried I'm overstepping. I don't care if I am, but given the amusement in Beast's eyes he's finding my outrage amusing and not offensive.

"Don't worry, I'll make sure Joey sees him. Fuck—" he says, wincing again.

"That hurt?" Dax asks, a smile pulling up his split lip as Beast presses against his side.

"Yeah, yeah, you got me good."

Despite his chest-beating bullshit, Beast hasn't come out of the fight unscathed. I'm fairly sure that his split lip and eyebrow have got to sting. Plus, there's a deepening bruise on his chest, so I'm guessing Dax managed to break a rib or two. Good.

"Guess you're not infallible then, yeah?" Dax grunts.

"Big word for a street kid. I'm impressed." Beast laughs, then coughs, then winces. "So you up for training with me?" he asks Dax, all friendly like he hasn't just beaten the shit out of him.

Dax chuckles, then groans as more blood weeps from his own split lip. He licks at it. "I've heard you're the best trainer in London. Yeah, I'm up for that."

"Just in London? Mate, I'm the best in *Europe*." Beast grins broadly and all I want to do is punch him in the face.

"Well, as much as this blossoming bromance warms my heart, I'd appreciate it, Beast, if you got the fuck out of my dressing room and fetched Joey."

Beast chuckles. "She's a keeper, this one."

"She sure is." Dax smiles then immediately groans again.

"I'll go get Joey. He'll have you sorted in no time."

An hour later, Dax has been cleaned and wrapped up by Joey, an old dude that looks more like a biker than a doctor. I'm betting the kind of training he's had isn't the kind most doctors get. Talk about shady backstreet *doctor*, and I'm using the term loosely here.

"You've got a mild concussion, bruising and swelling to your eye and cheek, and some nasty split knuckles. Other than that, you're good. There aren't many people who get in the cage with Beast and come out with relatively minor injuries like this," Joey says, clearly impressed.

"Minor injuries?" I scoff, clearly *unimpressed*. As far as I'm concerned, Dax needs to go to the hospital to see a proper doctor and have a head scan or something to check he hasn't got bleeding in the brain. I don't trust this two-bit backstreet doctor who smells of beer.

"Yes. He'll be good in a few days!" Joey says, slapping Dax on the shoulder before winking at me. "Beast tells me you'll be coming to the gym to train?"

Dax nods. "That's right."

"Good, then I'll be seeing you there, son," Joey replies, before giving me a wink and leaving the room. Urgh, arsehole.

"You're not seriously going to train with him, are you?" I ask Dax as he knocks back a glass of neat whisky and looks at me from his good eye, given the other is swollen shut. "You *hate* Beast."

"He ain't so bad."

"So now you're friends?" I shake my head in bewilderment. "Did those blows to your head scramble your brain or something?" I laugh but it comes out slightly hysterical.

Dax leans forward and grasps my hands in his. "I *owe* him and Grim for having your back when we couldn't. Anyone who helps you is a good person in my book."

"So that's two debts you owe, or have you forgotten the deal that was made the last time we were here?"

"I haven't forgotten."

"Dax—"

"Shh, it's all good," he says, leaning forward and kissing me gently. I allow him to pull me into his arms and bury my head into the crook of his neck momentarily. It helps to ease the building anxiety I'm feeling.

"I don't like seeing you like this…"

"I know, Kid."

Sighing, I press a kiss against his jaw, stroking my fingers gently across his lips. "I never wanted this for you. I'm scared to fucking ask what you all did whilst we were apart."

"Kid…"

"It's okay. I'm not a fool. I know it can't be good. But you know what?"

"What?" Dax asks, pulling back to look at me.

"I don't care. I don't care what you've done in Jeb's name. I only care about us from this point onwards. That's all. That's it," I say fiercely.

Dax sighs, then presses a sweet kiss against my mouth. "Fuck, Kid. Do you know how much I love you?"

"How much?" I whisper, my heart soaring.

"It's a tear-the-sky-down-and-rip-a-man-to-shreds-for-even-looking-at-you amount. A lot, Kid. So fucking much."

"That's pretty huge," I grin, unable to help myself.

"Yeah, fucking scary amount actually. I know the others think the same," he adds, as though sensing my need to hear that too, and I believe him, about Zayn and York at least. But Xeno…

"Where is he, Dax?" I ask, my heart hurting.

He sighs heavily. "I don't know. If I did, I would tell you. I swear it. The last thing he said to us before he snuck the fuck off was that he needed to get his head straight. I should've known he'd pull something like this."

"He's done this before?"

"Once, about a year ago…" Dax frowns.

"What?"

His response is interrupted by Nancy, one of the girls. "Sorry to interrupt, but we're up, Pen." She grins widely, clearly excited. I love her enthusiasm. It's about the only good thing that's come out of the mess; being able to teach the girls to dance and watch them flourish.

"Thanks, I'll just be a minute," I say, waiting for her to leave before fixing my gaze back on Dax who's looking a little unsettled.

"If your outfit is anything like hers, I might have to stab a few of those bastards sitting out there in the eyes," he mutters.

"Dax, stop sidetracking. What aren't you telling me about Xeno?"

"I'm not sidetracking, Kid. What exactly are you wearing under that robe?" he asks, pulling at the edge of the collar. I slap his hands away.

"Dax—!" I warn.

"Just go out there and knock 'em dead, Kid. Then we'll talk, okay?"

"Is that a promise?" I ask, getting to my feet and untying the bathrobe that's covering my outfit.

"That's a prom— Fuck me, Kid! There's gonna be *murders* tonight," Dax exclaims, his eyes popping open in shock at my outfit. Well, one eye at least.

I chuckle and let the robe slide from my shoulders, allowing the material to pool at my feet. An hour later I get to find out just how true his statement was.

40

Pen

I stand in the middle of the cage and wait. The lights are out, and the pyrotechnics won't start until the music does. There's a general buzz of excitement and a tension that fills the air much like it had that night I danced here three weeks ago. Except this time, I'm not second guessing what's happening.

This time *I'm* in control.

There's no fucking, there's only anticipation and a roomful of gangsters waiting to see *me* dance. For the first time in a long, long time, I feel powerful.

Surrounding me in a circle are the girls. They look amazing and a far cry from what these gangsters have come to expect. Grim agreed to trust my artistic streak and paid for the outfits to be made, no expenses spared. Each of the girls are barefoot and wearing black bodysuits encrusted with tiny black and silver gemstones which sparkle when the light catches them. The sides of their bodysuits have a section cut out of them, showing off their beautiful curves and acknowledging what they once were. I wanted them to use their sexual prowess as a weapon, much like I use dance as mine. Their eyes are framed by kohl liner and their lips shimmer with gloss. All six have their hair pulled back in a high ponytail and their legs are bare. In short, they look fucking incredible.

In contrast, I'm wearing the dress Zayn bought me. It fitted perfectly with the idea I had for the dance. From the ankles up, my legs have been painted on with body makeup, flames licking upwards—not as a nod to Malik Brov, The Collector, though I suspect he'll see it that way—but because I have a fire, a strength that *burns* within me.

Three years ago my brother and Jeb changed the course of my future, they took away my happiness, my joy, and I let them. They tried to dampen my fire, they tried to make me weak, and they almost succeeded, but tonight I'm rising from the ashes, like a motherfucking phoenix from the flames. From this moment on, I will not allow anyone to get between me and the men I love. Xeno might have disappeared, but I have to trust he will return. I have to trust that my love for him is enough to bring us back together, and when he returns I'm going to fight for us. For *all* of us.

"Ready?" I whisper.

"Ready," the girls respond in unison. We've practised every spare moment and they've got this routine down.

"I'm so proud of you all." And even though I can't see their faces clearly, I know they're smiling at me.

"Let's do this," Nancy says. She was the beautiful blonde who acknowledged me that night I first danced in the cage. She's the best dancer of the six.

Drawing in a soothing breath, I get into position. With my knees bent in a plié and my arms held wide, I drop my head and wait. Around me the girls raise their arms and rest their hands on each other's shoulders.

Thump, thump, thump, thump.

The opening beat of *Play With Fire* by Sam Tinnesz begins to sound out around us. It's the perfect song to represent how I feel.

Danger, secrets, past hurt, anger, all of it is funnelled into this dance.

Like a match lighting petrol, walking away from the Breakers had blown up in all our faces, burning us all. But now that the truth has been shared, I know we'll find a way to rise up out of the damn ashes. *All of us*.

Even Xeno.

I have to believe he will come back. I know I hurt him, but I also know he felt guilty. I saw it in his eyes, he isn't to blame. Jeb and David are, and one day those motherfuckers will get their comeuppance.

Drawing strength from the music, from the badass dancers surrounding me, I let the angry cadence of Sam Tinnesz's voice lift me emotionally. I'm fucking ready.

The first line of the song plays just as indoor flares rigged to each post of the cage go up in a burst of startling orange and yellow sparks, heating our skin in a fiery glow. With the next beat the flares suddenly go out and the cage is lit instead by a soft orange glow. This is the cue for the girls to begin to dance around me, and just like I knew it would be, their timing is perfect. Twisting and turning, spinning low, then sweeping back up high, the girls move like ash billowing from the flames of a fire.

As I watch them, my veins run with heat, with passion, with a raw intensity and a determination to prove my strength, to show my worth. I'm no longer weakened by Jeb and

David's threats. I've found a way to protect my sister and myself. It may not be foolproof, but it's a fucking start. I'm not that terrified, cornered girl anymore, I'm so much more than that. I'll only get stronger each and every day I'm surrounded by my boys.

My men. *My* Breakers.

This dance is for them as much as it's for me.

A breeze passes over my skin, lifting up my tulle skirt and fanning the flames that have always burned inside my chest. I spin on my feet in a series of fouetté turns, the girls mirroring me.

They're the ash.

I'm the flames.

The dress Zayn bought me moves fluidly, the tulle skirt light, perfect for dancing in. The material whispers over my skin, revealing my thighs, and showing off my dark, blood-red underwear as I move. Just like we practiced, the girls raise their hands in the air above them as six, topless men lower down from silk ropes and grasp their wrists. One by one they're lifted ten feet off the ground, as though a fierce wind has blown through the warehouse and has churned the ash rising up from the flames, *from me*.

Below the spinning, sparkling girls, I dance.

Every step is a word. Every line of my body, a story. I tell my tale right here in the club named the same. For some it will just be a pretty dance, a performance to thrill, but this isn't for the gangsters that surround me. This is for the Breakers. This is for *them*.

I transition from a fouetté turn into a renverse tilt jump, landing lightly then dropping to the canvas as I work the floor with long lines and smooth strokes. Bending at the waist, I flip forward into a split, then sweep my legs together before stepping upwards in one graceful move. I use every single part of my body to express how I feel. From the tips of my fingers to the tops of my toes, I burn the fucking canvas with my dance.

I feel.

Boy, do I feel.

This is who I am. This is who I was born to be.

A girl who dances like flames rampaging through a forest. Powerful, potent, oxygen stealing.

Out of the corner of my eye, I see someone step into the cage. Someone familiar.

My throat tightens. My stomach churns. My chest heaves.

My heart fucking leaps.

I come to a standstill, blinking back the shock, and holding my nerve.

Even if he wasn't dressed head to toe in black, even if his face wasn't covered by a black mask with just the eyes and mouth cut out, I'd know who it is.

Xeno.

He strides towards me, the taut muscles of his stomach contracting beneath his skintight top as he moves. My throat constricts as he ducks beneath Nancy's legs, stepping into the circle the girls are making around us as they're lowered back onto the canvas, the men dropping behind them as they fan out into a wall. Nancy captures my eye, giving me a look asking if I need help. I shake my head telling her it's okay, to just go with it. She nods and begins to dance, wrapping her long legs around her partner just like I'd choreographed. The other girls follow.

"You're back," I breathe out, my hands pressing against his chest, my fingers skirting over his bare skin between his top and mask. Xeno being here wasn't part of the plan, but I just go with it, and like the true professionals they are, the girls continue dancing. One by one they wrap themselves around their partners, grinding on them. It's sexy as fuck.

"Look at you," he whispers, bringing up his hands to cup my face. Electricity zings between us, the air potent and crackling, eddying with emotion. Passion. *Fire*.

"What are you doing here?"

"Dancing with you." He places his arm around my back, jerking me against him. Air whooshes out of my chest as my body slams into his. "Don't think, just move."

He dips me backwards, mimicking the couples around us, one leather-clad hand sliding up my thigh and lifting my right leg around his hip whilst the other holds onto me firmly. Xeno grips me tightly, the beat of a new song vibrating up through the canvas as we move. It's *Fire on Fire* by Sam Smith. My head tips back as I bare my neck to him, the ends of my hair reaching the canvas.

He leans over me, just like he did that first time he danced with me in the studio. This time he isn't hiding who he is from me, just the rest of the warehouse. I can see his beautiful eyes burn fiercely behind the mask he wears before he lowers his mouth over the bare skin of my chest. For a moment he holds me there, pressing a lingering kiss over my beating heart whilst the couples dance around us, their movements whipping up the air and covering my skin in goosebumps.

"Tiny," he laments, his lips sliding over my clavicle, and my neck as he lifts me back upwards. "I fucked up."

He presses a gentle kiss against my lips that is almost painful in how heartfelt it is. I'm all for passionate kisses, but this is something more. This is a promise of everything I've always wanted. There's a tremulousness to his kiss.

He's holding back.

This is the slow trickle of water through a crack in a dam, waiting for the moment to burst. This is the low heat of a flame flickering to life, waiting for the tinder to catch and burst into an inferno. This is a heart slowly cracking open, but not wanting an audience in that moment when it does. This is a boy called Xeno, kissing a girl he calls Tiny.

This is an apology, and a declaration.

"Xeno, this is dangerous…" I mutter against his mouth. My heart's pounding in my chest, not just because he's kissing me the way he is but because out there in the darkened warehouse are men who still have the power to hurt us.

"Keep moving," he responds, gripping my right hand within his and gently pushing against my left shoulder so that I spin away from him. He chases after me, catching me before I collide with one of the couples, and with his hands on my hips, he uses the momentum to lift me up above his head. My hands grasp his shoulders as I pull in my core and level my legs horizontally above him. It takes great strength and trust on both parts to be able to perform a lift like this. Being able to pull this lift off without practice just tells me what I've known all along, that Xeno and I were made to dance with each other.

The way we move together is instinctual, just like it is with the rest of my Breakers. He grins, baring his perfect white teeth as he lowers me down his perfectly toned body. Lust and passion—that sets my whole body alight—glimmers in his eyes.

Sam Smith sings about passion colliding, fires alighting, desire burning, and the timing couldn't be more fucking perfect. That's what we are Xeno and I, we're passion, desire, lust, hunger. *Love*.

I feel that.

As we dance, I *feel* his love. It's fierce. It takes my breath away.

Xeno presses another kiss against my lips, his teeth edging against my bottom lip, nipping at my skin with a low growl that rumbles through his chest into mine.

"Fuck," he mutters, before he pushes against my hip with his left hand, encouraging me to spin away again. I kick out in a series of fouetté turns across the canvas and behind me he performs a front flip without his hands, meeting me once again in an embrace that has my heart fucking soaring. He grasps the back of my head, tucking me under his chin and holds me close. The push and pull of our relationship so perfectly described within our movements. For a moment he just holds me as we sway together, my hand resting over his heart as it pounds like a bass drum. Every inch of me is pressed against every inch of him as he strokes his hand up my back and cups my face. When he bends over me, his mouth dropping to my ear, I shiver with anticipation, my senses telling me that something isn't right.

"I need you to trust me. Can you do that?" he asks.

"What do you mean—?"

His fingers dig into my bare skin, the urgency of his voice making me suddenly fearful. Around us the girls continue to dance, covering this brief, urgent conversation. "I'm sorry I let you down, Pen. I'm so fucking sorry for it all. Your pain," he says, holding his fisted hand against his chest, "It's *mine* now. That motherfucker won't hurt you ever again. I'll make sure of it."

"Xeno, you're scaring me! What are you talking about?"

My question is cut short when the lights suddenly go out, bathing us all in darkness.

"Fuck!" Xeno whisper-shouts.

"What?"

"There's no time. Know that I *love* you, Tiny," he says

fiercely, then I feel the sharp stab of a needle sliding into my neck and the cold intrusion of something liquid entering my veins.

My body goes limp as my mind fights to say conscious, but it's no good, the darkness grabs hold of me with sharp claws, dragging me under. The last thing I remember before I slide into oblivion are warm arms picking me up and the distinct sound of gunshots being fired.

The story continues in Breakers
Coming Soon.
books2read.com/AcademyStardom3

AUTHOR NOTE

Well, there we have it. *Lyrical* is done. Can I take a breath now?

Writing this book was like being underwater. Some days I felt like I was drowning under the weight of these characters' sadness and hurt. I needed regular breaks to breathe... *and* drink gin. Seriously though, writing *Lyrical* was an intense, emotional journey, and whilst all my books have a similar effect on me, this book took the cake. Pen and her Breakers have a lot to answer for!

That first scene of Pen at Grim's club took me several attempts to write. I knew I didn't want her to be raped by anyone, let alone one of the Breakers. I knew that Zayn, that *none* of the Breakers, no matter how much they thought they hated her, would ever cross that line. It was important to me that Pen found her strength and showed those boys what it truly means to be courageous. She did that, I believe.

Like lyrical dance, this is a story about expression, feelings, and emotions. This book is about Pen and the Breakers re-

AUTHOR NOTE

establishing their bonds. It's about wading through their past hurts and forging a new path. It's about their journey, and how their love of dance brought them back together in a way that's unique to them. It's about character growth. I hope I've conveyed that. If you enjoyed this book, please do consider leaving a review.

Next up is *Breakers*. This is the final book in the trilogy and will pull together all the story threads and wrap them up in a neat little bow. However, please don't be fooled by the analogy. *Breakers* will pack a punch. Xeno said: *'we're the Breakers, and we break things after all.'* No truer words were spoken, and that's reflected in the final book. There is a lot of things to cover in the next book. Lots. You might have a lot of questions. If I do my job correctly then hopefully all will be answered, but rest assured, all my stories end in a hard won HEA. There's just another 100k or so words before they eventually get there. Fair warning.

Now for the thanks. I always feel like a bit of a plum doing this. I've not won an Oscar, after all, but there are people who deserve a thank you, so here goes.

As always, dear reader, thank you the most for continuing on this journey with me. Thank you for your words of encouragement and continuous support. I swear it never gets old.

Thanks to my beta and alpha team. To Courtney, Janet, Gina, Lisa and Jennifer, you ladies ROCK! I love you all.

Thanks to my team of ARC readers, you're all amazing.

Thanks to my readers in *Queen Bea's Hive*, you make my happy place a joy to be in. Your endless support is incredible.

Special thanks to Dani Piantadosi and her young daughter who helped me put together a tap dance sequence for Pen. I'm so grateful!

AUTHOR NOTE

And lastly, thanks to my kids. 2020 made me your teacher. I'm so bloody sorry if I messed up. I swear to you, I love you more than you'll ever know, but I am *so* glad you're both back at school being taught by professionals and not by a harassed mother trying to juggle *all the things*. You were both brilliant. I'm so proud of you both for working hard and giving me those precious few hours to write when we'd finished 'school'.

To be certain that you keep up to date with all my new releases and author news, please do come and join my Facebook group, *Queen Bea's Hive*, where I'm most active, or join my newsletter here.

Once again, thanks for sticking with me. Here's to plenty more stories to come.

Love, Bea xoxo